William P. Wood

"Wood clearly knows the inner workings of the judicial system."
—Publishers Weekly

"Wood, a former prosecutor, knows well how to surprise and engross us."
—Vincent Bugliosi, author of Helter Skelter

"A natural storyteller!"
—Norman Katkov, author of Blood and Orchids

SUDDEN IMPACT

"A must-read for those who love a classic, hard-boiled detective novel."
—Publishers Weekly

"No one writes a better police procedural than Bill Wood, and *Sudden Impact* is his best one to date—lucid prose, meticulous legal detail, and unforgettable characters struggling in various moral quandaries. Terrific, unputdownable stuff."
—John Lescroart, New York Times bestselling author of The Thirteenth Juror and The Hunt Club

"William Wood is a master of suspense. *Sudden Impact* is Wood at the peak of his powers, tense and eloquent, with characters and a story of political intrigue and riveting tragedy."
—Steve Martini, New York Times bestselling author

BROKEN TRUST

"A spellbinding tale about the men and women who dispense justice from the bench."
—Associated Press

"Fast-moving . . . Fascinating . . . Convincing . . . Chillingly informative."
—Sacramento Bee

"A tour de force of compelling courtroom drama and spellbinding storytelling. William Wood . . . draws us suspensefully into a classic tale of the individual and the system, of decision and verdict, and of good and evil."

—Gus Lee

GANGLAND

"The nonstop action and relentless pace will satisfy fans of the hard-boiled thriller genre."

—*Publishers Weekly*

"The story never cools down and never plays tricks."

—*Kirkus Reviews*

RAMPAGE

"A taut courtroom drama . . . hard to put down."

—William J. Caunitz, author of *One Police Plaza* and *Cleopatra Gold*

"One of the better courtroom dramas in years."

—*New York Times Book Review*

"From first to last, *Rampage* is superior . . . Please do not miss this one."

—*Cleveland Plain Dealer*

Also by William P. Wood

Sudden Impact

Gangland

Pressure Point

The Bribe

Broken Trust

Rampage

Quicksand

Fugitive City

The Bone Garden

WILLIAM P. WOOD

STAY OF EXECUTION

A NOVEL

TURNER

Turner Publishing Company
4507 Charlotte Avenue • Suite 100 • Nashville, Tennessee 37209
www.turnerpublishing.com

STAY OF EXECUTION

This is a work of fiction. All the characters and events portrayed in this book
are either products of the author's imagination or are used fictitiously.

Cover design: Maxwell Roth
Book design: Glen Edelstein

Library of Congress Control Number: 2014954225

ISBN: 978-1-62045-473-2 (paperback), 978-1-63026-755-1 (hardcover)

Printed in the United States of America
14 15 16 17 18 19 0 9 8 7 6 5 4 3 2 1

*For the Kings, Emory, Shannon, Jessica, Emory Jr.,
and Zachary, friends in good times and bad.*

If Soules to Hell's vast Prison never come
    Committed for their Crimes, but destin'd be,
Like Bondmen born, whose prison is their home,
    And long e're they were bound could not be free;

Then hard is Destinie's dark Law, whose Text
    We are forbid to read, yet must obey;
And reason with her useless eyes is vext,
    Which strive to guide her where they see no way.
                         —Sir William Davenant

STAY OF EXECUTION

MAY

ONE

ROBERT CARNES SAT ON the bed in his underwear, his back against the headboard, and pretended to read *TV Guide.* The girl lay beside him on her stomach, a faded blue towel draped over her backside. The air conditioner in the motel room was on high, rumbling and hissing faintly, and from the bathroom, Carnes heard Lee singing an old Stones song off-key.

Carnes had been staring at the same page for ten minutes. He really did not see it. He owed a great deal of money, and he was waiting for the phone call that would save his life. He did not want the girl or Lee to know he was anxious.

"What do you think, Bobby?" Melanie asked. She said her name was Melanie, and that was fine with Carnes. He and Lee had picked her up at Rico Taco on Washington Boulevard as they came from the airport into Los Angeles last night. Melanie Vogt she called herself. She confessed to using Ginger or Amber sometimes. Carnes could not recall all the names he had used over the years.

"What do I think about what?" he asked gently.

"Your horoscope I just read."

"Sorry, honey. I wasn't listening."

She sighed slightly and turned back to the newspaper folded on her pillow. "I said, 'Capricorn.' That's you. 'Today will be a day of much activity. Watch for strangers and legal matters. Pisces will play a part as well.' Lee, he's a Pisces, right? See what I mean?" She stopped reading and looked at him expectantly.

"I don't know what he is."

"You should find out."

"I'm thinking about a few other things. I don't care about that stuff."

The singing from the bathroom was getting on his nerves. It was already past eleven in the morning and no phone call, and Carnes didn't think there was much to sing about. Spread on the small table beside the bureau were eight neatly folded sandwich bags of white powder, the very best methamphetamine Carnes had been able to get on short notice. The eight bags represented every cent he had and were the basis of his deal today.

One bag was nearly empty, open and deflated. Lee had been working on that pretty steadily since they got Melanie into the room last night. Carnes admitted only to a tablespoon in his coffee a few hours ago. The room still smelled of burnt coffee.

"I believe this." Melanie solemnly tapped the newspaper. "My daddy was a trainer, you know. Here in LA? LA's all I really remember, but we moved around a lot of tracks when I was a kid." She had a blithe way of talking about serious things and a solemn tone reserved for the frivolous, Carnes noticed.

"He get fired a lot?"

"He quit. Anyway, my daddy always got good jobs because he was good with horses."

"Some talent."

"It is. They liked him, he could just touch them, they knew he was okay for them. Didn't matter what happened, he always got jobs because horses liked him. We stayed the longest near Anita, you know? Santa Anita? You like horses, Bobby?"

"Could care less. Jesus, what's he singing so loudly about?"

Melanie went on, "Well, a man should like horses."

"Like Daddy?"

"They like you, it shows you got sincere qualities." She shifted a little so the rest of the newspaper under her crinkled. "See, horses are smarter than people."

"I believe it."

Lee shut off the shower and his bad singing was louder.

Carnes smiled at her gently. If anybody asked, he would say he was first attracted to her eyes. Violet eyes. Set in a small, tan face. He put his hand on the lower part of her back as she talked, feeling the warm skin, the rise of her buttocks where the towel just barely covered her. They had her for another couple of hours and he seriously considered paying her until they got back. It was her eyes. So wide and clear and innocent, although there was little real innocence about Melanie.

She wiggled unconsciously under his hand. He let her voice wash over his anxiety about the silent telephone. "Anyway, so my daddy always made fun of horoscopes, stars, the whole thing. People been reading them for thousands of years. So there's something. But he'd read the horoscope to me, made faces because he said my mother, who I never saw too much, he says she's always going, 'Watch out, the stars got it right, you better listen.' And he thinks it's really funny."

"Isn't it funny?" His white hand paused on the tan skin.

"No. It ain't funny. Nope. Nope. My daddy read this one, this's what I'm telling you, you're so smart. He read this one, maybe I read it for him. It goes, 'Beware of animals today. Trust your instincts and make travel plans, attend to loved ones.' He's a Taurus." She recited from deep memory. "And Jesus, that's the day a horse named Rose Queen went crazy and bolted from her stall, and my daddy tried to stop her, only she's scared of something, so scared she just keeps on going, and he's knocked against the stall gate, kind of snapping because Rose Queen bolted. My daddy hit his head and he went blind." She sighed again.

"Blind?"

"Can't see nothing. You hold your hand up, he don't see it.

Somebody's got to help him do everything. He can't even like walk around."

"Somebody else? Not you, honey?"

"Not lately." She pursed her lips in anger.

"You think this horse knew about his horoscope?" Carnes asked in his always gentle voice.

"No, dummy. It's just there's a lot goes on we don't know about. I don't mind taking advice anyplace I get it, if it's good advice. There's got to be something to this, it's so old." Melanie squirmed on the bed, the newspapers crinkling and crackling, until she was opposite his face. "I know my daddy always wished later he'd listened to that advice. He cursed the day he laughed at it."

Carnes grinned and stroked her head, amused at the melodrama, the cheap moral and ready sentiment. She believed in a simpler existence of signs and omens, determined ends laid down and as observable as sunrise. She did not, he saw, understand the chaotic vortex of people's lives. There were no guideposts.

Over the long, sleepless night, he and Lee taking turns with Melanie, Lee stopping only to recharge his battery with the very pure methamphetamine in the sandwich bags, Carnes came to know the signs of her excitement, real or feigned. She knew what was in the sandwich bags, and Lee had blabbed enough to her. She wouldn't say it directly, but she was obviously excited by two significant crank dealers buying her for the night.

Carnes also thought, out of vanity, that there was something intimate in her violet eyes, something she saved for him and not Lee.

"You having a good time?" he asked, stroking her shoulders.

"Sure I am."

"I like you a lot."

"I like you."

He let her kiss his hand, then lick his palm. "You like Lee?"

"Not as much as you, Bobby."

Carnes smiled. "Why do you like me?"

"I just get a good feeling. Right off. I mean this in a good way. You remind me of my daddy."

His hand drew back in irritation. "Thanks a lot."

Melanie rolled on her side, facing him, her small, hard breasts white against her tan. "No, dummy. I don't mean like that. I mean, you're steady Eddie. You know what you're doing."

"Sure I do." He laid aside the *TV Guide*. Lee was shaving and still singing badly.

"What about your folks? I told you about mine," she said.

"I don't have any."

"They dead?"

"No. I never had any."

"Like an orphan."

"No. I never had any mom or dad."

She smiled. "Okay. Everybody's got folks."

"Not me."

Puzzled, "That's a joke, right?"

"You think so?"

"Yeah, I do."

"I'm not lying to you. Trust me."

He felt a strange twinge of protectiveness toward her. She did seem to trust him.

The bathroom door opened with a rush of steam, and Lee strode out, a towel loose on his slender waist. "Rotich call?" he asked, sitting down at the table, brushing a small pinch of crank onto a piece of toilet paper.

"Not yet."

"Asshole." Lee rolled the toilet paper into a tube. "Let me call him. Get him moving."

"He said he had some arrangements. He'll call when he's done." Carnes suppressed his anger. Lee was a great partner and had helped close some lucrative deals in the last few months, but he was impetuous and grating during a wait. "Leave some, okay? I'd like to show Rotich a couple of full bags," Carnes said.

"We got seven, Bobby. The guy doesn't need to see any more." Lee licked his lips for Melanie's benefit, then slowly chewed the rolled paper and swallowed.

They made a strong bargaining unit, him and Lee. Carnes had the bland, blond face of a college professor, maybe a middle manager at a small factory, with gray frame glasses and a tall, slightly fleshy build. Lee, on the other hand, was an obvious hardcase, long brown hair in a rubberband ponytail, indoor pallor, thin. Excitable. I'm a better shot than he is, Carnes thought. And smarter.

He tossed the *TV Guide* at Lee. "Why don't you watch something?"

"Hey, after we're done, I'm taking you to Disneyland," Lee said to Melanie.

"I always wanted to go there."

Carnes broke in. "We won't have time."

"She's never been there, Bobby."

"We're going right back to Elko."

Lee grimaced. "Well, that's a new one. Tell me anything else you got in mind."

"That's all."

Melanie rolled onto her back. "Where's Elko?"

"Nevada," Lee answered.

"Near Vegas? I never been there."

"Not so close."

Lee sat down on the other side of the bed beside her. "You ready for a ride, sweet thing? Looks like we can't go to Disneyland for one."

"I guess I could be." She shrugged and stayed on her back.

Carnes felt another surge of protectiveness and told himself it was wholly wasted on Melanie. She had been fending for herself on Washington Boulevard, around Pico, sometimes Sawtelle, she said, with the Mexican guys who stood around with nothing to do, waving at passing cars like she did, hoping for work. She could handle Lee.

"How about giving us some room, Bobby?" Lee took off his towel, drawing Melanie to him. Then he said abruptly, "The son of a bitch's supposed to call an hour ago. What's taking so long?"

"I don't know."

Carnes slowly got off the bed and went to the window, pushing aside the heavy, flaccid drapes. A hot May Thursday outside the Half-Moon Motel, blurred cars rushing by on the broad street, passing a vast tire store, all-you-can-eat restaurants marked by signs of dancing chickens and cows, and above it all, the Los Angeles skyline in the distance in every direction, rising against the smudged morning.

Lee had no idea how much money Carnes owed or how little time the crew in Bakersfield had given him to pay it back. Twenty-four hours to get their crank or cash, he thought.

He heard the two of them on the bed and didn't want to look. Somehow it was different in the daylight, even with the drapes closed and all the lights off so it seemed like night in the room. Last night, in the genuine darkness, making love to Melanie was beautiful. It felt spoiled now.

"Maybe something's wrong, maybe he's doing something, Bobby." Lee, nuzzling Melanie, paused. "I don't like the guy. I never met him, I don't like him anyway. You say he's okay. I think he's fucking around."

Carnes went to the small closet and got out his black suitcase. Beneath Lee, Melanie hummed to herself on the bed. Carnes opened the suitcase, took out his three pastel button-down shirts and one white shirt and laid them carefully on the bureau. He slowly checked the .44 that had been under them.

"You got a gun," he heard her say. He looked up and Melanie was staring at him. "You both got guns?" she asked almost primly.

"Sure we do," Carnes answered. It looked almost comical, Lee vainly struggling on her, the crank finally galvanizing him and making him impotent at the same time, while she rocked and stared at the .44.

"Jeezuh H. Jeezuh H. Jeezuh H. Damn," Lee said bitterly, looking down at himself. "Won't do anything."

Carnes put the gun on the bureau. It was getting far too late, and the longer he waited, the angrier he'd become.

"I'm calling Rotich," he said.

For a while after the two of them left, Melanie enjoyed the rare luxury of a paid motel room to herself. She showered twice. She went to the Half-Moon's small coffee shop and bought a ham and cheese sandwich and a Coke with a lot of ice and took them back to the room. She ate happily and left the TV on and then tried to find any crank or money Bobby might have left behind, but he'd taken it all. He and Lee left with two large black suitcases, after emptying them, and two large guns. Bobby's few clothes were still in the closet.

She debated simply walking out. She didn't like guns, having a vivid memory of the small revolver her father used to keep beside the door wherever they lived. It was the same gun he hit her mother with, and the bruise stayed for weeks.

But, Bobby had paid her another one hundred fifty dollars to be there when he came back around two. Then the three of them would drive out to the airport and fly to Reno. It was the closest major city to Elko. Lee wanted to go visit San Diego if they couldn't go to Disneyland, and she had volunteered to show them around the city. She had not been there since her father worked tracks in Tijuana and Calexico. But Bobby was sharp. No side trips. No time.

She took off her jeans and sandals. Bobby had given her one chore to do with the airline while she was sitting around. She did like him. He was pleasant, even kind, not like Lee, who preferred roughhousing and struck her as undependable. She prided herself on forming instant and accurate assessments of men. She did not quite see why a solid type like Bobby was hanging around a guy like Lee.

"He's my partner," Bobby told her, "and I put up with things from him I wouldn't tolerate from another person on earth. You have to have a partner."

"Not always," she said, thinking of her own independent life.

"It takes two to do anything you really want to do," Bobby had said.

She knew all about sticking with someone. Her father had been drinking and getting thrown off tracks long before Rose Queen blinded him. She stayed with him through it all. Even when he hit her or ignored her for weeks. Because, like Bobby, he had a sweet side, too. She remembered the five small bouquets of mums he left around the apartment on her twelfth birthday. And the times he'd sneak her onto the favorite in some race, just so she could sit on the famous horse and view the world from that height.

Finally there were limits to what she'd put up with, after the cleaning, yelling, the taunting. The last time she saw him, he had moved into a duplex in a not very good neighborhood in El Monte. He shared it with a grossly fat Mexican woman who shouted.

She picked up the phone. She was unsure what Bobby had in mind after he and Lee finished their business with this man Rotich, who seemed to make them both very angry. She avoided things that made people angry, if possible. She tried to avoid bad influences. It was, she felt, an accomplishment more or less like avoiding drugs, which was astonishing at this time in her life. Someone she went out with was always offering her something. The Mexican guys, trying to get work, any work, from the cars that rushed by on Sawtelle, they smiled and offered her hits off whatever they were smoking. She said no. She had had an unpleasant experience several months earlier when three bikers had taken her to their clubhouse in El Monte, casually held out some blue capsules, and she gamely took them with beer. Her father was living only a few miles away, but he might as well have been on the moon. She didn't get out of the clubhouse for days and had the continual feeling, when she had feeling at all, that the top of her skull was about to blow off.

This business she was in now was only a temporary thing. She intended to go to cosmetology school soon. She had already gotten an application from a good one in Montebello.

For the moment she was content to wait for Bobby to come back, and she was looking forward to leaving Los Angeles for a while with him. He apparently liked her very much. He had given her his credit card number and his home address in Elko.

Now she was on the phone, listening to that insipid announcement that played over and over, waiting to make new plane reservations for the three of them. Bobby said he wanted a much earlier flight to Reno. He'd changed his mind after talking to Rotich. He told her as he snapped shut the empty suitcase, the second one. She wondered why he and Lee were taking two empty suitcases with them. And the guns and the crank.

If she and Bobby spent any time together, she would ask him to keep guns out of her sight.

He'd probably do it too, because he liked her. She thought this crank dealing might pay for school faster than what she was doing.

"Hi. Hi. Hi," she said, gripping the phone, looking down at the clear polish on her toenails, wondering if it needed touching up. "I got a reservation today. I just had a change of plans."

TWO

CARNES DROVE THE RENTED CAR, checking street directions he'd neatly printed on the city map, on the seat between him and Lee. Graceful as white paper gliders, seagulls circled and clustered in the sky as he watched, heard them keening, settling to garbage cans to fight over scraps. It was not a long drive from the motel to Marina del Rey, but once he turned off Venice Boulevard, the streets twisted suddenly. Two small sweat drops hung on his eyelids. Lee stared at the white houses and green lawns, the tattered palms reaching upward toward the flaring sun and the iron bar of pollution just below it. It was a leisurely day, the people on the sidewalks in shorts, bright cut-off shirts, their eyes clouded behind black sunglasses.

He made another turn, and there, like a gray-green cloth spreading out to the horizon, was the Pacific. Carnes tasted the faint bitterness of the marina's salt water. The air was hot, dry. Soundless and dreamlike, triangular sails moved across the water. Farther out, a long black freighter lay motionless.

Lee was silent, tensed for the meeting. He only laughed when a man in a wheelchair got caught in a crosswalk, buffeted by people who spun him and his chair in helpless circles.

Rotich lived on a palm- and elm-lined street. He stood on the perfect green lawn of a large ranch house. Tarp-covered boats waited in every driveway on the street.

"That's him," Carnes said, sliding the car up the wide driveway. "He's doing okay."

"That's why we're coming to him with this deal." He got out, holding one suitcase, Lee taking the other. Rotich strolled to them, hands in his khaki shorts. He was about fifty, balding, with skin reddened as if baked, and hairy arms and legs. He grinned.

"Good to see you again, Bobby." He offered his hand. "You must be the famous Lee."

"How come I'm famous?" Lee asked suspiciously.

Carnes said, "Barry thinks his phones may be tapped. I made all the calls using your name, Lee."

The news startled Lee, and he started to say something, but Rotich said, "I got everything laid out for you, but you in a rush?"

"We got a little time, Barry," Carnes said. He noticed he was sweating more and blinked away the burning salt in his eyes.

"Come back with me. I want to show off some stuff." Rotich merrily waved them forward.

Carnes gave Lee a little sign to go ahead, and they followed close by Rotich toward the house. Carnes could not recall how many different houses Rotich had bought and sold in the last few years.

Lee was disturbed. He said openly, "How come you used my name?"

"We can talk about it later. It's all right. The phones are fine."

Rotich, if he was listening, pretended not to hear. He said to Carnes, "It just gets better and better, don't it, Bobby? How long we been doing business?"

"Six years."

"Seven, my ass. How long you guys been working together again?" He pointed at Lee. Carnes knew Rotich's mannerisms and the unsubtle probing was characteristic.

"About a year," Lee answered, calmer, seeing Carnes so calm. He trusts me, Carnes thought. "Me and Bobby knew each other for a long time now, out around Reno, Tahoe. Elko. Grew up near each other, kind of lost track, worked with other guys, kept in touch, finally hooked up."

"Other guys?" Rotich led them to a blue-trimmed four-car garage and cracked the door open with a grunt.

"You probably know every sorry one of them, Barry. What counts here, right now today, is that you know me." Carnes ducked into the garage with the two others. It was hot enough that he had sweated through his white shirt, and his pants stuck irritatingly to his legs.

"Hell, yes," Rotich agreed, spreading his arms wide, bringing his fleshy palms together with a smack. "Hell. I'm curious is all. Now. Look at that. Pretty, right? I mean, down deep pretty?"

Carnes indifferently looked at the speedboat on its cushioned cradle, its sleek hull glimmering in the sunlight from a window. Lee smirked admiringly, and Rotich playfully slapped it and praised it.

"I'm getting a little thirsty," Carnes said to cut it short.

Reluctantly, Rotich said, "We'll go in. One more thing, come on around the side." He waved them on, his hairy arms flapping.

"I wished I had something like this," Lee said, glancing back at the garage as they left.

Rotich put his arm around Lee as if they'd been friends for years. "Bobby and me'll make you rich, you stick with us."

"Bobby ain't rich like you."

Carnes tensed, walking slowly. "I am rich. I just don't show it around."

"Hell yes, Bobby's rich," Rotich agreed. "You just won't find it. Keeps everything real secret, all the bank accounts he's got, money stuck around." They were in a tree-shaded backyard. "I believe in using money, my own self. Have fun."

Carnes paused, hands tight on the suitcase. A long yellow camper was parked in the backyard, bricks at its wheels. Two broken bicycles lay beside it. The plastic toy tanks and trucks alarmed him.

Rotich was grinning and showing off the camper when Carnes interrupted him.

"Anybody else home, Barry? I thought we were alone today."

Rotich apologetically wiggled his thick eyebrows. "Me, too. Then Joyce won't take the boy out. Won't take him to the park. He's acting up, so she's mad at him."

Lee shrugged and looked at Carnes.

Rotich went on, "It ain't no big thing. You know Joyce. She's been doing my books for years. Sam's only nine, so he don't know nothing, except he's got a bad mouth from someplace. Now. This camper is where I keep all my crank, moving in and out. I got the only key." He patted the side of his shorts.

Lee said, "Boat and a camper." He was delighted at the spoils.

Carnes cautiously wiped his sweating hand on his slacks. He decided changes had to be made sometimes in even well-designed plans. It was impossible to foresee every contingency, and Rotich leaving the kid and his wife at home simply added a new element. The rest was unchanged.

"Yeah," Carnes said. "Let's go see the family."

Joyce Rotich lay on the living room couch when they came inside. The air was cold and dry. Carnes noticed that all of the furniture was new, and there were stacks of boxes along the walls so the house looked like a showroom with its inventory displayed for sale.

She was a little younger than Rotich, dressed in a turquoise halter top and shorts, drowsy from the bottle of sweet wine on the floor by her and the ashtray of discarded joints she had been rolling and smoking. A stereo played too loudly somewhere.

Joyce Rotich's eyes were sunken, but she sat up, licked her gray lips, and hugged Carnes when he bent to her. "Who's this one?" She pointed at Lee.

"New partner. Lee Ferrera."

"No Doug? I liked him, very nice guy."

Carnes said, "Doug took off. I don't know where he went."

"You can't hold onto anybody," she said. "Everybody leaves you."

"I'm staying," Lee said, ignoring Rotich's sullen frown as he appraised Joyce.

She rolled a joint, offered it to each of them, and only Rotich took it, lit it, inhaled deeply, and gave it back to her. "You bring anything for Sam? He asked," she said.

"Couldn't find anything this time. I'm moving fast."

Rotich smacked his hands together. "Well, then hell. Let's not waste all this time. Come on back."

Carnes and Lee followed him to the rear of the house. Bottles and empty buckets of take-out chicken lined the hallway, covered with tiny ants. Here and there someone had started to write on the cream-colored walls but stopped, giving a startled, hasty appearance to the half-words. Carnes felt his drying sweat chill.

He interrupted Rotich's chatter again. "You still got that Glock 17, Barry?"

"Ammo's light or something. You shoot your own foot off, all seventeen shots come out. I got solid stuff, old shotgun, some pistols in the bedroom."

Carnes nodded casually. "Tell Lee about the time you shot an apple off Joyce's head." That recollection ought to distract Rotich.

Rotich laughed. "My birthday party four years ago. I got her against this old tree and put an old apple on her head, and I was so shit-faced I couldn't see the tree, much less the damn apple."

Carnes laughed, too, and Rotich took them into a veneer-paneled room he unlocked. "I couldn't even hold the gun steady, and she's got her eyes squished tight shut."

"What happened?" Lee asked.

"I got off a couple pops." Rotich locked the door behind them. "You saw her just now. What do you think happened?"

"I don't know."

"I blew her brains out." Rotich laughed loudly and settled behind a glass-topped desk covered with precision balance scales, four dark ledger books, several chemical bottles that gave off a dank, musty odor. Boat oars hung on the wall.

Lee, Carnes saw, didn't like being kidded. He frowned as Rotich bragged about the house costing four hundred thousand dollars, paying the down in cash, maybe selling it again soon.

"Let me show what I've brought," Carnes said, and Rotich pulled the top ledger and one of the delicate scales closer. Carnes opened his suitcase and took out the seven white sandwich bags and laid them before Rotich. Lee sat down on a small sofa jammed between file cabinets and more chemical bottles, his suitcase between his legs. He tapped his feet to the muffled stereo music.

Carnes thoughtfully watched Rotich open one bag, sniff, grin, spoon a small mound onto the scale, open one of the chemical bottles, and while he was doing that, Carnes took out his .44 from the suitcase.

"Give me the key to the camper, Barry," he said gently.

Lee was on his feet. "What's this, man?"

"It's all right. I know what I'm doing," Carnes said. Rotich had frozen, his large red face scowling.

"Not funny, Bobby," he said. "I'm real pissed here."

"Give me the key," Carnes repeated, bringing the gun close enough that Rotich could see down the barrel. "If you've got any pieces in here, you leave them alone."

"Put it down. There ain't any in here. Cool off." Rotich was instantly conciliatory.

"While Barry's giving me the key, Lee, please go bring Joyce and the boy in here. Let's have everyone together."

Lee hesitated. "I don't know."

"Please do it right now, Lee. Right now," Carnes repeated.

Lee jumped at that, as Carnes knew he would. He was a very predictable man in his own way and a perfect replacement for Doug. And the three others who had gone before Doug. Lee bolted to the door, unlocked it, and tromped cursing down the hallway, kicking a cardboard bucket.

Carnes said to Rotich, still holding an open bag of crank, "It's good stuff. You can keep it, Barry. Give me the camper key and open your lockbox and that's all I want."

Rotich licked his lips and slowly stood up. "You just fucking away your whole damn life, man, you know that? Nobody's going to touch you ever again." He gave Carnes the key.

"I don't like messing up a good business relationship either," Carnes said, shaking his head. He seemed to invite sympathy from the man he held a gun on.

Rotich went on grumbling, threatening, as he opened a set of sliding doors in one cabinet behind the desk. There was a shotgun propped inside.

"Don't touch it, Barry."

"I am not fucking crazy," Rotich said. "Not like some people." He brought a large steel box, worked its combination lock, and stood back. "That's the last I got around. I been paying cash for everything."

Carnes nodded, automatically reckoning the stacks of rubber-band-bound cash. "It's fine, Barry. Don't be ashamed." He carefully slid the money into his suitcase and locked it.

Lee returned with Joyce Rotich, who held a small boy, a smear of melted chocolate rimming his mouth. He was terrified, mute, and Carnes didn't think he'd had a bath in weeks.

"Go over there with Barry," he said to the woman, and she tugged the boy with her.

"You don't have to tie us up or anything shitty like that. Just take everything and get the fuck out," Rotich said, ignoring the half-terrified grab Joyce made at his shirt. Sam stared at Carnes in terror and amazement. He wonders why his pal is scaring everybody, Carnes thought.

"All I want you to do, Barry, is lie on the floor. You by him, Joyce, and you hold onto Sam. You stay facedown. Lee, please disconnect the telephone. Then you stay on the floor for a count of one thousand. I'll lock the door. You won't know if we've left or if I'm waiting right outside, so you stay down." Carnes spoke as Lee yanked the phone out with a bang.

"What? What happened? What's wrong?" Joyce stared and stammered.

"Please get down on the floor."

Lee stood by, eyes going from one face to the other. He held his .44 nervously, uncertainly.

Rotich nodded and clumsily got down to his knees. Sam started to whine, and Joyce absentmindedly put her hand over his mouth as they lay facedown on the carpet. It was unpleasant in the room, even with the air-conditioning on so high, the chemical smell and fear overpowering it.

Rotich looked up as Carnes stepped over him. "Stupid fucking move, Bobby," he said.

Carnes nodded slowly, put the .44 to Rotich's sun-reddened neck and fired. Joyce screamed and tried to stand, but Lee fired at her, and she fell down on Sam, who started to squirm from under her. Carnes quickly bent, firing into the boy's head.

Lee was pumped way up with shock and surprise. "You planned this all the time. You did. Fucker. Fucker. You didn't say nothing to me." He shook his gun as if it were hot.

Then he shouted as Carnes fired three more times standing over the bodies, into each head.

In a swift, seamless action, Carnes swept six of the sandwich bags into Lee's suitcase. Never take everything. Always leave a scene looking like it should, like a drug deal suddenly gone wrong. He dropped his gun into Lee's suitcase. He didn't look at the bodies again or the bloody explosions of flesh on the carpet. He never looked again.

He spoke calmly. "On our way out, Lee, let's try to find a bag or something to carry all the stuff in the camper. I don't think it will all fit in your suitcase, and mine's filled with money."

Lee chattered, waving his gun. "You didn't tell me you had a setup here. You said it's a buy. Just a buy."

"I didn't know this would happen."

"You did, man. You planned it all out, man."

Carnes strode out of the room, down the hallway, looking for the bedroom. "We don't have time to argue. Are you mad at me? You want me to do it over?" He didn't wait for Lee to reply. He went into the rose-tinted bedroom, the stereo banging out its beat, and tore open bureau drawers, flung open two large walk-in closets, adding more jumbled clothes to the heaps already in the room as he searched for another suitcase.

Lee sat down on the bed. "You should've told me. Jee. Zus."

"Well, you did a fine job." He found a battered blue suitcase and brought it out. "These people never cleaned up. I don't think I ever saw a reasonably decent home made into a pigsty so quickly. Barry's only lived here a couple of months."

"That's three people, man. I feel like shit." Lee's tautly stretched face was shiny, and he stood up jerkily.

Carnes walked out, carrying the suitcase. "Barry chose a high-risk profession. And Joyce knew what was going on because she helped him cook crank and cut coke and was a doper herself. You saw that. If it makes you feel any better, Lee, the kid wasn't theirs. He was Joyce's sister's boy. Joyce's sister is doing time in Kansas."

They went into the hot, hazy afternoon and emptied the camper of five large white packages of crank, enough to make close to two hundred thousand dollars from the right buyer. Carnes had no doubt he could satisfy the Bakersfield crew and have a fair return for himself, too. He helped Lee pack the suitcases with crank.

An old fig tree, gnarled and pendulous with green fruit, rustled in the hot wind. Carnes thought of picking some figs and letting them ripen at home in Elko, but decided he could buy any he really wanted.

They put the suitcase in the trunk of the rented car, and Carnes drove away, down the street of white wood and stucco houses. He passed two little girls in pink swimsuits chasing each other on the sidewalk and slipped into the unbroken weekday-afternoon traffic on Venice Boulevard slowly and invisibly.

On the Marina Expressway, Lee came to life again. He shouted, "Everybody's going to know it was us. Me. You used my name. He's your fucking bud."

"Barry had a lot of customers. I'm sure his neighbors noticed."

"What about me? I'm out there, man."

"Everybody's dead," Carnes explained quietly. "I don't think it matters." When Lee wouldn't stop complaining, he added, "You made a lot of money just now. Think about that."

They passed boat repair shops and the carelessly mingled-in, glassy blue office buildings and Carnes was again aware of the cold silence at the heart of things. No one knew Rotich and his family were dead, and when the news did come out, no one would care. The boats would go sailing, the planes flying, the people chatting and laughing on LA's sidewalks.

"So what was I along for?" Lee demanded. "You need some asshole to help you?"

"I needed a partner I could trust."

"All you did was fuck me, man."

"I play fair. You know that. Ask anybody."

"If I can find them. They all walked like Doug, man. Maybe they got smart." Lee's sinewy white arm dangled listlessly from his window.

"Maybe they did," Carnes said. He was watching the overhead signs for the turn to the Half-Moon Motel. His hands were dry on the wheel. His anxiety had passed mercifully like a summer storm.

He briefly saw the Pacific below the sandy, scrub-covered hillsides around the street and dreamed of faraway sails on the green water. Melanie lay tanned and naked on the boat deck, and her violet eyes fastened on him.

"You never tell me anything. You never told me shit," Lee burst out, kicking the floorboard hard.

Carnes smiled. He didn't want Lee upset and uncontrollable.

"I'll tell you something now. It's about Melanie. I trust you or I wouldn't tell you."

"Tell me what?" Lee asked sullenly.

"I think I'm in love."

It was about what she expected, even with Bobby's repeated promises and the extra hundred dollars he gave her as he and Lee packed up in two minutes flat. Lee, she noticed, was oddly quiet, paid no attention to her now, and had a gray sheen over his face that was disgusting. She wondered if he was sick. All the clothes went *whop,*

whop into a pile on the bed, and she wondered where their suitcases were.

"But I just changed the plane reservations for us three," she said when Bobby explained quietly that he and Lee were leaving right away.

"Well, that's no problem. We'll get something at the airport now. You cancel two of the other reservations and keep one for yourself. You can meet me in Elko later."

Bobby gathered some shirts across his arm. He was soaked with sweat from the heat outside, and his boyish, plump face looked so much like the kids she used to work with at the racetracks. He reminded her of a boy who used to give her Life Savers.

"I thought I was coming with you," she said, folding her arms.

"Not right away. If we didn't have business to finish, you could come." He stood close to her.

Lee was hollering again, "I want to go now, Bobby. Right now, Bobby," and cursed her a little.

Melanie looked at her pink repainted toenails as she pretended to sulk. "So what am I supposed to do?"

"Fly out and I'll meet you in Reno, take you to my house. Door-to-door service."

"No, thank you."

"Okay. Go home now. I got your address and I'll call."

"You won't call."

"I said I like you."

Lee snapped open the motel room door, and the heat flooded in. "I'll load up the car," he declared. He took a bunch of clothes and stomped out.

"What's he so mad about?" she asked, holding on to her hurt expression.

"Don't worry about him. Lee's not staying much longer. He's not staying long in Nevada."

She relented slightly. Lee gone would be nice. "You'll really call?"

"I swear to God. And I'll fly you to Reno, and we'll just take everything from there." He sounded sincere. She heard car doors slamming outside and Lee shouting for Bobby to get moving.

"I'm sorry you paid extra for nothing," she said.

"I'll get my money's worth later." He grinned. Another shout from Lee, and the car horn impatiently honked twice. "I better go."

"Between you and me," she confided, "I'm not sorry to see the last of you-know-who," and she pointed outside.

"Me, too. I'll see you very soon."

She unfolded her arms, stood a little on her toes because Bobby was about five inches taller than her, and kissed him hard on the mouth. She felt the bunched-up shirts he held against her chest. "Thanks for everything. I'll be waiting."

He kissed her back. He was flushed, almost as if blushing, and it struck her as very endearing. He didn't say anything, winked at her, and went out the door. She stood in the doorway and watched him load the car and Lee drive them away, squealing the tires across the hot asphalt of the motel's wide parking lot. Melanie felt a curious sense of loss and anticipation. She believed some of what Bobby told her. He would call and she would go to Reno.

It wasn't wise to believe too much of what people said, and her own family was proof enough of that. So many oaths to stop drinking, promises to hold a job, weeping apologies for blows struck when he was drunk. She'd heard every excuse people make from her father.

But Bobby was mostly truthful, she thought.

She stayed in the doorway, staring at the Half-Moon Motel's green and red highlighted sign, futilely burning against the afternoon's stinging sunshine and the city's paradoxical, edgy torpor. The motel's single story was a flat snaking building curled around itself in white and cinder-block sameness. It was bound by a machine-stamped dullness to the brown-tiled beauty salon and gas stations across the street, the frying oil smell drifting upward from Chinese and Korean and Southern restaurants that edged hopefully, like supplicants, toward the sluggish freeway streaming nearby. All one city, locked and interconnected freakishly and inextricably together. The dusty green eucalyptus around the motel quivered in the hot breeze. She closed the door to keep it out.

She had the room until checkout time at five so she decided to take a nap, pleasantly thinking about the future. She fell facedown on the unmade bed, into the sweat-tinged sheets.

She heard the ice machine two doors down rattling fitfully before she went to sleep.

SEPTEMBER

THREE

LATE, WYLIE MORGANTHAU thought, late, late. He hurried across the street, coat flapping, to the City Hall press conference that was already going on. The TV camera lights, stark white against the stone walls of the enclosed plaza, wavered in the crowd of reporters.

Morganthau puffed up the stone stairs, then leaned against a cool pillar. He cursed himself for not thinking how bad traffic was around City Hall and the Criminal Courts Building. He had been slowed to near immobility on Spring Street, the jackhammers and trucks tearing things up as usual. He stuffed two more pieces of gum into his mouth. He wished he were still smoking.

In the center of the lights, the loud questions, whitened and imprisoned, was George Keegan, District Attorney of Los Angeles County. Morganthau strained to hear, walking a little closer, bumping into people. He had wanted to see George before the press conference started, to wish him well on the first day of the Carnes trial. And to tell him the campaign for reelection was going splendidly.

More or less true, Morganthau thought. Keegan's opponent was one of his own deputy DAs, Celia Aguilar, and she was making his run for a second term a bitter war.

Two reporters near him recognized Morganthau and whispered greetings. He smiled dutifully. Being Keegan's campaign chairman was part honor and part drudgery. It was something he owed a very good friend.

A helicopter swept overhead and momentarily drowned out what Keegan was saying. The mayor flying out on some vital mission for the city, Morganthau thought sourly, timing his departure right in the middle of George's press conference so everybody knows he's here. Nelson Poulsby had been a rival of Keegan's for years, but in public he maintained a bland facade of neutrality in the campaign. As if he wouldn't like Aguilar to grind George into dust, Morganthau thought.

The engine's chopping roar faded, and he heard what Keegan was saying.

"I pledged to the people of Los Angeles that this trial would stay in Los Angeles," Keegan said in his familiar deep voice, finger out, eyes hard on the reporter who asked the question.

"What if the judge grants the defense motion to move the trial someplace else?" Persistent jackass, Morganthau thought, trying to remember if the portly man with his shirtsleeves rolled up was with the *L.A. Times* or a wire service.

"The judge won't grant the motion."

"You sound very sure."

"I believe Carnes can get a fair trial in this community," Keegan said. Then he smiled, a grim smile. "Besides, it would be wrong to move him to another city."

More questions. Morganthau squinted up. The City Hall's tall tower rose up like an ancient battlement, pale butter against the unusually blue sky. It had been used as a state capitol in many movies, stood in for grand office buildings, housed Superman's secret at the Daily Planet. It was an essentially Hollywood structure, both real seat of local government and imaginary backdrop. Keegan used to say he looked out from his office across the street, and almost every day there was a camera crew and lights and actors filming something.

The press conference was enclosed by a stone colonnade and arches on the plaza, and Morganthau thought it was exactly the right place to put George Keegan. In a plastic and pliable world, he was fixed and certain. He had principles and a center. The stone castlelike setting suited him.

He was pointing again, answering questions. Early gray hair, wide, hard face, and a stocky build in his dark suit, he looked like a man of character. He looked like a man you could trust as district attorney. Or even governor, Morganthau thought. Why not? People were talking about it if he won this campaign.

At the center of things, now joking, now rebuking, now grave, this was the best time to first see George Keegan. Looking at him in the wavering, hard camera lights, microphones hovering over him on booms, pointed at him, you wouldn't think he was in a tough reelection fight or about to personally take a major murder case to trial. Or that his wife had died in a car accident only three months ago.

Even after all these years, Morganthau did not know how George Keegan could present so solid a face to the world or maintain such confidence. He always seemed at ease in public. Three years ago, at Elaine Keegan's tenth birthday party at the Bel-Air Hotel, Morganthau and Muriel toasted their old friends George and Leah. He remembered the cake with yellow candles, the Guatemalan waiters who didn't use deodorant, the heavy silverware. While Leah and a slightly embarrassed Chris Keegan watched, George got up and sang "Happy Birthday" to Elaine. The people in the restaurant recognized him and applauded. He liked applause. There was nothing wrong with that. Shy Elaine, beside Leah, enjoyed the attention, too.

But what Morganthau remembered most was how George and Leah acted together. They were usually more affectionate in public than at home, which Morganthau thought odd. Leah patted George when he sat down after singing, kissed his neck, like they were just getting to know each other. With friends, they were more natural, a settled couple, Morganthau thought. Leah talked more. She talked over George, and he let her, which was something he didn't tolerate from others. At home or in public, though, George was different around Leah. It was hard to describe. Protective, maybe. Afraid for her for some reason.

He fended some people away from her. He made sure she had time for the committees and friends he didn't share, things she had taken up before they were married. He would try to slow her drinking down, too. You could see her slowly, steadily, taking one, then two, then three more cocktails at dinner, never losing her smile, the way she could make you feel it was good to have you there. That's the way the old Los Angeles families brought up their kids, and if it seemed haughty at first impression, Morganthau realized that Leah used manners and presence and social events as shields. She was about as opaque as George. You really saw a lot less than you thought you did.

And even during the campaigns, which she tried to get away from, there was George beside her, keeping problems away, like he was standing guard over her. Like he was personally responsible, every second of their lives together, for her happiness and well-being.

Morganthau frowned. Then this past June, when Leah's car went off Mulholland Drive one night, Elaine called, anxious and frightened. She was scared for her father. When Morganthau arrived, the Keegan house in Beverly Hills was filled with people, political friends, Leah's family, neighbors. He and Muriel didn't mingle. They stayed upstairs in a darkened bedroom until morning with George. He lay on the bed, fitfully asleep. He woke up often, talked, then fell asleep again, still wearing the running suit he'd had on when the police came and told him nervously, because he was county district attorney, his wife was dead.

Morganthau could not reconcile the man in the center of the lights, under City Hall's shadow, with the man who wept, mastered his weeping, exhausting himself that long night. This terrible effort was what had scared his daughter and her brother before Morganthau arrived, and why he and Muriel had kept vigil all night. Some kind of fight, an argument about the campaign, had sent Leah from the house, onto the high canyon road. George must think he's responsible somehow, he failed in his duty—if it wasn't love—to protect her.

Jesus, Morganthau thought, I tried telling him. You can't watch people all the time. You can't protect people like they're glass. It didn't do any good. There was, at the middle of George, some darkness that leapt out. He wanted to die, he said.

Morganthau believed him. It was the one time he glimpsed Keegan revealed. Before and afterward, the man was himself again. Confident. Impulsive. Arrogant sometimes, Morganthau admitted. Since Leah's death, he wondered whether George Keegan ever really joked or smiled naturally. He even wondered how much he truly knew about George before the shock of Leah's death.

It's that private school shit, Morganthau thought. You keep everything to yourself. Being in politics hadn't encouraged George to open up, either. Maybe that's why he liked it.

Muriel sometimes, usually at breakfast, would say that the worst things about George and Leah were their backgrounds. She's rich, old money, old manners, old obligations in public and private. He's restless, not rich, ambitious, and thinks everything in life, people and jobs, are tasks to finish.

"George's job is keeping Leah happy the way she wants to be happy," Muriel would say, reading the paper, eating a bagel. "She's not a happy person."

"Where do you get that? You see them at the hotel, snuggling, George singing to his kid? They're happy. They've got everything."

"I'm saying what I'm saying." Muriel rubbed her fingers on a paper napkin. "All we get to see is the floor show."

"Sometimes you get up," Morganthau snapped, "you got these insights from I don't know where about everybody. We could do a lot worse than be like those two."

Muriel looked at him, serious and irritated. "I love them both, but I wouldn't want to have their grief for anything."

"You don't know what you're talking about."

"Look," Muriel said, "I'll prove it. You know why we stay together, we get along?"

"Tell me," he said sourly. "I forget."

"You go your way"—she held a hand up—"I'm not criticizing. I go mine. We get together on the big stuff, the house, the kids, you know."

"Everybody's like that," he said.

"Not George. Not Leah. The way they been brought up, they're stuck together on everything."

Well, that was Muriel. She could recite every current pop psychology and she knew the history of most of the older Beverly Hills mansions. But, Morganthau admitted, she might be right about the Keegans, especially after that terrible night with George.

But right now, that morning, George looked sure and in control.

Morganthau took out his tasteless gum and brashly stuck it to a City Hall pillar. He unwrapped a couple of fresh pieces.

"You don't have any question about Carnes's guilt?" A TV reporter pressed closer to Keegan.

"None. He's charged with four counts of first-degree murder, and as I pledged to this city, I'm going to ask for the death penalty." Keegan's chief deputy and a few other senior deputies moved to him.

"How do you think doing the trial yourself will help your campaign?" A shouted question beside Morganthau. He glanced at the frosty young woman who asked it.

Keegan shook his head. "I'm not hoping for any campaign advantage."

"It's very unusual for the district attorney himself to try a case," she persisted. "It's extraordinary."

"Maybe more elected district attorneys should try it." Keegan smiled slightly. "I'm having a fine time." He looked at the Criminal Courts Building across the noisy, teeming street. "Carnes is guilty and he will be punished."

Before anything more could be called out, Keegan said, "I don't want to keep Judge Ambrosini waiting," and with his chief deputy, he strode across the plaza, the mass of reporters trailing, lights bobbing up and down like a disorganized army retreating before a foe.

Morganthau thrust close into the crowd and shouted Keegan's name, all the time moving down the stairs of City Hall, into the street, the traffic slowing, stopping.

"Terrific. Good luck. Just came to say good luck," Morganthau said when he was beside Keegan. The pace didn't lessen.

"Thanks, Wylie. You're not going to leave me alone at that fund-raiser tonight?" A grin. Keegan's eyes were hard but tired.

"I've been massaging these Koreans for weeks. I'm going to squeeze them for you tonight."

A quick pat on his back and he let Keegan march ahead, into the large glass doors of the building, held open by two city cops. The reporters dropped off, clustering together among the surly people outside. Morganthau counted only three signs condemning Keegan being paraded up and down by shrill petitioners.

He found himself near the woman who had asked Keegan the last questions. She agreed to have coffee with him. They walked, chatting about the smog and the noise around the court building. Buses with Keegan's campaign ads splashed on their sides, KEEGAN'S THE WAY FOR DA!, rumbled by them.

They sat down in a small Chinese coffee shop around the corner from the Criminal Courts Building. It was surprising to find embroidered cloth napkins on the plastic tabletops. The city cops would come here in a few hours for lunch. Only two old men slurped soup now.

"I'd take you for a drink, but I gave up drinking," Morganthau said. "Smoking I gave up, too."

The woman nodded. She had that detached, indifferent expression that passes for clinical objectivity among some reporters. Her nails were short, bitten off. She was maybe thirty, he guessed, her face flushed to health with makeup. He had run into her a few times during the campaign. Her name was Mary something.

"I get a question for every one you ask me," she said. The waiter brought very hot coffee in pasty, heavy mugs.

"Sure, sure. I'd like to get a feel for things from you. How's his going to trial look to you?"

She stirred in several packets of sweetener. "Grand-standing.

Like the time he went out to Santa Monica and had every camera in town there so he could blast some polluters."

"They were polluters. Right into the ocean there."

Mary shrugged slightly, blowing on her coffee. "Keegan knows good pictures and good sound bites."

Morganthau nodded. He loosened his tie. He wished he were still drinking and Muriel had not laid down an iron edict about giving liquor up or her. This campaign had been a sore test of his willpower. Rather than put his used gum in the cloth napkin, he dropped it into the ashtray.

Mary asked, "Tell me why he's still in the campaign at all, Mr. Morganthau. Most of the people I talk to think it would've been more natural for him to drop out after his wife was killed."

He winced at the hot coffee. "George Keegan has a very strong sense of public responsibility. He really thinks he owes this city to run."

"Does he want to be governor?"

"Who knows?"

"You should. You've known him for a long time."

"Since before he was city attorney"—Morganthau put up one hand—"ten years. When he was working for his father-in-law's oil company. My construction company did some work with him."

"But he hasn't told you?"

"Look, Mary, you know his reputation in public. He's a straight shooter. In private he's very private. He keeps to himself."

They sipped, and an argument in Chinese began behind the counter. One of the soup-eaters was pointing angrily at his bill.

"You're supposed to be bankrolling his campaign." She smiled, waiting for his reaction.

"Me? Bullshit. No offense. I made my contribution. And I take him around to meet businessmen in southern California."

"You've got one of the biggest construction firms in Los Angeles. You could pay for his campaign."

"That's what Aguilar says." Morganthau felt himself getting annoyed. He was trying to get a reading from an outsider on George's campaign, but talking to a reporter meant giving in return. It was highly irritating. "George Keegan's campaign records are perfect, look at them."

"I did."

"So you see he gets his money from some businesses, which is terrific because he's tough on environmental laws. He gets money from movie people, cops. People. That's his secret. There's no horseshit with George, and people see that."

"So the latest polls have him and Aguilar apart by about six points. He's not very popular if he's only beating a political baby like her by six points."

"When the votes are in, he's going to beat her. Okay, I got one for you. You think he's showing off taking a big case to trial himself, right? You going to cover it?"

She nodded and pushed away the coffee. "Yeah. Everybody is."

"So it's not such a dumb idea."

"I didn't say it was dumb."

Morganthau had been part of the strategy sessions in July and August when Celia Aguilar began her campaign. Her main attacks on Keegan were that he was an aloof, arrogant administrator. He was not, like her, a veteran of the courtrooms, or had not been for years. He didn't know what went on in the very courtrooms below his eighteenth-floor office in the Criminal Courts Building. He was a general who stayed away from the front line.

Well, Morganthau and everyone else argued that she was partly right. The district attorney presided over an office of nearly a thousand deputies serving seventy or so cities in the county. He was primarily an administrator.

But George, even then, was thinking. Leah's accident was too recent for him to be listening, Morganthau thought. We all figured he was grief stricken, he didn't care what happened in the campaign. I thought he'd quit myself.

But he didn't quit and he was grief stricken and he did announce that Aguilar's attacks couldn't be ignored. Fight her, he said. I can see him standing in that cold living room, Leah's face in pictures on the piano, and he was saying he could prove to the people he was worthy of their trust. He could try a case himself.

He said it with vigor, and there was no argument from then on, even if his campaign people were doubtful.

But they were wrong, Morganthau thought gleefully. Me, too. George was right. This trial was going to be a long soap opera, with him the star. It would occupy TV and the major newspapers, the campaign itself until November. Aguilar was already reduced to reacting to his boldness.

Imagine. The DA himself in court on a major drug-murder trial. Los Angeles loved a show.

Mary took out a small spiral notebook and a black pen. She started jotting. "Keegan's smart. We're all going to be in court watching him. But that means he's raised the stakes. He's got to win the trial. He can't blow it."

"He'll win."

"He hasn't been in a courtroom for years."

"Look, Mary, George Keegan's absolutely convinced Carnes is guilty, and he's going to absolutely convince the jury." He looked at her pen moving in the notebook. "What are you writing?" he asked suspiciously.

"My shopping list." She smiled at him. "Okay. But why this guy? Why did he choose this case, Mr. Morganthau? I mean, he's got everything from drunk driving to serial killers, and he picked a guy who kills a family and his crime partner."

Morganthau hunched forward. There was hardly anybody around to hear, and he suspected no one left in the coffee shop spoke much English anyway. But some things gained solidity by being underlined. "Off the record, I do not know why he wanted this one, but it's the one he wanted from the beginning. I don't know his reasons."

"You make him sound more interesting than a politician."

Morganthau dropped his voice. "Mary, he's the most unusual and fine person I know. No bullshit. The truth."

She watched his face and was satisfied at least he believed it. "Well, I'll watch him with a little more insight, maybe."

He leaned back, dabbed his mouth with the napkin. "Be fair. That's all I ask. How about you meet me for dinner tomorrow? I can go into some detail about our plans to beat Aguilar. Things like that." She was not bad looking, he thought. And she was smart. Her smile was mocking, coy, and the pen paused.

"People talk about you, Mr. Morganthau."

"What? You believe it?"

"Of course not. But I can't have dinner with you."

"Positive?"

She shook her head. "Yes, I am."

He sighed good-naturedly. It had been worth the chance, and he was inwardly pleased that a sort of reputation existed about him. "Well, we'll be talking, I bet. Can I drop you someplace?"

"I'm going to stay and work on my shopping list awhile."

He left her and headed for his car in the lot up the street. He was harshly panhandled three times, wet eyes and dirty hands pushed at him. Morganthau was content. George had at least one reporter thinking of him as something other than a known quantity, and that meant more coverage. The sun was prickly warm, diffused pale light filtering through smog. He stuffed more gum into his mouth and walked by city workers smoking, eating on the grass by the parking lot. He squinted up, thinking it was true he did not understand George Keegan very well. I put buildings up. I know lots and bounds and unions and so many tons of gravel and steel, but George thinks about things you can't see or touch. Justice and responsibility, honor. Sweet Leah, God rest her, once confided that her husband was the most ambitious idealist she ever met. Or ideal something. Morganthau no longer remembered the exact words.

The touchstone for him and George was ambition. I understand that and why George wants to get reelected and maybe go higher. That's real.

The sunlight beat around him. He thought of Keegan a little while ago, bathed in the cameras' lights. I don't think of George any other way, he realized. The light always shines around him.

FOUR

WHEN GEORGE KEEGAN entered the Criminal Courts Building, he had paralegals with him and two deputy DAs carrying the trial files, and county marshals had to link arms to keep back the disordered crowd that surged tidally in the vast lobby. He saw the gray flat stage in the middle of the lobby, which looked permanent. It was supposed to be an escalator, but after twenty years only a hole in the building existed. It was, for Keegan, a reminder of the ramshackle inadequacy of human justice. If we can't make it work, we just cover it up, he thought.

He was used to crowds and people calling his name. He took it for granted that the elevator would be held for him and rush him and his assistants to Department 57 on the twelfth floor. He wasn't nervous, but he did wonder about the tremulant excitement he felt. Stage fright? Doubt? He didn't know. He had to stay clearheaded for this first morning's all-important challenge.

A double line of people were trying to get into the courtroom as spectators stretched back along the corridor, like an audience for a sporting event, the people chatty and buoyant. Several threw high signs at him, and he smiled back.

At the end of the corridor, just before the courtroom's tan doors, two security checks were working. At the first, three harried marshals cursorily patted people, passing them to four more marshals at a metal detector. The machine gave out whines, and the few lucky people squeezed through like toothpaste oozing out a narrow tube.

Keegan walked in. The courtroom was filled already, half the seats taken by reporters, the others by the first panel of jurors who glanced apprehensively at the spectators taking the rare empty seats. Keegan was always disappointed at the banality of a working courtroom. The lights were high and fluorescent, the walls flat brown, the seats really long benches like pews, and the whole scene was scarcely distinguishable from a crowded government passport office or hospital waiting room.

The sheer volume of crime and suffering in the city overwhelmed any impulse at individual solemnity. Take a number, Keegan thought, as he brushed by the long L-shaped counsel table just in front of the bench and the flat-toned linoleum on which the court clerk and bailiffs desks rested. File folders and books were set out at each place on the table; people with eyes down moving papers and books for the trial lawyers. It was like one of his son's lacrosse or football games on Saturday afternoons. The expectant crowds and the pointing at every newcomer were the same, Keegan thought.

In his coat pocket, unknown to nearly everyone, Keegan carried his motive for taking on the Carnes trial, perhaps for staying in the campaign itself. He touched the letter to make certain it was still there. He would read it again before the judge called them all to order and there was no turning back.

Keegan looked back at the faces, all hungry and waiting, and knew they wanted the same thing he did. Some sense out of death and slaughter, a balancing of unknowable terror against justice, even dispensed in this mass-produced, unsingular setting.

He was cynical enough to see that they wanted to be entertained, too. The murmuring rose as he passed the bench on the way to the judge's chambers.

Judge Serse Ambrosini sat at his black oak desk, slowly stirring a tall glass of orange liquid. Keegan put out his hand. The judge didn't take it.

"We watched that circus across the street," the judge said in his nasal, impassive voice.

Keegan thought Ambrosini was taking on a royal pronoun until he noticed Carnes's lawyer, Cynthia Goodoy, on a couch at the back of the chambers. On the wall over her, instead of photos with the famous or his diplomas, the judge had hung a large oil painting of a Renaissance gentleman in bottle-green hose regarding the observer haughtily from a marble palace window.

Poor Speedy, Keegan thought, using the judge's courthouse nickname. He wants marble and he gets linoleum.

"There's a high public interest, Your Honor," Keegan said. He was not going to bend at all to this judge. It's my trial, not his, he thought. He had been extensively briefed on the judge's autocratic and dour manner.

"You intend to give the defense a change of venue like she wants?" He stopped stirring and grimaced at the glass.

Goodoy got up and joined them. "I think Mr. Keegan just made my argument for me. What kind of impartial jury can Mr. Carnes expect when the DA is out holding press conferences? In front of this court?"

Keegan folded his arms. He was not going to let the trial leave Los Angeles. "The people wanted to hear where I stand. I didn't comment on the witnesses or the evidence. I'm not going to."

The judge drank from his glass. A faint orange mustache was left behind. "Miss Goodoy filed her change of venue motion this morning. I have already told her it is untimely."

"Then deny it," Keegan said. Goodoy started to speak, but the judge put up a thin finger.

"Don't interrupt me here or in court. Either of you. It is untimely, but we will hear it. This requires sending the whole jury panel back to the jury commissioner and wastes a great deal of public time and money."

Keegan had heard rumors that Ambrosini, whose brothers were vice-presidents at Bank of America, had worked out a time-table for buying his family's clothes and counted the number of steps from his courtroom to the garage and his car, calculating the wear and tear on his three pairs of brown wing tips to determine when replacements would be needed. He was a slight, dark-haired man who wore short-sleeved white shirts. His brown frame glasses glimmered over filmy gray eyes. His large-veined nose had been broken and badly healed.

He got his nickname Speedy as a candidate for the state Assembly a decade before. He was in a Fourth of July sack race, dressed in a pearl gray three-piece suit, when he tripped and broke his nose. He regarded politicians, especially successful ones, with contempt and antagonism.

He was, unfortunately, the only judge available to hear what was planned to be a four- or five-week death penalty trial. Keegan had to take him.

Goodoy was quite different, he thought, looking at her. He found himself measuring her again, as he did every woman since Leah died, searching for some trait, expression, that would recall in life what was gone. Cynthia Goodoy did not resemble Leah much. She was younger, in her forties, tall and upright, with a patrician simplicity and intelligence. She had been in the public defender's office for almost eighteen years. Her voice was per-petually a little amazed, as if even after all that time, those babies beaten, guns fired, vehement lies, she was capable of surprise at human behavior. Juries tended to like her. She was remembered as a grade school teacher.

On one side I've got a petty tyrant who'd like to see me fail and on the other, a deceptively mild defense lawyer. For an instant, Keegan shrank against his own pride and need. It was a rough path he was on. But he wouldn't let anyone know it.

Ambrosini pushed aside the glass and stood up. He was only five feet six or so, but his upraised chin gave him a truculent air.

"Mr. Keegan, I am ready right now to impose a gag order on this trial on my own motion. I assume you would not want a gag order."

"The people have a right to know what's happening in this court," Keegan replied bluntly.

"If I say so. If I allow reporters. If I allow a camera," the judge snapped. "I may not. I am thoroughly annoyed with both of you. My ground rules are simple. All motions are to be filed in advance of any hearing. Any questions about evidence are to be brought to me before court. Not during a witness's testimony." He went to the small bathroom off to his right and carefully rinsed out the glass. He held it up to the light for inspection.

Keegan hadn't moved, face set, arms folded. Confidence was a pose sometimes, useful, imperative for survival. He found himself adopting it more and more in the last months, pulling assurance around his public and private person plate by plate until he was covered, impenetrable.

"Anything else that might delay us from going on the record?" the judge asked, hands on his hips.

"I'm ready, Your Honor," Keegan said.

Goodoy braced herself on a chair back. "I haven't gotten an answer from Mr. Keegan about whether he's subpoenaed a particular witness."

"Well, tell her," Ambrosini said.

"Melanie Vogt," Goodoy said, studying Keegan. "She's the main prosecution witness. Do you have her?"

Keegan turned to leave. "I don't have to give you my witness list."

"I don't want to waste time, Mr. Keegan. I am directing you to tell Miss Goodoy if you've subpoenaed this witness."

Keegan paused. "She's cooperating."

"Your Honor," Goodoy said, "if for some reason Mr. Keegan loses track of this witness"—she raised her hands—"his case will collapse."

"You will not get a continuance, either," Ambrosini said. "I'm assuming you haven't put this witness under subpoena."

"She's been cooperating, Your Honor. She's in a secret location because of my concern the defendant will try to harm her."

Goodoy chuckled. "That's ridiculous. She's the one attacking him. If you produce her, I'd like any deals disclosed."

Keegan nodded. He wasn't fearful of truth except when there was nothing to temper it. No trial to help make a wife's senseless death coherent.

"All right, I'll see you both in court in ten minutes," the judge said. "Mr. Keegan. You may be looking at a motion to dismiss without a solid case. I may be forced to keep it from going to the jury."

"Then a murderer would walk free, Your Honor."

Ambrosini grinned. "We know it happens every day."

"I can't believe you'd let a travesty like that take place."

Ambrosini's white, stringy arms looked tough as pale jerky. "Speaking abstractly, I think the travesty is allowing an officeholder to use the apparatus of justice for his own benefit."

Keegan reflected the judge's bitter contempt. "I know you couldn't possibly mean me, Your Honor."

"No. I couldn't possibly."

Keegan walked out, Goodoy following him. At the sight of them both coming into the courtroom, a flurry of movement went off, people talked and found their seats, bailiffs busily made final placements of water carafes and cups on the bench and counsel table.

Seated farthest from the empty jury box, Carnes picked at something on his hand. He wore a white, long-sleeved shirt, tan slacks. His doughy paleness disgusted Keegan, like an illustration from morning chapel of infernal corruption and decay. Carnes smiled at Goodoy. Another assistant public defender was with him at the table, a young man fumbling nervously with legal pads. Two watchful deputy sheriffs stood behind Carnes.

"You could still challenge Speedy," Goodoy said.

Keegan paused with her in front of the bench, the audience taking them in like matinee theatergoers. "The trial would be delayed, and I'm ready to go."

"I'm being selfish," she admitted with a small smile. "He's very annoying. Maybe he's supporting Aguilar. How about that?"

"I don't care. I'm not going to paper him, Cynthia. I want to go to trial today."

She sighed. "No offers? You still won't make me any kind of deal?"

"No."

"Even if you've witness problems? Even if you're going to juggle a campaign and a trial?"

Keegan put on his broadest, most warm smile. "I'm having the time of my life."

He sat down beside his own assistants. For a moment he couldn't even remember the name of the young man and woman who would keep count of exhibits and witnesses, pass information to him, prompt him on objections or points of law he might have forgotten since he was last in court. This inability to place individual faces and names was starting to worry him. It was recent, too, perhaps merely a byproduct of the restless nights in the last few months, the faint opacity that seemed to cling to everything lately.

He looked around. People were still trying to find seats, two women grinding over toes as they crept to empty spaces near the back of the courtroom.

He took the creased letter from his coat pocket. Pity can stir us to boldness or recklessness. Taking this case might turn out to be a master campaign stratagem, but its impetus came from pity.

The letter still had its routing slip, from the Santa Monica branch of his office, to Central Operations downtown, to his chief deputy, finally to him. The pain was tangible. This is how I should feel about my wife's death, he thought.

The letter was two months old. It was addressed to him from a woman in Kentucky. Her oldest daughter had been killed in the Marina del Rey shooting. He read, hoping to be moved again.

I do not know what my daughter was doing with Mr. Rotich at the time of their deaths. I have been told there was evidence of drug use, but my Joyce did not use drugs in my home.

I understand that a man named Robert Carnes has been arrested for the murder of my daughter and my grandson Samuel. I cannot imagine what would make this man murder my daughter and the sweetest child on earth. But, on behalf of my husband and our surviving children, I am terrified that some technicality may allow this man Carnes to go free or receive less than the full punishment he deserves.

My fears are prompted by the news that another man named Lee Ferrera was first suspected by your office. Since he has now been discovered shot himself, you charged Carnes. I fear more mistakes may be made. I implore you to use your personal prestige to punish this murderer.

Our family is devastated with grief and my surviving children are heartbroken. We all fear death now and are sick in spirit.

I am grateful you will consider a Mother's plea for justice. I miss my little girl and still do not believe she is gone. In May, my husband and I buried her remains in a lonely little graveyard beside the Missouri River. We did it with our own hands and it was a very hard thing to say good-bye to her. I mourn her every day.

Please help me. This monster must be punished. I cannot eat or sleep well and am tormented that this man will go free. I know you are a very busy man and cannot take personal control of this case, but you can put very good people on it.

I respect you and know your reputation for justice and Law.

It was signed, in thick strokes, *Adele Harrold.* Keegan got many letters like this, pleas for help or mercy, cries for vengeance. Most were answered by deputy DAs for him. He had dictated the reply to Mrs. Harrold himself, but could not put into it how much her words had affected him. Even before Leah's death, he had begun saving small photos sometimes sent with the letters he saw. Sons, daughters, fathers, friends, always smiling, the sun shining on them or they were posed in front of blue backdrops. The pictures multiplied, and Leah found them in his pockets at home or in bureau drawers. He shrugged them off when she asked. He did not know why he was drawn to these faces or their tragedies.

Mrs. Harrold's letter alone hadn't impelled him to take the Carnes trial. It was one more cry added to a heap of pain and it came when his own was most acute and said things publicly Keegan had trouble saying even to himself.

The courtroom clock jerkily moved its hands, someone laughed behind him, someone joined in. His assistants were studiously showing him how deeply they worked, muttering over papers while waiting for the judge to appear.

Keegan suddenly had a sharp memory. It was far from the stale, anticipatory courtroom, years ago back in Connecticut before his family came to LA. He had gone to a private school, red brick, the gravel driveway glistening in fall rain, muddy legs playing football for the shouting parents, and egg-salad sandwiches on Friday eaten on the grass. Morning chapel began every day. Keegan listened and could hear the organ, hear the men and boys singing. From the fearless headmaster he took, was engraved with, a flinty command often repeated as the morning lesson. It was II Timothy, "*Study to shew thyself approved unto God, a workman that needeth not to be ashamed, rightly dividing the word of truth.*" He had no trouble showing his public indignation at lawbreakers. He held press conferences beside bales of marijuana and cocaine bundles, walked gang-riven streets with reporters following along. He testified in Sacramento before politely listening committees. He could show outrage and indignation. He knew how to charm people at luncheons, as he would at the fund-raiser cocktail party that night.

Goodoy glanced from her deep conversation with Carnes, looking toward the bench. A bailiff struggled to his feet and the courtroom seemed to expel a sigh of satisfaction. Speedy Ambrosini, his trial ledger under one arm, marched to the bench.

But grief, Keegan thought, coming to his feet with the people behind and around him, I can't get around it. I can't touch its oily contours like the woman who wrote that letter.

"All rise. Department 57 of the Superior Court of the State

of California is now in session. The Honorable Serse Ambrosini judge presiding," a thick-middled bailiff called out briskly.

Keegan put his hands on the counsel table and looked at
the judge.

His trial was about to begin.

FIVE

AMBROSINI KEPT HIS EYES down as he firmly announced his preliminary housekeeping rulings for the trial. Keegan sat back in his creaking plastic chair, waiting.

I will not, he vowed, to himself, let this trial leave Los Angeles.

"The court makes a ruling that one pool camera, representing the following news organizations, will be permitted to videotape the proceedings." Ambrosini nasally read off all of the TV stations in Los Angeles, several in Riverside, and one from Mexico. "One pool photographer will be allowed to photograph the proceedings as well."

He looked up, sourly. "In addition, a section reserved on a first-come basis for the press has been set aside for the trial's duration at the front of the courtroom. I expect every news representative to behave with decorum."

Keegan saw the photographer unscrew a lens and replace it. He also knew that the TV camera, almost hidden at the rear of the courtroom, was implacably taking in everything he did. He sat quietly. Carnes passed a note to Goodoy, and she shook her head.

50

There was no impatient, fearful figure beside Keegan. The dead kept to themselves.

The judge went on, "Before we start jury selection, we have a motion filed by one of the parties to consider." He smiled gloomily at the two sides of the counsel table. "This will require excusing the jury panel until called. Thank you, ladies and gentlemen."

The surprise was obvious as people grabbed their coats and bags, books and sewing, from the benches and pushed slowly from the courtroom in an ungainly muddle. The rude vacancies in the benches suggested no one was interested in the case.

Keegan used to brush her aside when Leah sardonically patted his arm and said, "George, all you really want to do is be LA's big principal. You want to tell us all how to behave."

If I don't, who will, he thought.

The bailiffs closed and locked the doors, and Judge Ambrosini wrinkled his large nose. "Call your first witness, Miss Goodoy."

Keegan had his briefing papers thrust to him by an assistant. The witness who got to the stand was small, tiny hands and face, a tiny beard, and round glasses. He perched rather than sat on the witness stand. His name was Walter Tisdel, and he was a political scientist from Cal State Northridge.

The purpose of a change of venue motion was simple. The defense wanted to demonstrate that there was so much publicity about a case, it could not fairly be heard and must be moved elsewhere. Since no evidence had been heard or jurors questioned, a change of venue motion existed entirely as a theoretical exercise. Experts could be hired to argue it either way.

Keegan's strategy was to discredit Dr. Tisdel. He despised the dishonest witness, whose testimony bent with his fee, and the little professor liked speculation far more than concrete things.

Keegan made notes as Goodoy questioned her witness. If the judge granted this motion, it would be a disaster for Keegan. He would be trapped in a trial away from the city during the campaign.

More than that, he thought justice owed the people of Los Angeles the chance to hear the case.

From her seat, Goodoy asked, "Dr. Tisdel, did you conduct personal and telephone interviews?"

"My researchers do both," he answered in a startlingly deep voice. "First we contact people by telephone, then do a more detailed in-person follow-up."

Carnes was rapidly writing, and Keegan wondered what was passing through that febrile mind, down his hands, to the legal pad. Evil, he realized, was easy to recognize, frightening in its energy and resolution.

"When were these contacts made?" Goodoy asked blandly.

"Oh, within the last six weeks."

"Since the time Mr. Keegan announced he would take the trial himself?"

"Generally."

Keegan underlined the word and put a red circle around it.

Goodoy stood up, graceful and reassuringly polite. "How big was your overall sample?"

"We interviewed eight hundred people. I wanted a larger than normal sample for this trial to minimize any possibility of error."

One of Keegan's assistants, a young man with wide eyes and thinning hair, chuckled low. Keegan listened and wrote.

"What areas did the questions in your sample cover?"

"Two broad categories." Tisdel grinned up at the judge. "The first was to establish if the interviewee had even heard about this case. Did the person know the name Robert Carnes? And the second broad group of questions was to establish if the interviewee had therefore prejudged the case."

"You mean made up his mind without hearing any evidence in court?" Goodoy asked, to make the obvious even plainer.

"Well, decided on a verdict of guilty based solely on information in the public arena."

"Newspapers? Radio, TV?"

"Even gossip," Tisdel said. He wiggled a little, checking the placement of his glasses, very pleased with his work.

Goodoy asked her next question carefully, looking at Tisdel as if the answers to come were wholly unexpected. "On the basis of your research, Dr. Tisdel, did you reach any conclusions?"

"Yes, I did."

"All right. About the first general kind of questions you asked, what percentage of potential jurors said they'd heard about this case?"

"The figure I recorded was seventy-two percent had heard of Mr. Carnes or something about this case."

"And how many had formed an opinion?"

"Objection," Keegan said, hand raised, then lowered self-consciously. It had been a while since he wanted to catch a judge's attention. "Speculation."

"We haven't heard the witness's answer yet. At the moment it's merely vague," Ambrosini said. "Your objection's premature."

"I'm sorry, Your Honor," Keegan said with practiced ease from years of rough political meetings and personnel sessions with the deputy district attorneys association. "I was trying to save some of the court's time."

"Oh, let me worry about that, Mr. Keegan. That is my job. Yours is to be a vigorous advocate."

"I am, Your Honor," Keegan said.

"I realize that," Ambrosini said with sarcasm. "Go on, Miss Goodoy."

Although Keegan had done practice sessions for several days with veteran trial lawyers in Major Crimes and Central Operations, he was still a little rusty, but it would all come back.

Goodoy had waited, looking at Carnes, then the jury. "How many of your sample had formed an opinion?"

Tisdel said, "Well, it was very high."

Thank you, Keegan said. He rose quickly. "Objection now, Your Honor. That's conclusionary and relative."

Ambrosini nodded. "Sustained. State the figures, Mr. Witness. Let me decide their significance."

Tisdel made a half-bow, puppetlike, at his seat. "I'm sorry. I discovered that sixty-seven percent of the people who'd heard of the case had formed the opinion that Mr. Carnes was guilty."

"Guilty or responsible?" Goodoy asked curtly.

"No. They said guilty. He had committed murder."

"Based on your experience as a pollster and statistician, Dr. Tisdel, how does that sixty-seven percent figure compare with other cases you've researched?"

"Objection again," Keegan said, putting his pen down to show irritation. "It's this trial that matters, not any others."

"Sustained."

Goodoy had three large notebooks and several videocassettes brought to her by her assistant. She took them to Tisdel, who touched them, examined them pleasurably, like a child with new toys. "Do you recognize these items, Doctor?"

"Yes. These are files of the newspaper accounts and TV stories that appeared in the Los Angeles media market on this case."

"You used these stories in formulating your questions?"

"Yes. And I viewed all of the TV coverage myself."

"Did you ask any specific questions about Mr. Keegan, the county's district attorney, personally trying the case?" Goodoy pointed at him.

"Yes. The effect was to heighten any awareness of the case."

"And therefore increase the percentage of potential jurors who already thought Mr. Carnes was guilty?"

"Yes," Dr. Tisdel said, disappointed he couldn't say more about it himself.

It was a clever tactic. Keegan became the focal point of Carnes's prejudicial publicity. Like I clobbered the case from the start, he thought. Lynch mob leader, political opportunist.

There was no question that local TV stations and newspapers had lovingly covered his interest in taking the case. The horror of Carnes's crimes moved from page one of the Metro section in the *Times* to Page One. It was, as Keegan intended, no longer a statistical killing, but one with real people. That was the risk he chose.

He was startled from the deepening reflection by Goodoy's almost pedantic recital. "Your Honor, I've shown these items to Mr. Keegan, and I'd like them marked in order. Defendant's A

through G, and entered into evidence." She pointed at the notebooks and cassettes.

"Objection, Mr. Keegan?"

"I've looked at them. Everybody's seen them."

Ambrosini smiled coldly. "Perhaps I haven't. I haven't owned a
television for several years. Mark and enter these exhibits, Madame
Clerk. I'll review them at the end of the testimony."

While the clerk, suddenly conscious she was the center of
attention from reporters, counsel, and Carnes, fumbled a little
putting small red stickers on the notebooks and entering them in
her evidence log, Goodoy went back to her place. Carnes smiled
at Dr. Tisdel, who smiled back.

"Nothing further, Your Honor," Goodoy said.

"Mr. Keegan," said Ambrosini with anticipatory relish, hoping
for a stumbling effort. "Cross-examine."

He got up, buttoning his coat. All his life he had been directed to
take responsibility, sought it, and now the weight of Mrs. Harrold's grief fell on him, mingling with his own. He thought of Leah
and his own children and a stranger's child buried beside a river.
So many eyes turned to him at that moment, in the courtroom,
beyond it in the city through the cameras, beyond them even.

His voice was calm, though. Confidence and bluster were the
tools of life and politics and the law, and he had mastered them.

"May I approach the witness?"

The judge frowned. "Do you have to?"

"I would rather question him standing up, Your Honor."

"Go ahead," Ambrosini said reluctantly.

Keegan walked to Dr. Tisdel. The little professor smiled at him,
like a physician about to calm a hypochondriac.

"Would you say that statistics, your field, is a neutral one,
Doctor?"

"You mean objective?"

"Is your field one of science instead of speculation?"

Dr. Tisdel beamed. "Well, there is some speculation involved. Drawing inferences and implications from facts."

"But you do start with facts, don't you?"

"I do."

"And then you try to stay objective and reach whatever results those facts point to?"

"Yes."

Keegan came closer to the witness. The light overhead made Tisdel's skin look plastic and the judge's nose shiny. The animate turned sickly in the courtroom's flat glare.

Keegan said abruptly, "How is it that you've testified in eighteen different criminal trials in this county, Doctor, and seventeen times reached a conclusion favorable only to the defense?" He pointed, realized it was a melodramatic gesture, something he'd done at press conferences denouncing dishonest school administrators or several of the mayor's appointees on city commissions.

Goodoy said loudly, "I object. Mr. Keegan closed the door on other trials or cases himself a little while ago."

The judge began speaking, and Keegan turned, looking up at the imperious voice. "Your Honor," he said, "I'm exploring this witness's overt bias. He isn't an expert. He's a spokesman for the defense."

"Now. Really," Tisdel blurted out.

The judge closed his eyes, a small smile briefly on his face. "This is not a public meeting, Mr. Keegan, this is my courtroom. You will state your objection, and you will let me rule on it." He opened his gray eyes wide. "Clear to you?"

Keegan nodded. This was not the time or witness to engage Speedy Ambrosini's authority. There were important witnesses to come, and Carnes himself, and Keegan wanted to reserve any chance he risked being held in contempt for them.

"My objection," he said steadily, "is that Dr. Tisdel's opinion in this case is exactly like his opinion in almost every other case in this county in which he comes in for the defense."

The judge blinked, to Keegan's surprise. "I suppose that does go solely to his present testimony and not his past opinions."

"That is my point," Keegan said.

Goodoy argued briefly, and Ambrosini said, "Overruled. Ask your question again."

Keegan faced Tisdel again. "How do you explain that amazing run of your opinions?"

"I based my opinions on the responses. That was how they came out," Tisdel said with a shrug.

"Not the way you put the questions?"

"No."

"Don't you think it defies probability, Doctor, that you'd come out for the defense nearly one hundred percent of the time?" Keegan saw the judge grinning. He knew whoever was watching TV had the answer, too. A trial can be theater and politics as much as a search for truth, he thought.

The little professor put his tiny hands up. "Mr. Keegan, it's random. I could just as easily come up with seventeen occasions favorable to the prosecution from now on."

"Could you?"

"Certainly."

"Even if the public defender paid your staff, your fees, and paid for your report like this case?" Keegan asked sharply.

"I'm compensated by the county for my time, not my opinion."

His senior trial attorneys had prepared a list of questions for Tisdel, based on their own experiences with him. But Keegan put it aside. He had a much faster way of discrediting the witness, a way he understood instinctively better than his trial staff did.

He picked up another piece of paper.

"On direct examination by defense counsel, you said your interviews covered a period of time that included my announcement, right?"

"You were a factor. People knew you would be trying the case. It increased interest. Memory."

"You care who wins the district attorney race, don't you?" Keegan said, folding his arms, the paper hanging down.

"What?" Tisdel asked, startled.

"Objection. Relevance. No foundation," Goodoy said quickly.

"Overruled. But do you really want to ask that question, Mr. Keegan?" the judge inquired too delicately.

"I do."

"Then go ahead." A smug smile at what he believed was a politician's foolhardy inexperience in court.

Dr. Tisdel shook his head. His chin went up. He looked back at the TV camera at the rear of the courtroom. "I have no interest in your campaign at all. Or anybody else's."

Goodoy smiled and made a note and whispered to Carnes, who grinned back at her. The reporters suddenly grew quiet, their own instincts sharpened. One of the bailiffs squeaked his plastic swivel chair.

Keegan said as he thrust the paper onto the witness stand, under Tisdel's gaze, "I have a certified copy of a financial statement filed with the Secretary of State's office in Sacramento."

"Has defense counsel seen that?" the judge asked, sitting forward.

Keegan didn't answer. "Please read the twenty-fourth name down, Dr. Tisdel."

As the little professor counted, the judge asked with greater sharpness, "What is that document? I want to know if the defense has seen it."

Goodoy stood swiftly. "I haven't, Your Honor. I don't know what we're doing."

"I'm establishing the political motive behind this motion, Your Honor," Keegan said.

An astonished Goodoy shook her head as Dr. Tisdel finished his count and said, "I've read the name. I'm frankly surprised."

"Mr. Keegan," said Ambrosini, his face hardened, "stop what you're doing and answer my question."

Keegan spoke to the reporters and camera. "I am showing the star defense witness a campaign disclosure statement filed this last quarter by Celia Aguilar. Who is running against me."

"I would like to see that paper. I would like a break to examine it." Goodoy was agitated.

Keegan knew he now had the complete attention of every reporter and the judge, so he spoke over Goodoy. "Whose name is listed at the twenty-fourth space, Dr. Tisdel? Who gave nearly four hundred dollars to my opponent's campaign?"

"Mr. Keegan," said the judge loudly.

"Your Honor," said Goodoy.

"My wife," said Dr. Tisdel, staring down again at the paper.

━━━━━

"You are unprincipled," said Judge Ambrosini, sucking angrily on a silver toothpick in his chambers. His robe was still zipped up, and he roamed from his desk to the window. Goodoy and Keegan stood beside his desk.

"He's a biased witness," Keegan said. "I only exposed it."

"You knew how inflammatory that information was. You knew it was only marginally relevant," the judge said.

Goodoy opened her palms at Keegan. "No one has ever accused Dr. Tisdel of fraud before."

"Did he tell you?" Keegan was tired of this show. "About his wife giving money to Aguilar?" he asked Goodoy brusquely.

"No, he didn't. He says he didn't know about it. They're not that close."

Ambrosini put the toothpick, an heirloom from his father, in his desk. "You deliberately played to the press, Mr. Keegan. I won't tolerate that. I will not."

"You needed to know how unreliable Tisdel's opinion is," Keegan said firmly. "It's my duty to show it to you."

"I will not have you bringing your campaign into this courtroom. If you are going to try anything else, I will personally arrange for the attorney general to take over this case," the judge said.

"He should be sanctioned," Goodoy said. "Some punishment."

Keegan looked out the window, at the tops of old buildings and stretching farther past them, the arterial lines of the city streets, and it was all his responsibility. Leah was right, at least, about one thing. He could never release the feeling that whatever sins or crimes ended up before him in the city were his to resolve.

"I'm going to consider the matter of sanctions before I make a ruling tomorrow on the venue motion, Mr. Keegan." Ambrosini dropped into his chair, glared up. "You are unprincipled," he repeated.

"I have my own standards, Your Honor," he said.

SIX

COURT RESUMED FOR SEVERAL HOURS. Goodoy made strenuous attempts to rehabilitate Dr. Tisdel, but the damage was irreparable. Keegan thought the judge would have to take the public perception of bias into account and deny the motion. He could hardly grant it when the reporters would point out that the defense's expert was tainted by support for Keegan's political opponent.

When court recessed, Keegan and his assistants went quickly to a freight elevator, pushing through the lines of people. He had a special key and used it to take the elevator straight up to the eighteenth floor of the building. In the morning, when he was driven from home to work, Keegan went directly from the basement garage to his office by way of that elevator. When he was downtown, he was driven everywhere, even the three blocks for occasional drinks in the Otani Hotel's bar. The chief of police, the sheriff, they also never walked in public. We're too recognized, he thought, the elevator opening onto the gray marble and concrete of the shining corridor. Private hates, public hopes, all gravitate to us because we're the symbols of order.

60

And power. As the chief liked wryly to remind them all when they got together at the bar. Keegan suddenly realized that except for family business or occasions, he hadn't seen anyone else socially since the accident.

But I campaign. I go to lunches and dinners. Tonight I even make some money doing it.

What Aguilar and his enemies did not understand, what he himself had only come to see recently, was that the campaign for reelection was a refuge for him. It was the sole validation remaining in an iron-bound world he was sure would fly apart if he quit or was defeated. By force of effort alone he could hold it all together, family, work, justice.

He said hello to the tiny black city cop sitting in front of his outer marble-fronted office. Behind her was the seal of the district attorney. She signed in everyone who came to see him. He asked about her sick daughter. He knew about everyone's family. He sent cards on every birthday and anniversary. He went to many of the baptisms and marriages and bar mitzvahs.

A man threw his arms around Keegan.

"I loved it, boss. We couldn't have gotten better. KCOP did live coverage outside City Hall. You've got actualities on every radio station. I got calls coming from *Newsweek*. The Fighting DA."

Keegan disentangled himself and kept walking. He was still disconcerted by his Public Information Officer's impulse to embrace him. Klein was a big man with a black mustache, and he smoked cigars in the building. "Remember what I said last week, Phil. No comments about the trial. Get me today's media log. I didn't get a chance to see it this morning."

Klein doggedly panted beside him. "I'll bring it right over. You're getting great coverage. Aguilar's going nuts probably."

"Good coverage so far," Keegan agreed, based on what he'd heard. This was the part of any day he enjoyed the best, the restless yet purposeful movement going to his office. He and Klein went through the outer office, his white-haired receptionist smiling behind her glassed-in fortress, striding to his inner office, where two secretaries typed busily. They had been with him since he was city attorney. Twelve years ago, and already it struck him as a life-time. He waved as he went by them.

Keegan took off his coat, hanging it in the paneled closet beside his private bathroom. He was in a bubble most of the day. Leah called it his cocoon. Drivers and elevators, special seats at meetings and events, half of the eighteenth floor dedicated to ful-filling his wishes and the other half anxious to be seen helping him. People and memos came to him. He rarely went to them.

It was swaddling, and if he wasn't careful, it made him believe his judgments were infallible. Or it had until recently.

After Klein left, Keegan told one of his secretaries to send Barbara Cabrerra in. She was nominally a special assistant, but really on loan from the governor's office to help him with cam-paign strategy. She had been aghast when he announced he would take the Carnes trial. It was unexpected, and professional campaigners hate surprises.

After her he had a meeting with a popular actor and his lawyer. In fact, fingering the thick stack of phone messages and notes from his executive assistant and secretaries, he saw he had meetings and problems that could take up every minute of the day. The illusion of purpose such activity created was also comforting.

There was a perfunctory knock on his door. He waited.

From his window this high up, he looked out onto the KRKO Radio tower and the New Otani Hotel with its orange circle logo burned in like a setting sun. J-Town, Japan Town, crowded against the hotel, separated from Hispanic shops and bustling tourists by a single street. City Hall loomed before him, too, and all the new banks in blue glass and silver, One Wilshire planted like a stone leg above them all. Directors from sever-al of the banks were on his finance committee. Farther west, shimmering in the late afternoon haze, was Long Beach and the indistinct hump of Catalina Island, where his jurisdiction and responsibility ended.

He fingered the silver dolphin cuff links Leah had given him on their eleventh wedding anniversary. Tokens of their honeymoon on Catalina, in Avalon, where they danced at the Casino festooned with lights. A vast fleet of pleasure boats rocked in the harbor, including the one that brought them. He had just married into one of the city's richer families, her father in oil just as his used to be, even if their positions were grossly different.

When he and Leah made love that first night on the island, he could truly say he experienced one of the rare moments of peace in his life. In part it was because he was in love, in part because the future had been scrubbed white, all blackness and shadow obliterated.

He had been wrong to believe that. The shadows had crowded around more quickly than he imagined they could.

On the second or third night, he didn't remember which now, they ate a long, full dinner, and he sensed she was different. She had very blue eyes, and as he and Leah went from one bar to another in the small island city, she never looked at anything, just glanced and moved on. She never let go of me all night, he realized. Walking, or in the little electric carts, she held on to him, and her laughter was sharper and lingering.

Somewhere they ran into a couple, the Rabkins, old friends of Leah's parents, and somehow they all ended up on the boat, sitting and drinking, the harbor black-watered and yellow-lighted from the city and the other boats. Keegan smelled the heavy brine of the ocean, heard parties in the darkness farther out, lone yells, a scream, across the water.

The next thing he remembered, the Rabkins had left. Leah sat alone on the deck, head down, long dark hair around her shoulders as if she were releasing the bands and springs that kept her laughing and seeming so normal.

He went into the main cabin. He kissed her as he left. He rubbed her leg. I said I'd be right back, he remembered. He also remembered the sudden, improbable, stricken look on Leah's face as her glass slipped and broke.

He made a joke and left her.

I was in the cabin, what for? Another glass? Drink? The whole golden-wooded, carpeted interior wobbled and rolled with the tide and his drunkenness. I was only down there a second.

In a second, Keegan discovered that lives change, things come into them and remain, darkly flowering over the years.

He came back onto the deck, and she was gone. Her chair was tipped over. He called her name. He looked along the sleek boat's deck. He put his drink down.

He heard the tiny splashing sound as she perhaps meant him to. He looked over the side, into the few feet of water between the boat and the dock, the dark waters more agitated between the solid surfaces, the reflected yellow party lights glistening here and there. Leah was between the boat and dock, facedown in the water, arms out, as if she were peering down to the ocean floor.

Keegan leapt in, coughing, swallowing sour seawater. He pulled her closer to the dock. Her face rolled up to him, white and composed, hair dragged across it, a torn small artery pulsing blood over her eyes that the water washed away instantly, replaced, washed away.

He didn't remember actually pulling her onto the dock, bending, frantic, calling out, breathing into her slack mouth, then shouting. It was hard to be heard over the night's multitude of boat parties. Finally, Leah coughed and breathed and opened her eyes, and her hand squeezed his arm tightly. Four people ran onto the dock from nearby boats and helped him.

Later, at the small hospital behind the Casino, he was alone with her. She sat on the narrow metal-framed bed, bandaged, weary.

For a long while, Keegan had been soothing. Now, seeing her alert and apparently not seriously injured, he was angry.

"You scared the hell out of me," he said.

Leah looked up. She had on a man's cotton shirt, her skin at the neck and rolled sleeves tanned. "Don't let me go, George," she said.

"You have any idea how much you scared the hell out of me?" he said again, more loudly. He sat beside her and she sank to him, too wearily even for the trial she had just gone through.

"I'm sorry. I didn't mean to do that. I thought you were gone."

"Just inside. For a minute. I said I'd be right back."

"I don't know what it was. I felt so lonely."

"You do not go swimming alone off the end of the boat." He rocked her gently like an errant child.

"I didn't mean it."

"You fell in?"

She shook her head. "I jumped."

"Look, honey, if you'd waited a minute, I'd have come in with you." He kissed her and she kissed him back, hard and clinging.

"Don't leave me alone, George."

"We just got married."

He got up and started to help her up. He held her hand, like a knight and his lady. The doctor appeared, in shorts, stethoscope hanging on his bare, tanned chest, looking like he was annoyed to have been yanked away from a party of his own.

"Get your own physician to check the stitches," the doctor said. "This is just first aid."

"She's all right?" Keegan asked.

"I wouldn't do any more drinking tonight." The doctor grinned.

Keegan took Leah and made sure they left with everything they had dropped in the confusion of getting her to the little hospital. He handed her her sneakers, and she shook some sand from them and carried them out.

The circular street around the Casino was clogged with people, faces oddly colored as the lights strung overhead turned tans splotchy. Leah walked slowly, barefooted on the hot asphalt, people pushing, shouting happily past them.

Keegan was sober, completely clear. "Accidents happen. We have to be careful."

Leah looked around her. "I was afraid of being alone out there."

"I won't leave you alone. I'm going to watch out for you," he said.

She held him tightly as they walked, stumbling sometimes past the grinning crowd, heading for the dock. "Promise you'll hold on to me, George. I'm going to depend on you."

He made a joke. "Hope to die. I promise." But she was sober, too, and serious in a way he didn't fully understand.

The pledge was given, unheard and unnoticed in the revelry of others, but that didn't matter. I gave it, Keegan thought. I took up the responsibility for someone else's happiness and life.

They made love gently in the small bunk bed on the boat, in darkness.

Leah fitted her body against his later. "I won't be too much of a burden," she said. "Maybe it was seeing the Rabkins. Listening to them. Like all the people I know. All my life. Sometimes," she breathed against his face quietly, "I get tired of everything."

"You have me now."

"I have you," she said, and they rolled apart, and a little after that, made love again, and the night slipped heavily across the ocean, stilling the parties and voices.

He had not reckoned how deeply she needed him, the bottomless reassurance she demanded. It smothers everything finally. It was the first time that he really saw her and realized her despondency. She was too good with the masks, he thought. I never suspected until that night in the Avalon hospital that she might want to kill herself.

Over the years he protected her. He made an effort to satisfy the frightened and ever-lonely woman. When the kids were born, things were best. She seemed content, preoccupied with them. Then they grew up.

Keegan fingered the cuff links again. Love gives way to fear or pity or simply a sense of responsibility. But we're only human, he thought. We had our frictions over and above anything else. The night she gave him the cuff links, he had taken her to dinner at the Bel-Air. She usually wanted to go there for special occasions because her family always had. She was drinking more seriously. They fought about her father again. Leah insisted on paying for dinner, embarrassing them both. My family's got the money, she said loudly.

I had ambition, he thought. Maybe I used politics as an excuse to spend more time away from Leah, who was growing older and more desperate. I couldn't do more for her.

He pushed aside the memory. I didn't want to do more. I broke my word.

It was as basic and devastating as that to Keegan. He had failed her, willfully, after giving a solemn pledge.

There was another knock on his office door. He looked up.

"Come in," he said.

Barbara Cabrerra was eating a poppy-seed muffin, holding it in her hand and nibbling so that yellowish crumbs fell to the floor. She was stout and thick-lipped, her eyes small and playfully wicked behind her glasses.

"You're going to keep the trial here. Hooray," she said, flopping into a chair in front of his desk.

"It looks that way."

"Have I come at a bad time?"

"Why?"

She peered at him. "You looked far away."

"I'm right here."

"Well"—she settled back—"we're putting together a new radio ad, George. Old clips from your speeches about fighting for a decent life, clean air, clean water, clean streets."

"Aguilar's been hammering me for being aloof and incompetent. How does that help?"

Cabrerra finished the muffin, wiped her hands briskly, and dangled her arms over the chair sides. "George, the voters think you don't care. They like how you sound most of the time, but there's uneasiness. We get it in our tracking polls."

"This is going to show the real me?"

"George Keegan. He cares."

He rubbed his eyes. "I do care. Jesus, I spend all my time caring."

"Of course. All we're doing is pointing it out. People need to have a reason to vote for someone else," she said with a smile. "Celia's trying to come up with the reason."

"So why aren't I farther ahead of her?"

Cabrerra yawned without covering her mouth. "George, after all the years you've been around LA, people are getting bored. That's all it is."

"I don't want to bore anybody," he said mockingly. In truth, Cabrerra didn't care very much whether he won or lost. To her the

campaign was mechanical, so many points for this ad, so many sub-
tracted for that mistake, and the winner determined by adding it all
up. He was her cause of the month. Because the governor wanted
to make sure an ally stayed in office.

"Well, I was worried about your going to trial. I thought, Hey,
it will look like a play. But I watched you today." She beamed at
him. "It was poetry. Good guy versus bad guy. You should do this
more. You've got a natural presence."

"So I'm home free?"

She stood up again. Cabrerra either reclined bonelessly or was
in frantic motion. She had switched to motion. "Unless there's a
major fumble."

"Like losing the trial?"

She nodded.

He helped her. "I've got a lot to do, Barbara." She could hurry
out without appearing rude now.

She was already at the door. "Oh. One quick thing. Our
globe-trotting mayor, the Honorable Poulsby, is passing the word
he's for Aguilar."

"He's going to endorse her? That's a big damn change." Keegan
angrily threw down his pen.

Cabrerra smiled sweetly. "The mayor never does anything
straight. He's going to stay neutral in public."

"Bastard. Thanks for the good news."

"He's jealous, George. He'd like to be governor, too."

She waved too broadly and left. Keegan cursed again. The fact
was that after being district attorney and city attorney, he inevita-
bly carried the burden of hasty decisions, misstatements, failures,
like Marley's clattering ghost. He had authorized trials that took
too long, the public thought, cost too much, achieved too little.
Prosecuting a landlord whose building burned and killed eight
people took months, cost two million dollars, and Keegan personally urged conviction. The jury could only find minor technical fire-
code violations, and the whole effort looked like a straining grasp
at publicity for the DA.

There were other trials like that over the last few years. Keegan had been told he was growing too inflexible. Not every public wrong was a crime. "But there has to be punishment," he said at the staff meetings. "Don't walk out of here telling your deputies we can bargain everything."

Now he was paying the price for such harshness.

He told one of his secretaries to alert Win Conley, the head of Investigations. "I want to go check on our witness. Tell him to be ready to go in a half hour." He checked his watch. That would crowd the fundraiser, but Melanie Vogt deserved special handling. His case would collapse without Melanie Vogt's eyewitness placement of Carnes and Ferrera and the victims all together and the time she spent with Carnes in Nevada. He needed Conley along because the ex-cop had much more experience handling snitches and nervous witnesses than he did. Besides, they were old friends.

He grinned. Conley would like this next meeting with an actor. He was an old-movie fan, grumbling often about how far pictures had fallen. I get to talk to a real star, Keegan thought.

"Tell Early and his lawyer to come in," he said to his secretary.

"I didn't see your last movie," Keegan said to the two men sitting in front of him.

"Just did eight million dollars in Pakistan," Max Early said, his big shoulders hunching in feigned surprise. "Pakistan!"

He was an oversized action star, and he had chased his latest girlfriend through the usually quiet streets of Beverly Hills late one evening. The chase attracted police attention because they were both in Maseratis and speeding nearly ninety miles an hour. He tapped her rear fender.

On his desk, in a stack nearly as thick as a telephone book, Keegan had the Beverly Hills Police Department's exhaustive investigation of this major crime, with reports, pictures, statements.

"Thank you for seeing us." Early's bald lawyer, incongruously named Charles Boyer, sat with his knees together. "We're anxious to end this incident and go on."

"I voted for you," Early said, fingers up. "Three times."

"Mr. Early, I haven't decided what charges should be brought here. I agreed to see you and your lawyer as a courtesy."

"We appreciate it. We do. Very much," Boyer said quickly, legs pressed together more tightly.

Keegan went on, "Do you want to make a statement?"

Early stood up straight, a stiffening Keegan recognized from his movies. Just before unloading a thousand rounds at someone. "Me? Say what? I'm being nailed because I'm me. I've got the money. Look, I gave her the car. You know what she's doing? She's suing me for three and a half million. Bitch's suing me." He looked with incredulity at Boyer, who nodded up and down.

"Don't get excited, Max," Boyer said. "Don't lose it."

It occurred to Keegan that he was watching a scene the two of them had worked out. Or maybe improvised on the spot, but it was a structured episode, and the big line was coming. He envied actors on that score. Life for them was a matter of pretense and certainty. Everything fitted into a pattern of drama or comedy.

"I might decide to file a reckless driving count," Keegan said, seeing the silver-framed photo of Leah, Chris, and Elaine on his desk, trying to recall why they were all smiling and so young. "We could dispose of it with a plea to that."

"No plea. No way. I didn't do a damn thing," Early breathed.

"Don't get excited, Max."

Early said to Keegan, "What would it take?"

"I told you."

"Right. Right. Forget this bullshit. It's over. I mean, later. You're in a campaign, what kind of help do you need?"

Boyer stared down at his shoes. He was along as an accessory. A star didn't travel without an expensive lawyer.

"Money and support are always welcome," Keegan said, forcing a smile. "This is a big county."

"I said I voted for you. I'll do it again," Early said, poking Boyer in the shoulder. "How about a party at my Malibu place?"

"I'll have my campaign treasurer call," Keegan said. It was now his turn in the script. He opened the telephone-book police file and flipped pages while Early stared at him and Boyer coughed. They had been escorted up the freight elevator for privacy like all celebrity witnesses or suspects, one of Keegan's courtesies. These arrangements were not for the public. He closed the file. "Well, I'll have to make a final decision. But there's no question you were both speeding."

Early stared. Boyer sighed gratefully. "Pay the two dollars, Max."

"I enforce the laws equally," Keegan said.

Early nodded, the symmetry coming clear. "Okay. That's all I'm asking. A little fairness for me, too."

They shook hands, and Keegan walked them to the door, Early pausing to sign an autograph when one of Keegan's secretaries shyly asked for it.

He went back and dictated a memo for the Early investigation file, directing that speeding tickets be filed against both the actor and his girlfriend and a letter of commendation be sent to the Beverly Hills detectives who had worked so long to make the case. He clipped the tape to the file. So much effort for such nonsense. The whole Early case was worthless, a waste of time for everyone. I only salvaged a little from it and I gave nothing real away. He knew it was a thin rationalization, but clung to it more tightly for that reason. Every day there were similar problems and offers: *Give me a break on this coke possession thing, it's Mickey Mouse. I can help you.*

It was always the same wheedling, smug voice, tinged with fear. Because I have power, Keegan thought.

And I want to keep it. He acknowledged it very seldom, but there was pleasure of a deep kind knowing your reach extended from mountains to the sea, across seventy cities and millions of people.

Just below him, so the angle distorted the peeling billboard, was the fading face of a blue-aura'd evangelist named Dr. O. L. Staggers, who had died and yet lived on in the billboard, one brown hand upraised, his eyes staring upward toward Keegan's office.

Like a docile imp, his wife, Miss Velma, was shown playing a tiny organ at his side and raptly gazing upon him. Large demonstrations against the mayor or Keegan were usually held on the weedy concrete floor on which the billboard was based. Last summer a convocation of irate witches had camped out, chanting, singing, banging metal, to protest a city ordinance banning their parade.

Keegan uneasily looked into the paper-and-ink eyes below. The city promised every few months to tear down the old billboard, but so far Dr. Staggers had endured.

Keegan had to get out suddenly, the compression of his chest threatening to strangle him. He called one of his secretaries. "Get Win Conley up here. We're going to see Melanie Vogt."

SEVEN

MELANIE BLEW A PERFECT SMOKE ring into the air.

She stood outside the American College of Beauty in Montebello with six or seven other students. The women wore blue smocks, and they smoked and gossiped during their break. Melanie was very tired after the morning's facial session and tinting lesson. The students worked on women who couldn't afford professional treatment, and Melanie had tangled with dry, stiff, and dirty hair of every description. She smelled of lemon tint and rose crèmes.

"It's not so bad," she told her friend Carmen. "It's like any regular job. You got to have an attitude. You're going to work."

Carmen sent two straight plumes of smoke from her little nose. "All those guys? Not me. I don't like many guys."

Melanie shrugged. "I didn't mind."

At her side, Danuta, the fat woman from Bangladesh, said something vehemently, but since she, like many of the students from Mexico, India, Korea, El Salvador, and Brazil, spoke English poorly, Melanie and the other women nodded automatically. At the American College of Beauty, Melanie had learned to swear in a half-dozen new languages, and this pleased her.

She was so pleased to be the center of attention at breaks because of her former life. It had been, she now admitted, quite adventurous and different from the other women's experiences. She also tried to appear nonchalant about Bobby's trial. That, however, was difficult. He still frightened her, not only because he had turned out to be so untrustworthy, but because he was so much more intelligent than she first suspected. The weeks in Elko with him had shown her a cunning side that was disturbing.

Melanie was also annoyed with herself for so badly misjudging his capacity for wickedness.

Day by day, as the trial approached and she knew her testimony would be required, she grew more nervous. The other students said they were impressed by her bravery. She was not, she knew, at all brave. She simply had no other choice. Mr. Keegan himself had made that perfectly plain when they worked out the deal that allowed her to start her courses at the beauty college.

After the break, she trooped back to her chair with the other students, to the women sitting patiently under thin plastic drapes to be curried, clipped, and washed.

Mrs. Hanover, pouchy-eyed and huge-hipped, walked from chair to chair exhorting her students. Melanie had become her favorite, in part because she was a diligent and conscientious student, and perhaps more, Melanie thought, because she and Mrs. Hanover could hold a complete conversation without resorting to sign language or an interpreter.

The students were joking about going to work for movie stars or almost anyone who lived on the Westside of LA, had two cars, one a Rolls, a pool, and required home visits twice a week.

Mrs. Hanover interrupted Melanie in midlaugh. "You have some visitors. I'll finish your client." She already pushed toward the soapy head Melanie had been working on.

"Who?" Melanie asked. She rarely had visitors, and whenever anyone knew she was working here, it was unpleasant. Cops. Or people working for cops.

"Some people from law enforcement," Mrs. Hanover confirmed, voice lowered, hands scrunching in the woman's hair. "In my office."

Melanie nodded quietly, dried her hands, and walked back to the office. A few of the students watched her. She felt like she was going to her own execution.

I can't change it, she thought. It was bound to happen.

She had seen the start of the trial on TV that morning.

What she saw in Mrs. Hanover's office was Mr. Keegan waiting for her to come through the door. He had that look again. He could be very charming, but the look was into his heart, and it was stony. He had his hands in his pockets.

Beside him was an older man, gray-haired, bent over a little, in a seersucker suit with a pin on the lapel. His shoes, she noticed, were very shiny, and that reassured her. A man who tended his shoes that carefully was not planning anything that might scuff them. He was peering closely at the pictures of old movie stars Mrs. Hanover had on the walls.

"Hello, Melanie," said Mr. Keegan. He did look tired. "This is Win Conley. He's head of the Bureau of Investigations in my office."

The older man smiled at her. It was a nice smile, but an old one, like he wanted to say something soothing to her because so many terrible things went on in the world.

"Hello," she said, hand out. She noticed his loving attention to the pictures. "Mrs. Hanover used to work at Paramount."

"No kidding?" Conley said. "I had a friend who was a guard there."

Mr. Keegan braced himself against the desk. She couldn't help noticing the bronzed baby shoes right behind him that Mrs. Hanover used as paperweights. "I want to make sure you're ready to appear in court," he said directly.

"I guess so."

"Good. I may not need you for a week, two weeks. We've got to pick a jury first. But I'll probably put you on near the start of my case."

She folded her arms. They were being very polite, but she sensed there was no sincerity. They were here to make her testify, and that was all there was to it. "I've been thinking about things," she said.

"What?" Mr. Keegan asked sharply. "You haven't had any problems here, have you? You get your tuition covered, and I've made sure you have a place to live. Is there something you haven't mentioned?"

"What it is, is I'm thinking about what happens when Bobby finds out where I am," she said.

"Nothing will happen. Your protection will go on as before. He's staying in jail, then he's going to prison, and then he'll be executed."

One, two, three, she thought. Mr. Keegan is always so sure of himself. At first, she was calmed by his assurance, like a skittish horse stroked by a confident trainer. Now, she didn't know. He was too sure, maybe.

"But it's more public now. I didn't think it would be so big. Everybody's watching."

"He was going to find out. You understood that from the beginning. I told you."

"Yeah, you did," she admitted. She appealed to the more sympathetic-looking Conley. "You mind if we go someplace else? People like to listen around here."

Conley nodded even though she didn't think Mr. Keegan was all that thrilled to take the short walk through the rear of the beauty college up some stairs into the parking garage. It was low-ceilinged and cement and empty, only them and the cars.

"I looked up your horoscope," she said to Mr. Keegan. "You got to be careful about business and financial matters."

"The trial isn't business, and there's no money," he said. "So much for the stars."

Conley leaned against a car and looked out onto the traffic below them on Greenwood Avenue. "You don't believe that, do you?" He smiled at her.

"Well, you believe in God, don't you?"

"Yes, I do. Mr. Keegan and I even go to the same church."

"Well," she said with conviction. "It's the same thing."

"I hadn't thought about it. Maybe it is," Conley said.

He agreed a little like he meant it, but she thought he was playing the soft part for her while Mr. Keegan kept up the pressure. She was intrigued by the idea that they were friends. Mr. Keegan, though he could be friendly with her, struck her as someone who didn't have many real friends.

"Melanie," Mr. Keegan said, "I'm going to ask you again what you testified to at the grand jury. Nothing more. The defense lawyer's going to try to attack your story. Your character. I'll protect you."

"I know all that. You explained that the first time we met."

"Then I don't see the difficulty."

"Bobby isn't stupid. He'll find out where I am, and he'll do something. Look, I didn't know this was going to turn into such a big deal. People are going to recognize me everywhere."

"I guarantee your safety."

She glanced at Conley. He yawned. Mr. Keegan actually seemed to believe he had that power.

"You're the safest person in the whole city," Conley said. "You've got the whole Bureau of Investigations keeping an eye on you."

Mr. Keegan obviously detected her unease. He motioned her to come to the edge of the open garage. She did. They looked down on the cars and people, a woman with four kids trying to keep them in line. An old man waving up at the sun. A bus with Mr. Keegan's face pictured on its side shuddered past. "What do you see?" he asked. It was not a polite question.

"People. Cars. People."

"I see voters. Human beings. I see the citizens of this county, who count on me to keep them safe. I balance the scales again when bad things happen."

He sounded emphatic, and she grew even more nervous. It was like he said it to pump himself up as much as her. He went on, "Carnes is a very bad man, Melanie. You and I can balance the scales again by making sure he's punished."

He acted like she was a baby or a fool. Conley smiled at her and said, "I'm putting on patrol checks while you're on the stand and afterward. Until this guy goes away."

"Yeah, okay," she said to placate them. "I see. Okay. I was just thinking, you know, worried before. I wanted to hear you tell me how much I'm going to be protected."

Mr. Keegan smiled, a professional's mastery of expression, just as she had mastered it at an early age. "I've taken you into my protection. You are safe."

"Then I'm ready, I guess." She opened her eyes wide, put her hands out. They were not going to let her walk out of this deal. Go along. Think. Make them happy first, she thought.

"I'll show you how easy it's going to be," Mr. Keegan said. He put his hand on her shoulder. "I'll ask, Did you know any of the victims?"

"I never met them."

"Carnes never talked about them while you lived with him? Not a name?"

She licked her dry lips. It was a game to him. Or there was something else going on she missed. He clearly had never lived in her world. She answered with forced ease, "Bobby does not, repeat, does not talk like that, Mr. Keegan. You don't know the man."

Conley broke in, "You'll help us. You want to, I can see that."

"You took trips with Carnes," Mr. Keegan said, turning his back on her, his voice hollow in the man-made cavern of the garage. "Where did you go?"

Conley's eyes were on her. Cop's eyes, the ones that went all the way back in his head, that saw everything. He wasn't fooled by her cooperativeness. She worked harder. "We looked at places. We went sightseeing. Ghost towns. Gambled a little in Vegas, three days there." She smiled. "It was fun."

"Where was Lee Ferrera?"

"I don't know. He wasn't around."

"Did you ask Carnes?"

"I did. Once. I go, 'Say, Bobby, where's Lee at?'"

"What did he say?"

"He goes, 'Oh, Lee left like I told you. He's gone.'"

Mr. Keegan turned back to her, and she saw he had deep lines cut down the sides of his eyes. She hadn't noticed them when they first met, right after she came forward in June. He's gotten real old-looking suddenly. Then she remembered about his wife.

Maybe that was why he was rock-hard with her. She had known men who held themselves together by not giving an inch. If they gave even a little, they were afraid they'd come apart completely. She had spent more than one night in a motel room with a raging or sobbing straight arrow.

And I'm in his hands now, she thought, looking at Mr. Keegan.

"Did you ask him where Ferrera was or where he'd gone?"

She shook her head. "You do not ask Bobby too many questions or he just turns you off."

"Ignores you?"

"Turns you off," she repeated, as if he were the child or fool now. "You don't exist." She took a deep breath. Maybe Conley would hear her. "I got scared when they found Lee's body in the desert and he was shot."

"You suspected Carnes?"

They both studied her, like it was some kind of high-school exam, and they were teachers. "I *knew* it was Bobby. He turned Lee off. That's how I knew he killed that family. When he turns you off, you're dead."

Conley nodded, and Mr. Keegan patted her arm. "Answer like that and everything's going to be fine."

They left her standing in the garage after some more chatter about keeping an eye on things and talking to her again before she had to take the stand. She waited until her heart stopped its uncomfortable thumping. It was like one of those rare but terrible nights when her father had come into her room, scaring her awake. He was drunk, sometimes he brought friends with him. It was easier once she was awake, and the startled first moments, the worst part, were past.

The fear seemed to go on today, and it was light outside.

She went back downstairs to where Mrs. Hanover and the others stood around awkwardly like they had been waiting for her. She thought of the old man's smile, sorrowful and cruel at the same time. A cop's smile. No friend there.

Water slushed around from the dozen open faucets, and the machines whirred and buzzed, and the place was cloying like a spice cake of mixed scents. It looked very normal.

Melanie tapped her front teeth thoughtfully.

"You so serious." Carmen paused, rinsing some hair.

They all watched her, Mrs. Hanover, Danuta, Carmen, the rest.

"I'm going to be famous," Melanie said bitterly.

EIGHT

FROM HIS SECOND TIER, Carnes watched the others ambling across the red-painted concrete to the exercise yard at the Men's Central Jail. His pale arms, showing through the jail's short-sleeved red jumpsuit, hung over the cold metal railing. His plastic ID bracelet itched. It was just before dinner and time for recreation, and he hated Bridge Day.

His appetite coming to the first day of the trial had not been good. To provoke it, he chewed thoughtfully on a roll he'd saved from lunch at the courthouse lockup.

He strolled across the concrete as if walking alone among the men talking, smoking in groups. The other inmates, black and Hispanic and the reedy, flat-faced whites, generally kept away from him. He thought about lunch so he wouldn't think about the trial or the bridge game. At the courthouse, the food had been dished out by obese trusties wearing shower hats. It consisted of whitish sauce on grayish meat and more Jell-O. He had a mild curiosity about why the county's jail food had so much lime flavoring in it.

It was hot in the narrow yard, the concrete on all sides reflecting the heat and sweat and anxiety. He looked around and saw men exactly like the late unmourned Lee with the same watery brains. He tossed the rest of the roll away. Most jail food soured very quickly, and it had already become hard as stone.

It was time for the Killers' Corner.

At the far end of the exercise yard, close to the half-naked tattooed men grimacing with black iron plates hefted up and down in their trembling arms, was a small concrete table. A half-slant shadow from the jail's cement wall fell on the table and the three men around it.

"I'm not playing with Seymour today," Carnes announced, sitting down.

"Why not?" demanded Seymour Belik, flat-headed, brightly sunburned, wearing sunglasses.

"Because you can't remember the cards," Carnes said gently. "All right?"

"I don't care. I do not care. No. I don't like this game anyway. No." Belik tapped his short fingers on the concrete table. He was waiting for his trial on twenty-eight counts of killing prostitutes in Hollywood and dropping their remains, more or less complete, around the San Diego Freeway.

"I'll play with Fred," Carnes said.

Frederick Townsell, the "Bad Boy Slasher," nodded agreeably. He was going to be transferred to San Quentin for killing eighteen young men. At his trial, the former architect made sketches of the press people sketching him. These sketches of his sold for several hundred dollars.

Townsell said, "Yeah. Let's make it Carnes and me against you two. Brains versus bozos."

"Shut up, Freddy," drawled the last man, on Carnes's left. He had three cigarette butts neatly laid beside him on the table. He always collected butts, his used napkins, his hair from shaving. His name was Larson Kaplow, the "Santa Monica Strangler." He killed five men and five women in five years, strangling them all and neatly wrapping them in large plastic trash bags. Several inmates had suggested he could profit from his crimes by endorsing the strength and durability of those trash bags.

Carnes chafed a little at the knowledge he had only four murders to his credit and thus was technically low man at the table. He did not, though, mention his former partner Doug or several others to his fellow bridge players in order to raise his total.

The four bridge players drifted together at recreation periods because virtually no one else in the population would be seen with them.

Each one, Carnes learned, had certain usable quirks. Belik, the former truck driver, was the stupidest and most easily inflamed. This provided Carnes with his only true recreation.

"Let's play," he said briskly. "It's getting late."

"Who's got the cards?" Kaplow asked.

"Belik's supposed to bring them today," Carnes said.

"Not me. Not this time. I don't have them." Belik pounded his fists on the table. "Nobody told me."

"I told you," Carnes said. "Before lights out."

"Did not. Did not. For shit sake, did, did not." Belik knew the others were ready to pounce on him. He screwed his face up as if to cry.

"You are so stupid," Townsell said. "How're we supposed to play, Seymour?"

"He's so stupid he forgets his own name," Kaplow said.

Carnes let them go on picking at Belik until it wearied him and he said, "I brought some cards," and took out a deck of cardboard cards from the commissary. They were jail issue, without stiffness or edges, and they fell apart quickly. They also couldn't be made into weapons.

"Why didn't you say so?" Belik shrilly demanded.

"I thought you had them."

"Just because you're on TV now, you think you're big shit." Belik started to rise. "Mr. Big Shit."

"Sit down, Seymour. We're your friends," Carnes said, pushing the cards to Kaplow to deal.

It was small sport, ganging up on Belik, but there was little to do between going to court, seeing Goodoy, or sleeping, Carnes admitted to himself.

They played sedately for a while. The weight lifters paused every so often to comment on the rancor in the Killers' Corner.

What occupied Carnes very much was finding Melanie again. He had utterly lost track of her when she left him and returned to LA. She would be a very bad witness. She no longer loved him, and he didn't think much of her anymore.

Thus far, finding her had eluded Carnes. Then, Kaplow, in the midst of describing a spider bite he'd gotten on his hand sometime in the night, said, "My movie guy's coming over today. He's got someone interested in my story."

A bell started ringing, signaling the end of the period and dinner. Like school, Carnes thought. He gathered up the cards. He and Townsell had triumphed over Kaplow and Belik.

"Ask the ACLU," Belik said boastfully. "I've got a better story."

Carnes had an inspired thought. "I forgot about your movie, Larson. What was the problem again?"

Kaplow smiled. He was doing better lately, more consistently pleasant and cooperative after a change of his psychoactive medication. He squeezed off the lit end of his cigarette, the ash falling to the ground. It must hurt to do that, Carnes thought.

"This guy. He's a producer," Kaplow said, leaning forward. "He read about me. He's been trying to get the rights. You have to get the rights."

"I don't quite understand," Carnes said with interest.

"Look, Bobby, you get well-known, all kinds of people say blah, blah they know blah, blah about something that happened. You been on TV so much now, they're going to go blah, blah about you. All kinds of people." The four men stood up and walked toward the jail's open doorway.

"Your little pal." Townsell winked, nudging Carnes. "What's her name?"

Carnes didn't answer. LA County sheriff's deputies counted and noted the inmates passing from the dusty sunlit yard to the cooler dark jail. Clipboards and guns were displayed as the men walked by.

"These people, they want a piece of everything, that's what my movie guy says. So you got to get their rights first," Kaplow said. He blinked one eye.

"Melody. Melissa. Mel. Mel," Townsell said, tapping his forehead. He winked at a deputy. "What's her name? You keep talking about her."

They were about to split up. Belik started sneezing, his red face purple each time. The other inmates swaggered by them, wary and contemptuous. Carnes tried to sound casual. "So your producer has to find these people, the ones who say they know things? He locates them?"

"He says so. He's good at it. He's been doing movies a long time. He showed me the names. He's been sued a lot, so he tries to get these rights right away."

"Would you mind if I talked to him?"

Kaplow had his hands in his pockets. He had picked up the butts from the card game, and he counted them now in his palm. "Why do you want to talk to him?"

"I think he could help me."

"Do what? He's doing my movie," Kaplow said. "Not yours."

Carnes put his hand on Kaplow's soft shoulder. It was like pressing mud. "I'm not going to interfere, Larson. Trust me. I want his advice finding someone."

Townsell's saturnine features leered. "I know who. I just can't get her name. What's her name, Bobby?"

Carnes smiled. "Okay, Larson? Can I talk to him?"

"I guess it's okay." Kaplow put the butts carefully into his pocket. The flat-lit corridor smelled of fried fish and stale smoke. Otherwise it reminded Carnes exactly of the schools he had briefly attended as a child. He was sorry, a little, that he had been expelled so often. The jail brought back all the old associations, routines and bad food and unpleasant company. He liked the one school, with elms around it, and sunny beige walls. But even the most tolerant principal couldn't overlook one student partly blinded and a teacher with a fractured skull. Carnes had forgotten their names.

Kaplow said, "He's coming after chow. Eight. Instead of my fucking lawyer."

"We'll say I'm working on your movie or your appeal. Whatever to get me in with you," Carnes said.

"My movie," Kaplow said warningly. "Not yours."

Carnes nodded and headed for his own cell, then to the high-ceilinged room with its vats of food.

Townsell was beside him. "Melanie. That's the name. You're still looking for her, right, Bobby?" He grinned. "The little hooker."

Carnes didn't answer.

The three men sat in the visitors' room after dinner, more officers than usual outside watching them.

The movie producer was named Frank Goldsmith. He sat opposite Kaplow at the plastic-topped table. He looked dried out to Carnes, browned, and his face and skin had an odd tautness like a too-tight drumhead. He seemed to want to be younger than he was. He dressed in black—jeans, loafers, shirt—like an aging delinquent, and he kept absentmindedly pressing the back of his springy brown hair.

He was also very impatient, about to bite off every final word Kaplow or Carnes said. But he was otherwise very professional, and Carnes was impressed with the movie credits he mentioned. They were all, he noticed, about ten or twenty years old, but some were famous.

He had been excited to meet Carnes. "I watched you on TV today. I had a meeting over at Metro, some time to kill, so sure, like everybody, I watched the trial. One word of advice, okay?"

Carnes frowned as if concentrating. "Certainly."

Goldsmith had his hands up, lips pursed. "Don't stare into the camera, okay? I was watching, I thought, Oh, shit. This guy comes across like Al Capone, staring like that."

"I didn't realize I was staring."

"Who does? It's a trick. Look, just ignore it, do your thing. What's the guy? The gangster? Gotti? He knew cameras. Very good. He didn't look, didn't make faces, and when he saw a camera he couldn't avoid looking at"—Goldsmith split his tight face into a gruesome expression—"he smiled."

Carnes nodded, and Kaplow, who had been petulant at sharing his producer, said, "I want to meet the guy who's writing the script. I want to make sure he's getting it right."

Goldsmith shut off his acting lesson, was solemn, sincere, in an instant, and this also impressed Carnes. It suggested an unfixed character, and that was useful.

"Larson," Goldsmith said, "I've got some great interest at CBS, and you are going to have input every step, because this is your story. Nobody can tell it like you. That's my promise."

"I don't want any jokes about garbage bags."

"We're not even thinking like that, Larson," the producer said, and then, as Carnes watched and listened, he earnestly described the meetings he had had about making a television movie about the legal problems of Larson Kaplow. Why anyone would want to know more about Larson was beyond Carnes. He liked Goldsmith's patter, though. It was smooth. It had rhythm and energy. He seemed to believe some of it.

When Kaplow sank back against his plastic chair, satisfied at last, Goldsmith looked at Carnes. "So, you're helping out on the project? How? Exactly how?"

"Well, not really, Mr. Goldsmith. I've got my own story to tell you."

Goldsmith inched his chair across the concrete with a nerve-scratching sound. "Good. Good. Because, you know, as I watched the trial, I thought, Here's a story all done. A man up there, his life on the line, ambitious DA going after him." Goldsmith made a sour face. "Keegan's kind of a menace. I don't know what you know, but I've got friends, good friends, good people he's nailed for really trivial, small shit. A little dope. A little money stuff. I know the stories. I know the people involved. So I know how Keegan's screwed them over, so I know, or I think I know, how he's using you to help get reelected."

"I'm not crazy about him," Carnes said. "Do you want to hear my story?"

"Okay. First, you should know I've got my own production company. Goldsmith Productions, and I've got development deals all around town, but mostly a first-look arrangement at Metro." He spoke breezily as if the connections were mundane. "So what I'm saying, going in, no promises, nothing, because I haven't heard anything, is that I can take your material and do a variety of things with it. I've been around for a long time." He stood up, pacing. "Okay. Go." Carnes then told his story, simply and directly, how his ex-partner had lured him into a drug deal and wantonly killed a family. How enemies of his ex-partner had taken revenge by shooting him in Nevada and dumping his body in the desert. How the authorities had wrongfully concluded that Robert Carnes was the culprit.

"It makes the whole thing easier for them, Mr. Goldsmith." Carnes got up, watching the producer pacing, head down, hands in his black jeans, muttering a little to himself. He sounds a lot like Larson, Carnes thought. "They blame everything on me."

Goldsmith eyed Kaplow. "What do you think?"

"I don't want you to drop my story."

"Number one, I have commitments on your story, Larson. Number two, I do not, unlike so many people in this business, make idle statements. Number, number three, we have a deal, you and me."

Carnes watched the nervous, emphatic gestures. Goldsmith sucked in air loudly. "There are some interesting things here. Okay. I can see some possibilities, dramatic things going on with drugs and family and shit, okay?"

"Thank you, Mr. Goldsmith," Carnes said.

"But, it's soft, okay? It could use a great deal of work."

"I think that's your department." Carnes clasped his hands together. "I'd leave that up to you."

"Of course. Sure. Look, I've got a commitment to Larson first, okay? Then, what you told me, it's interesting, it's got some worthwhile elements, but it's not"—he shaped his hands, his face animated—"coalesced," he said. "So what we'd have to be talking about here, assuming I can clear some time, some space, is taking this on and that's it. It's a project for Goldsmith Productions."

"That would be the most important thing that could happen to me," Carnes said, sitting down. Kaplow played sullenly with two cigarette butts.

A relieved grin appeared on Goldsmith. He apparently had thought convincing Carnes to come over would take more persuasion. Carnes suddenly had a vision of an aging movie man, frantically tap-dancing his way from place to place in Los Angeles, always glancing up at meetings with people who were growing hostile or indifferent, to see if they were bending, wavering. Even feeling sorry enough for him to say yes.

He had the contacts. That was what mattered. And he was hungry.

Carnes saw that, too.

He would like to own my story. "You'll need to get rights from some people, isn't that true?" Carnes asked.

"Maybe. You tell me."

"Well, as you probably know, a great deal of this story depends on one person." Carnes unclasped his hands and looked at Goldsmith. "She was with me. She can substantiate a lot of what I've said."

"The girl? What's her name?"

"Melanie Vogt. I don't know where she is. I think the police are hiding her."

"Sure they are," Goldsmith said. "Friend of mine, he got picked up by LAPD, he was a little high, all right. He got thrown into a room full of fifty screaming guys downtown. Fifty. A regular guy. Think of it. Have you ever been thrown into a room of fifty men?"

Carnes shook his head, and Kaplow nodded.

"That's how Keegan and this bunch of Nazis treat people. And this guy is a respected actor. You'd know the name. Treated like he's some fucking bum, and he's still shaken by it. Still," Goldsmith said angrily. He tapped one brown fist into the other.

"Can you find her, Mr. Goldsmith?"

"Frank. No more formality here, men." He spoke to Carnes

and Kaplow like a drill sergeant glad to be back among his platoon. "Find her? She's in town, I can find her. I know everybody in town. I know places and people nobody can get to."

"Are you married, Frank?" Carnes asked.

"Not now. Couple years. I was."

"Children?"

"I got a daughter living near San Francisco."

Carnes wanted Goldsmith to feel a bond with him. "Melanie and I were married in a spiritual way, Frank. We shared ourselves. I know if you find her, she'll help us."

Goldsmith was moved by some great emotion suddenly, as if the mention of his new friend's tribulation and his own former marriage stirred him. He was, Carnes concluded, an emotional person. Goldsmith put out both of his hands and firmly grabbed a startled Kaplow's and Carnes's. He said fervently, "My handshake is my word, men. That's my way of doing business. Always has been. Always will be. You know what the people like me in the entertainment business have to carry?"

Carnes shook his head, and Kaplow, who disliked physical contact, worked to free his hand from Goldsmith's grip. Carnes was interested.

"We carry a whole shitload of responsibility because we've got the greatest tool for fighting injustice in the whole fucking history of the world. T-fucking-V. Robert, Larson, you'll go straight into the living rooms, the hearts, of a couple-fucking-million Americans, and they'll see what this goddamn maniac Keegan is doing here."

He released their hands. Kaplow wiped his hurriedly on his pants leg, and smiled shyly.

Carnes thought Larson liked the idea of being in a million living rooms. Unsuspecting living rooms.

Goldsmith gave them both a defiant fist in the air.

In fact, Goldsmith Productions, like its proprietor, had seen much better days. It led a gypsy existence, moving from one temporary office to another, which was not unusual at all in the TV or movie business; but most companies changed locations with jobs, not because the rent was delayed one time too many.

Aside from the upbeat end of the day with Kaplow and Carnes, Goldsmith's day had been rotten. His only surviving deal, a tentative movie about whaling ships and a UFO, had died that morning.

But, as he cantered, his usual pace, into the Almont Hotel just before nine P.M., his mood was better. Things were happening again.

The Almont was just off Wilshire Boulevard in Beverly Hills, which gave it a little breathing space as a permissible lodging, but it was creaky-looking, with pebbled walls and hangings from the 1950s. Most of its tenants were husbands in the movie business thrown out of their homes for various domestic misdemeanors. Actors, a small-time director or two, a few producers, slouched around waiting until their wives would unlock their doors.

Goldsmith was recently divorced. His house on Camden Drive was for sale, and the Almont Hotel's fading charm was his refuge.

He went directly to the bar. The TV was on, most of the small, white, cloth-covered tables empty. The regulars gave him a quick glance, nod, glare, then went back to their rattling newspapers as they drank and sulked. Two men in very out-of-fashion sport shirts argued about horses running at Santa Anita.

Greta waited for him at a table. She was dressed in a blue outfit with small pearls. Her wrinkled face was thin, but at a distance her figure was good, especially from the rear.

She had coffee, and he jauntily ordered a vodka tonic.

"You're in a good mood," she said.

"I'm always in a good mood," he said, taking out his appointment book. "You know me. Cheers." He raised his glass to her.

"I heard you lost out at Metro," she said. "No deal anymore."

"It was flaky to start with. Something much better's coming."

"Oh, goody."

He felt very energized, electric with the possibilities of hooking the defendant in a major, public trial. But first things first. He said to Greta, "It's out in Pasadena"—he wrote out the address for her—"Here's the detail sheet," and handed her a page of notes. "The woman's a widow. She asked for you. She's seen every movie you did five million times."

"Surely only two million." Greta smiled, smoking well into her second pack of the day.

"She's a major-league fan. It's a party for some old friends going to Europe, and she wants you to come about ten, make it a big entrance, big surprise, and give her a kiss on the cheek."

Greta sighed. "Oh, dear. I'm a very good friend?"

"Close personal, but she's always respected your privacy so she hasn't told anybody." He finished his vodka and ordered another. It was a celebration of a new, golden day dawning. "You went to college together."

"I didn't go to college," Greta said with a grin. "I was standing in for Judy Garland at Universal when she fell apart. I think I went to college in one picture." She frowned thoughtfully.

"Her name's Mrs. Francis DeCarterret."

Greta took a look at the detail sheet. "I'll know my part by the time I get there. Do I have to stay for the whole party?"

"She's paying five hundred."

"How about until midnight, Frank? I've been to three of these things this week. I've got so many close, intimate friends now I can't stand it."

"She didn't sound like she'd like you to leave early." He closed the appointment book. "I think she's used to getting her way."

"Oh, goody," she sighed. "Show time."

"You'll be great. We'll split tomorrow morning. She's sending a check over."

Greta nodded, familiar with the routine of Goldsmith Productions. "Anybody else making the party rounds tonight?"

"Earl is. Wally. Leroy. He's got two. One on the *Queen Mary*. He's an old friend of a retired colonel or something." Goldsmith slugged back half of his vodka. Power surged in him as it had not for weeks. Months even. The sour failure of the morning's rejection washed away. "Then he's the former boyfriend of some woman in Holmby Hills."

"It's about the same as when we made movies. I did one with Leroy." She put out her cigarette, instantly took out another, held it up. "We did two dance numbers. You should dance with me. I'm very good." She lit the cigarette, and her face was hazy in the smoke, like a shot through gauze in one of her later movies.

"Well, this pays the bills until the big one hits." He tapped the table. "And it's coming pretty fast."

"Oh, goody. Get me in."

"I'm sorry you got to go out on deals like this."

"You're a true fan," Greta said gently. "I don't think people appreciate how sensitive you are, Frank."

"I love the business. I care about friends."

"Well, this is a little like acting, so I'm not complaining. It's work, which God knows I wouldn't be getting at all except for you. It's make-believe. We all get by on it in this town. But I am grateful for your kind thoughts." And he heard the same cultured, delicate voice Greta had used in so many films. He hated to admit that Greta and Leroy and the others were the most reliable source of income for Goldsmith Productions. Perhaps there really was a change coming.

"You better get going," he said.

"Tell me one thing." Greta stood up. She spoke in a cultivated, patrician tone. She was in character for the Pasadena widow.

"What?"

"Is Leroy getting more than five hundred a pop for his routine?"

He said no, and she left. Goldsmith took his empty glass to the bar, had it refilled, and quickly got into a conversation with four men, writers and a director, he'd known for years. He told them about Carnes and Kaplow, bragging about his courage being alone at the jail.

"These are killers. Stone killers. But I gave them the yak-yak, my best bit, the producer."

"Frankie, aren't you worried one of us will take this and try to get something going before you can?" asked the bald man to his right.

Goldsmith shook his head. It was a terrific day, terrific night, and he thought it might be a more terrific night if he called a woman assistant director he'd run into that morning at MGM. She was usually free and very acrobatic. He looked at the man who'd asked the question. "I've got witnesses. My friends. So I'm not worried. Besides, we're talking about the Strangler and Carnes. If I thought somebody was dealing me out, I'd tell those guys."

Goldsmith finished his drink and thought of how he would go about finding this woman Carnes described so meticulously for him before he left the jail, her habits and thoughts, her appearance. I can find her, and then I've got the whole deal, and I can take it anywhere, and this project's going to fly.

"I think I heard that in one of your movies," someone said. There was a little laughter. The Almont Hotel was informal and tense with waiting all the time.

"I'd tell Carnes," Goldsmith said seriously. He had their attention. "This guy Carnes. He's got a quality."

"Like what?"

"Quiet. Looks like anybody. Voice is quiet." Goldsmith lowered his own, the ring of faces like boys around a campfire. "But the eyes. It's in the eyes."

"What?" a tiny man asked, a shrimp appetizer poised in his fingers.

"He's been there. It's there in his eyes."

NINE

SEVERAL HOURS BEFORE Carnes met Frank Goldsmith at the jail, Keegan took Win Conley home with him for dinner.

Keegan drove, which he sometimes did going home from work even when he had a driver. His routine required variation, if only so he didn't think it completely ordered his days.

It was the hour in Los Angeles when most people agree the city looks decent and beautiful. The sunset washed pale gold from the mountains over the crowded streets to the sea, vanishing in darkening mist. Because he was nervous about the fund-raiser and tired from the first day of the trial, Keegan took a familiar route home. From Spring Street downtown he swung onto Olympic Boulevard, and then up to Wilshire, even though at that early evening hour the traffic was heavy. He liked seeing Beverly Hills at that golden time of early evening and thought Conley might, too.

"She's going to be a good witness," Keegan said, still thinking about Melanie Vogt's answers. "I think I made her understand how important she is."

Conley, whistling quietly, glanced quickly at Keegan. "She's a hooker. She knows deals. She knows she loses this deal if she backs out."

"Maybe that's how it looks to an old cop, Win."

"That's how it is. Take my word for it."

Keegan knew Conley had seen and done a great deal as a cop in Beverly Hills when he was younger and then in LA. It made Conley's romantic fascination with movies intriguing. He otherwise didn't tolerate illusions in life.

Conley said, "Well, I'm going to keep an eye on her myself until you need her."

"You have enough to do," Keegan said.

"No problem," Conley said. "Who's at home tonight?"

"Just Elaine and Innocencia. Chris's at school."

"Everybody all right?"

Keegan nodded. "We're all fine. Elaine sometimes wakes up at night. I hear her crying." Keegan dropped the subject.

"You must be awake yourself," Conley said. He didn't go on, either. His own wife had died in January, his daughters had grown and moved away, and he lived alone. He was the one who had called Keegan's fourteen-year-old son, Chris, at school in the Valley to tell him that Leah was dead.

They were on Wilshire already. Keegan lamented the changes in the city, most of the movie theaters gone, record stores, hardware stores, the family restaurants, replaced by trendy little places that were crowded and sharp. He was glad Chris and Elaine at least had grown up while many of the city's old stores still existed, before they were turned into banks or closed. The Ontra Cafeteria—where Chris choked on a piece of halibut when he was very young, and Keegan remembered shaking him in panic—was gone. So was Owl Rexall, where Leah bought cough medicine and got their prescriptions filled. The only places still around were the tailor on Brighton Way where Keegan got his suits made, just as he had since he worked at Signal Oil for Leah's father, and the Italian barber on little Santa Monica who cut his hair, told dirty jokes, and kept a gun collection.

Conley, as if listening to Keegan's mind, looked at the cold art galleries and new restaurants. "Place has changed so much. I'm glad I only come out here to go to church now."

Keegan nodded. "Christ, you go back to Howard Hughes, Win. Of course it changes."

And we lose it and the people, and only our memories, false and alluring, remain, he thought. He didn't want Conley to know how much he missed the city he'd grown up in. Conley, as a very new Beverly Hills cop, had been one of the first on the scene when Howard Hughes crashed his plane in the city. For years he received Christmas cards, which he saved carefully, from Hughes.

"Last weekend, I helped Ray Massey to communion," Conley said.

"Is he on one cane?"

"Two now. You'd know if you still went to church. Stood up with Randolph Scott, too," Conley said with pleasure.

"I don't have time since the campaign picked up," he said. It was not true. He had stopped going to All Saints', only six blocks from his home, a little before Leah's death, about the time he began keeping the photos from letters and putting them in his pockets. The withdrawal from All Saints' bothered him, though. It suggested a greater, more terrible withdrawal from faith, but he didn't want to examine that possibility very much. He said to Conley as he turned onto Rexford Drive, "It doesn't seem the same now. It's changed, too," and he hoped Conley would think only of a dead wife and the church where he and Leah had been married.

Where Chris carried the Yule Candle one Christmas as the lead acolyte. He missed his son and wished he wasn't away at school. Even if the school was only in the Valley, Keegan made it a firm rule that visits were to be no more or less than holidays and end of exams. Leah hated the rule. "The last Victorian parent," she called him when he argued that being away from the family would make Chris rely on his own resources and character, build him up.

Still, I wish I could see him more often.

Keegan parked and got out, a briefcase in each hand. Trial material, campaign material, papers to read and check.

His house was on a gentle hillock, bordered by perfect low hedges maintained by industrious gardeners, like all the houses on the block. It was a white house, green-trimmed, with a wide front window, like almost every other house, and it had been built in 1928. He and Leah bought it for fifty thousand dollars, the down payment loaned by her father and recalled at every later meeting in some way.

The only remarkable thing about the house was that the front window had been replaced by bulletproof glass when he was elected county district attorney. And the button. Don't forget the button. In the master bedroom there was a hidden button that would summon the Beverly Hills police in two minutes. Elaine had proved that four years ago when she accidentally found it, and the house was suddenly besieged by black-and-whites and worried BH cops.

He and Conley went inside. He heard voices in the kitchen. Keegan put his briefcases down on the dining-room table. Leah would have hated that. He saw Conley take a deep breath and rub his hands going into the kitchen. Elaine loved seeing Conley. He always gave her a dollar and took an interest in her latest problems in school.

Keegan checked the grand piano, Leah's major snobbery, glowing with polish near the front window, silver-framed family pictures around it. Sometimes Innocencia didn't dust it, and he had decided it should look as Leah wanted it to, as if she could walk in even now at any moment. Sit down on the long beige sofa, offer him a drink. From whatever she had been drinking for several hours.

All day. That day.

Keegan went into the kitchen. He saw Conley talking to Chris and Elaine, while Innocencia stirred pots at the electric range.

"Look who's here," Conley said, pointing at Chris.

"This is a surprise," Keegan said. Sometimes he and Chris shook hands, but not now. "It's good to see you."

"I wanted to make it a surprise," Chris said. "I watched you on TV, everybody did. It looked good. I got a ride into town from Mr. Vaughan."

Elaine and Conley, like conspirators, watched Keegan's reaction. He was very pleased to see Chris. His son was growing tall, his hair as black as his mother's, but with Keegan's square face. He had not cried or shown more than decent grief since her death and that, too, was something he had inherited from Keegan.

Except he never saw me that night, Keegan thought. My weakness. My guilt. My crime.

"It's good you came," Keegan said, sniffing the air. "That's really good." He pointed at the pots.

"We're having corned beef and cabbage for your dinner."

He looked at his watch. It was later than he first thought. He was also suddenly uneasy about the memories these people would raise and what he might say. Better to stay in motion.

"I haven't watched the time. I'll have to miss it. Can you save some?"

Innocencia, slim and excitable, stirred quickly. "The potatoes get mushy."

Conley patted her. "Don't worry. I'll eat enough."

Keegan said, "I've got to change for a campaign thing. I'd like to talk to you, Chris."

His son followed him back to the bedroom. The memories rushed in, as he had feared they would.

It was the reelection campaign that started her off. For the months following his announcement, Leah drank more than usual, and her sensitivity increased. She had been seeing a psychiatrist on Bedford Drive, walking distance from home almost, a Beverly Hills convenience. The sessions weren't productive. "We're paying a lot of money, mostly mine," she would say later, "for him to tell me I'm unhappy. I know I'm unhappy. How about it, George? What's your professional opinion?"

They fought much more often in those last months.

But the last night was interchangeable with many others. I should have seen something, he thought. By that time, he was deliberately closing his eyes, figuring his duty and pledge were honored because he and Leah stayed together. Because we were a great-looking public marriage.

He came home that last night, like tonight, with only a few

minutes to spare before going out again. He was tired. Leah sat at the piano in the living room. She didn't play anymore, but she liked to drink at the piano.

Small talk, he remembered. We started with the usual back and forth about our days, Leah working on some charity, seeing a dozen people.

He sat down beside her at the piano, his own drink in hand. He touched her glass. Coldness seeped around Leah and him.

"Play something," he said.

She smiled. "Oh, I don't feel like it."

"I love listening to you."

She nodded, hand brushing over the keys. "I don't think I can remember any notes. Everything slips away."

He stood up. "I've got to change. Morganthau's nervous about money this time. I keeping telling him, I'm the incumbent, I've got a good record, downtown's going to contribute like they did last time."

"You're going out again?"

"I told you. Last night."

"You didn't."

"I'm fairly sure I did," he repeated, walking upstairs. He cringed now, thinking of his tone. For so long he had gotten into the habit of acting as if Leah were forgetful or worse.

She came up beside him as they walked along the hallway. "Well, we can't have Wylie Morganthau getting nervous."

"No, we can't. He knows too many people."

"I don't think you told me, George. About going out."

"Does it matter? I have to go. He's set up a meeting at his house with some bankers."

"That's what you say." She put her glass down on the bureau in their bedroom. She had started, only a short time before, to make vague accusations against him.

"That's the way it is. A campaign meeting." He grew exasperated. "I'm in politics, darling. I have to see people all the time."

"So if I checked with Muriel, who won't shut up, if I checked with Muriel, I'd find out about this meeting you say is at their house."

"Yes, you would."

Leah folded her arms. She closed her eyes briefly, and she shook her head slowly. "I don't want to be a burden, George. Honestly, I don't want to put pressure on you."

He touched her gently, went on changing his clothes. Contrition usually followed her accusations. He knew the whole performance.

"I know you don't," he said. "And you aren't."

"I know I am."

"I'd tell you. I don't lie to you."

She sat down on the bed, then lay down. As if laid out almost, stiff and unseeing, eyes unfocused looking up. "I wouldn't know if you did. You could tell me almost anything."

"I save that for press conferences."

"You always make jokes out of things I say."

Keegan paused, smiling for her. "Nobody says I have a sense of humor, Leah. It's one of my shortcomings."

"They should see you at home. See us together. Without any phony—" She swallowed and groped for a word, then sighed. "Phony, phony, phony."

"It won't be a late meeting."

"Stay as late as you want." She pulled herself up. "I won't do anything this time, George. I mean it. I won't go out in public or shake hands. I will not do it."

His exasperation broke through again. "We'll talk about it. Later, please."

"Nothing's changing. I am not making a public show for you." She had found his sore spot and somehow decided to dig in that night. "I won't do it."

"Then don't."

"Thank you, Governor," she said, face flushing.

"I'll see you later," he said, not wanting to fight or push against her again. It was one thing to hold on to a passive form, keeping her head above the water. It was something else when the drowning victim fought against you.

He said, "Leah, this is very important to me. It's not simply a job I go to. It's part of me. It's not something to use for ammunition when you feel badly."

She pulled her legs toward her, arms around them, and looked at him angrily. Why, he wondered? What did I do except love her, and when that flickered and failed, kept faith with a promise to stay by her.

"Do you love anything except yourself?" she asked, low, bitter. "I don't think you do, George. It came to me finally. You don't love anybody else."

"You're right. No one else." He caught himself. "Maybe Innocencia. She makes wonderful meatloaf."

"Make jokes about me again. You only prove my point."

"I'm trying to make you see it's ridiculous."

"Everything's ridiculous except you and what you want."

"All right, Leah," he conceded. "I surrender. I'll go quietly."

He turned, and she said something, angrily, then called his name, and the anger, he thought, was gone. It was, he thought later, more like a cry.

Sometime after he left the house, Leah drove into the early June twilight to Chris's school. Looking for peace. For unqualified love, Keegan thought.

He was only slightly concerned when he got home later and found her gone. There had been one or two missing nights in the past. Then the call came, and he was flown by a Highway Patrol helicopter to the site. From the air over it, he saw tiny figures, lit up like fireflies in the dark, clustered on the slope of Mulholland Drive, red and white flares from the fire trucks parked like toys, and the long line of backed-up cars. Keegan got a full briefing from the Highway Patrol when he landed, and he still didn't believe it. It was too much like a policy meeting at the office or the campaign meeting he had just left, earnest people trying to persuade him of their viewpoint.

Only the views were cold. The skid marks on the winding, hairpin curves of the high road meant Leah had been doing fifty miles an hour. A tire blew out. He didn't understand. She should have been on Coldwater Canyon. It was the easiest route to the school.

The car, their old station wagon, careened over the side of the brush-covered canyon, down sixty feet. Her last view would have been of the city lights starting to come on against a rosy, blue-lapped twilight.

Standing at the site, Keegan listened to the officers, watched the mechanical flurry of machines and men pulling and prying at the car. To his horror, he realized he felt relief. His burden was lifted. He was disgusted with himself, ashamed.

The sheriff himself brought word an hour later at the hospital. She'd been drinking. Keegan acted as if the news were unexpected. Then the sheriff whispered, "Didn't cause the accident, nobody else hurt. Won't be any paperwork. Won't go any farther than you."

Through the public funeral and cameras following to the grave, the newspaper stories about the loss of one of the city's most charitable figures, Keegan sank lower inside. Accident or deliberate, he turned the facts over and over again; he had failed her, let her go when he should have struggled hardest against his absorption in the campaign. How much of an accident could it be when a woman who drank heavily sped along a high mountain road? The tire exploding didn't relieve him at all.

He sat for hours afterward puzzling it time after time, thinking how it might have been different if he had missed the campaign meeting.

Or if, he thought, I had only turned back to her when she called my name that night.

He went on, with work and the campaign, and the trial, too, to make his own order from the murky disaster, but he never felt the same again. He had the sense of being a stumbling runner, constantly missing a step, forever feeling the lost cadence.

Chris sat down on the bed, hands braced. Keegan took off his coat. He changed shirts.

"Everything's fine?" he asked Chris, as he went into the bathroom and washed his face, then hands.

"I have an English exam tomorrow. But it's okay. You should've seen everybody in the lounge, watching the trial."

"What's the verdict?" Keegan slowly dried his face and hands.

"A lot of the teachers think it's a stunt. You're playing politics."

"The judge told me that today in so many words." He came out of the closet, knotting a new tie. "What do you think? Your opinion matters a lot more to me."

Chris nodded. "It is a good way to win the election. I mean, Aguilar's wrong now. You're in charge."

"Well, my own opinion, my hope," he corrected, "is that the voters realize Ms. Aguilar's grasping at anything. I hope they see I care. I do care. I don't sit in my office shuffling papers around. I try to make decisions that are right. I try to make the just result possible. Even the trials that went against us, they should have been put to a jury. No, Ms. Aguilar's made a big mistake thinking she can attack me for being deskbound. I'll admit I was nervous this morning, first morning back in a courtroom since"—he paused in this unexpected headlong rush of words, impressions—"I did the Harbor Commission trial when I was a city attorney. I had to prove two commissioners were stealing city money and I did. The problems weren't any bigger than this trial. And"—he grinned at his son—"I've got a superb witness. I interviewed her again tonight. Oh, no. Aguilar, the mayor, the *Times,* they're all making a big, big mistake if they think they can smear me. The people are going to see what I believe every day."

He suddenly realized how boastful he sounded. Chris had been nodding, but there was a confused element in his expression.

"You looked great, Dad."

"Thanks. The point is convicting Carnes," Keegan said, hastily finishing dressing. I said too much. I would've said more in a moment. "Now, Chris, it is good to see you. But you know the rule about coming home."

"This's a special occasion."

"It still doesn't mean you can just leave school. You know that."

"Yeah, I thought you'd like it."

"I do. But it was wrong."

"I'm not going to apologize." The strange steel Keegan didn't comprehend showed itself in Chris again.

"I don't want an apology. I want you to follow the rules. They're good rules. Stay at school. I'll come to see the game."

"This weekend. It's Saturday at two." He played forward in lacrosse, an East Coast game transplanted uneasily under the blue sky and palms.

"Saturday." Keegan paused. "All right. I'll try."

Chris stood up, ready to leave the room. "You won't be there. Mom said you don't like us all very much."

Out of nowhere. Brewing and seeking a chance to reveal itself, a bitter verdict. "When did she say that? It's not true," he said heatedly to his son.

Chris paused at the door. "I never see you. Elaine doesn't. Mom didn't see you."

"She saw me every day," Keegan called out, but Chris was gone. Keegan sat down on the bed, feeling unsteady. He sat for some time, then got up carefully, like a man who thinks he's broken a bone.

He was late for the fund-raiser. Elaine, Chris, and Conley were eating in the kitchen, on the red and white oilcloth-covered table. The chatter as Innocencia served died out when he came in.

"I'll say good night to everybody. How will you get back to school, Chris?"

Conley said, "I'll run him out. I've got one of my guys bringing my car."

Elaine looked at her brother. "It's kind of nice having him here during the week."

"Well, I'll see you all later. Good night, Innocencia," Keegan said. His control was remarkable, and he complimented himself. Chris didn't look away, but watched him constantly.

Keegan went out to his car. He sat at the wheel. The white-curtained front window was like a cataract-covered eye, yearning for vision. I've got to go, he thought. I can't be too late.

Conley was at the car window. "You all right, George?"

"I forgot something. I'm fine." They were informal after hours. He started the car. "Thanks for staying for dinner. And giving Chris a ride."

"I'll give you a little advice from an old hand. You should be with them both more. You go too hard on him. I wish to God I'd known half what I do about raising kids when I had my own at home." The sad Conley smile appeared briefly.

Keegan's hands were tight on the wheel. "I know my own family. I don't need your analysis."

He backed the car out and drove down the street and saw Conley, back turned, head down, slowly going back into the house.

The fund-raiser was held at the home of Park Sol Lee, a K-Town jewelry importer. His office was a small, dusty storefront near Western Avenue, but he lived in a mock English manor house above Sunset Boulevard in the seclusion of evergreens and palms. When Keegan drove up, the wide driveway was already filled with Mercedes, Bentleys, Rollses; and pink-waistcoated young women, all achingly beautiful, parked his car for him.

The house was lit up like a colored lantern with strings of lights and decorations. Park was informally known through Koreatown as the Godfather, because he helped with anything that needed attention, from vaccinations to fire code compliance. There were rumors about other things, too. But Keegan had Morganthau check Park out. There was nothing politically harmful. He was simply a powerful man in his community. And downtown, where he had many friends on the City Council.

Keegan then checked him in the bureaus at the DA's office. There were no pending cases or investigations.

I can take his money with a clear conscience, he thought. He tried to put the problems at home to one side. It was a technique he had mastered over the years, so his days were not so much continuous incidents or personalities, but strictly defined boxes, like the trimmed, green hedges that so neatly separated the houses on his street.

Morganthau was nervously waiting in the foyer when Keegan came in. Morganthau raised his eyes in relief.

"George. Great. I was having an attack. Go away," he said sternly to the white-jacketed Filipino waiter with white gloves who tried to offer Keegan something delicately seasoned on a silver tray.

"I thought it wasn't formal," Keegan said, irritatedly looking at his campaign chairman's tuxedo.

"Smile, George," Morganthau said, shooing away another waiter who urged something on them. "You're the main course. They've been talking about you all night. You know this house?" Morganthau took his arm and headed them toward the lights and noise of the living room.

"No. I've never been here before."

Morganthau's wife, Muriel, appeared as they walked, pecked Keegan on the cheek. She was sixty, silvery haired. "Is he talking about this place? Hello, George. I took the tour. Six-car garage. In back, he's got a mile-long swimming pool. They've got this little copper porthole near the bottom of the pool." She giggled. "You can stand in the little room and look through the porthole at everybody swimming. It's a wonderful old house." She patted Keegan as if she expected him to buy it.

Before Keegan could answer, a large man with a pinkish bald head stared, put his drink down, and began a rhythmic clapping with his tiny hands. The other people stopped talking, jewel-heavy women and men in black and gold, and soon the room filled with applause.

Keegan responded automatically, waving a hand in the air and smiling. His nervousness evaporated, and he completely forgot about the guilty moments at home earlier.

As he moved toward Mr. Park, people patted him on the back, moved aside. Keegan answered with ready words. Morganthau, at his right, whispered, "Three-fifty a couple, George. Plus the people who bought and didn't come. You're having a great night."

Muriel Morganthau leaned to his other ear, and she wafted over perfume. "It's like the old days, isn't it? Leah'd love this."

Public people with private lives scarcely indistinguishable from each other. Me and Leah, he thought.

The large pinkish man bowed. Keegan said, "Mr. Park, I'm overwhelmed by your hospitality. Thank you for having me in your home." He looked at the small, ink-haired woman smiling at him from Park's side. "Thank you, Mrs. Park."

"This is my cousin. My wife is ill again this evening," Mr. Park said in his oddly high-pitched voice. "This is another cousin." And he motioned to a similar small woman at his other side.

At once, Mr. Park clapped his hands again, the musicians stopped. He said something loudly in Korean. Morganthau translated. "He told us he'd do this, George. It's a tribute to you."

"What's he saying?"

"You're the savior of Los Angeles. They can see it for themselves on TV. You make the city safe. If they work for your reelection, their kids can go to school without fear, they can go to work, everybody can make a fortune."

Muriel Morganthau nodded. "I have a feeling. The bad times are over. My feelings are always good. You know that. I pick up things."

"Oh, don't go with the ESP again. George, all day now, she's talking ESP," Morganthau complained.

"As long as I win, you can tell me anything, Mur," Keegan said to her, and she smiled. Even mysterious powers were easier to cling to than the notion of senselessness or personal fault.

"I knew you'd listen," she said. "Not like him." She shook her head at Morganthau.

Keegan smiled and waved as a shout in Korean went up and the room broke into mechanical, enthusiastic applause again. He turned, waved, turned, waved, smiled, and turned, as if spitted and rotating in the center of attention.

It was a lengthy evening. At the impromptu receiving line, beside an enormous fern, Keegan shook hands with each couple. He held a glass of champagne in one hand. Morganthau and Muriel worked the partygoers on his behalf through the house.

Many of the men, Keegan began to notice, were acupuncturists. Each time he asked someone his occupation, he was told the same thing. He asked one man, "Is anybody here doing something else?"

The man slowly peered around. "No. We're all the same. I know everybody. We know each other." The receiving line moved on.

By eleven, Keegan excused himself to find a bathroom. It was an unbreakable rule of politics. Never leave a bathroom unused. It could be a long time to the next one. His father-in-law, who before rising high in Signal Oil used to be a roustabout, had laughed with Keegan about the rawer aspects of life on the campaign trail. Leah would groan or playfully nudge her father when he grinned as Keegan talked about the food he had to eat, the people he had to meet, the strange places he found himself. Keegan often saved ribald stories for Leah's father. It was a way of pleasing him. There's nothing wrong with trying to make your marriage easier, he thought.

He also admitted that he liked to be liked. Maybe too much sometimes.

Keegan got as far as the foyer, Filipino waiters gliding in and out with trays. A thin, solemn man took Keegan's hand abruptly. "Thank you. Thank you," he said gravely.

"You're welcome."

"You must visit my school," the man said. "Very modern and very professional facility with good parking." He had one hand inside his tuxedo jacket, and he was nervous. Some people were nervous around Keegan because they'd seen him on TV.

"What school is that?" Keegan asked politely, reflexively.

"The Western States School of Acupuncture." He dipped his shiny, glistening black head down, his hand still in his jacket. Keegan had the swift impression he was going to pull a gun.

Not here. Not with so many people around.

"I'm a great, great admirer of you," said the thin man. "You are a great crime fighter. I feel better every day with you."

"I appreciate your support tonight." He paused.

"Dr. Sung. I am the dean."

"Dr. Sung, the name of your school rings a bell. Are there other schools here tonight?"

"Oh, yes. But they aren't as big as mine. We have seven buildings and a library, and we are near the Gramercy bus stop."

Keegan's mind had caught a stray focal point. "You have to give exams to your students? Graduating exams?" Suddenly, he thought Morganthau had made a terrible mistake. There would be no money from this crowd tonight.

"My graduates meet very high standards." Dr. Sung nodded, pleased at Keegan's interest. "I give strict examinations twice a year."

"Nobody can practice acupuncture without passing those exams."

"They must be well trained."

"They need your blessing."

It was a magical word, and Dr. Sung smiled. "Mr. Park said you understood everything. Yes. Yes." He took his hand from the tuxedo jacket and pushed a thick white envelope into Keegan's coat. "From a grateful citizen," he gasped and darted back to the party.

Keegan felt the bulk of the envelope as if he'd been punched. His anger grew. He went into the bathroom off the foyer. It was cluttered with gold fixtures, thick mauve towels, cinnamon scented. He locked the door.

In the mirror's expanse, lit by gold lamps in the shape of gaslights, Keegan watched a scene and a single player. He saw an angry middle-aged man, skin too white and loose, shades of an earlier vigor in his broad shoulders. The man took out an envelope and opened it. He held four one-thousand-dollar bills in his hand. Keegan looked at his own face, the anger mixing with fear. They thought I would take it, he thought. Was there some sign they saw? Was there a visible taint of guilt and corruption that they could detect?

He jammed the money back into the envelope. The door opened and Mr. Park came in, pocketing his key.

"You've seen Dr. Sung?" he asked. He swayed a little. He smiled. He was drunk.

"Yes. Just now. You son of a bitch."

A frown. "He presented you with his gift?"

"I thought it was yours. So I wouldn't investigate schools that took bribes to pass students. You're the Godfather."

"It was the gift of a friend. One new friend to another." The large man stood still, as if he were afraid he would topple over.

"You're bribing. You were trying to bribe me," Keegan said furiously.

"There are many others here who wish to honor you."

"Bribe me."

"There is a misunderstanding. You're offended. What can I do?"

"I'm leaving. Get out of my way." Keegan started to push by, but Mr. Park wouldn't move. "Get out of my way," he said and grabbed one of Mr. Park's arms, pulled him roughly. The force startled the large man, and he bounced from the marble sink, arms flailing for purchase. He slipped on the floor and fell beside the elegant toilet. He stared dimly at Keegan and then giggled.

It was a revolting, taunting sound.

Keegan rushed out, found Morganthau talking to an old woman with stiff, high hair. He shook the envelope at Morganthau. "The fat bastard tried to bribe me."

Several people lowered their voices, stopped talking, drinks frozen in their hands.

"Calm down, George. What'd he do?" Morganthau asked.

"He gave me money to prevent an investigation of these people."

Morganthau shook his head. He looked into the envelope. "I don't believe it. He's been straight."

Keegan said, "Give it all back, Wylie. Every cent. Tomorrow."

"What're you going to do? Okay. Whatever you want. Jesus." He took his head in his hands. "Let me think."

Keegan saw Mr. Park wobbling into the living room. His white ruffled shirt had come up a little, but he was smiling. His cousins rushed over, uttering soothing cries.

The trio played, and Keegan strode to Mr. Park. He threw the envelope. It struck the large man on his forehead and the people around him gasped. "I'm returning the bribe," Keegan said.

"You are witnesses," Park said, picking up the envelope and holding it up. "What a joke. How funny." And he laughed, repeated the words in Korean, and threw the bills at his cousins, who scrambled for the money. The trio played "For He's a Jolly Good Fellow," and the applause was loudest this time.

They're happy with my little joke, Keegan raged. What fun. What a show. What a laugh.

Park had wounded him in the most sensitive spot he had. It was not so much that I was offered a bribe, Keegan thought. It was that they all thought I would take it.

He shouldered past people, outside, waited impatiently for his car. Muriel and Morganthau came out, too.

"All I need is for Aguilar to get any of this," Keegan said. "So every cent goes back right away."

"Sure, George, sure. I'm sorry. I didn't know. The bastard was always so okay."

"George. George," Muriel said soothingly. "One thing that woman can't get anybody to believe, you being dishonest."

"It's the suspicion, Mur. Rumors that kill."

"You're very upset. You want us to come home with you? Have a drink maybe?" Morganthau asked.

Keegan shook his head. "I am upset. But I'm perfectly fine, Wylie. Good night." He left Muriel with a quick cheek peck.

In the space of a short night, he had gotten angry with three old friends, loyal people who had stood by him during the heat of campaigns and the depths of grief.

But they were wrong, he thought as he drove. Conley should mind his own business. Wylie and Muriel left me exposed to an opponent's attack.

The argument didn't settle. He drove along Olympic and

then, on an inchoate impulse, pulled into the Vendome liquor store. Two people were out at that hour, a man pushing a shopping cart filled with bottles, a woman judiciously studying a wine label.

He had not been here for a long time. He found the bottle he wanted and brought it to the only open checkout line.

"Mr. Keegan. Remember me?" asked the young Japanese woman at the cash register.

He was embarrassed for a moment. "May. How are you? How's your father?"

"He's got two jobs instead of just doing your gardening, and all the other people on your street." She shook her head. Her father had worked for Leah and Keegan and then, like almost all the Japanese gardeners in Beverly Hills, had been displaced by Mexicans.

"Say hello for me. I hope he's doing well."

She nodded, chirpy and unaffectedly pleasant. "You see your pictures outside? We put up one of your signs in the window."

"No. I didn't. Thanks."

"You get a lot of votes around here. I remember when Mrs. Keegan used to come in." She rang up his liquor and put it into a brown bag. "Same brand as she bought. I give you the same fifteen percent discount I gave her. She was a steady customer."

Not to hurt, not to ridicule, he realized. It was simply a business statement. Leah used to come in here and buy all of her liquor, by the cartload.

"Mrs. Keegan, she was always happy when I saw her. Smiling, you know, with a good attitude. She always talked about when I was a little girl, you know, and I came over and helped my father do your backyard. I pushed the leaves with my feet. She remembered that. She liked to talk about when I was little." The young woman smiled. "I liked her a lot."

"She enjoyed talking about our children when they were little," he said, uncomfortably. The last months before the accident, Leah faded often into dreamy reminiscences of Chris and Elaine's early years. As if the days when I worked at Signal Oil were far preferable to my standing on my own.

He took the bottle and drove the few blocks home. It was dark and quiet, and he was surprised to find Elaine watching TV with the lights out, waiting for him.

She helped him heat up some leftovers from dinner in the kitchen. He took the bottle, still in its brown bag, into his bedroom. He put it on the bureau, where Leah's cosmetics used to preside. He didn't know what he was going to do with the bottle or why he'd even bought it. He didn't drink often, but when he did, it was usually to get drunk. He took off his coat and tie and shoes.

He opened some windows to let the sea breezes in. The orange-headed bird-of-paradise plants in the front yard swayed a little.

Elaine sat at the kitchen table with him, legs curled under her. At thirteen, her braces had just come off, her ash-blond hair was tended more carefully. She was lithe, airy, and he was glad she stayed up for him.

"You look like Chris when he had a bad date and came home early," she said, grinning. Elaine had little of Chris's reserve. She spoke everything aloud.

"I had a bad night," Keegan admitted. He gingerly tasted the hot food, pulled a piece of bread apart.

"We never get to eat together."

"Things won't settle down until after November."

"Is the trial going to last until the election?"

Keegan chewed and nodded. "Oh, yeah. I've got thirty or thirty-five witnesses. There's no estimate on who the defense will put on for Carnes. He might testify. I'd like that."

"I'd come down and watch you do your cross-examination."

"We'll see." He ate carefully, but didn't taste the food. "Did Chris get off all right?"

"Mr. Conley took him like he said. I did kind of like seeing him again, not like a weekend or holiday," she said, rubbing an invisible spot on her leg. "It was like we were all together again."

"We're doing all right."

"We talked about switching schools. He'd go someplace

near here. Maybe Beverly."

Keegan tore up another piece of bread. "You both worked it all out?"

"We talked about it. He's been thinking about it for a while." She sighed. "A lot's changed this year."

"Well, that's all the more reason to keep things as they are. It's a bad habit to give up on something, your work, your school, whatever it is, just because it's unpleasant. Even if it's very unpleasant," he said, talking to fill the air as much as anything. "My parents didn't think that way."

"Grandma didn't?" Elaine asked in surprise.

"She and my father both believed you couldn't force things. So we moved a lot when I was your age. My father changed jobs a number of times."

"I wish I'd met him. I wish I'd known Grandma longer. I only remember her a little now, like when she gave me pennies."

"I learned the lesson of working through the difficult problem of challenge myself, honey," he said. He got up and put the dishes in the sink. He was tired. Elaine wouldn't remember much of his parents, except what he told her. How could he describe the nights his father came home, genial, soft, and ineffectual, quieted with drinking after work? How could he justify to Elaine a man who went from being an oil executive to a glorified debt collector at Pacific Gas and Electric because he was too meek or pliant?

He couldn't stand up to his bosses, Keegan thought, heading for the living room. But he was a whiz at getting people to pay their power bills. Who could turn down that smiling, soft man who seemed about to cringe? Hell. He made them feel sorry for him.

It was an example Keegan was determined to avoid. He felt his father's was a hateful life.

"Tell me about your day," he said. He lay back on the sofa. It was almost normal. Night breezes rustling the elms outside, the jagged edges of the palms night-black. Leah could come in at any moment, sit beside me, close enough to feel her warmth and smell her.

Elaine didn't sit beside him. She leaned against the piano. It was a disquieting lounge-singer pose and made Keegan irritable. Maybe Leah was right talking about them when they were younger, trying to hold on to that image.

"Two more people in Drama got parts in a commercial."

"Don't ask me again, honey."

"Mr. Nelson says I'm good. I could get work if you gave your permission."

"I'm not giving my permission. We've talked about it a lot. You know my reasons."

"They're not good ones. I can get work."

"I know it sounds exciting. I'm sure your classmates' doing it makes it seem harder for you not to." Keegan sat up. "But both your mother and I were sure you've got to finish high school before you start acting."

"It's too late." Elaine was suddenly childlike again, pushing away from the piano, arms folded. "Years too late."

"You'll have to accept that I know what's best."

"Mom would listen to me."

Keegan got up. "She's not here," he said. "And that's all there is to it."

"Just because you say so." And she turned from him.

"Yes." He was weary. "It's late for both of us. I've got to be in court, and you've got school."

Later, alone in the bedroom, he sat on the edge of the bed. It was quiet in the house, a preternatural stillness that he hadn't adjusted to and found as jarring as banging or shouting. Elaine was asleep probably, or like him, awake and unquiet herself. He would have liked to say he was sorry, gratify her wishes.

He would have liked, more than anything, to ask her if she blamed him for the last months, or that terrible day itself.

What did I do, he wondered again. What could I possibly have done wrong? If your upbringing was solid, your guides tested and sure, if the goals you aimed at were laudable, how could there be blame?

He undressed. Somehow fate had thrown Carnes in front of him at the exact moment when convicting a vicious killer made sense out of personal confusion and tragedy and galvanized his campaign.

If I lose this trial, then it means I've been wrong all along. My standards are false. If I lose the trial, he thought, I lose my job and my sense of meaning in the world. I can't live in a senseless world.

He put the liquor bottle in the cabinet under the sink in the bathroom. I won't drink any. I'm not Leah or my father.

TEN

THE NEXT DAY, THE AIR POLLUTION Control District predicted only moderate eye irritation in the LA basin. Pockets of thicker smog would hover over the San Fernando Valley and south-central Los Angeles. It was a warm September day, cloudless, hazy.

Keegan spent the morning meeting with his senior staff, the bureau chiefs from as far away as Long Beach included. He had delegated much of the daily office operation to his chief deputy, but it was necessary before court to catch up on the most bothersome problems. Anything could become a major problem for the elected district attorney, a car-tapping and speeding like the actor Early, an undercover investigation of the mayor of Lakewood for embezzlement, a stabbing in Southgate between a white man and a black woman, a sheriff's SWAT team breaking into the wrong house on a drug raid. Keegan still had to sort through which threatened him more. He had to guess over and over.

He did not mention the incident at Park's home. He was the

only witness as well as being the object of the bribe. He did not want to put more obstacles in the way of the Carnes trial than there already were. He sat through the meeting on personnel matters and a change in office vacation schedules, and then, at nine forty-five, he went down to Judge Ambrosini's courtroom to find out what would happen to the trial.

At that hour, his challenger for the office of district attorney was forcing herself through the second morning-coffee meeting, this one in Glendale. Forty women crowded into a living room to meet her. Celia Aguilar smiled, which she did not do very naturally, and told them how she would remake the district attorney's office into a dynamic, responsive organization. Her media advisors had selected "dynamic" and "responsive" as two very popular and very vague goals.

At nine fifty-nine A.M., Judge Ambrosini took the bench to announce his decision on Goodoy's change of venue motion. Instead of simply stating his decision, he cleared his throat, gazed out at the stuffy and overcrowded courtroom, and read a ten-page opinion. He had decided to be as judicial as possible.

"All he has to do is say whether it's granted or denied," one of Keegan's bewildered, bored assistants whispered to him.

"He wants to look like a judge," Keegan answered. He drummed his fingers on the table. Carnes, he saw, kept rubbing the back of his neck, as if he'd gotten a cramp from sleeping badly. Goodoy stared up at the judge as he read and read.

Motorists on the bumper-to-bumper San Diego Freeway southbound or the Santa Monica Freeway or the twisting and ancient Pasadena Freeway heard Judge Ambrosini's decision reduced to a flash as they drove home. People near TVs saw live coverage outside the Criminal Courts Building break into game shows and soap operas. Local stations were berated by viewers who hated missing a few minutes of regular programming.

The *Los Angeles Times,* as the largest-circulation paper and the paper of record for the whole county, further reduced Judge Ambrosini's thudding style to a few words in large, black type:

CARNES STAYS IN LA

The boat moved languidly with the late tide, and around the private docks, strings of bright white lights hung like shiny beads, firing the other massed hulls, and slim, sculpted shapes moored for the night, with a bleached hardness. The exposed yachts rode in the water, white on black, like the tips of icebergs.

Two men walked down the dock, feet muffled in rubber-soled sneakers. The shorter man had trouble with his balance on the slightly undulating dock. He tried to keep up with the other man, but kept wiggling one arm for stability. He clutched brown file folders to his chest with the other arm.

The two men climbed onto the boat. Nearby condominiums and restaurants shimmered in the bluish night, and a dry wind stole past even the best security guards and iron gates.

In the boat, the men bent low, straightening up in the main cabin. Celia Aguilar sat by herself, sipping from a tall gin and tonic, her shoes off, eyes closed. She was dressed for the six tiring campaign stops she'd made that day, muted colors, her red scarf, and trademark dragonfly brooch. The brooch was a play on her nickname as a campaigner and prosecutor, "The Dragon Lady."

"Trouble finding it, Celia?" asked Nelson Poulsby, the taller man and mayor of Los Angeles.

She slowly opened her eyes. "I dropped off. No. No trouble. Hello, Martin," she said to the shorter man, Poulsby's vice-mayor and assistant.

"Fix us up, okay, Marty?" the mayor asked, sitting down in a chair beside Aguilar while Koenig dropped his files on the bar and poured and mixed drinks. He was a sallow-faced man with thin mouse-colored hair. It was rumored he had had scurvy two years ago, because he worked so hard and relentlessly for the mayor he forgot to eat properly. No one could recall a case of scurvy in City Hall for easily a hundred years.

Aguilar yawned. "There are moments when I know, I know, I know it is not worth it." She blinked, suddenly alert.

Poulsby laughed. "Public life, Celia. Get used to it." He was sixty, tall and tan, with eyes so close they sometimes looked crossed. He took off his shoes, wiggling his toes.

"My eyes hurt," Aguilar said. "I didn't think that was possible. I would love to be home right now. My husband and I would eat dinner. I'd actually talk to my children again. I think I have two."

Martin Koenig handed the mayor a milky mixture and drank thoughtfully from a glass of Scotch himself. "Was everything you needed in the Carnes file I gave you?"

Poulsby laughed. "Give her a minute, Marty. She's tired."

"Try doing a multiple-defendant death-penalty trial like the Dillon brothers, Nelson," she said, finishing her drink. "That's really tired. I'm still adjusting to campaigning."

"All right. Tell me. What did you see in the file? What about this trial Keegan's doing?" Poulsby put his drink down.

Celia Aguilar sat up a little straighter. "The boat rocks just enough to make you drift off. I'd like to own one someday."

"Who wouldn't?" Poulsby agreed. "Guy who owns this and four others parked around us doesn't live on the same planet as we do. He's my wife's sister's second husband. Real estate."

"Was there enough in the file?" Koenig persisted, elbows resting on the bar.

"Yes," she said. "Keegan's got quite a case to put on. I don't want to ask how you got a copy of the DA's case file, Martin."

The mayor answered stiffly for his assistant, "It's open to people who trust me," he said. "There's nothing wrong."

"I'm not probing, Nelson."

"It sounded like you were accusing."

"I'm not accusing."

"We're all together. We all want Keegan out and you in."

Celia Aguilar held her glass out, and Koenig reluctantly came over and took it from her. "Oh, I agree. I think LA will be much better off with me in office. I'm just a line prosecutor. I'm not a politician like you or Keegan," she said calmly. "But I do know there's something very wrong with a man who won't get out of a race when his wife is killed. You have to wonder. You have to think he's such an egomaniac nothing will stop him."

"Keegan's an asshole. He likes power. That's why he didn't quit." Poulsby sourly shuffled his feet on the carpet.

Aguilar smiled slightly. "I think my judgment of Keegan's a little less biased than yours. You hate him because he's sent five commissioners of yours to prison."

"It's more than that."

"And he says he'll convict more people you appointed."

"I make five hundred appointments to boards and commissions. I can't be responsible for every single one. I choose people who look solid, the best." He waved an arm at Aguilar. "Some people are bound to be crooks. Keegan's acting like they're all crooks. He's got power under his skin."

"Nelson, what on earth are those?" She pointed at his glittering cuff links.

He proudly displayed them again. "I can get you a pendant like this, Celia. See how they catch the light." He proudly twisted his arms, the cuff links shining. "They're smog. You take about one or two hundred cubic feet of LA air, and you compress it, and you end up with, with"—he groped.

"Particulate," said Martin Koenig at the bar. He gave her a drink.

"Yes. You get the particulate matter compressed. Looks like gems, doesn't it. Some smart alecks at Cal Tech made them, but I'm wearing them to show off."

She grimaced and drank. They waited impatiently until she was ready. "Well, the Carnes trial is going to be a problem for Keegan."

"Can he win?" Poulsby asked bluntly.

"It depends on what you mean by win. He could come away with a first-degree and a couple of manslaughter verdicts. If it was my case, if it wasn't being used as a campaign gimmick, I'd even think about dealing it out."

"Plea-bargain? A killer like this guy? Everybody would go wild." Poulsby stood up and rubbed his chin. "Four people. Jesus. How do you guys figure things in the DA's office?"

Aguilar slipped her shoes on and got up, drink in hand. "An experienced trial deputy, someone who's done this kind of trial often," she began.

"Like you?" Poulsby interrupted.

"Like me. An experienced deputy could show the jury how Carnes planned and set up the whole situation. It requires all of your eyewitness evidence and circumstantial proof coming together, but it could be done."

"Keegan's not experienced," Poulsby said.

"He's a politician," she said.

"So he's going to lose?"

"There's a very good defense. Carnes is going to blame the whole thing on one of the victims, this Ferrera."

Koenig picked up one of his brown files, took a quick look. He sat down, shrewd eyes on Aguilar. "He killed Ferrera. The hooker says so."

"Yes, she does. And it would be nice if a gun matched up or there were some physical evidence to show Carnes shot the Rotich family. There isn't."

"Sounds like a tough case," Poulsby said. "Good. Keegan can fall flat on his face."

"Some of the evidence is solid, but a lot of it depends on one witness."

Poulsby peered out a porthole at the rocky bounds of the marina, the small lighthouses glaring redly in the night. "How long before he finishes this jury picking?"

Aguilar put her glass down, yawned again, and crossed her arms. "They've been working at jury selection for two weeks. They've got almost a full panel. They only need a couple of alternates. I think Keegan could say he's pleased with the jury in a few days."

"Then the evidence starts?"

"Then the jury's sworn, and there's no going back. If Keegan makes any mistakes after the jury's in place"—she was hard, the dragonfly brooch steely in the cabin light—"Carnes walks free."

"Oh, would that be great?" Poulsby said. "The bastard would be dead."

"Which bastard?" Aguilar asked.

"There's only one, Celia. I'm getting very sick of hearing on the news about every burp and fart Keegan makes. Jesus. Two weeks of him walking in and out of the courtroom, people all over him. Aren't you sick of it? I mean, Jesus, it's creamed your campaign," Poulsby said. "You get ten seconds of some lunch speech someplace. He gets thirty seconds, a minute every damn newscast. He looks like Godzilla compared to you."

"Well, there's the difference between us, Nelson. I'd like Keegan to lose the election, but I'd like Carnes to be convicted, too."

"In this life, you can't have everything."

She studied Poulsby, then Koenig, and shook her head. "I don't know what I expected when I got into this campaign. I think I was naive about what I'd be doing, all the meetings and handshaking. The people I've had to like." She looked at her watch. "Do we have anything more?"

"Tell me one thing." Poulsby grinned briefly at Koenig, then said to Aguilar, "About the rumors. You and Keegan. You really fight as much as I hear? Is that the reason you're running?"

A powerboat roared by in the darkness, engine whine rising then falling, and a slap of water rocked the yacht. Aguilar stayed upright, steady. "There are two main reasons. Dillon and Anda. Two trials Mr. Keegan interfered with while I was trying to hold them together in court."

"What'd he do?" Koenig leaned forward.

She thought for a moment, as if debating whether to tell the mayor and Koenig her thoughts. "Every afternoon, after court, Keegan made me come to his office and tell him what happened in the Dillon case. Four gang members shooting up a house in Pacoima. He would tell me how to handle the case." Her voice was sarcastic. "As if he had any experience. He would tell me that it was important for the office not to lose. As if I didn't know, as if I was a level-one deputy."

Poulsby nodded and glanced at Koenig.

"In the Anda trial, he tried to make me lay back because Mr. Anda, the slumlord whose building burned down with eight people killed, was a campaign contributor."

"You've got to use that," Koenig exclaimed. "That's dynamite."

"Martin. Keegan never gave me an order. He never told me to prosecute less vigorously."

"What did he do?"

"He pointed out my mistakes. Every day. Every detail. He had his gofers in court, and he would show me how weak my case was getting, how expensive the trial was getting, how I was losing the chance for conviction."

"Oh. Keegan's not a straight arrow," Poulsby said. "A shock."

"He's a hypocrite," Aguilar snapped. "An egomaniacal hypocrite."

"No question," the mayor said, his smog cuff links glittering again as he put his hands out to Aguilar. "I'm going to call old Sanders in the Ninth District tomorrow. Get some more bodies out for you. Since he had that stroke, I've been carrying him. He'll help us out."

Aguilar looked at her watch again. "Right now they're sitting down to dinner. I actually miss my daughters fighting at dinner."

As if rehearsed, Koenig said, "It might be worthwhile to talk to this hooker."

"See how she stands," Poulsby said, slipping behind the bar, making another drink.

Aguilar sensed an ugly suggestion. She put her glass on the bar. In the chastising manner she used on wayward jurors, she said, "You can't tamper with a witness."

"Jesus. No. No."

Koenig shrugged. He touched his thinning hair as if checking to make sure none had come loose in the last few minutes. "I only meant a little exploration. To find out if she's actually going to appear. For our own information."

Aguilar said, "My husband's a big supporter of yours, Nelson."

The mayor smiled.

"I try to tell him what a fool and jackass you are every morning, but he still thinks you're a good man. You'd make my point by going after a witness."

"Marty only mentioned meeting with her. That's all. Tell your husband I'll send him copies of my last couple of speeches."

"He'll treasure them."

Poulsby sighed luxuriously as he drank, sat down again on the soft sofa, legs out. "The one thing I'm still working on, Celia, is whether Keegan's a fool like me. Like you say I am."

"Why worry about that, Nelson?"

Koenig had found the controls to the stereo system beneath the bar counter, and the cabin was filled with a lush, enveloping throb of strings. He watched Aguilar.

Poulsby said, "If this is such a messy, tough case, he's got so much that can blow up on him, why does he take this one? I mean, you said he's been away from court for years. Why pick a lemon for his comeback? Why put everything he's got on a tough trial?"

She waved to Koenig to turn down the music. "That's why he's an egomaniac. He thinks he can do anything."

"You better go home to the kiddies and poppa," the mayor said. "My wife and I, we have schedules. Tonight I'm scheduled to get some peace and quiet. She's in Santa Barbara."

Aguilar picked up her papers and looked around the cabin for anything she might have left. "One last thing, Martin. Leave the witness alone. Stay away from the trial."

Koenig's impassive, sallow face moved up and down.

Poulsby said, "I think Keegan's got something going in the trial we don't know about. I'd like to know what it is."

ELEVEN

A CERTAIN ELECTRICITY IN THE courtroom, an undercurrent of anticipation and impatience.

It was nearly eleven in the morning. The courtroom was filled. The jury box was filled. Four chairs were set alongside the jury box, and three of those four were filled.

The clerk called a name. Mrs. Francis Sandoval. A woman wearing a dark pantsuit, glasses in one hand, two paperback books in the other hand, took the seat. On the bench, even Judge Ambrosini was fidgeting, checking his pens, his water glass, sitting back, leaning forward.

Keegan stood a few feet from Mrs. Sandoval.

Everyone knew that very soon, perhaps in a matter of minutes, there would be a jury sworn to hear the case. Only questioning the final alternate juror remained.

Keegan held a legal pad in one hand. He was calm, as if expecting everything. The hand he gestured with was moist, and anyone standing close to him could see the drops of nervous sweat on his forehead, under his eyes. But to the cameras, the spectators, he was glassy smooth and cool.

"Mrs. Sandoval," he asked firmly, "you've heard all the questions that have been asked here in the last few weeks?"

"Yes, I have," she said, hands folded, slowly, almost imperceptibly chewing on gum or her inner lip.

"Would your answers to any of them be substantially different from what you've heard?"

"No, they wouldn't."

"Well, specifically, will it cause you any problem to sit on a jury, if a juror is unable to serve, if I am the prosecutor?"

"No, it will not," a slight singsong. She moved her shoulders.

"You have no feelings either way about hearing this case based on the public attention it's gotten?"

"I haven't heard any evidence. No one's put anything in court, have they?"

Keegan turned from her. One of his assistants smiled. She had listened and knew the correct answers. Show no prejudice toward one side or the other, nothing to indicate prejudging the case. Three full panels of one hundred possible jurors each had been weeded through to get the twelve in the box and the three sitting beside them. Mrs. Sandoval wanted to sit on the case. She hadn't tried any of the usual excuses, my husband's at work, my children need me at home, my job will suffer, I've got an illness. I hate cops. I love cops. I hate George Keegan. I love George Keegan.

Judge Ambrosini cleared his throat. He had begun combing his hair differently. Keegan thought his wife must have said he looked better with his hair at an angle to the camera.

"I have a question before you proceed, Mr. Keegan," the judge said. "I need to know if you are acquainted with any of the parties in this case?"

Keegan waited as Mrs. Sandoval slowly looked around the courtroom, lingering on Goodoy, Carnes, and the two assistants at the defense table. She looked up at the judge.

"I believe I know you, Your Honor," she said.

"You do?"

"I'm not sure. I think so. Didn't you used to shop at the Thrifty in Culver City? I think you did."

Ambrosini's grayish face reddened a little. He coughed. "I believe my family did shop there."

"Then I saw you. I used to work at the pharmacy."

"Will it influence you in any way to sit as an alternate juror having seen me or my family?" the judge asked coldly.

"Oh, no. I only mentioned it because you asked." She stared again and then added the one comment that ended the tension and brought the courtroom to a full laugh. "I thought you were much taller, though. I guess it's true that the robe makes the man."

Ambrosini hit his hand twice on the bench to end the chuckling. Keegan sat down, rubbing his hands in his handkerchief. "I pass Mrs. Sandoval for cause," he said. He would be happy with her.

Carnes was thinner, losing weight, and his shirt collar, open as always, hung loosely. He sat back as Goodoy asked her questions. Keegan never forgot the campaign and the trial were wound together.

Goodoy reminded him again.

"Have you ever voted for Mr. Keegan?" she asked the potential alternate juror.

Mrs. Sandoval smoothed one wrinkled leg of her pantsuit. The courtroom, reporters, spectators, and clerks listened.

"I've heard of him. I know who he is."

"Well, my question was, have you voted for him?"

"No."

Goodoy nodded, a small smile. Ambrosini had permitted this much latitude on the issue since Keegan's position was unusual. But now, at the very last, Goodoy suddenly said, "Well, are you going to vote for him?"

Keegan got up. "Objection, Your Honor."

"Sustained."

"Nothing further," Goodoy said.

"Please tell defense counsel that kind of stunt isn't permitted, Your Honor." Keegan stayed on his feet.

"Don't play games again, Mrs. Goodoy," the judge said. "Don't order me, Mr. Keegan." He paused. "Pass the juror?" he asked Goodoy.

"Pass," said Goodoy, nodding to something Carnes whispered. "Mr. Keegan?"

"I'm satisfied with the jury. As I've said before."

Judge Ambrosini smiled, as if he'd just locked and bolted the thickest, heaviest steel door on earth behind them. It was, in truth, exactly what was about to happen. In another moment, Keegan knew he had no choice but to go forward. With a jury in place, Carnes could be tried only once for the murders of the Rotich family and Lee Ferrera.

No matter what might go wrong during the trial.

Ambrosini said, "You may swear the jury, Madame Clerk."

Keegan strode into his office, with Phil Klein, cigar unlit and soggy, in tow.

"Get a car, all right, Phil? And get Conley up here, too."

"You've got the *Newsweek* gal. She came early. She was over in court watching you."

"Where is she?"

"I stashed her in my office," Klein said, shaking some saliva off the end of his cigar into an ashtray. "Remember you said this was important?"

Keegan sat down, quickly sorting through the messages and the folders. Personnel problems, an assistant bureau chief in Narcotics had to be demoted. Problems with the level-three attorney exam, note from his chief deputy. City Council questions. Luckily, almost everything was being shunted to his chief deputy, but like the airy debris from a great explosion, some of it still sifted down to his desk.

"Send her up here and get that car."

"Long trip, short trip?"

"Marina del Rey."

Klein nodded. "I'll bring her in."

Keegan composed his expression, and just before the door opened again, his executive assistant bringing in the tall woman, blond hair and green-tinted glasses, he put his head down. He wondered, in the course of an average day, how many people he saw, and spoke to, and sat with? Although the trial had drastically cut down the numbers, he suspected he still saw a hundred people about something, in groups or alone. Here was another one.

It was possible, he had discovered, to be very lonely and disconnected even among the most ardent throng of people. Or with someone paying absolute attention to everything he said or did.

It was possible to be absolutely alone at home, in your own bed, beside your wife, with your children only a few doors away.

"Lorrie Noves," she said, shaking hands with him. Klein waited briefly at the doorway, winked, and left.

"It's a pretty name."

"I think my parents shortened it from something much longer. They were from Peru."

He nodded. His desk was cleared; all files with names or identifying colors had been hurriedly put into drawers. "I'll let you know if something's not for attribution as we go, all right?" he asked. "Would you like something to drink, some coffee?"

She shook her head and took out a small tape recorder. "Do you mind if I tape?"

"No tapes." He smiled. "We'll just talk."

"You are being careful."

"I'm in a trial and a campaign."

She took out a notepad. Keegan saw she had thin fingers and long legs. "You've caused some interest with your campaign and trial back east."

"I'm flattered." He used the natural, easygoing manner, the bank officer listening approvingly to a loan application. Leah's caption for it.

He noticed her nudge a large olive green bag with her foot. She must have carried it in. "Did they search you outside?" He smiled again.

"No. Mr. Klein vouched for me. It's just a camera, some films, some lenses. You mind if I get a few pictures?"

"No. I thought you'd have a photographer."

"I like doing my own. I know what someone's talking about when I interview them. I can catch it." She opened the bag, took out a black camera, and began taking pictures.

"This interview's taking a while to get started."

"We started." She got up and went to his large window. She took a few shots, then pointed. "Who is that? That seems so California."

Keegan came to the window. She was pointing at Dr. Staggers and Miss Velma. "He's been looking up at me ever since I got here. Why is he so California? Because he looks ridiculous?"

She shook her head, then froze, snapping a view of the peeling billboard. "I guess it's theatrical. Even religion is show business out here. You're religious, aren't you?"

"I've gone to church all my life."

"Maybe that's not the same thing."

"It works out the same."

She smiled again. "You are careful."

"Why don't you ask whatever questions you've got, Ms. Noves? I'm going to be leaving in a few minutes."

"All right. As I said, you've caused some interest where I come from. It strikes people as, well, theatrical to take a murder trial during an election."

Keegan shrugged. "I'm a DA. I prosecute criminals."

"You? Yourself? Nobody does where I live. I talked to several DAs in New York. They say it's hard enough trying to run their offices. Add campaigning and add a big trial. It won't work."

"I'm muddling along."

"You don't strike me as a man who muddles through anything."

Keegan sat down again. "I'm no different from anybody. I try to do what I think is right."

She put the camera in the bag and stared at him thoughtfully. He tapped his fingers on the polished wood of his desk. She said, "I watched you in court today. Yesterday, too. You've certainly gotten a lot of attention from this trial. I guess what I don't know is why you're doing this one."

Keegan reached into his coat and took out the Harrold letter and gave it to her. "I think that sums up my reasons."

She read slowly. Then closed the letter. "It's very touching. But don't you get a lot of touching pleas just like this?"

"No." He meant: None that touched me so properly, so timely.

"All right." She made a note. A helicopter lazily swung around the spire of City Hall and floated off to the east, into the brownish haze of the late morning. "You've probably heard all the things people say about you. Arrogant. Stubborn. Ambitious. Generous."

"I hadn't heard that." He smiled. She was easy to talk to, and he didn't mind that her presence was a trap and the questions bait.

It wasn't friendship for her, but another assignment. He knew that, and yet, he wanted to go on talking to her.

"The thing I haven't heard anyone say, your friends or your enemies, is that you're sentimental. Soft. That a letter like that would move you."

"It did. There's nothing complicated. I had to answer that letter's appeal myself."

"Mr. Keegan," she said, same tone, same bland look, then the barb he hadn't expected, "did this trial have anything to do with your wife's death?"

He got up, and her eyes followed him.

"Most people would have retired, temporarily anyway, from public life. You got more involved."

Keegan said, "I told you I'm no different from anybody. But my private life is private. I'm a public man. I do things in public because it's my responsibility."

"You don't like my questions?" She leaned forward a little.

"They're irrelevant."

His phone buzzed. Conley and the car were ready. "See if Barbara's free, too," he ordered. "Tell her we'll have lunch out." He grinned at Lorrie Noves. "That should bring her. You can come, too."

"Where?" she said, already hoisting the olive bag.

Keegan held the door for her. "The Death House. That's what the media called it."

"It just looks like an empty house," Cabrerra said when the car parked.

"It is an empty house," Keegan said. "For sale." He pointed at the sign on the brown lawn. Conley and Lorrie Noves followed him to the door, Conley coming up and using a key to open it.

"Don't expect a showplace," Conley said. "LAPD went through it pretty thoroughly in May."

"Why are we here?" Lorrie Noves held her camera up.

"I want to look at it. I'm going to start putting witnesses on and I want to see where it all happened," Keegan answered. He held a diagram, made by the police, room by room, *X*s indicating bodies like a treasure map. "I've seen all the photos. Read the reports. Talked to everybody. But I want to see it myself."

"It's like a field trip at school," Cabrerra said chattily to Noves. "I had a couple projects to finish, but it's liberating just dropping it all."

"I wanted Ms. Noves to meet you, Barbara," Keegan said.

He heard the hissing, abrupt sound of the camera. Let this woman see everybody he had around him, the old friends like Conley and the hard-edged professionals like Cabrerra. That was his world.

They all stood for a moment inside the front door. Keegan inhaled the dull, musty smell, emptiness mingled with desertion. Sunlight filtered through tan paper hung over all the windows, like skin. He led them through the house.

"I haven't been to many crime scenes," Noves said soberly. "I expected something more."

"I've been to a lot of crime scenes," Conley said. "They're all about the same."

"This is my first," Cabrerra said. "It's actually peaceful."

"My first homicide, I had to wade into a canal in South-Central, and haul out a body floating in it." Conley grinned without pleasure. "I was a lot bigger in those days, so I got all the good jobs."

"How did you know it was a homicide?" Noves asked, her

camera held up like a talisman.

"Guy started leaking from every hole he had once I put him on the sidewalk," Conley said. "They're all about the same, like I said."

"I thought there'd be something more," Noves said as they walked. "To show three people died here."

"Like what?" Keegan asked. "Groans? Rattling chains?"

Conley chuckled, and Cabrerra said to Noves, "He means that respectfully. He's very aware of the suffering here."

"Barbara's job is to tell me to say the right things and tell other people I've said them."

"George," Cabrerra said. It was a caution. The atmosphere had been awkward with a journalist, but Keegan felt suddenly relieved and couldn't hide it completely.

"So you are affected?" Noves asked when they stopped.

"In my own way. You know I am." It had been a test coming here. At the crash site in early June, the wound was open and raw, a vivid cut in the earth from a burst station wagon on a hillside, rescue workers tearing it apart to get at his dying wife. Here there was silence and dust and peace, even if only the peace that follows a cataclysm. I can face this kind of death, he thought.

Maybe I'll face the other.

They stood in the den. The floor was bare, stripped down to the wood, then pieces of wood pulled up. A few circles, from blood spray, were left on the veneer walls, but most of the veneer was gone, too.

"Like an animal was here," Lorrie Noves said, looking at the damage.

"Los Angeles police. Collecting evidence," Conley said.

"No, I meant before them."

Keegan saw her disquiet in the house. She started taking pictures of him holding the diagram, crouching down beside the gaping hole in the floor, down to the dirt. She was not a tough reporter, and that was intriguing.

They ate at a small seafood restaurant. The Pacific curled and rushed beside rocks, sometimes misting the restaurant windows.

"What kind of article are you doing?" Keegan asked. He finished his crab salad and had iced tea.

"I don't know yet. It might be a feature. They might cut it down to a sidebar on something else," Lorrie Noves said.

"One thing you've got to understand about George," Cabrerra said, her glasses gray in the shaded indoor light, "is he's very outspoken."

"I know that. I read our file."

"He asks questions most public officials wouldn't."

"I know about the time he blew up at the chief of police over some secret intelligence files." She glanced at him, arms on the table. "Everyone said you had a temper tantrum."

Keegan sat back. Conley sat beside Noves across from him. "It got everyone's attention. I didn't like my police department maintaining files on ordinary citizens."

"You did it just to get attention?"

Keegan smiled. "I was mad."

Conley grunted. "People, I mean cops, were ready to hang old George out."

"But you came to work for him," Noves said.

Conley shrugged again, squinting at the ocean, then at the barely furnished room. "I knew George from church. I knew his kids and his wife."

Keegan nodded. "Win and I are old friends."

"Well, I understand loyalty," Noves said. "It was interesting to see how people react to you. When we came out of the house just now, you went over and talked to the neighbors on their lawns."

"They were waiting for me. They must have recognized me."

"You could have left. You could have waved."

"I really do like talking to people, Ms. Noves. I enjoy running."

She hadn't taken out her notepad. It was a good gesture, because the atmosphere became much looser than earlier.

Conley shook his head. "Now that's one very strange thing about this man."

"Are you staying in LA for a while?" Cabrerra asked.

"A few days anyway. You're starting the opening statements in the morning?" she asked Keegan.

"Ten o'clock. I'll make some changes tonight probably."

Cabrerra burped quietly and ate another roll. Keegan wondered why he tolerated her smugness and bad manners. Because I'm ambitious, and she helps the ambitious, he thought.

Lorrie Noves frowned. "I think I know some things about criminal law. But aren't you worried what happens even if you convict Carnes?"

Keegan and the others looked at her. "How do you mean?" he asked.

"Suppose the jury agrees he should get the death penalty. Do you really think he'll be executed?"

"Why wouldn't he?" Keegan was interested in her probing.

"Look at how hard it is for anybody to be executed. At the last minute they can get somebody to grant a stay, what is it?"

"A stay of execution. But that only delays a sentence already in place. Judgment has been pronounced."

"You make it sound like fate or something. Carnes is destined to be executed."

Keegan shook his head. "I know that a doesn't change anything, Ms. Noves. Carnes shaped his own destiny."

"That would apply to everybody, wouldn't it, George?" Cabrerra swept a few crumbs from the roll into her hand.

Keegan stood up. Conley had raised his eyes a little, as if in exasperation. Noves zipped her camera into the olive bag. Keegan said, "I'm not a philosopher. I do believe we can't escape ourselves, who our parents were, how we're raised, what happens to us. How about that, Ms. Noves?"

The olive bag pulled one of her shoulders lower than the other, so she seemed weighted down by his words. She looked at Keegan.

"If you really believe that, I think it's one of the saddest things I've heard."

"Why? Why should we be sad about it?"

"I guess because even Carnes gets someone to grant him a stay of execution. Temporary reprieve. We don't have anybody."

Cabrerra said to Noves brightly in the parking lot, "I don't want to forget to give you the latest *Times* poll. We're ahead by four points."

TWELVE

"SHE'S BEEN TO YOUR CAMPAIGN headquarters," Cabrerra said before court the next morning.

"She's doing a story," Keegan answered from his chair.

"She's asking about your contributors, George."

"They're fair game. We're filing everything on time. Wylie Morganthau is keeping everything very open."

"You're not nervous about her."

"No."

"George, let's be practical, all right? In a little while—" she began, mouth pursing when he broke in.

"Ten minutes."

"I forgot you like everything spelled out. Ten minutes from now, you'll go into court and make your opening statement. Now, George, this is also a campaign statement. The people are listening to you as a prosecutor and a candidate."

"I worked very late. I didn't get these bags under my eyes by accident."

"What I'm saying is that you are walking a tightrope. Do you

139

really want an out-of-state, national media reporter going every-where, talking to everyone, right now, right this minute?"

"How can I stop her?"

"I can stop her. I can keep her busy."

"I think she'd see through that, Barbara."

"I think this is very dangerous."

"There isn't much we can do about it."

"George, you can subtly suggest to our people that they keep back a little. Nothing spectacular. Make Ms. Noves get bored and go away."

"I think she'd see through that, too."

"She's not a clairvoyant, George."

"She's a smart woman. She'd start to wonder why we're being evasive. That would be a lot worse."

"I see now."

"Good." He pressed his face, as if to push the fatigue from it. "She'll be gone in a day or so."

"You like her."

"Not particularly." He tried to chuckle.

"Oh, my God, George. Oh, goddamn. George, do not, please do not even think about this woman as a woman. She is a reporter. Reporters are either your enemies or your garbage dumps. They are not people."

"Thanks, Barbara. For spelling it out."

"You don't have to sulk. God, George, please think about the little people. Like me. Like what happens to my reputation if you get destroyed in a *Newsweek* story."

"Leave me alone. I know what I'm doing."

"All right. This is only professional wisdom. Gathered over the years. You're my eighteenth campaign. I do have some experience about candidates and affairs and reporters."

"Who said anything about an affair? What are you talking about?" he snapped. He grabbed loose yellow sheets of legal paper, roughly tapping them straight.

STAY OF EXECUTION   141

Hate is a peculiar emotion.

Carnes didn't understand it very much. He did feel something very unpleasant, very definitive about Keegan, but when other people talked about hating someone, he didn't really know what they meant.

"Good morning, ladies and gentlemen," said Keegan, going to the lectern set before the jury box.

Carnes counted again. Eight men. Four women. The alternates all women. Since this was his first trial, he was surprised how casually dressed everyone on the jury was. From TV and movies, he assumed they would be in suits and dresses. But his jury was in short-sleeved shirts and pullovers. Mrs. Ozal in the back, at least she wore a nice blouse. Carnes was disappointed and worried.

He glanced at Goodoy. She sensed it, looked at him, smiled, and put her finger to her lip. She didn't want to miss anything Keegan said in his opening statement. Carnes sat back. Goodoy was always attractive. Today she had on a black dress and a simple white scarf.

He listened, his mind fixed on the dramatic way Keegan flung his arms out. It was irritating the way Keegan seemed to have gotten so much of it right. How the Rotich setup went and how the drugs ended up in Elko, even how Lee died.

Carnes bit the side of his right thumb. The skin was already down to red soreness. Keegan must be getting this information from Melanie. She was the one. If he hated anyone, Carnes hated her. But he found most emotions difficult to conjure up, except love. He already felt the stirrings of it for Goodoy.

She hadn't grown up in anything like his home or Melanie's, he realized. None of the raging, furniture-wrecking scenes, the miserable early mornings when someone, mother or father or sisters, was crying wildly in the house. Goodoy's upbringing would have been quieter and serious. He imagined she took piano lessons.

He ran a finger around his moist, loose collar. He always seemed to be sweating these days, and he didn't eat well. It was all about finding Melanie and making sure Keegan couldn't gloat over him.

Just a few minutes ago, Keegan swept into the courtroom, little bearers around him with files and papers. He walked like he had a stick up his back, and he sat down, hand on his chin, acting like he didn't know everybody in the courtroom watched and talked about his entrances and exits, and how the reporters all jumped up to follow him.

He was a vain, ambitious man. Carnes had dedicated his life to anonymity, doing his business without attention. Now Keegan had thrust him into the light, and he very much didn't like that.

Maybe I hate it, he thought. Maybe this churning is hate.

One thing was simple and clear. Keegan couldn't keep Melanie; and this trial, such a showcase for that vain man, couldn't go on as he thought it would.

Carnes glanced at Goodoy again. She was scribbling as Keegan intoned to the jury.

I might be falling in love, he thought.

It was no different from any speech, Keegan thought as he spoke. The only difference is that these twelve people, four more with the alternates, can't ask questions. They only stared. One or two looked down to avoid his eyes. One crossed his arms. A lady at the end, closest to the judge, kept looking at Ambrosini.

Keegan had a rule that no speech should go over fifteen minutes. He was violating that a little this morning, but not by much. People started to forget things, he discovered, after fifteen minutes, like the sermons he heard at school. Only the babble stayed after a while, a white noise.

"After killing the three members of the Rotich household, the defendant Carnes and Lee Ferrera returned to their motel. They packed and drove to Los Angeles International Airport. They took the methamphetamine and sent it by air freight to Reno, Nevada."

Goodoy looked up. "That is a misstatement of the evidence, Your Honor."

Judge Ambrosini shook his head. "This is opening statements,

Mrs. Goodoy. This is what Mr. Keegan hopes to prove. Objection's overruled."

Keegan waited until the courtroom and the jurors had stopped wiggling in the seats at the interruption. He had been giving speeches for seventeen years, luncheon meetings at Kiwanis and Rotary when he was at Signal Oil and Leah's father wanted to show him off. Then, his own speeches, sidewalks and auditoriums.

If I can't give a knockout one this morning, I should give up, he thought.

"What did the defendant Carnes do in Nevada? He spent money. This money came from the home of his victims. When his partner Lee Ferrera grew nervous, the defendant Carnes killed him, too. Shot him. Just as he shot the victims in Marina del Rey. You will hear from police officers and pathologists. They will describe the kind of bullet, the kind of gun, the kind of consistent wound in both Marina del Rey and Elko."

He saw Goodoy smile and whisper to Carnes, who also smiled. They must be happy I don't have the guns from any of the killings. But I've got to put the story in front of the jury, get them thinking about the same guns.

He dropped his hands from the lectern. Every seat was taken in the courtroom, a collage of faces and reactions. Several of his own deputies sat listening to the boss.

Keegan pointed at Carnes. "What you will hear is evidence from eyewitnesses and evidence you can take and touch in the jury room. This evidence shows a clear plan by Robert Carnes to go to the home of Barry Rotich and murder him and his wife and their small nephew. He was a child." Keegan paused. "Shot in the head. You may hear the defense pick at some small pieces of this evidence, or that witness, trying to throw sand in your eyes. But, you can pick at City Hall here and there and stand back"—Keegan moved a step from the jury—"and still see it's City Hall. It's solid and immovable.

"But never forget that small child, alone with his killer, facing his killer." Keegan pointed at Carnes again and Goodoy got up, huffily.

"Your Honor, this is outrageous. Mr. Keegan is arguing. He's not making a statement. He's trying to save his case."

"I'm showing the jury the evidence that convicts that man," Keegan said sharply.

Judge Ambrosini put up his hands. "Wait. Not two of you at once. Mrs. Goodoy is correct. This is the time for opening statements. You argue at the end of the trial."

"Your Honor," Keegan said roughly, "I know the order of a trial. I don't need any sarcasm from you."

It had come out faster than Keegan could stop it. He didn't regret the retort. He thought the jurors, however much they looked up to a judge, would resent the judge playing favorites.

He turned to the jury without waiting for the judge to rule on Goodoy's objection. There was a rustling, skittish sound of feet on the hard floor as the spectators shifted around in their seats.

"Mr. Keegan, don't turn your back on me," Ambrosini said.

"I thought you were finished," Keegan said.

"I am not finished. We have a difficult trial ahead of us. I am not going to start it by tolerating displays of disrespect or anger in this courtroom."

"I can't do this trial without being angry," Keegan said.

"You'll have to try. We'll all have to try. I want everyone to act with respect and decorum in my court."

The profile in the *Times,* requests for interviews from around the country, did get to him. Speedy Ambrosini's as vain as anyone, Keegan realized. A full page of photos of him at his desk, the bust of Holmes beside him, walking hand in hand with his wife on their evening stroll, sitting on the bench, had done wonders to his personality.

"I'm going to apologize in advance for any rudeness or anger I may show, ladies, gentlemen," Keegan continued. "If you hear me getting angry with defense counsel, I'm sorry. I don't mean it against her personally. But there is a lot to be angry about in this trial. As you listen to the evidence I'll present against Robert Carnes, think about how he manipulated people. Think about how he selfishly and brutally used people to get money and drugs. And affection. You'll hear from a woman he used just as selfishly."

Keegan was aware of Carnes shaking his head, muttering to

Goodoy. Melanie Vogt was still a sensitive spot. Goodoy sat, lips tight. She could not object after Keegan and the judge had danced politely. She would appear petty.

"Listen to all the evidence," Keegan said, looking closely from juror to juror, "against this master manipulator. Then I know you will agree on the only verdict. Murder in the first degree with special circumstances."

He nodded curtly and took his seat. His assistants leaned over, whispering congratulations. Keegan swallowed to moisten his throat. He drank a glass of water. As he turned from the jury, he had looked around the mosaic of bodies, clothes, faces in the courtroom, trying to see Lorrie Noves.

"Mrs. Goodoy, you have an opening statement?" Ambrosini asked, glancing up, pen in hand.

"Yes, Your Honor." Goodoy came to the jury, but didn't stand at the lectern. It made a good contrast to Keegan's stolid, fixed recital.

She spoke almost apologetically, like a guest in a home.

"I agree with the district attorney. You must listen to the evidence very carefully. What he didn't say is that you must listen to all of the evidence, not just the evidence he puts on. Because when he finishes with his case, you haven't heard the whole story." She shook her head. "You haven't heard half the story. And I know none of you make up your minds about anything before you hear all the facts."

Keegan watched several of the jurors nod. It was a good, commonsense appeal to them. Goodoy was going to make this a hard trial.

"The defense is going to present a case, and you must listen to it before you decide whether my client, Bob Carnes, is guilty of anything." She stressed the last word. "There is a lot of manipulation going on in this case, but he's not part of it. I'll let you decide who is manipulating the case and the evidence."

She didn't look at him, but Keegan knew the implication was clear to anyone in court. Even the judge frowned, his newfound meekness preventing a comment from the bench.

"So, all I can say, listen to the witnesses against my client. See who has a motive to lie or gain something. See who's telling the truth. Because you have to decide who's telling the truth, just like you do at home or at work."

Another appeal to common sense, and Keegan irritatedly fiddled with his legal pad. She had trapped him, too. Her argument was as inappropriate as his had been, but to point it out would now make him appear petty. The modest gestures, somber dress, quiet speech, obviously were layered over a shrewd courtroom tactician.

"The defense case is very simple. You may be surprised how much of the defense case Mr. Keegan himself will put on." She smiled briefly in his direction.

"Our case is that the wrong man is on trial. You will not hear any evidence that puts a gun in Bob Carnes's hand at a murder scene. You will not hear any evidence that he threatened anyone. You will not hear any evidence that he killed anyone. No evidence."

Keegan saw more than a few jurors sitting forward, caught up in Goodoy's patter. He did not know if she believed any of it herself. But he burned imagining how many times Goodoy, prim and sincere, had come to other juries, pleading for other killers, and said very much the same thing.

I won't show it, he vowed, although for the first time he truly thought what she was doing was abominable.

It was an abomination, an affront to justice and honesty.

A glob of spit on the dead.

Keegan felt his hands sweating again.

Goodoy inclined her head slightly. She was finishing. "All of the evidence you will hear, from the district attorney, and the defense, will point to one man. Lee Ferrera. He is responsible for the crimes charged against Bob Carnes. He is the master manipulator Mr. Keegan talked about."

Who cannot be with us, fortunately for Carnes, Keegan thought.

Goodoy sat down. It was barely quarter to twelve. Not a judge to waste even fifteen minutes before lunch, Ambrosini said, "We've heard opening statements now from both sides. Mr. Keegan, you may call your first witness."

A moment passed. Ambrosini said, "Mr. Keegan?"

"Yes. Yes, Your Honor."

"I said, you may call your first witness."

Keegan announced the first name on his list.

He had been waiting in the dark bar off the Biltmore's lobby for twenty minutes. It was nearly seven, and the early-nighters had come in. He sat at a table near the back. He had had two drinks, and stopped because if he didn't he would go on.

Lorrie Noves came in, talked briefly to the bartender standing beneath the hanging glasses around the bar. He pointed to the rear of the bar.

She came over, stood uncertainly, then sat down across from Keegan.

"I'm sorry I'm late. I didn't want to be."

"It's all right. It's the first quiet time I've had all day."

The waitress took their orders. "I couldn't refuse an invitation from a subject to talk to him." Noves smiled. She had the olive bag with her and she put it beside her feet. Her hair was combed back, and she had high cheeks. Keegan, for the first time, noticed a small scar at the edge of her upper lip. It gave her a rough, reckless air. Just that small line of white, thickened skin on a lip, he thought.

"I thought this would be more informal than my office or in court. I had the impression yesterday I was being a little pompous."

"I've had tougher interviews," she said.

"Well, I don't want you to think I didn't want to answer your questions."

"Most people in public life answer just what they want to, Mr. Keegan," she said. "I've learned that much."

He nodded, hands on the table. Thick hands, thick fingers, like a ditchdigger. He felt an old, old uneasiness, something from adolescence, and realized it was because he wanted this woman. Some things don't change, even with success, a family, age.

"Were you going to say something?" she asked slowly. The

waitress brought their drinks, and the piano player, a bald man in an ill-fitting tuxedo, ran arpeggios experimentally on the keys.

"Were you in court?" Keegan said. That was easiest.

"Yes. I heard it all. I covered trials in Brooklyn for about two years, so this looks about the same."

"Criminal trials?"

She shook her head. "Strictly white-collar lawsuits. X saying he was owed X million because he completed the apartments on time. Y saying he used cheap concrete and the whole thing would fall down."

"I see."

"Not the most exciting reporting, but I learned a lot. I managed to get better assignments and I got better jobs."

"Well." Keegan looked at her through the glass chimney of the candle between them. Tongue-tied like a kid. He knew Cabrerra was right, too. This was dangerous; more than that, it was foolish. "How did the opening statements strike you? Did what I said make any sense?"

"Very much. I thought your opponent made some good points, too. I'm sorry I won't be able to see how it comes out. It's like catching the first act of a play and then getting a call from home."

"You'll write your article before the trial's over?"

"The magazine likes me, but they don't like me enough to spend their money at the Bonaventure in Los Angeles for all that time."

Keegan nodded again. He drank quickly. "You should stay here. At the Biltmore. It's the older, Spanish side of the city. It's a beautiful restoration."

"I like the modern stuff. Do you mind my asking about your wife? You didn't like it yesterday."

"No, go ahead. Ask anything."

Lorrie Noves lit a cigarette, pulled the crystal ashtray to her. Where did she get that scar, Keegan wondered.

"I really don't want to upset you," she said. "If talking about personal matters upsets you."

Keegan said, "I'll ask you a question. Are you married?"

She smiled. "A good lawyer knows when to turn the tables. Yes. I am married. I have a daughter named Chelsea. My husband works for the corporate counsel in a mining company based in New York."

"Do you miss your family? When you're away on trips like this? I find"—Keegan drank his glass to the bottom, put it down slowly—"now I miss a great deal, but I can't take a plane and get to wherever I should be."

"I'm sorry. I know it was a tragedy for you."

"Well. I've got two children. We're still close. We were a very close family," he said. "Very close knit."

"Your son's at Harvard School in the Valley, and your daughter still lives with you," Noves said.

"You've done your homework."

"Just the basics. Some people, when a major trauma hits, change things. But you didn't change anything. Your son stayed away at school."

"His education didn't get worse because his mother died," he said, the edge back in his voice.

She didn't mind. "No, I didn't finish. You only changed one thing in your life."

"Yes?"

"You took this trial. You didn't drop your campaign, you didn't bring your children closer, you didn't take time off." She was studying him. "I wonder why."

"You have an idea?"

She smiled. "All I'm interested in is some insight. Something that helps me understand you. Something I can write about."

He paid the waitress who came up. "People do things because they're right. Because they're honorable."

"I suppose some do."

"That's a cynical attitude."

She put her hands on the bag. The piano player was louder and the bar more crowded suddenly. "I grew up on a dairy farm in Vermont. Small town called Cornwall. So I saw a lot of cows. Everything's very basic on a farm. When I started covering trials and lawyers, I added realism to how I saw things. I haven't met anyone like you. You seem to be expanding my horizons."

He stood up. "Do you have to be anywhere right away?"

She followed him out of the bar, into the baroque, red-tile and stone lobby. "I don't have to be anywhere."

He drove them down Olympic, then turned up to Wilshire around Highland, following it west. The night was warm, a smokiness in the air. He parked in Beverly Hills, on north Canon Drive.

"This is where I grew up," he said. "Not a farm." They got out to walk.

"Not exactly." She laughed. She slung the bag over her shoulder, and she looked younger and simpler.

"I thought I'd show you a little of my past. For your insights." They walked past other people, some tourists, an occasional woman in a maid's uniform heading for a bus stop. Keegan, for the first time in months, perhaps not since Leah's accident, felt like talking normally, without weighing every word or thinking that every conversation had to be thought through in advance.

Without making life like a trial. Making people into witnesses or defendants to be used, threatened, vanquished.

"I meant it when I said I didn't want to upset you."

"You haven't," he said in surprise.

"I meant that personally, too. Not just because I'm doing a story."

He took them into Baskin-Robbins, and they bought ice cream cones, holding them with napkins, and then went walking past the Italianate beehive that stood where the grocery store Keegan had shopped at for years used to be.

"My father and mother weren't rich people," Keegan said, licking his cone, watching Lorrie Noves lick hers. "They wanted to look a little richer than they were. I grew up with people who took money as a standard."

"You married a wealthy woman."

"Leah was wealthy. Or, Larry, her dad, was." The sour tone was unmistakable. "I've tried to keep my own kids from thinking about money and status. I want them to have character."

"I think your daughter wants to be an actress?"

"Who've you talked to? Elaine's been pretty shy about telling people."

"Not that shy," Lorrie said, and it was chiding, playful, and warm all at the same time.

He wiped his fingers with the napkin. "Some of my staff warned me about you. They thought you were being aggressive about checking on me."

"Me?" she asked, and nudged him gently in the shoulder.

"They thought you were clever and persuasive and only interested in a sensational story."

She wiped her fingers, too, and nodded. "I am looking for a big story. But you trust me enough to take this tour. To talk to me."

"How stupid am I?" he asked.

She smiled. "Can I tell you my dream?"

"Yes."

"I have had, for half my life, this fantasy, this dream, of buying something on Rodeo Drive. That's stupid."

He took her several streets over to Rodeo, where the tourists were out, even at night, strolling from brightly lit window to window, pointing and taking pictures, as if they were at a theme park. He was intrigued and amused at the apparent sincerity of her admission. He also realized she had avoided answering him.

They went into several stores, and in one she bought a very expensive yellow nightshirt, had it wrapped in thin paper, and put in a carry bag with the store's colors.

"Thank you for coming with me," she said. "I've been to LA, but I've never had the courage to do that."

"Your parents came from Peru and dairy-farmed in Vermont, and you buy clothes in Beverly Hills." He smiled at her. "Nobody knows where life is taking them."

"You can only plan so much," she said. "Things happen."

They walked back to his car. "I'll take you back to the Bonaventure."

"Would you mind showing me your home? Not inside. Just where you live?"

"Do you mind a tour? A short one?"

"I'd like one."

He drove along Sunset this time, turning toward Benedict

Canyon. It was still vaguely rural, the street planted with palms thickly, and most hillsides deep with ivy, the homes hidden up drives or higher on the slopes. "Leah and I lived here when we first got married. We couldn't afford to buy it. We rented for a couple of years." He pointed up at a Spanish mission-style home. "I was working for Larry, her dad." He chuckled quietly. "It was one of those odd moments when you think life is planned out. My father had been an executive at an oil company based in Connecticut. We moved out here and he promptly got fired. Well. Promptly in about three years. He got a job at PG&E. Good job. But he liked pleasing everybody, and he never got mad," Keegan said, still looking at the house where his marriage had started. "He started drinking, and then he was collecting overdue bills."

"I thought you grew up there in the city of money and movie stars."

"I did. We lived just over the line from LA. No pool. No maids. One car. But it was Beverly Hills."

He turned around, and came down the winding street, heading back into the city. She had said very little. He was attracted to her enough to want to stop the car, but afraid of the idea, too. The strange thing was that the more he talked about his life, and his wife, the more he wanted this strange woman who probably posed a threat to him.

Maybe that's what I want, he thought.

"One more stop," he said, driving them back toward Beverly Hills.

"Is something wrong?"

"Why?"

"You're not watching the road. You're staring at me." She made it sound complimentary.

"I'm sorry."

"I don't mean to embarrass you."

Keegan, who had never felt too out of his depth in any situation, didn't know now how to talk to her. He put both hands on the wheel.

"You've got a scar on your lip," he said. "I wondered about it."

She leaned toward him a little, close enough for him to smell faint spicy body lotion, to hear the rustle of her clothes. She looked briefly in the rearview mirror, then sat back with a chuckle. "I don't even notice it. You're the first person who's noticed it. Maybe my mother did."

"It's not a war wound or something?" he asked, a small smile.

"Foreign correspondent shot at by marauding bands bravely keeps reporting? Wonderful things these plastic surgeons can do with some spit and needles? I wish. No. When I was six or seven I fell down a ladder in our barn. My bottom front teeth went up, and I cut through my lip."

"That's all?"

"Sorry. Just a little childhood accident. But thanks for being so observant."

The remark warmed him. They drove up Camden Drive so he could show her All Saints Church and tell her Humphrey Bogart had his funeral there, then down the street to Rexford. He got out of the car, and she followed. They stayed in the middle of the quiet street. It was pretty and still, the sky above almost starless in the LA air, the palms and high elms cutting ragged spaces as Keegan looked up.

"That's where I live." He pointed. "Looks like Elaine's asleep."

"She puts herself to bed?"

"She's a year ahead, a freshman in high school."

Lorrie Noves folded her arms. "I meant, she's used to going to bed with no one else at home?"

"Since the accident." Keegan felt the old coldness settle on his chest. "Before then. I had a lot of late nights."

"All right," she said softly.

Then, because he couldn't stop talking again, Keegan said abruptly, "Someone tried to bribe me recently. Don't ask who it was. Don't bother checking around, because there aren't any witnesses and there's no evidence."

"Why tell me?"

"I'd like your objective opinion. Do I look like the kind of man who could be bribed?" It was angry and defiant.

"You're the last man I'd think of."

"Yes. That's what I've always thought."

She sensed his agitation. "What's wrong then?"

Keegan said, "Why did they even try? What was the point? Did I look that weak?"

She took his hand. It was not sexual as much as it was kindly, the reassuring of a bleeding victim after an accident.

"Don't try to read much into people's motives," Lorrie Noves said. "They had their own reasons. Probably had nothing much to do with you except that you're powerful."

He squeezed her hand, then touched her mouth very gently. A pair of headlights swept slowly by them, the darkened car turning slowly to avoid them. It was a police car, slowing. Keegan waved his hand, and it rolled on.

With a wave of my hand, he thought. That's how powerful I am. How powerless.

"I'm going to take you back to your hotel. Right now," he said.

"I think that's a good idea." She let go of his hand, and they went to his car. "I'll still be here for another day or so. Who's going to be your next witness tomorrow?"

Keegan started the car and drove. He knew the instant had passed, for now, and was both grateful and furious it had. Lorrie was professional, her shield, and he slipped back into the role of a subject. Not a man or a father or even simply a person. Just the impersonal facts and observations clumped together in a news story.

"Tomorrow. I'll start with one of my eyewitnesses. Try to build the Carnes testimony logically so the jury follows it more easily."

She had the olive bag in her lap, and she nodded, fiddling with it, her hand then going through her hair, wind coming through the window. Along Olympic heading downtown, the signs changed from English to Spanish to Korean, mixed, blinking in neon, and Keegan's own campaign billboard rose over a medical building with no English on it at all. People floated around all-night markets and bus stops.

"Oh, hell," she said quietly, looking out.

"I agree," Keegan said. "Yeah, I do."

THIRTEEN

WIN CONLEY PAID for his two apple fritters and coffee with a lid, and the wide, white-uniformed woman behind the doughnut shop's counter said coyly, "You're turning into a regular."

He grinned back at her. "I can't stay away with you here."

"Oh. It's just ten and here you are. I can tell time by you."

He glanced into the darkness outside, over at an RV lot and its flatly lit shiny metal shapes. Cars passed soundlessly, and from the back of the shop, a small radio played tinnily. "I get hungry the same time every night," he said.

"You come back like you do later, and it's a free cup of coffee."

He grinned widely, showing he was beguiled by the prospect. "I bet I'll be lonely, he said. He gave her a small high sign as he left.

In his car, Conley sipped carefully from the boiling-hot, sour-tasting coffee and thoughtfully ate half of one apple fritter. It was thick, doughy, reassuring, and filling. He put the car in reverse and backed out of the parking lot. He was surrounded by auto repair garages and dark apartment buildings. On Artesia Boulevard he followed the path he'd been on for a week, traveling a mile.

155

Groups of men, laughing and yelling, stood on the corners under the cones of streetlights, the shadows around them inky. Conley drove by one of the KEEGAN'S THE WAY FOR DA! billboards flanked by fading giant beer cans frosted in white and torn beaches hanging off the billboard in strips. He wondered if Celia Aguilar would take in enough money to buy as many signs and billboards as Keegan had. He hardly saw any of her campaign stuff anywhere.

It was hard to see why she was so close to Keegan in the polls. Except maybe people were tired of George. Who knew. In LA anything could happen.

He went under a freeway underpass, soaring concrete arches. He took tiny drinks from the hot coffee, driving with one hand, as he used to do when he was a patrol officer years ago. He slowed, almost by instinct, passing a garishly bright liquor store as five young men and women swayed out, bottles upraised, voices high, and drove on.

Once, when he patrolled downtown LA on a summer night, he and his partner had seen a car parked, dome light on. There were four men inside, hunched over. It was a high drug area, heroin kits discarded in the gutters. The car's windows were closed on a hot night.

He and his partner had slipped up. Four dopesters fixing would be a decent bust. But when, with guns drawn, commands barked out, the car doors were opened, Conley found four young Mexicans hunched over a child's storybook in English. They were painstakingly making out the foreign words.

Even now he could recall the frightened, truculent faces turned to him. Guns pointed at them, men in uniform, it must have seemed like they were still at home, he thought.

It was one small lesson in his education. Appearances in the city of movies and dreams were often misleading. Conley grinned to himself. Maybe he liked movies so much because there was no question in them. They were shadows and illusions plain and simple, and all they wanted to do was amuse you.

He used his radio only once as he drove, to let the car coming to the end of its shift know he was going to be on the scene in three minutes. Enough time to eat one of the apple fritters, he had discovered.

He parked half a block down from the graceless square apartment building with ferns and stunted palms planted around it, vainly attempting to hide its mottled ugliness. GARDENVIEW TERRACE was posted with a light, two letters crooked.

Conley saw the other car from his Bureau of Investigations drive away. He was alone. The shift was his.

He would watch very determinedly for the first two hours; then the night, the heaviness in his stomach, the lethargy, would creep over him. He recited numbers and dead men's names. He rubbed his eyes hard. He finished the cooled coffee with the second fritter.

He had his attention focused on the third floor, right side, fourth set of double windows. Melanie Vogt was in residence, he saw, both windows alight. She had come home from the college of cosmetology at six-thirty. Sometimes, pushing his glasses up, Conley could even see her scattered shape moving behind the bland drapes. He rubbed his ankles and tenderly touched the varicose vein on his left leg, which had started aching again with these late-night surveillances. He had until two A.M., when a relief car, with two investigators he had personally chosen, would arrive. Conley yawned and tried to find a more comfortable position in the car seat.

Watching the apartment windows, he thought of his wife. He had been with LAPD for five months when he met her. Margerie's apartment on Western Avenue had been broken into, and Conley took the first report. She smiled at him. She worked in the script department at Republic, reading batches of material and writing summaries. She was, Conley knew instantly and profoundly, the most beautiful and desirable woman he had ever seen.

He came back to the apartment for two weeks afterward. Parking outside at night, like this, watching her windows, trying to find the willpower to knock on her door. He saw her come and go. Carry in bags of groceries, walk her terrier. At the end of two weeks, Conley finally introduced himself again, awkwardly asking if she'd had any more trouble with break-ins.

They went out for several weeks. He remembered the first time he and Margerie made love. It was in her apartment, on a Murphy bed that folded out from the wall, so they were in the middle of her living room. He had visions from old silent comedies of the bed flapping back into the wall at the worst moment. She thought, she told him later, he was only being very gentle with her.

Conley could see her now, hear the faucet dripping in the kitchen, the terrier scratching at the bathroom door, where he'd been confined. Smell roses in a vase. The beer he'd finished. The pungent sweetness of her skin from the bath. He was clumsy and nervous and ardent, and at the very end, Margerie reached both arms up around his neck, pulled him down gently, and kissed his closed eyes.

Conley, so many years later and so alone, looked away from the Gardenview Terrace for a moment. It was the wrong time to remember.

In the next hour, six men and women passed his darkened car. Four used keys and went into the apartment building. One couple embraced, broke, embraced again before walking on.

Conley pissed into the empty coffee cup and closed it with the plastic lid. His leg ached. One window in Melanie Vogt's apartment went dark, and he sat up sharply. His hand paused at the car door, about to shove it open. The remaining light stayed on. She had only moved into one room.

Near midnight, the street was busier, and Conley watched with cold fascination. Two young men set themselves up on the corner. At intervals, cars drove up, someone leaned out, hands passed back and forth, and the car drove on. Conley could not see what was being passed to the cars.

Two more young men, black in black jeans and warm-up jackets, joined the others, and they all began talking and laughing.

Halfway up the block, he saw Melanie Vogt come out of the building at a trot, her hands around a heavy suitcase. She stood on the walkway, looking up and down the street. Conley carefully opened his door.

A Mazda rushed down the street, pulled up in front of the

apartment building. Conley noticed one of its headlights was out. A blue Mazda, and he couldn't see the license. It was happening very fast. He was still coming out of his car.

The Mazda honked twice, and Melanie walked to it, swinging the suitcase into the backseat, getting into the passenger side herself in an almost seamless movement. The men at the corner turned to watch.

Conley closed his door quickly, and headlights off, swung his car toward the Mazda, cutting across one lane of traffic in an arc.

He was startled when the Mazda tried to drive past him and broadsided his car instead. He rocked forward, then back, hands still clenched around the steering wheel, and felt the car quaking. The noise was explosive, like a steel hammer on a bucket of glass.

Melanie Vogt was in the street, standing up, shouting something, and then running. Conley pushed his door open and ran after her. He shouted at the Mazda, but it backed up with a fierce grinding sound and clattered away up the street.

She ran ahead in a narrow alleyway between the Gardenview apartments and another building. Conley wished he had brought a flashlight or radio with him. He felt the same shocking blur as the night Hughes's plane went down. Wreckage, burning, wings in Beverly Hills. These things were not supposed to happen.

He lost sight of her. He heard her sandals slapping ahead, and breathing heavily, feeling heavy and inert, he gasped forward. He had his gun out.

At the end of the alleyway was a steep, concrete-lined embankment, hung over with dead and fecund eucalyptus, dropping away into a long, fenced drainage canal. In yellow arc lights, the smear of water in the canal was black. Conley heard Melanie running along the concrete, then the liquid of her feet splashing in the dirty water.

The canal was fenced on all sides and ran true and predictably. Conley ran back toward his car, down the alleyway, to call for help and then drive along the canal himself.

The four men who had been at the corner were clustered

around his car, yanking at it, pulling, and Conley shouted at them, his gun raised.

As if in that same unimagined dream, the men shouted back, and began shooting at him

Conley dropped to the street, instinctive, reacting, and he fired at them, trying to move some distance from them at the same time. He was suddenly in the wet earth smelling a tangle of ferns and azaleas and birds-of-paradise around the apartment building. He thought he could get into the entrance, amber and shadowy, and hide.

Three of the men started toward him, still shouting obscenely. One had a gun. One had a knife. He saw something dark, bulky in another's hand.

Conley fired again, and broke from the clinging plants, husking breathlessly, shoving at the streaked glass door, pushing inside, running down a half-lit hallway, thick with old smoke and ammonia. He ran up a flight of stairs, breaking into the second floor, into a twin hallway, and he pressed against the wall opposite the stairwell door. From down on the street, through a window at the far end of the hallway, he heard the brittle disintegration of glass.

No footsteps. No pursuit. Quiet.

Behind the doors along the hallway, Conley listened to yelling and TV, music and voices in Spanish and English. His face was hot and wet, and his leg throbbed painfully. He slid along the wall, rasped through his coat by the uneven, stippled paint. He listened. Stillness outside, the faint, retreating derision of a human howl.

Conley knocked roughly on a door. Then again and again until it opened. A woman, small, swarthy, and fearful, stared at him. Three young children skittered among the toys and clothes on the floor.

"I need your phone. Call the police," he stammered, his gun slipping back into its holster. The woman stared wider, and he fumbled for his DA Investigator badge. "Okay. Okay. Call the police."

He had a chance to show her the badge just before his stomach heaved and he vomited violently.

Keegan wore gray slacks and loafers without socks, all hastily pulled on. He had put on his Harvard School sweatshirt, a gift from Chris.

Conley sat on the living-room sofa, a light Scotch in his hand, his coat crumpled at his side. Elaine, hands crossed on her knees, in a saffron robe, looked at Conley from the hassock.

"More, Win?" Keegan pointed to his own half-empty glass.

Conley shook his head. Keegan worried about the pallor and the dark-circled eyes he saw.

"Don't apologize," Keegan said. "I don't want it."

Conley nodded. "Right."

"I've talked to Marv Hickcock. He's put a half-dozen extra LAPD units in the area," Keegan said. "The cops are checking up and down the canal and the streets coming off it."

"Marv and I started at the Academy together," Conley said. He didn't drink, he winked sadly at Elaine. "Now he's chief of police. I'm running Investigations for you. Two hundred people working for me. That's success."

"No self-pity," Keegan said. "I can't afford it."

"Right," Conley said.

"I don't think they'll find her."

"Not if she's running."

"I have to assume some responsibility. I have to assume she's running because of me. Too much pressure. Too much attention because I'm doing the trial."

Keegan finished his drink. Three Beverly Hills police cars had pulled up in front of his house, lights on, a courtesy, after LA's chief of police called to explain the effort his men were making to find the wayward witness. Beverly Hills didn't want to appear unconcerned about Keegan's problem.

"Don't blame yourself," Conley said. "She's like a lot of witnesses. It's not you."

"She was my responsibility."

"Right." Conley winced at the knowledge.

"I've got Mintline and Klein on their way over," Keegan said, tapping his glass as he thought about what his chief deputy and public information officer could do to help him get out from under this disaster. "I can get some trial strategy from Mintline, and Phil may have a few ideas about how to play the thing to the media."

"Klein can give you an angle," Conley agreed. He seemed empty himself, sucked dry.

Keegan thought of Conley sitting in the same spot, less than five years ago. A captain about to retire from the police, Keegan's fellow communicant at church, sitting here with others when Keegan announced he would run for district attorney. Leah was unhappy with the decision. She hated politics and campaigning. Only Win instantly put out his hand, shaking Keegan's up and down, he was so unabashedly happy.

"I'll have to get to Ambrosini in the morning," Keegan said. "I've got to get some time from him." He glanced at the gently ticking, quarter-hour chiming mantel clock. Two A.M. Already morning.

Elaine spoke for the first time. "I think the neighbors think we've been robbed." People stood on the sidewalk, under the streetlights, in their running suits and bathrobes.

"More complaints to the City Council about us living here," Keegan said to his daughter. "Go back to bed, honey."

"It's going to be noisy around here. I might as well stay up."

Conley leaned back, sighed, sat up. He put his glass down on the mahogany coffee table, knocking off a stack of magazines. They spilled to the floor. Stricken, he grabbed them up. "I'm so sorry," he said.

"Leave them, Win," Keegan said.

"I thought it was a little added protection, me taking a shift, watching. Looking out."

Keegan shifted uneasily. He was tongue-tied and embarrassed. He didn't like Elaine seeing Conley's humiliation.

"Shit, George, I wanted to. You know, help out. You know what burns me the worst? I knew"—he tapped his head—"I had a feeling she was going to take off."

"It's done. Now we have to find her."

"Maybe she went home," Elaine said with her mother's unafraid impetuosity.

"Please, honey," Keegan said warningly.

"Where's home for her?" Conley answered sourly. "Her old man? We've got someone going to him."

"Win, the others will be here soon. There's no reason for you to stay. You look tired," Keegan said, picking up Conley's glass, putting it on the piano as an unequivocal sign of dismissal.

Slowly Conley got up, coat bunched under one arm. "Thanks. I can't really tell them anything now."

"We've got enough information from you now. I can get the rest later this morning."

One of the senior investigators from the bureau would drive Conley home, to the empty house, made sullen and remorseful by his failure.

Keegan didn't want to face the implication of that failure. Conley had taken on a job usually handled competently by one of his investigative teams. Like I took on the trial.

And Conley had failed.

"I'm going to work on Ambrosini," Keegan said walking Conley out. "I think I can put off the trial for a week. I can handle the media."

Conley nodded. Keegan knew he had eased the old cop's guilt a little by his show of false optimism.

"Call me, George. Anytime. I'll be in first thing."

Keegan patted him on the back. It was a formal gesture, from a fund-raiser. "At least LAPD got two of the guys who came after you."

"I want to find the bastard in that Mazda," Conley swore.

"Tomorrow. Get some sleep."

Conley left, into the night, and Keegan knew it was only a short time before the TV news vans arrived and yet more reporters camped on his lawn. He put up a hand to some of his neighbors, to mollify them a little about this latest inconvenience. Like the tour buses that ran up and down streets pointing out movie-star homes to out-of-towners. The cops milling pointlessly outside tried to look purposeful when they saw him. One young cop started making gestures to push back to the neighbors.

Elaine took his hand when he came back. She hadn't done it for a long time, perhaps since Leah's funeral.

"He looked really unhappy. I hope I never make a mistake like that."

Keegan squeezed her hand. "You can't condemn him for one mistake, honey."

But it was untrue. In his own heart, he had done just that to Conley.

He heard cars driving up. "Play hostess for me, okay? I'll be right back."

Elaine went to the front door to let in the first of the senior staff from the DA's office, and Keegan went to his bedroom. He called the Bonaventure. Lorrie answered on the second ring.

"Did I wake you?" he asked.

"No. Just reading. It's very late, though."

He heard the professional's aroused curiosity. Or was it personal interest? He sat down on his bed, in the oddly deserted room he and Leah had shared for years.

"A story's going to break very soon. I know you've got a longer lead, but you might want to jump on a few people right away."

"I'm ready. Go ahead," she said. There was no mistake. Lorrie's tone was clinical.

Keegan said, "About an hour and a half ago, my key witness vanished into thin air. It was some kind of prearranged escape."

Silence. Pensive, he thought. "What are you going to do?" she asked.

"Get her back. Find her."

"I'm sorry."

"Not as much as I am. Or Win Conley. She got away from him."

"He's a nice old man. He should be sitting with his feet up in a boat on some slow river. Fishing."

Keegan didn't think she meant it viciously. It was almost a wistful daydream. "I'm meeting with my senior staff in a couple of minutes."

"Can I watch? Strictly for background?"

"No. Not this time."

"I understand. I had a lot of fun tonight. I'm really sad it's ending so miserably for you."

"I've had worse nights. I'll survive. I've got to go."

"Tell me who I should talk to," she said in a rush. His heart sank, hearing the reporter anxious to cling to a source.

He rattled off names, some in his office, an assistant deputy chief in LAPD who would know everything and might not be as shy as the chief.

"Thanks for the break, George. If I tried to catch up in the morning . . ." She let it dangle. He had given her a big present, and she knew it.

"Will you call me tomorrow? After court?" he said. "I'd like to see you again."

"I'll call."

He hung up. Cabrerra was more accurate than she realized. The danger from Lorrie Noves was aimed at something more hidden than his political future. He had not loved his wife for some time before she died, and knowing that made grief obligatory and endless, as a penance. Loving someone now exposed him far more than the risks of the campaign or the Carnes trial. He would have to embrace his own failure in the past. I'll put myself in the open.

For a woman who may not care at all.

He left the bedroom, lights dutifully turned off, for the confused welter of voices awaiting him in the living room.

FOURTEEN

HIS CAR SLOWED SO HE COULD CHECK the house numbers, his driver silently obeying his sharp commands.

Keegan wore dark sunglasses, sat on the passenger side of the county car, the radio spitting out a mixture of police calls and music. The eastern dawn was still in pink bars over the city. At four that morning, a sudden wet wind had rushed in off the ocean, and the fashionable, antique homes along the street were smudged with leaves and branches, the clipped lawns dirtied with bits of paper and garbage.

"Here it is," Keegan said. The car slowed, parked.

The radio was tuned for the moment to news, and the dramatic flight of Melanie Vogt was the lead story. Keegan had waded through a bath of camera lights and shouted questions twenty minutes before when his driver arrived and he strode from his house to the car.

He took off his sunglasses. As he was about to head up the white sidewalk to the ornate old home, a small, briskly striding figure came toward him.

166

"Good morning, judge," Keegan said.

"Hello, George," Ambrosini said nasally. He was dressed in a gray three-piece suit already, a raincoat, collar up, unbuttoned. "You've got an emergency."

"I have a problem," Keegan said.

"Come in," Ambrosini said glumly. He led them into the dark foyer, then to a dark room off the kitchen where a table was set for one, coffee in the cup, orange juice.

"I'm sorry to interrupt your breakfast," Keegan said, sitting down.

Ambrosini took off his raincoat, checked his cuffs, and sat down without looking at Keegan. He drank some orange juice. He sat waiting in sour anticipation.

"I shouldn't even be seeing you. I thought you'd wait until we got to court. Goodoy will be there."

"It can't wait. I need a couple of days to get this witness in custody," Keegan said. He hated coming to Ambrosini for a favor. Their previous encounters before the trial had been perfunctory, courteous, and empty. Handshakes at county bar meetings. Nods at dinners for the Music Center or one of Leah's committees.

"She wasn't under subpoena, was she?" the little judge asked. He pinched his bulbous nose. He seemed to be waiting for something.

"I had her under surveillance. I had her cooperation. I had every belief she was going to voluntarily appear. She's the center of the case against Carnes."

"Your case," the judge said. He glanced up. He tapped his silver fork softly on the white tablecloth.

"I'll make a formal motion this morning, but I've got to give Marv Hickcock and my staff time to find her."

A thin, smiling woman in a print dress wafted in carrying a plate with a steel cover. She put it down in front of Ambrosini and whipped off the cover.

"Oh." She looked at Keegan. "George Keegan. I didn't know you were coming for breakfast."

"It was unplanned."

"It's all right, Estelle," the judge said, glumly going to work on the steaming food.

"It's scrapple this morning. Do you like scrapple?" she asked, holding the steel cover like a cymbal she wanted to bang. "My husband is very partial to scrapple."

Keegan shook his head.

"Oh. Well. All right." She paused in an equally light departure. "How was your walk?" she asked the judge. "He and I always take our morning walk, and then I come back, always ten minutes ahead, and get breakfast started. I eat later. But he has to have his food right at six. Right at six." She smiled.

"Because I have to go to court, Estelle. That's why we must eat together at six." He went on mechanically putting food in his mouth, eyes down. "When we do eat together."

"Well. It was good seeing you again," she said to Keegan. "Even though he'll probably ask for more, there's some scrapple for you, if you'd like?" she offered again.

Keegan again shook his head, and she left.

Ambrosini instantly pushed the plate away, wiping his mouth as if it were unclean. "I detest scrapple. She knows that. It's another one of her little jabs."

Keegan stood up. He was very tall standing over the judge.

"Will you give me a continuance?" Keegan demanded. He would not wheedle or grovel.

The judge washed his mouth out with coffee. He put his hands on the table and got up. "No."

"I told you Carnes might go free if she doesn't testify."

"No," the judge said again.

"You son of a bitch," Keegan said. "He's a killer."

The insult didn't touch Ambrosini. He said, "You came here this morning to see me behind everybody's back. Because you're in trouble. I said you were unprincipled. You've never done anything to make me change that opinion."

"Do it for the sake of justice," Keegan said roughly.

"All I'll do is keep this meeting between us." He glowered. "And my wife."

Keegan left, furious he was in the position of asking for a favor from a man who delighted in denying it to him.

He put on his sunglasses, the elegant homes darkening, and told his driver to head downtown.

"My late wife's father used to call Hancock Park the place where every old asshole in the city waited to die."

His driver chuckled, surveying Ambrosini's neighborhood. "They're still some pretty nice places."

"They're still full of assholes," Keegan said.

Parker Center, the headquarters of the city police, was named after one of the cruder, longer-serving chiefs in Los Angeles history.

Keegan met on the top floor of the white boxy building with the present chief and his staff. They were in a room on a floor divided again and again into a succession of rooms, like littler boxes multiplied inside the larger one.

"I'll try again in court this morning," Keegan said, standing at the head of the conference table.

In front of him, all of the senior police officials were in civilian clothes, like a bank's board of directors.

"I can't promise you anything," said the chief, stout, gray, and mustached. "Until she starts using a credit card, shows herself to buy something, someone sees her." He put his hands up.

"Her father was a trainer. Can you keep an eye around the border if she goes south?"

Hickcock, the chief, folded his hands. "The Border Patrol is alerted, George. I've put three extra teams of detectives on it."

"All right. That sounds like the best for the moment." Keegan gathered his papers. He knew what the chief would probably say next.

"A lot of overtime hours are going into this, George." Hickcock looked at the nodding faces around him.

Keegan nodded, too. He knew his own part in the performance. "I know, Marv. I appreciate it. I owe you a major favor in return."

In his own office on the eighteenth floor, Keegan made notes as his bureau chiefs and chief deputy offered advice. He ate bits from a muffin, sipped from a china cup. He had gone out without anything before seeing the judge.

The sky was porcelain blue, early autumn outside his window, and the city stretched away into the distance.

"To sum up," he said, "you all agree Speedy will not grant me any continuance?"

His chief deputy nodded along with the heads of Special Operations, Branch and Area Operations, Major Trials. Cabrerra and Phil Klein sat together whispering.

"Boss, he has complete discretion to make a call like that," the chief deputy said. Keegan had not told them about the morning meeting.

"Is it appealable? Can I take him up to the District Court of Appeal?"

"No. We'd lose anyway. It's a discretionary decision by the trial court, and he's got grounds for making it."

Keegan chewed another piece of muffin. It was cold, cottony in his mouth. He had decided that his weapons were no longer legal. He would have to fight Ambrosini on political terms.

It was a great risk.

"What's the word on the Mazda?" Keegan said. "Any identification?"

He looked around.

The chief deputy cleared his throat. "Boss. Win hasn't come in yet. We're using the License Division in Sacramento. We're running through dealerships around town, car repair shops."

"All right. Barbara," he called out, drank some coffee as Cabrerra looked up. "Assessment?"

"I've made a few calls this morning, George." She puckered her mouth, dabbing at a stray streak of lipstick in a corner. "I don't see any damage at the moment. It's all very much wait and see."

"Wait for what?"

She smiled at him. "What you do. How you handle it."

Keegan nodded and put down his pen. He ate the last, dry piece of muffin. "Phil. What's coming from the local media?"

Klein had unwrapped a cigar. In deference to the people on the eighteenth floor, he did not light his cigars anymore, merely held them or chewed the ends. He used this one as a pointer. "Everybody wants a statement. Everybody wants an interview with you, boss."

"No statements," Keegan said. "I mean that. Whatever is coming out of this comes from me. In court."

They nodded.

Cabrerra spoke up. "I know it's not exactly germane, but have you talked to Morganthau?"

Keegan sat back. "Not yet. Wylie's on autopilot anyway, keeping the dinners going, get-out-the-vote operations, phone banks. He won't have anything too much to offer this early."

His chief deputy stood up, a little nervously. He was a thin, running man, and his face sometimes looked cadaverous when he trained for a marathon. He said, "Boss, we'd all like to wish you the best today. We're all working our hardest for you."

Before Keegan, touched and ready with a practiced platitude, could answer, his chief deputy and the other men all flipped their ties up. They whistled for him. On the underside of their ties, from top to bottom, were KEEGAN'S THE WAY! campaign buttons.

Keegan rose before the impishly, owlishly perched judge on the bench, who looked down at him with as bland and empty an expression as a snake with an already paralyzed meal in front of him.

Carnes sat back, crossing his arms. Goodoy listened, hand on her cheek. The crowded courtroom, reporters nearly outnumbering spectators, was silent.

"Your Honor," Keegan said. "Based on the discussion we have just had in chambers, I am filing a motion for a continuance of this trial based on the unavailability of a major witness."

"Give the documents to the clerk, Mr. Keegan. They will be filed," Ambrosini said blandly. Keegan's assistant passed the papers to the court clerk, who stamped them and noted them, handing one batch up to the judge. "Do you have anything you wish to add to these motions?"

Keegan walked into the cramped space just in front of the bench. He was in the center of the camera eye, and everyone in the courtroom was focused on him.

"Your Honor, new information, recent information, has come to me that the absence of this witness was not caused by her actions alone."

"You mean someone helped her? Someone was there to pick her up." Ambrosini nodded, his glasses catching the lights. "I know. I heard you just now. I can see that in your moving papers. It doesn't add much to your request."

Keegan was poised on the brink of a dangerous statement.

He was not going to give up the trial so easily or knuckle under to the judge.

He was going to use the weapons he had. "Based on information from a witness, Your Honor, it is clear there was a planned attempt to take this witness out of this city."

"Planned? To do what?"

"To prevent her from testifying against the defendant," Keegan said, facing Carnes, the cameras, and people. "There is a plot to prevent this trial from continuing."

Goodoy got up, hands waving before her. "Your Honor. Your Honor. This is the first I've heard of this accusation."

"Are you accusing the defense?" Ambrosini's thin mouth turned down, he glared at Keegan. "Where is this accusation in your papers, Mr. Keegan?"

"This information became available to me only in the last few minutes, Your Honor."

"So it's not here?" the judge demanded, flipping through the papers on the bench. "I don't have it before me?"

Keegan smiled grimly. "Yes, you do, Your Honor. I'm telling you right now."

Ambrosini stood up, papers clasped to his side. "Ten-minute recess," he snapped.

The reporters, barely held back by the bailiffs, surged toward Keegan, who remained rooted to his place in front of the deserted bench.

"I'm not accusing you," Keegan said to Goodoy in the judge's chambers. "I'm sure you've got nothing to do with it."

Goodoy, standing by the window, fidgeted with the side of her hair, pressing it down over and over in agitation. "Thanks for nothing."

"I think your guy's behind it. Or people working for him."

"Where? How? Show me," Goodoy demanded.

From behind his desk, robe buttoned tightly, dark and furious, the judge said to Keegan, as if Goodoy wasn't even there, "Not in thirteen years on the bench. Never before. My courtroom turned into a show, a comedy."

"I'm not joking," Keegan said. "I've been working with Marv Hickcock, Sacramento, my own staff all morning. This was a premeditated assault on the trial. Not just me."

Ambrosini's small dark eyes widened behind his glasses, like a switch had been thrown. "Amazing. Now the whole spectacle is really for my benefit, too. I'm at risk, too? My standing as a judge?"

"I'm not blaming you, either."

"I don't think there's any point you'd stop at. You know what I mean, Keegan. You know exactly," Ambrosini said, head lowered, squeezing his nose angrily.

You can't talk about our dawn meeting now without it looking like some kind of collusion, Keegan thought. Sure I know. And how mad it makes you to be silent about it.

"Judge, I'd like to see the DA's evidence. I'd like to have some proof before we go any farther," Goodoy, her gentility put aside abruptly, demanded.

"Where is the proof?" the judge exclaimed.

Keegan was on surer ground. He had spent years with people who either loathed or feared him and had still gotten his way in politics. He had never wanted to use the tricks in court.

"I'm still gathering proof."

"Tell me what you have."

"The timing, the car, the packed suitcase, the attempt to run down my investigator, the flight of both the car and the witness."

Ambrosini got up and came to Keegan. His normally pale cheeks were hectic with anger. "You have nothing. You've got a shaky witness who had every right to leave or take a drive or do whatever she wanted to do."

"It was a plot," Keegan repeated.

Goodoy said, "I'm moving for a mistrial. The publicity is going to ruin any chance of a fair trial."

Keegan nodded, as if in agreement. At least with a mistrial, he would look like the victim of sinister forces, and Carnes would stay in jail until a new trial date could be set. I could still get justice from this case later.

But the judge shook his head. He had his hands on his hips, his robe around him like a small, dark courtier from the Renaissance painting in his chambers. "No. No mistrial. No continuance. Mr. Keegan has calculated that I would give in to his grandstanding. I'm not going to give him what he wants."

"Judge," Goodoy said bitterly.

Ambrosini put up his hand. "No mistrial. Period. No continuance. And Mr. Keegan, I am watching you like a hawk. One step and I will impose a contempt judgment on you that will curl your hair."

Keegan nodded. "I'm not going to be threatened, Your Honor." Least of all by you, he thought. Or what you could do to me.

I'm threatened by memories and fears far worse. They went back into court, and it took Judge Ambrosini nearly another ten minutes to quiet the noise before he could announce his decision. He said twice he would clear the courtroom.

Keegan noticed that Carnes, frowning, was watching him with puzzlement and concern.

FIFTEEN

LORRIE NOVES SAT THROUGH a breakfast speech by Celia Aguilar at the Garden Grove Merchants Association. Fruit compote, chilly scrambled eggs, coffee, in a low-ceilinged, bright room at the Goldcrest Hotel on an industrial strip. Mostly men, about forty, black, white, a few Asians. Lorrie made notes. Aguilar wore gray, gestured frequently, had problems with the portable microphone.

Points about Keegan: He was high-handed. Aloof. Miscalled several major trials in the last few years. Spent too much money on wasteful prosecutions. Spent too little on local, basic crimes.

Like crimes against merchants. Thefts. Petty thefts. Robberies. Burglaries soaring under his administration because too many cases were dealt away.

Many heads nodded, coffee was sipped, mouths wiped.

Questions: What about the Carnes trial? Aguilar declined comment because it was still going on. Her small smile indicated clearly she thought it was another high-handed, expensive stunt by a man who had done the same kind of thing over and over.

She took questions for another fifteen minutes, then bustled out, a large black purse bursting with papers and notes under one arm. Applause was generous.

Lorrie met up with her again at her campaign headquarters on Wilshire and Western, near a blackish, formerly ornate old movie palace.

Celia Aguilar dropped behind a gunmetal-gray desk, put her feet up, and began calling people. She spoke, clipped, tartly, and took a plastic cup of coffee from a shy teenaged volunteer. Around her were lawn signs in stacks, posters on the floor in stacks, five men and women working the phones. A large brightly colored banner hung on the back wall. AGUILAR FOR DA. FOR CHANGE.

Aguilar hung up, hands poised over the phone.

"Give me a minute," Lorrie said.

"Barely," Aguilar agreed, hand lowering. She rubbed one foot carefully. "I need new feet."

"Did I just hear your standard campaign speech?"

"More or less. I have to keep adding the crime stats because they change. But I don't tailor my message very much."

The volunteers on the phones added a persistent hum to the traffic noise floating in from Wilshire with the sharp morning sunlight.

"I noticed you wouldn't take any questions about the trial."

Aguilar put her feet down, sat as though she were at her desk back in the Criminal Courts Building. "It's still going on. Unlike George, I still have respect for the judicial process."

"You really do believe he's using it?"

Aguilar shook her head. "I know you're from New York. LA is the land of show biz and hype. But a trial is sacred. I don't ever want to see our courts turned into political game shows."

Lorrie wrote, and Aguilar said, "I mean, just look at how George lost a key witness, for God sake. He's making a major trial into a media event, not a search for the truth."

"You wouldn't have lost a witness, either?"

"Ms. Noves, in all the years I tried cases, I lost witnesses. But I never had one run away from me who wasn't under subpoena. I got them back."

Lorrie glanced up as one of the phone volunteers jumped from his seat and darted to a small color TV on the makeshift table. He turned it on.

Aguilar said, "What's going on?"

"Keegan's just said there's a conspiracy to screw the trial," the volunteer said breathlessly.

Both Aguilar and Noves went to the TV as a special bulletin was mumbled, stumbled, from outside the Criminal Courts Building.

Lorrie watched in confusion. Keegan hadn't mentioned anything like this last night. Had he found out more since then? She felt betrayed that he hadn't alerted her.

Aguilar breathed heavily, eyes fixed on the TV. Everyone in her headquarters stood watching. She said, "A conspiracy. My God. George's lost his mind."

"It's impossible?"

Aguilar said coldly, "The people I know who'd like this trial to fall apart couldn't find their shoes."

"Who do you know?" Lorrie asked, already taking pictures of the worried volunteers and Aguilar's stony expression as they gazed at the TV.

"I mean all the voters who want to retire George Keegan."

"You sounded more specific."

Aguilar, arms folded, traffic bustling behind her outside, the TV babbling inside, said calmly, "I wasn't being specific at all."

Lorrie went on taking pictures, but at that moment she knew Aguilar was lying.

You're probably very believable in front of a jury, Lorrie thought, but I've been covering lawyers for too long. I can hear the lies.

She wondered if she should tell Keegan.

The mayor and one of his vice-mayors, surrounded by a small band of friends and favor-seekers and a straggling reporter, walked leisurely along the marble- and stone-vaulted corridor of City Hall. Their voices carried upward into the proud stony vastness as if they were in a great train station or a Spanish tomb.

"Hurry it up, Marty. I've got a meeting in five minutes with the Parks Committee," said Nelson Poulsby. Several councilmen drifted alongside, like small ships trailing a great liner.

Koenig, files in hand, smiled uneasily. "He's claiming a conspiracy."

"So?"

"I thought you'd be interested."

Poulsby spoke loudly for all of the attending seekers. "I'm always interested in whatever George Keegan says. Everybody is."

Several ribald comments followed, addressed to Poulsby's ears.

The vice-mayor leaned close to Poulsby. "I think you'd like to hear everything."

"Do I really need to hear it, or do you only think I need to hear it?"

"You really need to hear it," Koenig said, low.

They passed an alcove, scallop-shaped, in the marble hall, in which a greenish hologram of the Mayor raised its head and smiled, ghostly, disquieting, as the observers walked.

At the gold-doored private elevator that would rush the mayor to his high office, Poulsby paused, leaning to Koenig. "Marty," he said, "have you done something you shouldn't have?"

A short, thick-lipped man past middle age sat on the witness stand, a small plaid cap in his hands.

His name was Russell Dagowitz, and he was nervous. Keegan, after his assurance in facing the judge in chambers, was nervous, too. Dagowitz was the first significant witness who could connect Carnes to the victims. With Melanie Vogt on the run, he had become even more important.

There was a thick, vibrant unsettledness throughout the courtroom, as if Keegan were expected to pull some extravagant gesture every moment, topping the last. Keegan took a breath, then started.

"Mr. Dagowitz, in May of this year, what was your address?"

Bass-voiced, head thrust out, he replied, "3414 Canterbury Way in Marina del Rey."

"Where is that in relation to 3417 Canterbury Way?"

"Across the street. Not directly. Kind of kitty-corner." Dagowitz made an oblique angle with his hands.

"Did you know who lived at 3417 Canterbury Way?"

"A family. I thought they were a family."

Goodoy said swiftly, quietly, "Objection. Non-responsive."

"Sustained," equally swift from Ambrosini.

So it's going to be a team act, Keegan thought. He smiled with practiced ease at Dagowitz's puzzled frown, then smiled at the jury. They were the audience, too.

"Did you know the people, Mr. Dagowitz?"

"To see them. Not to talk to. They had a boat. I'd see them with that sometimes. Going out. Coming back."

"Let me show you some photographs." Keegan put them on the witness stand, and Dagowitz relinquished his plaid hat. "Are these the people you knew?" "Objection," Goodoy said. "Are these exhibits or what?"

Ambrosini, resorting to benign sarcasm, said, "Yes, Mr. Keegan. The custom is to identify the exhibits so the court, the defendant, the jury, know what you're talking about."

"Also vague, Your Honor." Goodoy pressed her advantage.

"Sustained. Tell us what you're asking the witness, Mr. Keegan."

Keegan didn't answer, holding in his anger. He didn't look at the judge or jury. He knew they were following the acrimony with hungry interest.

They won't think the judge and defense attorney are ganging up on me, either, he knew. I'm still the DA. I'm the big one in this court. If I act weak, I'm doomed.

He said carefully, "Mr. Dagowitz, I'm putting some photos in front of you. They're marked People's Number Three Through Six for identification. Do you know the people in these pictures?"

Dagowitz shrugged at the delay. "Sure. That's the family at 3417."

"Photos of Barry Rotich, his wife, Joyce, and his wife's nephew, Samuel," Keegan said, pointing for the jury.

"Objection."

"Why, Mrs. Goodoy?" Ambrosini asked as if he cared.

"No question. He's making a statement."

"Sustained. We ask questions in court, Mr. Keegan, on direct examination."

"I'll try and remember."

"Sir?"

"I was addressing the witness, Your Honor."

"Well, as we tell witnesses, keep your voice up. I can't hear you," Ambrosini grumped, writing something in his large trial ledger.

Keegan instantly returned to his witness. He didn't want the jury distracted. They had to listen to Dagowitz closely, and his words had to sound more important than they were.

Until we find Melanie.

"Think back to May fourteenth of this year, Mr. Dagowitz. Did you see any of the people in those pictures?"

"The People's exhibits, Mr. Keegan."

"Thank you very much, Your Honor. Did you see any of those people in the People's exhibits on May fourteenth?"

"You mean these pictures?" Dagowitz pointed in a little confusion. "I hear people this and that. I don't know what you mean."

"Objection," Goodoy said, chin out. "Vague."

"Mr. Keegan," said the judge, "be more specific. Sustained."

"How can I be more specific, Your Honor?" Keegan's temper burned brightly too soon.

"I'm not instructing you how to present evidence or question a witness," the judge said, hunching forward. He would like to pounce on anything right now, Keegan thought. "Continue your questions, if you have any more."

"I do, and I'd like to ask them without being interrupted so much."

"Then ask them properly." Ambrosini's voice was lulling, false. Behind their hands or with lowered faces, the bailiffs grinned. They knew the judge's moods well, and this deceptive gentleness was the herald of his wrath. Two bailiffs slid closer to the courtroom doors to block them. The judge liked to order them blocked.

Dagowitz leaned back, puzzled. He glanced at Carnes. He raised his eyebrows, and Carnes raised his back.

"They were proper," Keegan said. "I'll make them more proper for you and Ms. Goodoy."

"Do we understand each other?"

"I've never been in any doubt."

"Would you like a recess, Mr. Keegan?"

"No, Your Honor. I'd like to let the jury hear this witness."

The judge smiled. Not now. Later, he seemed to say. I will wait for a much better time to drop the net on you. "Go ahead and try it again, Mr. Keegan." He used both hands to push his glasses up.

From the jurors, hard, impatient faces looked at Keegan.

He took another breath. This is my trial. My witness. My campaign, he thought.

He said coolly, "Mr. Dagowitz, when you saw the Rotich family"—he pointed at the photos—"did anyone else arrive at 3417 Canterbury Way?"

"Yeah."

"What time of day?"

"Around noon, a little after. I was home because I had a stomach bug. Something like that."

"What did you see?"

Dagowitz put his cap on the witness stand. "Well, I'm looking out my front window, and across the street I see a car drive up."

"Did you notice anyone around 3417 when the car drove up?"

"The guy. The older guy." He tapped one of the photos. "This guy."

Keegan held it up for the jury. "For the record, a picture of Barry Rotich."

Carnes leaned to see and nodded. Goodoy listened, and behind her one of the deputies guarding Carnes sneaked a small piece of chewing tobacco into his cheek.

"Where was the victim?" Keegan asked. He knew it was a provocative question.

Goodoy did as she was expected to do. "Objection. No crime has been established yet. There isn't a victim."

"He's dead," Keegan said. "Shot in the head. Like his wife and the child."

The jurors snapped to the judge, who said curtly, "Please do not answer objections, Mr. Keegan. Let me rule. And I overrule the objection. And I warn both of you not to make talking comments to each other or for effect when you object."

Keegan nodded graciously. The jury had heard what he wanted-ed, and the judge seemed to agree.

He said carefully to Dagowitz, "Where was the victim?"

"On the lawn. No. In his driveway. Standing there. Like he was waiting."

"How long had he been outside before the car arrived?"

"Five minutes. I don't know. I didn't stay watching."

"Did you see anybody get out of the car?"

"No," Dagowitz said sadly. "My wife was sick that day, too. So I was running around. All I caught was the car."

"Could you see how many people were in it?"

He shook his head. "A couple."

"More than one?"

He nodded. "I think so. A driver and somebody else."

Keegan nodded, pausing for the jury, drawing out the image of two people arriving, as he said they had in his opening statement. It was, he knew, an inflexible rule of trial practice that the jury should be able to fill in the spaces of an opening statement with testimony or evidence that fit exactly. Like coloring in white spaces on a design laid out in black ink. Dagowitz was an early colored space.

Keegan sat down at his place, voice firm. "Can you tell us what this car looked like?"

Dagowitz nodded and looked up to the ceiling. "Small. Kind of brown. New looking. It had a big Hertz sticker on the back."

Keegan spoke to the jury. "It was a rented car?"

"Objection," Goodoy said. "Leading. Also calls for information beyond the witness's personal knowledge."

"Sustained," said the judge.

"I have a signed rental agreement for a Hertz car matching this description, rented on May thirteenth, Your Honor." Keegan stood up with the paper handed to him by an assistant.

"Are you submitting now, Mr. Keegan?"

"Yes. I would like it marked People's Number Seven."

They went through the tedious motions of passing the paper to Goodoy, who showed it to Carnes, who gave it to her, and she gave it to Keegan, who took it to the clerk, who marked it, and gave it to Ambrosini, who peered at it, sniffed, handed it back to Keegan, who gave it to the clerk, who put it atop a pile of photos.

Keegan sat down. The jury would peer at the agreement as they deliberated. They would remember Dagowitz and see that Ferrera had signed for the car.

Goodoy began her cross-examination abruptly.

"Sir, do you see anybody who was in that car on May fourteen in court now?" She swept her hand to take in the whole crowded courtroom. Carnes stared at Dagowitz. Daring him to make an ID in front of the jury, Keegan thought irritatedly.

"No. I don't." He lingered on Carnes. "No."

"Weren't you shown some photographs by the Los Angeles Police Department, too?"

"A lot of pictures."

"You didn't pick anyone from those photos either, did you?"

Dagowitz shook his head. He had gray hair at his temples, and it had come loose with sweating. "Nope."

Goodoy had all of the photo lineups shown to Dagowitz marked as evidence. She said, "For the record, Your Honor, I want it noted that the photos include pictures of both Robert Carnes and Lee Ferrera."

"Mr. Keegan?"

No choice. "Agreed, Your Honor."

Goodoy walked toward the witness stand. She had resumed

her soothing, calm teacher's manner. Kindly. "Mr. Dagowitz, don't you wear glasses most of the time?"

"Only when I'm driving. Or like, long distances. I don't wear them in the house or at work."

"And you're not wearing them in court, are you?"

"I can see you. I can see everybody okay."

Keegan rubbed his own eyes. He wished someone had information about the Mazda or where Melanie was. He thought of Lorrie Noves, too, and it amazed him that he would think of her now, in the middle of this examination.

He sat forward, bracing his concentration. No time for dreaming.

Goodoy had changed direction.

"On May fourteen," she said to Russell Dagowitz, "when you were ill, did you take any medication?"

"Only some Tylenol."

"Nothing stronger?"

"I had a beer."

"One or two? Maybe more?" she pressed helpfully.

"One. I got sick afterward." He smiled ruefully at the jury, and one or two nodded sympathetically.

"How far away was this car you say you saw?"

"Maybe fifty feet."

"Maybe sixty or seventy?"

"Maybe."

Goodoy pointed. "Could it be as far as from where I'm standing to the back of the courtroom?"

Dagowitz squinted. Keegan tapped his pen at this demonstration of the witness's weak eyesight. "Yes. Might be."

"Your Honor," Goodoy said, hands clasped, "could the record reflect this distance is sixty-five feet?"

"Yes." Ambrosini stirred a little.

"Were you wearing your glasses when you looked out the window at 3417 Canterbury Way?"

Dagowitz frowned. Keegan already knew these answers. The man was able to handle himself, however nervous he might be on the stand. "No. I wasn't wearing them. I was in the house."

"But you say you could see a car sixty feet away?"

"I said so. I saw it."

"Could you see what the man in the driveway was wearing?"

"I don't know. I don't recall."

"Could you see in the windows of his house?"

"I don't think so." Dagowitz sounded testy. He folded his arms.

"And you couldn't read the street numbers, could you?"

"No."

Keegan said, "Objection. What's the relevance of what else he could see?"

"Overruled," said the judge.

Goodoy walked closer to the witness. "So it's fair to say you couldn't see five feet farther than the street, isn't it?"

"Maybe I couldn't."

"Well, Mr. Dagowitz," she said sorrowfully, "how far could you see?"

And Keegan smiled when his witness pulled through.

Dagowitz glared at her. "I can see the moon. How far's that?"

SIXTEEN

CARNES HAD DISCOVERED that he was a celebrity in the Criminal Courts Building lockup. He spent the lunch hour acknowledging his name when other prisoners, some in chains and their jail jumpsuits, shuffled by him. He was getting used to being recognized.

He sat on a long wooden bench, off to one side of the bank of pay telephones, where prisoners were dialing, whispering, grinning, or grimacing. One man with tight curls danced from foot to foot as he spoke.

Lunch was a thin sandwich of some meat on white bread with a plastic cup of bright-tasting fruit juice. Carnes, his ankles manacled, ate slowly. He was deeply offended by the morning's court proceedings. It was clear to him that Keegan, the campaigning DA, was willing to pull all kinds of public relations stunts. This struck Carnes as dishonest, almost like cheating, and his sense of propriety was disturbed.

Beside him was a large, very muscular man, his legs and arms bound tightly with handcuffs and chains. His name was Blue

186

Williams, and Carnes helped him to eat, tearing the sandwich into small pieces. Unlike Carnes, who was in street clothes, Williams was still in his red jumpsuit. He was telling a story.

"So when the pigs shot him in the hand, right hand," he said, some sandwich falling from his mouth to the concrete floor, "fucked up fifty percent of his social life in the joint." Williams laughed heartily. Four guards attentively watched as the men talked or ate.

Carnes learned that his accidental lunch companion was on trial for the contract stabbing in prison of a visiting attorney. Williams was a member of a prison gang, the Aryan Brotherhood, and visible on his thick neck were twin greenish lightning bolts.

"He didn't die?" Carnes asked about the stabbed attorney.

"Shit no. Shanked him four times," Williams said. "Didn't get anything that'd nail him, like heart or anything, man. So that's why I'm getting jammed now by some of my so-called brothers." He swallowed and motioned for a drink of juice. The guards stared at him and Carnes and nudged each other.

"How about your attorney on this beef?" Carnes asked quietly. He seemed to quiet and steady the bitter white gangster.

"Fuck. I don't got a lawyer. I'm doing this one my own self. Pro-fucking-per."

Carnes thought Blue Williams sounded a little like the producer Goldsmith. The same intense verbal swagger, the intent to show craft and ruthlessness. The difference was that Williams could break Goldsmith into six separate pieces before anyone stopped him.

Carnes was also disturbed that he hadn't heard from Goldsmith about Melanie. Or about anything really. A few notes of cheer. But nothing to indicate he was having any success locating her.

Or even that he was trying.

Carnes was nearly at the point of concluding that Kaplow's movie pal was a waste of time. But Blue Williams, on the other hand, was an interesting individual.

"What about your trial? When's that?"

"I got a secret." Williams leaned over, chewing fast. "Ain't going to be no fucking trial."

"No?"

"I'm pleading. Why not? I'm in for life anyway." He spat as two Hispanics strolled by. "But they're going to make it an assault, and the fucking judge's promising if I cop to it, I get a liter of Coke Classic and a dozen doughnuts. Cake doughnuts. Pizza, too."

"You'd plead for more time just to get a pizza?"

"Lookee, Roberto, man. I ain't had a pepperoni pizza in seven years I been up at Folsom. So I go into court this afternoon, I cop, I get my very own pizza the way I like it and my own Coke and doughnuts."

A truly interesting, cockeyed individual, Carnes decided.

Bells clanged behind the walls, the regular sound of ordered life in the courthouse. Carnes thought, finished his own juice, the tang of it taking the roof off the top of his mouth. There wasn't much time left in the lunch break. The guards would come to take them all back to the courtrooms upstairs.

"You're having a tough time, Blue," Carnes said, emphatically and softly. "I'm having a tough time."

"Man. I know it. You got the whole fucking city watching you. Man. It's LA. Fame and everybody knows your name. You get a lot of pressure, right?"

Carnes nodded. Blue Williams was a man for whom time had a different value from other people. He was pleading himself into a much longer prison term than he might have gotten in a trial, and banking that his stoicism would prevail. Carnes knew that attitude was useful.

"Blue," he said sincerely, "I believe we can help each other."

Frank Goldsmith spoke into the pay phone on Sepulveda and Sawtelle. He had to put one finger in his free ear and shout into the receiver. There were too many cars going by and a group of Mexicans—mothers, fathers, and several infants—were arguing near the open doorways of the Miramar Court Apartments. Goldsmith kept looking over anxiously, because the Spanish words sounded threatening and some of the men had started to shove each other. It was afternoon, brown-hazed, warm, like tea sitting in the sun.

"Okay," he said into the telephone, "look, I got you her name, she used to work around here. Melanie. Right. Right. Right. Yes, I'm outside. I wanted to call as soon as I thought of this, so I'm at a pay phone. Yes. It's noisy. Yes."

Goldsmith swore.

"I gave you her age, when she was here. What? What? I know there are a lot of hookers. Look, you get the AD, the one who's always telling everybody how many he's screwed. Yeah. The guy who worked on my last picture. No jokes about how long ago that was, all right? Thank you."

Goldsmith glanced up. The Mexicans had begun pounding on doors in the motel's courtyard, and faces peeped out. One woman shook her small daughter like a rug being freed of dust in spring.

"No. I did not have anything to do with her taking off. No. I know what Keegan is saying. I read the newspapers, I listen to the radio, Russ. Swear to God. Would I be asking you to find her if I was the one who got her? Would I?"

More banging. More angry pounding.

"Look, I can't talk now, things are happening. Look, you owe me this favor, Russ. You get that assistant director. He's got names and places, and he knows the whole, the whole . . ." Goldsmith's words failed. "Hookers' subculture, okay?" A car honked loudly going by. "Here's something else. Melanie, she's got ambitions to be a hairdresser, okay? She's got something for some cosmetology school around here, too. Look, Russ, you know all the faggots and their schools and everybody who's hairstyling."

Goldsmith ducked instinctively when a small rock went by. They were throwing rocks in the courtyard and the babble was sharper.

"I am not, swear to God, insulting you, Russ. I am not calling you a faggot. I am saying you are a guy who's very successful, who owes me a favor, and who will check out these leads for me. Yes. Melanie wants to be a hairstylist. How do I know? A source. An impeccable, close-to-the-bone source. No. I will not tell you who."

Then: "I apologize for calling from a phone booth. I'm an impulsive guy, you know that. I get an idea, I have to act on it. Yes. I remember when you found me outside Madame Wu's. I do appreciate you picking me up off the sidewalk so nobody in the business would see me stinking drunk outside the restaurant. That was a long time ago, Russ, and I've done you too many favors to start mentioning them to you one by one, okay? No sarcasm, Russ. Okay? Without the remarks, just do this for me?"

A man, yellow-shirted and heavy-bellied, suddenly punched a man turned sideways to him who was talking to a woman and her small son. There was a screech, and then a ball of humanity, legs and arms coming out in all directions, raised dust and bounced toward the pay phone.

Goldsmith's eyes widened.

"Excuse me, Russ. I gotta go," he said, hanging up, scurrying to his car.

Narrow-topped palms reached high into the blue sky, planted as thickly as the streetlight standards arching over the bustling avenues, and the power lines stretched vertically across the horizontally laid freeways. It helped sometimes to think of LA as a big checkerboard, everything in some square, some color, and every move already plotted out someplace.

It was how she thought of the city anyway. A city, more than any other, fixed to the migrations and vibrations of the stars. All stars, on earth and in the heavens.

Melanie, temporarily named Tiffany, shook her head at another motel on El Segundo Boulevard. "Not that one. No pool."

"You are the fussiest gal," grumped the car's driver, belly against the steering wheel, one arm out the window. "That's number six."

"I didn't like it."

"Well, we don't plan to swim, do we?"

"I might. Later."

"Little Miss Tiffany," said the car's driver, his ardor going down with each passing minute, "I have a perfectly good room back at Ana-heim. A suite."

"Well, it's okay. You want to have me come in and stay and have all your friends and those other lawyers you know see you, they come into your suite"—she drew it out—"for a drink later, well, okay. Suit yourself."

She had taken the measure of this delegate to the State Bar Conference fairly quickly. He was past forty and fat and married, and when he met her in the hotel's bar and they began the spirited bidding that led to this ride through the neighboring cities, she calculated that he could provide a safe haven for at least the evening and perhaps into the next day.

By that time, Melanie would have sorted her thinking out.

The wild events of the previous night had left her bewildered. She had also run away without any clothes or money and could not go near the Gardenview Terrace, either.

She found it unconscionable that Keegan would have kept her under surveillance. He did not trust her, obviously, and she had done nothing, not one single thing, to leave him with that impression. She was attending school every day. She was available in the apartment his office had gotten for her.

No. This surveillance trick had been underhanded.

As it was, it had taken her several quick turns last night to make enough cash to get some distance from the scene of her recent trouble. She was truly shocked at the ruckus her disappearance was causing. Face on TV. Face in the newspaper. Name on radio.

I am famous, she thought.

And wanted.

She had no doubt that many of her former friends, even some of the beauty-college students, might try to cash in on her fame by telling someone, maybe Keegan or Bobby, where she was.

So she ran.

With a frosted wig and artful manipulation of her makeup, she looked reasonably different from the solid student of the American College of Beauty.

"Now, how about this little place?" He pointed out his window at another motel coming up. "It's got a pool. TV. Sauna even. How about that?"

She did not want to keep him out so long he got discouraged. They were some distance from Anaheim. She hadn't gone through so much upheaval and fright—plain mindless, terrible fright—since she ran from Bobby. That first night away from him had been the worst, because she knew he intended to find her. And he would. He was smart.

But I'm not too dumb, she thought, examining her chipped nail polish. Sudden changes of plans played hell with your appearance.

"Okay, Miss Tiffany?" he asked again, a little impatiently.

"I suppose."

"Fine. Fine. Fine." He had his old glimmer back. He had liked telling jokes about two women together and various clerics and animals, back at the bar. Hope it gets me going, she thought.

His lone asset was cash. Credit cards, too. But cash was better.

"You go check us in. I'll wait here," she said.

He parked and went into the motel. She watched a family, three children, mother, and father, toting orange bags and a video camera, lumber into the motel. Probably been to one of the amusement parks nearby, maybe even traveled from Disneyland.

So many hopes had bloomed with Bobby. He had seemed so much better than anybody else.

Then he turned out to be so much worse.

She wondered at the strange confluence of forces that must have occurred at her birth to bring her and Bobby together like that. She wondered how the pattern had been set. She had no doubt that it had been or that it was even now unreeling before her.

Her new friend took her hand, squeezed it, pressed it to his side as he took her down the winding walkway to their room. She was alarmed again as they passed newspaper vending machines. On several front pages was her face, an old school picture, smiling, never realizing the part it would play in her dilemma years later. There was no recognition from the man who opened the room door, sighed loudly, and began slipping off his tie even as he held the door for her.

The snoring kept her alert.

Melanie lay still. Beached, belly-up, her friend lay beside her on the king-sized bed, all of its covers on the floor. His mouth was half-open. The bathroom lights were on, so was the TV, the sound way down. He insisted on having the TV picture as company.

She had made several irrevocable decisions. First off, she was going to stay as far away as possible from that little guy, Koenig, because his assurances had turned out to be worth absolutely nothing. At the first sign of trouble last night, he drove off and left her to face whoever was after her from Keegan or the cops. Money and safety he'd promised. She blew a quiet raspberry. It was dumb to believe him. She'd seen that eager, phony servility in other men. I should've listened to myself.

Her friend made an especially loud snore, and there was a long silence in the room. She glanced at him. Then he snored again, like an animal at peace. It must be about three or four in the morning, she thought, checking her wrecked nails critically.

She slipped naked out of bed, and went over to his clothes, thrown into a chair. No hangers for this guy. When he thought she wasn't looking, he'd put his wallet and keys into one shoe, then stowed it under a chair. Melanie shook her head. The ones who pretended to be smart were the easiest.

She put the money and keys in her dress.

"What're you doing, honey?" he asked murkily from the bed.

She grinned shyly. "Had to get up."

"Come on back."

"You get ready, I'll be right back."

She went into the bathroom.

"Don't lock the door," he said.

She sighed and sat down on the closed toilet seat. Her toenails were also ragged, she saw. She sighed again. She missed the people at the College of Beauty already. She was heartbroken, thinking about it now, that her time there had apparently come to such an abrupt end.

But if I testify against Bobby, all that publicity, all that attention. He'll get me.

She had hoped the trial might be delayed long enough for her to finish the course and leave the city. Then Keegan stepped in, and everything was suddenly in a white-hot spotlight, and she couldn't move. She wiggled her toes, pink against the black and white floor tiles. Ambition. Her father had it. Best trainer in the West. Best pal to a lot of rich horse-owners. His ambition had blinded him. Literally.

"I'm ready," her friend called out.

"Just a minute."

"Hurry up."

She turned on the sink faucet, watching the silver column of water.

Everything would have been fine without Keegan and his ambition to get reelected or made king or whatever he was doing this trial for. I never wanted to be in the papers, she thought sourly. She had never gotten used to the squalid feeling of being used, either by her father or men or Bobby or Keegan. She wasn't going to put up with it.

Melanie turned off the faucet.

"Come on, honey. What's going on? Do I have to come in there?"

She sprinkled some complimentary cologne on her face and neck, her breasts. One last time should keep him quiet.

She languidly opened the bathroom door, arms spread on each side of the frame. "I didn't know what I was getting into with you," she said.

He smiled at her, arms reaching out.

She walked toward him, a pout deepening on her face. "Oh. I thought you said you were ready."

Melanie drove along gray streets, the lights overhead white dots and the sunrise flushed behind the black squares of the buildings. She intended to leave the rented car someplace in a parking lot where it could rest for several days before being found. It was hard to tell what kind of story her friend back at the motel might use anyway. He didn't impress her as the type who would own up to the sort of theft he had just suffered.

One lesson she had learned from Bobby was never take any-thing close to where you lived or could be located. She had no ties to Anaheim, the man, or the motel. Without the car, she left no path to follow.

She pulled into an all-night restaurant. Eggs and spaghetti, chicken and fish, all you can eat. Blue awning over the front door. It was half-full with early birds.

She sat away from the door, after carefully picking only the most delicate pieces from the long stainless-steel food counter. She drank water and nibbled. Some she would wrap in a napkin.

She had a newspaper folded open to the day's horoscope. Out-side, she saw the sun top the buildings, black wires slashed across its yellow disk, more movement on the streets as people came out.

She read. Beware of long travel or any change of scene. Changes are going on and you need time to adjust. Good advice, she thought.

She knew exactly what would happen if she defied the warning and started to run in earnest. It was impossible to leave Los Angeles.

I'd get away for a while, she thought, far enough to think I'd be okay. She salted a chicken thigh and ate. But I'd be running right into Bobby. The farther I went, the more I'd think I'm getting away, the more I'd be running into him.

So her task was to stay clear of Bobby and Keegan and Koenig as long as her fate compelled her to remain in Los Angeles.

It can't be long, she thought pleadingly. Please. Please. She never prayed to a god but had a vague image of great gears and shafts moving inexorably. She didn't think it possible to slow them or stop them or influence them in any way.

She merely said *please.*

"Something wrong?" One of the few waitresses stopped at her table.

"Oh, no."

"You looked like something went down wrong. You want some water maybe?"

Melanie put on a modest smile. "Maybe I did take a big bite. It's all right. I'm going to tell my friends to come here."

SEVENTEEN

THE PRECEDING EVENING, as Melanie was settling in with her temporary companion, Keegan attended a long-scheduled fundraising dinner at the Beverly Hilton Hotel. By coincidence, Aguilar had also scheduled a dinner that night at the Beverly Wilshire Hotel. The conjunction of the two affairs gave the city's press the ability to intensely cover both easily and ask many questions about the mysterious conspiracy George Keegan declared was out to ruin his trial of a murderer. The night's twin campaign affairs were headlined as "Dueling Dinners" in many editions around the county the next morning.

In the dimmed banquet room, waiters artfully glided between tables lit by flickering candles. The large assembly of well-dressed people appeared more intimate in the candlelight.

"You all know the hardest thing for a political figure is to keep his mouth shut," Wylie Morganthau said with a grin. He spoke from a podium at the head table, the sharp, upthrust light giving him a Halloween grimace. "You can imagine how George feels tonight, not being able to say anything."

A gentle laugh spread across the room. Keegan, at the head table and beside Morganthau, smiled gamely.

"You know how much he'd like to talk about what he's been doing during the day. Especially today. But you also know he can't. So you'll have to put up with a bunch of people talking about him." Morganthau had warmed them up with jokes and a few mildly ribald cracks about Celia Aguilar's femininity. There were groans, a few hisses, and some chuckles.

"So you can look at George. There he is. You can talk to him. But you can't listen to him."

Morganthau, Keegan knew, had a good sense of timing. He paused.

"And it's for that privilege of blessed silence that you're paying five hundred dollars a couple." A burst of applause, and a drummer gave Morganthau the proper punctuation.

Keegan was tired after the long day, but even more, he was acutely conscious of the hungry eyes on him in the dimness. Since his charge in court, he had been pressed with questions and yells going to his office, driving into the hotel. Even as he entered the banquet room to a standing ovation.

What do they want, he wondered. He tried to see some particular face in the crowd. They all paid to be here, they all support me, they're working for me, and yet they want something from me. Leah hated fund-raisers most of all. At civic committee meetings or with people of her own group, the same schools, churches, businesses, she was at ease and charming. But at campaign rallies or fund-raisers like this, even in Beverly Hills, she was anxious, nervous. She was the girl who worried about saying something wrong or stepping on some sensibility by accident.

Until that moment, though, Keegan had prided himself in taking a robust pleasure at mixing and talking to any bunch of people. He recalled Leah angrily answering him back one night after a rally. "I'm not a snob," she said. "It's got nothing to do with thinking I'm better than them."

"It sounds the hell like it to me," he'd said.

"George, do you really notice how these people look at you?

When they shake your hand? Their eyes? Do you?"

"Oh, for Christ sake, they like meeting you, Lee."

"Oh, no. It's the way they stare. They're hungry."

"Oh, for Christ sake," he said and went out, and she had a drink from the bottle kept in the bedroom by that time in their lives.

But now, Keegan felt it. The hunger, the desire to ingest some part of him. Maybe the controversy over his courtroom accusation, perhaps the titillation of the murder trial itself. But even these sophisticated contributors wanted to engulf him in some way, possess him.

Not as grossly as the partygoers at Park's perhaps. But Los Angelenos were hungry and had to be fed. It was a diet of power and dreams of power and violence.

Morganthau said, "All right. A surprise for you all and for George, too. For the first time in this campaign, we're going to have the whole Keegan clan in one place. And you"—he pointed out into the banquet room—"lucky, wonderful friends of theirs, you get to show how much we love them all." He started clapping, and Keegan was startled to see Chris and Elaine enter from the left side of the head table, come to him, while the band played loudly. The room came to its feet, and there were cheers.

For a moment he was annoyed at the gimmick, but Chris stood straight beside him, mouthed hello against the noise, and Elaine took his hand.

It was not such a terrible deception after all, to bring them all together.

After everyone had finished eating, the evening broke into knots of people who expected him to stop by. The band added sprightly old tunes to the voices and laughter.

"Well, you've made your debut," Keegan said, alone with his children briefly, at one side of the room. "I'm very proud of you both."

"He thought you'd be mad." Elaine pointed at Chris.

"Why?"

Chris, in a blue blazer and gray slacks, was as tall as his father already, but thinner, serious. "You didn't want us around this time,

Dad. Last time, it was okay, with Mom, we all had our pictures taken, went to things like this."

"I'm not mad. I love having you both here."

Elaine looked at him curiously. "Really? I hardly see you at home."

"I wish I had more time."

Morganthau wandered over, embraced an unenthusiastic Chris and Elaine simultaneously. "Okay, George? They're a big hit. You don't mind I keep them out for some duty on a school night?"

Keegan shook his head. "Why does everybody think I'm going to have a fit because my kids are with me?"

Morganthau grinned. "You're the one always preaching. Keep them out of the campaign. But look, George. Everybody loves seeing them."

"It was a great idea, Wylie. Maybe we can raise a couple thousand more." The irony was inadvertent. "I didn't mean that," Keegan sighed. "It's been a long day."

"Hey. Don't stand around back here. Mix. Mix," Morganthau urged, darting off to jolly some older contributors.

"Spend the night at home, Chris. We'll get you back to school in the morning." Keegan said it casually, but the thought of them both with him filled him with calm. It was a calm he did not want to cultivate because he might never part with them again.

"Sure," Chris said, looking around the room. "Is somebody really trying to mess up your trial? A couple of my teachers think you made it up."

Elaine groaned. "Is that dumb?"

Keegan said grimly, "Tell your teachers to ask me, Chris. I'll straighten them out."

Chris grinned. "I'd like to watch."

They strolled onto the floor, and the lights came up so the recent diners were revealed, glasses in hand, well dressed and satisfied, the settled Westside money that gave to causes all over the world: starving children, polluted waterways, peace in the Middle East, park expansions, and also worked to make sure the Beverly Hills City Council had members who would keep streets clean, vagrants out, and the fountains lit at night. Keegan was one of them, first by marriage, and later by his actions.

Mrs. Helft tugged her husband, Alvin, into view. "George, it's good to see you all out again. I feel so good when I see your kids here." She wagged her head at Chris and Elaine.

Keegan said, "Thanks, El. How's the frozen fish business, Al?"

Mr. Helft, shoulders of his custom-made suit too wide as usual, shrugged. "Could be better. Chile's a son of a bitch right now. Nothing's coming through."

When Keegan turned a little to his right, Lorrie Noves was there, and he flushed, childishly, pleasantly. "Hello," he said. "This is a pleasure."

"I need to talk to you," she said.

Keegan realized the Helfts, his children, were silent and watchful. "Sure. Now? Not now. I've got to meet someone."

"Can we meet later?"

"Sure. Come by the house about ten. We'll all be up." He grinned, putting a possessive arm on his children. "My son and daughter. This is Mrs. Noves. She works for *Newsweek*."

Hands were shaken. Mrs. Helft said, "I read your magazine every week. Faithfully."

"She doesn't have any opinions until she does." Alvin Helft pulled her arm, and they walked off.

"Mrs. Noves is doing a story on the campaign," Keegan said, embarrassed at his impulse to keep explaining. The odd thing was that he didn't think he sounded embarrassed. In the months since Leah died, he didn't think he'd sounded as he felt more than once or twice.

"It's a pleasure meeting you both," Lorrie said. "I'm looking forward to seeing you later."

Keegan smiled again and walked into the crowd, felt hands patting him, heard the compliments. His son walked beside him. Elaine was waylaid by a group of older Keegan supporters.

"Can I tag along?" Chris asked.

"What?" Keegan realized his son was still there. "No. I've got to see someone by myself."

"I'd like to listen in. I'd like to learn how you do this."

Keegan shook his head. "I don't think you would, Chris."

"Don't you like it? I thought you liked things like this."

"Doing something and enjoying it are often two different things," Keegan said. "I'll see you later."

He walked on, toward an exit near high-hung curtains around the stage on which the head table sat. His campaign banners ruffled and moved slightly from the air-conditioning and the swaying bodies below.

He wondered what Lorrie needed to see him about. He also wondered why he treated his children so cavalierly in public when he wished to have them so close now.

And more, he wondered what this man Frank Goldsmith wanted to see him about so urgently.

Keegan met Conley at the hotel's rooftop exit.

"Is he here?" Keegan asked.

Conley nodded. "I put him out there myself, George. Like I told you, he's what he says. A movie producer. I think I even saw a couple things he did."

"No record or anything?"

"Nothing. I checked with friends in the business, and Goldsmith's a little bit of a joke now. He's got some friends, though." Conley rested his weight on one leg, the other halfway up a stair. It was cramped and dark in the exit's stairwell. "You think he has any information about her?"

"Win, right now I'd listen to Celia Aguilar if she knew where Melanie Vogt was." He smiled slightly. "Before you leave, make sure you get a drink downstairs. Wylie's paid for the bar."

Conley smiled back, his lined face easing a little from the strain of tending to Goldsmith, and trying to expiate his own mistake in letting a witness get away. "Thanks, George."

"For the moment, stay here and keep anyone off the roof. There are reporters all over the place."

Keegan walked up the stairs and out, sure that Conley would guard the roof zealously. It was a misshapen landscape, rude bumps and odd stacks from air-conditioning units and vents, a few bottles from old visitors lying around. Standing near a rumbling vent was a taut-faced, tanned, slender man in black.

He came to Keegan.

"I hate heights. Hate them. Look. Up here you can see the Y, Robinson's." He pointed at the YMCA across the street below them and the blocky shape of the department store. "Christ. It's making me dizzy." He raised his eyes to the coal-dark sky.

"I didn't want anybody to know we're meeting. It's hard to find places."

"Yeah, okay. I know. Okay. This sounds stupid, but I get dizzy looking at crane shots in movies. On the screen." He put his hands up.

"Where is Melanie Vogt?" Keegan asked.

"I can find her."

"You don't know where she is?"

Goldsmith frowned. "Maybe yes. Maybe no."

"If you know where she is now and you don't tell me," Keegan said, "I'll have you arrested."

"Me? Arrest me?"

"For obstructing justice and harboring a fugitive. I had a warrant issued for her this afternoon."

"I didn't know. All I hear is, you say some big plot's going on, keeping her hidden or something." A siren faintly whined below, and the traffic hum along Wilshire was dull, heavy. To Keegan's right, the placid streets of Beverly Hills, the homes expanding in size and opulence as the streets advanced northward, glimmered against the night. It was chill. Oil-scented.

"I charged her as an accomplice when she didn't appear," Keegan said. "I don't have a choice. I won't hesitate to charge you."

"Hey. No threats. I came to you, didn't I? Let me ask, anybody approached you about this story?"

"What story?" Keegan asked in irritation.

"This. The whole thing. We trade, okay? You agree to give

me an exclusive deal on the story, the trial, you doing it. I give you this woman."

Keegan was astonished but tried not to show it. He thought of Robinson's and shopping there with his mother and father, buying Chris's scouting gear when Desmond's in Westwood closed. He walked past Goldsmith, a blast of hot air from an air conditioner vent blowing across him.

He tried to hold on to his scattering thoughts. A roomful of friends downstairs, a faithful man guarding the stairs, my kids with me. He thought of them rather than the past or the unknown future. He wished again for Melanie's certainty about life.

"Okay? What do you say?" Goldsmith followed reluctantly, worried about moving on the roof's expanse.

"Why do you have any ability to find her?" Keegan stopped suddenly, bringing the other man to a sharp halt.

"I can. I have contacts. I have information about her from a very reliable person." He nodded as if to underline the point.

Keegan came up to him. I'm still in charge, he thought again. "You helped her get away," he said harshly. "You were driving a Mazda."

"What? Me? Mazda? Help her? You kidding? I don't want to help her go anywhere," Goldsmith said, hands flapping in the air. "I just want the rights to develop this story for TV. Maybe for a feature."

"Who's your information from?"

"That is a proprietary, trade secret. But it's good. Believe me."

"If you don't want to be arrested, produce her tomorrow, Mr. Goldsmith," Keegan said. It was a bluff in part. Keegan could not arrest the man on what he had at the moment. But bluffs often worked in politics. He saw no reason one shouldn't work here.

Goldsmith held his head. It was a comical gesture. Then he said, "I'm only talking about a business arrangement. There's nothing to arrest."

"I'm not joking."

Goldsmith stared, bit his lip. A long screech of tires on Wilshire floated up, and even Keegan felt depressingly cut off up here on the hotel's dark roof.

"I was hoping we could help each other. I don't have her," Goldsmith said.

"You have no idea where she is?"

"No."

"Mr. Goldsmith, maybe this kind of bullshit works in movies but it doesn't in the law. Don't screw with me. You can't afford it," Keegan said. He walked toward the stairwell door.

"Look, Mr. Keegan, I admire you. I want to vote for you. I can do a terrific story about this whole thing. Christ Almighty, we used to be practically neighbors, I used to live on Wetherly, you're over where, over there on Rexford." He pointed behind him.

At the stairs, Keegan said, "Stay up here for a couple of minutes. I don't want people connecting us. Don't try this again."

He tapped Conley, and they walked down the stairs. He heard Goldsmith cursing, a tin sound as something was kicked.

"Anything?" Conley asked.

Keegan shook his head. "He's a flake, Win. He's got nothing."

It had been a long time since Keegan recalled so much pleasant coming and going around the house.

He left the kids with Conley and took Lorrie into his study. She dropped her bag and looked at the crowded walls.

"You've got pictures with everybody," she said, studying the celebrities and politicians in the framed and signed photos.

"It's my rogues' gallery." He sat on the sofa, shoes off, tie off, waves of fatigue and nervousness rolling over him.

She turned. "I like your kids. Can I get some shots of them before I leave?"

"You're still leaving tomorrow?"

She nodded. "I'll try to come back for more of your case, the defense. Right now all you're going to be putting on are cops and doctors, right?"

He smiled. "Building a foundation for my star witness."

"Any more on her?"

He shook his head. "We're all looking. We've got investigators checking on the car, but it's an awfully big field."

"You've got a clock to run against."

"I gave myself a little room today by going public with the conspiracy charge. Not much room."

She sat down opposite him in a padded chair, legs out on the footstool. She looked at him.

"You're the one staring this time," he said. It pleased him.

"I'm debating."

"What about?"

"Something I might tell you." She shifted uneasily. Her hair was long, falling more to the right side, the slant-light of the chair's lamp highlighting her eyes and cheeks. She looked so young.

"Let me know when you decide," he said.

"I suppose I should," she sighed, obviously not happy with her decision. "I think your opposition has an idea who swiped your witness."

"Celia Aguilar? What do you mean?" Keegan got up.

"I was with her this morning, George." He noted the familiarity Lorrie used. "We saw the TV about your accusation. She . . ." Lorrie paused, struggling again. "She slipped, something about the people she knows not being able to tie their own shoes, much less engineer a thing like hiding a witness."

"I don't believe Celia would be involved," Keegan said. "I know she hates me, but she's always seemed honest."

"I don't think she had anything to do with it. I think she just knows who did. Or thinks she does."

"No names?"

Lorrie shook her head. "She got awfully formal after that."

"That is Celia," Keegan acknowledged. "Thanks for telling me."

"Well, you gave me the tip about losing the witness. I got some good material from people before doors started closing today. I beat a lot of people who were after the same thing."

He put out his hand and shook hers, then wouldn't let go. He was thinking of two things at once: who Aguilar knew who also hated him enough to tamper with a trial, and how much he wanted Lorrie Noves right at that moment.

"I get the point," she said, her hand pulling back slightly.

"Do you?"

"Oh, I think so."

He bent down and kissed her, his hand letting go of hers, resting first on her shoulder, then sliding to her breast. She moved only a little. He pressed harder and then she pushed back, lightly, then enough to break their lips and his touch of her body. He stepped back.

Pulling her legs off the footstool, she sat up straight. "This isn't my style," she said. "I mean it, George."

"I'm sorry. I think you're very beautiful." He paused, the desire melting away, replaced by a sadness he hadn't felt much before. It was inchoate, and he couldn't fix it on any person or thing. It seemed to lie, fatty and heavy, in the center of his chest.

"I know this isn't your style, either. Not from what I know about you."

"Have you ever cheated on your husband?" he asked, going to his desk. He had several small airline bottles of rum, tucked in a drawer after he and Leah came back from Barbados two years before. He brought them out, offered Lorrie one, she took it, and they sipped from the tiny bottles. The voices of Chris, Elaine, a loud laugh from Win Conley, carried into the room.

"That's an old-fashioned word," she answered finally. "Did you?"

"No."

"I only did twice," he said, finishing the little bottle. It was smooth and hot going down. "Both times I was out of the city. An ABA convention in Chicago. National District Attorneys College in Baltimore." He hadn't thought of those hasty, yet enjoyable nights in a long time.

"I don't think you want to tell me anything else."

"I can tell you anything I want to."

"George, I might have to use it sometime. It's my job."

"You won't use anything like this."

"Don't trust me," she said, putting down her little bottle, switching off the lamp beside her, her face going into shadow. "It's not personal. Look, I know you've had a hard day, a lot of hard days. I don't want to take advantage of you."

He laughed. "I got the impression that's what I was trying to do."

"I think you're very lonely."

"Do you? Let me tell a little story. From my childhood. I was about eight. Maybe nine, and I went to a boys' school back east in Connecticut. And one morning, with some of my friends, I went running through the halls, down through the basement. These two old German refugees sold candy to the boys. They cooked, too. Anyway, my friends and I went running through, and I scared the hell out of these sweet old people. I didn't mean to." Keegan grinned, and he wondered what she was thinking since he couldn't see her face. He listened to Chris arguing with Conley about some part of police work and was pleased his son wasn't intimidated. Like me, he thought.

He said, "My bad luck was the headmaster, Dr. Mead. We were all terrified of him. He was an old public-school type, very stern, very official, you didn't do anything less than your very best around him. Well, Dr. Mead caught me, and he wouldn't let me go."

"He hit you?"

"No. He put his arm around me. I tried to get away again, but he was pretty strong for an old man. He held me that way, and he walked me over to the two refugees, an old guy and his wife, and he made me apologize, and I did. Did I. And then, with his arm on me, Dr. Mead marched me up and down every hallway in the school. He stopped in every classroom and showed me off. And all the time, with me being dragged from place to place, he was singing 'Me and My Shadow.'"

"Sounds very embarrassing."

"It should have been. But I enjoyed it, Lorrie, I had a fine time," Keegan said. "I was the center of attention, and I knew it. I've lived the rest of my life just like that. Showing off. Being shown off."

"You're being too hard on yourself. I know you've accomplished a lot."

"I can't wait to read the story you're going to write."

She got up, and he opened the last little rum bottle and drank it. The liquor hit him hard after the anxieties of the day, and he didn't care that it did.

"If you want my own opinion . . ." she began.

"I'd love it."

"My own opinion is that you're still grieving. That's natural. You should take some time off with your family and get it together."

Keegan got up, restless suddenly. "What's the difference, you think, between grief and guilt?"

Lorrie frowned. "Grief is like being sad. When you lose someone you love. Guilt. I don't know. When you've done something you're sorry about."

"Or something you haven't done. In my church we talk about things done and undone. Left undone," he said. "What do you think about my wife's accident?"

"How do you mean?"

Keegan was blunt; he wanted some decisive statement from someone, and at that moment because he had desired her, he wanted it from this relative stranger. "Accident or suicide? You have an opinion?"

"The reports all say accident."

"You've talked to my friends, her friends. You've seen me. Would you like to add to the reports?"

He felt the sadness thickening, and Lorrie shook her head. She's upset, and she doesn't like being put on the spot. "Do you think your wife killed herself and you had something to do with it?"

"I wouldn't say that at all," Keegan replied.

"Neither would I. That really does make you the center of attention if you blame yourself for someone else's death."

"I certainly wouldn't want to blame myself," Keegan said. "Not at all." He put his hands in his pockets to keep from touching her again. He was lying over and over to her.

"Look, George, you are tired, you're keyed up. I did what I needed to do, telling you about Aguilar. I better go back to the hotel." She shouldered her bag and got up.

"Just a minute. Wait here for a minute? I have to do one small thing, and I've got something I need to say to you."

He spoke firmly, but there was a deeper, imploring sound to his words. He turned and left her, uncertainly standing in the study, the mute, false pictures of fame around her.

He followed the voices to the kitchen. Conley was at the stove, spooning reddish chili into bowls. At the table, Chris and Elaine bickered. Conley said, "Sure I boxed when I was a kid. It's good for your reflexes."

Keegan interrupted. "Win, first thing tomorrow, put your people on Aguilar's campaign manager, a couple of her top staffers, her husband. See if anyone uses a Mazda. Or's been doing anything odd lately."

"All right. Aguilar? Doesn't sound like the Celia I know."

Keegan was impatient. "Then check on Poulsby, Koenig, that bunch around the mayor. Maybe the commissioners I went after. Celia apparently knows who set up the Vogt escape."

Keegan heard the front door close and from the quiet street, an engine start, the sound fading as the car drew away. He knew the study was empty. He switched on a smile. "Everybody have a good time?"

Chris nodded, taking a hot bowl from Conley. "Yeah, Dad. Great. People were nice. There were so many of them."

Elaine rolled her eyes a little. "He was going nuts because everybody wanted to talk to us."

Keegan laughed, hearty, bluff. It even sounded authentic. "You've got a lot of friends, kids. They all liked seeing you tonight."

He sat down with them, eating some of Conley's special chili, which tasted flat and lumpy to him. Win had several war stories, and Keegan wondered why Chris was so interested in them, listening with hardly a comment, intent. He wondered, too, what kind of pattern was being laid down for his son at school, as his own had been set out, day after day not only at school but at home.

They talked a little about the lady reporter and how friendly she was, and Keegan said nothing.

He said good-night to Conley later, and by twelve-thirty, the house was quiet again.

Keegan moved in the silence. The palms outside rattled in the breeze, asking questions, making judgments he didn't want to hear. He went to his bedroom and carefully dug out every one of the photos he'd accumulated over the last months. Ersatz memories, vicarious bits of lives lived while he held them. And he took the photos and put them in the kitchen garbage. He did not want to have them around.

He opened the window over the sink in the darkened kitchen. The thin white curtains flapped, the moon loomed overhead.

I am a good father, he thought. I've seen my kids together tonight. They are turning out very well. I can raise them alone if I have to.

He walked to their rooms, continuing his inner pep talk. At Elaine's room, the door was still cracked open slightly. He glanced in. She was asleep, breathing quietly, the rock posters sliced into wedges by the hall light.

I am a good public servant. I am trying to do the best I can for the people who depend on me. The suffering ones. The weak ones. The injured ones.

He didn't open Chris's door. His son was a light sleeper, and the hinge creak would wake him. Keegan had nothing he could put into words to his son and so did not want to face him.

He sat down on his own bed, the lights off, the palms crackling outside as the wind rose. Lots of leaves, dried in the desert wind, would be littered across the lawn, the sidewalks, and streets. The place sucked everything out, leaving outward shells, forms of what had been.

He got the bottle he'd bought and left under the bathroom sink. He unwrapped the cap, and poured a little into a glass. He took the bottle to bed. He would drink only a little more, enough to sleep without thinking of how foolish and sad he must have appeared to that woman and how ashamed he was for showing himself that way.

There were terrible unanswered questions, he knew. And he

could not supply the answers, nor did he want to know them really. How had Leah died? What did their lives together mean? What did his mean now, as he struggled so hard to win again, and then to climb higher? He drank a little more, and still dressed as he had been at the fund-raiser, more or less, and later in the study with Lorrie, whom he desired and feared, he fell asleep on the bed, uncovered.

OCTOBER

EIGHTEEN

THEY BURNED THE FILES.

Keegan thought of it again and again as he presented his case against Carnes. One of the first things he learned when he became district attorney was that one of his predecessors had burned all of the office files up to 1960. The record of a raw, rich, rambunctious organization and the county it served went up in deliberate flames. Los Angeles was a city of five thousand when the files began, it was a city of millions when the files burned.

Into the smoky air went the smoke of interviews and statements, photographs, hates and hopes, the documentary evidence of corruption in city government, bribes to earlier district attorneys, murders not prosecuted, cases dismissed. Thousands upon thousands of brown and white files, actors and drugs, payoffs, unions bought, fighting in the thirties as the entertainment industry changed. Keegan imagined the records of the Sleepy Lagoon riots, uncounted ordinary robberies and burglaries, into the furnace one day, the column of smoke from all of that turbulent human drama floating mistily into the sky, unnoticed by the commuters on the freeways, drifting across the pastel bungalows and poinsettias until it became vapor and was gone.

No room, his chief deputy had explained when Keegan found out about the destruction. No storage space for so many old records.

Nothing had been spared.

It was, Keegan realized, an act of willfully cutting memory out. When living minds died, there would be no written or photographic contradictions left around. It was Los Angeles living for the moment in a grand way, desiring amnesia about anything ten minutes earlier.

At first, he was appalled at the waste of so much archival material. It could have been given to UCLA or USC or some scholar interested in the explosive growth of the city or movies.

But, Keegan decided that there was peace in deliberately forgetting so much, making it irretrievable.

No shame. No guilt. No remorse needed.

Absolution by fire.

Each new day was really new and could be faced with enthusiasm and aggressive confidence. In a way, as the trial went on, Keegan came to admire his predecessor's courage.

Burn the files. Burn the memory. Burn the evidence.

He could hope that one day, some future district attorney would do him the service of cremating the records of Carnes and the campaign; and the pain of Mrs. Harrold's letter, the pictures from the Marina del Rey house, would vanish into the hazy sunshine over the glittering city.

In the days after his last face-to-face meeting with Lorrie, after she returned to New York to work on her story, Keegan forged ahead. He put on blood-spatter experts to say that the victims all died at the same time. The experts thought two people had been in the room, but Goodoy made them admit it could have been three or one.

At breaks, back in his office, as the search for Melanie Vogt went on, Keegan wondered whether the upraised hand of Dr. Staggers on the billboard was a warning or a rebuke. It might be a greeting, but he could not piece out what the dead evangelist was saying to him.

In court, his demeanor didn't change, but he was worried and nervous as each day passed. His supply of witnesses was dwindling, and thus far he had been unable to put all of the actors on the same stage at the same time. It was a gaping hole, and Melanie Vogt was needed to close it.

An afternoon session was about to begin. Piled on the counsel table were files and reports, and when a particular document or bit of testimony was mentioned, Keegan had it at hand, passed to him by one or two ever-present assistants from Central Operations.

Carnes, he noted, no longer busied himself with note-taking or whispering to Goodoy or her assistants. He watched the witnesses with his arms on the counsel table, hands clasped. He rarely looked at the jury, and when he did, his doughy face was thoughtful, and Keegan sensed a complex analysis was going on.

"Are you going to move your examination a little more briskly this afternoon, Mr. Keegan?" Judge Ambrosini asked querulously.

"As fast as the evidence allows me, Your Honor. So the jury isn't missing anything."

"Oh, I don't think they miss a thing." The judge glanced at the jurors. "You are catching everything, aren't you, ladies and gentlemen?"

The jurors nodded. Ambrosini implied he sympathized with how much they had to put up with.

Another Los Angeles Police Department detective sat on the witness stand. The exhibits crowding the witness stand had grown, as if alive themselves. Diagrams of the house at 3417 Canterbury Way, large photos of the death room, the neighborhood, were on easels by the jury box or on the wall. Piles of the victims' clothing, tagged and returned to their plastic bags, were laid neatly on the clerk's desk. The courtroom had a few empty seats finally, but very few.

Keegan held a small black notebook in one hand.

"Detective Dowden, were you assigned to do any investigation at 3417 Canterbury Way on May twenty-fourth?"

"The twenty-fourth?" the very fair, tanned detective asked.

Keegan put his hand up. "I'm sorry. I meant May fourteenth." He could not permit slips like that. The camera still watched and pitilessly carried his actions around the county.

Dowden nodded. Even though he was a young man, he had spent a lot of time before juries since he had been assigned to Narcotics. He was direct and believable. "Yes, I was part of the investigation."

"What was your specific part?"

"To locate physical evidence. To note its location and remove it."

"Did you do that?"

"Yes. I removed a lot of evidence from the house."

"Were the victims still at the scene?"

Dowden shook his head. Several of the women jurors watched him with more than usual attention. He looked like a Venice Beach fitness fanatic. "No. The bodies had already been removed."

Evidence removed. Bodies removed. Equivalent material without humanity. Keegan's problem was still trying to make the dead Rotich family come alive for the jurors. The detective didn't help by equating their corpses with other evidence.

"Where did you begin your evidence search?"

Dowden twisted to look at the chart of the house, each room a large green-shaded square or rectangle, posted on an easel beside him. "I started with the front room." He got up, using a blue felt-tip pen to mark the rooms. "It's a living room. I found several kinds of stereo equipment, TVs and three stereos. I tagged them."

"What do you mean, tagged?"

"Well, when you locate a piece of evidence, you put little tags on it, just a plain white tag. You put your name and badge number, and you put the date."

Keegan nodded. Very thorough and professional. He said, "Did you do that with every piece of evidence you found that day?"

Dowden also nodded, pen in hand. "We all did. I was with four other detectives, and we followed the same routine."

Goodoy raised a tentative hand. "I have an objection, Your Honor."

Ambrosini said, "You're never shy, Mrs. Goodoy."

She got up, frowning as if in deep confusion. "I think I missed the question about the equipment in the living room. Why did the detective think it was evidence anyway?"

Keegan thought she had nicely done that. He had tried to lead the jury from the point, but Goodoy forced him back.

"I can clear that up," Keegan said to the judge. No gain in hiding it now.

"Go ahead then."

Keegan stood up and came toward Dowden. "Why did you tag the TVs and stereos?"

"I thought they might be stolen property."

"Did you find out if they were?"

Dowden nodded. "Yes, sir. They came from a burglary in Compton in late February."

Goodoy smiled at the jury. See? These dead drug dealers were thieves as well.

Keegan decided to make his own point forcefully. He put the black notebook in front of Dowden. "Do you recognize this?"

"Yes, I do. It's a notebook I found in the rear room. Where the bodies were located. It was located on top of a metal cabinet."

"Your name, badge number, and initials appear on the notebook?"

Dowden opened it, displaying it for the jury. "On the front cover. I put them there and I logged it into evidence later on May fourteenth."

Carnes gently nudged Goodoy and she whispered to him. I'm sure he's fascinated by the notebook, Keegan thought.

"Why did you seize this particular item, Detective Dowden?"

Dowden folded his arms. "Well, it came from the crime scene itself. It looked like a diary or record. I could see narcotic paraphernalia and what looked like possible narcotics in the room."

Keegan looked at the jury. "So this might help you discover who killed the victims?"

Before Dowden answered, the judge gurgled and inhaled disapprovingly. "Mrs. Goodoy, are you satisfied with this line of questioning?"

"Oh, yes, Your Honor. I will agree Detective; Dowden is very qualified to testify about drug use and drug equipment."

Keegan was grim. Ambrosini thought I was getting away with something, letting the witness mention drugs. Goodoy doesn't want this witness to talk about anything but drugs.

Dead drug dealers who probably got what they deserved. From someone. Not her client, of course, Keegan thought.

Keegan wanted to move along swiftly to get away from this area. "Did you find any suspected drugs in the rear room?"

Dowden nodded. "On the desk I observed scales and a small bag of what looked like white powder. I seized all those items."

"Was the powder analyzed later?" Keegan made it sound routine, of no significance.

"Yes, sir. The bag contained thirty-four grams of methamphetamine."

The jury was quiet, taking in the sober accounting of drugs and death, like an inventory. Reporters in the first two rows of the courtroom, uncomfortable on their benches, made notes about how the jury looked or the spectators acted or how Keegan brusquely put his hand out for papers from an assistant. He had been unable to provide any more information about a plot to spirit his witness away and was looked on now as fairly untrustworthy. News accounts tended to emphasize how few points he made in court, according to the reporters' evaluation of the evidence.

Keegan plowed on, knowing his performance was being graded poorly. He had the notebook marked for identification and gave it back to Dowden.

"What does this item, now marked People's Sixty-seven, appear to be, Detective?"

Dowden held it like a missal, in both hands. "I examined it, sir. Based on my experience in narcotics, I thought it was a record of drug sales, transactions."

"Thank you," Keegan said. The worst part now was laying the victims' business before the jury. I'll have to work up some sympathy later, he thought. Move over this rough spot first.

"Please look at the entry for May fourteen," Keegan said. "What does it indicate?"

Goodoy stayed in her seat, despite the puzzled glares from the judge. She wasn't about to interrupt Keegan's blackening of his own victims.

"On that page"—Dowden stared, struggling with the script—"it seems to say, 'Ferrera. Eleven a. Elko. Speed.'"

"Speed is what, Detective?"

"It's one of the street names for methamphetamine."

Keegan impatiently motioned for another page from his assistant, who, flustered, handed it to him. "I have a stipulation, Your Honor. Both Ms. Goodoy and I will stipulate that the handwriting in People's Sixty-seven is that of the victim, Barry Rotich."

"Mrs. Goodoy?" asked the judge.

"Yes. So stipulated, Your Honor." She half-rose, a curtsy to the bench.

Ambrosini turned to the jury. He scowled at them as if angry.

"Ladies and gentlemen, both parties have entered into a stipulation. It means they have agreed the fact stipulated to has been proven. You are to treat such a fact as evidence."

"Nothing further," Keegan said. His aim was to link Carnes with Ferrera as often as possible, and at least the notebook put Ferrera in the right place at the right time. The problem was adding Carnes.

He braced for what Goodoy would do.

She came near Dowden, almost hesitantly. "You read through all of this notebook?"

He nodded. "I did."

"The names Carnes or Robert Carnes or Bobby don't appear anywhere in it, do they?"

"I don't recall."

"They don't, do they?" she persisted.

"I don't believe so."

"Only the name Ferrera appears, isn't that true?"

Dowden, who obviously disliked saying anything that might help the defense, looked over Goodoy's head, off into the court-room's middle distance. "Yes, it does. There are other names."

"But none that involve this case, isn't that true?"

Keegan frowned and whispered to his assistant that if she said "isn't it true" again, he'd gag. He sat back trying to bear with the damaging testimony.

"I believe that's true."

Goodoy nodded. She sighed. "Detective, I want to ask you a question based on your experience. How long were you a narcotics officer?"

"Four years."

"During that time, if you found people shot, and you found some drugs, in packages, and scales and records of drug sales, what would you think had happened?"

Keegan said, "I object, Your Honor. Detective Dowden is a fine officer, but he can't speculate what happened. He wasn't there."

"But, Your Honor," Goodoy said in amazement, mocking Keegan. "The district attorney put him on as an expert in narcotics. I can ask a hypothetical question based on his years of experience." She smoothed a corner of her lace collar.

Keegan argued, at least so the jury would realize that no mat-ter how infamous the activities of Rotich and his wife, they did not deserve to die, nor did a child. Goodoy's trial strategy was common, sensible, and effective. To the extent a jury of ordinary people decided the victims were criminals themselves, the harder it became for them to vote for a first-degree murder conviction against Carnes. He thought again of the burning files. Crimes gone into the atmosphere and forgotten. We all want to forget pain we've caused others. We all want to let responsibility slip away like smoke.

Keegan did not blame the jury. He understood the desire for that kind of blithe forgetfulness in himself. I may have caused a death by inattention or callousness or ambition.

Carnes smiled, the reporters were writing, and Keegan and

WILLIAM P. WOOD

Goodoy stood arguing before Ambrosini, who finally said loudly, "Well, Mr. Keegan, you did bring forth this witness as an expert, didn't you? That's what I understood. That's what the jury understood, I'm sure." He gestured at the jurors.

You just made damn sure they did, Keegan swore inwardly.

"You may go ahead, Mrs. Goodoy. Objection is overruled."

Dowden, when bidden by Ambrosini, said, reluctantly, "If that's what I had, I'd probably think a drug deal had gone bad." He crossed his legs and stared at a crease in his gray slacks.

"A drug deal gone bad," Goodoy repeated.

"Yes," he repeated unenthusiastically.

"And based on your years of experience in narcotics, was the home at 3417 Canterbury Way consistent with what you've seen in other drug dealers' homes?"

Keegan waved Dowden's frown down to reassure him. "Objection again, Your Honor. Vague. Vague."

"Sustained," the judge agreed quickly.

Goodoy nodded her head as if she, too, agreed that the question was too far beyond normal understanding. Keegan simply wanted to end this witness. It was highly unpleasant having to sit and listen to his victims savaged and not be able to really counteract the attack.

Remember they were people like us, just like us in more ways than they were different, he wanted to say to the jurors.

Goodoy closed in for a high finish of her examination. She put a hand toward Dowden. "Detective, when you read the name Ferrera just now in court, you knew he'd been charged with these murders at one time, didn't you?"

Keegan was on his feet, his pent-up anger showing. "I object. There's no relevance to that question. She knows it."

"Well, Your Honor, his office obviously saw the point if they charged Lee Ferrera with three murders," Goodoy began.

Carnes raptly watched her.

Ambrosini hit his open palm on the bench. His thin-lipped face was stony. "No comments, Mrs. Goodoy. No argument." He barked to the startled jurors, "You are to disregard the comments of counsel. I continually warn them, but you see the result. Comments of counsel are not evidence. The jury is not to speculate about the answers to questions or comments to which an objection is sustained." To the reporter he snapped, "Sustained, Mr. Keegan. We'll be in recess for fifteen minutes."

Keegan rose as the jury slowly filed out, the courtroom murmuring and alive with the last, abrasive moments of the witness's appearance.

Goodoy and Carnes put their heads together, the deputy sheriffs hovering close. Keegan wiped his damp forehead. He wondered what all the effort was for when the records would be burned soon and in five or fifty years it wouldn't matter at all what was happening today in this courtroom to these people.

Or to me, he thought. When I'm nothing more than another picture on the wall in the DA's office, will any of this mean more than those other lost files, spectral passions drifting among the ozone and particles of the basin's filthy air?

NINETEEN

THE WILD PARROTS OF WEST Los Angeles, refugees from homes that no longer wanted them, flew in massed colors in the night, shouting and shrieking over the sound stages and partygoers at Twentieth-Century on Pico Boulevard. Frank Goldsmith raised his head at the odd sound and drank deeply again from his never-empty plastic cup of warmish champagne. He loved the movie business. He loved movies. He loved wrap parties.

Around the end of the Western street, just off the high-rise tenements and ads and wildly strung false phone lines of early-1900s New York, a buffet table decked out with moose-antler candelabra and red cloth accommodated actors and the crew of a TV movie recently finished shooting.

"You know why I love movies?" Goldsmith said slowly, dreamily, to the burly construction foreman standing beside him.

"You like the retirement bennies?" Cheese and cracker bits dotted his blue T-shirt.

"Who retires? You just stop." Goldsmith indulgently watched the young crew members chasing each other, a young woman trying to drop some food down a man's shirt. "What's so fucking great about movies is you can change anything. Change everything." He nodded. "Someone dies one day. You look at the dailies and it looks rotten, so you go back and reshoot, and the guy's alive this time. Or you got a woman. You edit things one way, she's stupid, she's a joke. You edit another way, she's beautiful, great in bed, smart. One way she's the center of your life. Next time she's a bit part, walks on"—he wiggled his hand in the air like a swimming fish—"walks off."

"I worked for a guy, first picture," said the foreman, "he shot everything four ways. Four, Frank. So he's covered."

"Tell me life wouldn't be better, I mean, just one hundred fifty percent better if you could get four different takes on anything. Shit." Goldsmith shook his head. "You'd always get the woman you wanted. Marry her. Have a family. Don't marry her. Whatever. You'd have the greatest job in the world. You'd make gross-profit deals every time, and you'd win every award."

"Life ain't like that, I have to tell you."

"It sure as hell ain't. You don't have to tell me. One take. One setup. Story's over. You're over." He was suddenly depressed in the middle of the merrymaking.

"That's the way it is, compadre."

"Okay. So life isn't movies. That does not mean I've got to take every shitty thing that happens. I can still make some things happen," Goldsmith vowed, head going up and down, a little of the champagne falling into the street's dust, making little black spots.

From several honey wagons, the trailers where the actors were dressed and refreshed during a shoot, people whooped in, jumped out, yowling and slipping to the ground. Goldsmith smiled lovingly at it all. It was the exuberance of an after-game party, football on Saturday, which he had been denied as a young man and found here among his industrious colleagues.

"You got something coming up, Frank?" asked the foreman. "I'm open right now."

"I got a few projects cooking." Say too much and people would steal. It was the way of the business.

He ambled over to a buffet table. He loved listening to actors talking seriously.

"London School of Acting," one woman said to a man holding a prawn by its tail. "We did baroque dancing, you know, gavottes, gigues."

"We did improvs." He stared at her intensely.

"You know when my character goes into the saloon?"

"At the end?"

"Right. The last stuff we did. I used the movement, the dancing stuff, getting the right balance." She sipped her champagne and watched him chew the prawn.

"I noticed," said the prawn-chewer, staring. "Very natural. Great look."

Goldsmith got his own plate and dropped prawns and some dark vegetables on it, had roast beef sliced, filled his glass. He chatted with everybody. His worries about the Carnes project were distant here, even though he'd had little luck finding Melanie Vogt, nailing down Keegan, or advancing the project much more. Here he knew things would be all right. The luck of things was with him, here among the busy, the prosperous, the successful. It was the luck of the draw, life in Los Angeles, which could end in a moment's great earthquake or soar with a deal. It was a hustle and a con game, without permanence or certainty, and Goldsmith was at home.

He noticed the sadly smiling older man suddenly at his side. "You following me?" he asked.

"Nope."

"Nope. Right. You just show up here?"

Win Conley nodded. "The transportation captain's an old pal, so he said to come over."

"You're not following me?" Goldsmith nibbled a little roast beef. He noticed again how Keegan's sidekick had the same stiff formality, the uprightness of Gary Cooper, Tracy, maybe an older Harrison Ford. "You ever play a cop?"

Conley shook his head, smiling that sad, old smile. "I was a cop."

"You could play cops or sheriffs."

"Well, right now what I want to do is find Melanie Vogt."

"Who doesn't?"

Conley leaned toward Goldsmith, who noted the old-style hair oil smell and too much coffee. "Time's running out to find her. You watching the trial?"

"A little. I mean, it's getting old. Keegan's got to come up with something pretty fucking fast, right? I mean, everybody's going, Okay, okay, so there's a conspiracy, so your witness's missing. So show us something." Goldsmith grinned. "Entertain us."

The old marshal, because he looked that way to Goldsmith, stopped smiling. Suddenly, Goldsmith didn't like him, the expression he saw was very hard. Reflexively, Goldsmith checked around. People everywhere, somebody would help him if this old guy started anything.

Conley said, "We used to do a lot of bad things in the bad old days."

"Great line."

"So if you find Melanie, you call me. Don't screw around, Mr. Goldsmith. I've been around a long time. I don't care if I don't stay around a lot longer."

"Right." Goldsmith cocked a finger, gunlike, at him. It was hard to take seriously.

"I mean it," Conley said. "Here's my card. Maybe we can talk about the movie business sometime, too."

"Right," Goldsmith said again. Keep him jolly, that's the ticket. He went on smiling as the old guy strolled off, mixing into a clot of people roiling around the saloon set. Just like the marshal, Goldsmith thought fuzzily from the champagne.

There was a crash. The buffet table and red cloth were on the ground, three people squirming over it. A circle of boisterous chanters formed, urging on whatever was happening.

"Hey, Frank. This's over, man. They're getting rowdy." The burly foreman swayed. "Buffet looked like it was left over from Liberace's funeral."

"Yeah, it is over." Goldsmith dropped his half-eaten plate of food to the dusty ground.

"I got a chick we can check out." He made thrusting move-
ments with his hips. "Let's go now."

"What chick? Who? What?"

"This hooker. Melanie. You know. I told you." Goldsmith did
not recall ever hearing the name except from Carnes or Keegan or
the old cop. He tried to clear his mind. "You know where she is?"
The luck of Los Angeles, ever-changing, quixotic, invigorating.

"I'm parked right outside. Let's get out of here."

After an elaborate exit from the Twentieth lot, making certain no
cars were following, especially ones driven by Gary Cooper, Goldsmith had his pal drive east on Pico, then up to Beverly Boulevard.

"Who you looking for?" the foreman asked, seeing Goldsmith frequently putting his head out the window. "Someone
following us?"

"I do not believe so," he answered slowly.

"I don't do any stunts anymore, Frank. Fucked up my shoulder last time."

To distract himself and Tommy, the foreman, Goldsmith
started talking about old actors. "I sent Lawrence out on a job.
He's doing a party of World War II vets, wives, kids, everybody."
The car spun through the city's night streets as though its wheels
didn't touch the asphalt. "The guy who single-handedly destroyed
the Japs."

"He was the oldest private in that Iwo Jima picture."

Goldsmith nodded. "So all he's got to do this time is be there.
These vets just want to see him. Bring back memories. So what happens? Lawrence is still doing some kind of cocktail with, you know,
formaldehyde and grain alcohol. His back, he always tells me."

"My shoulder. Legit," said Tommy defensively, afraid he'd be
accused of deadening pain in some unacceptable way.

"Well, *his* back. He fell off some rock on Catalina doing a
Bataan movie or something. So he shows up for me at this party,
he's falling out of his chair, he's falling into people, he's falling on

the floor. Then. Then"—Goldsmith grew irate, recalling the fury of the host who had paid seven hundred dollars to have the actor at the affair—"he stands up, calls everybody names, falls over with a heart attack."

"He get up?"

"He's dead. He didn't get up." Goldsmith was triumphant. "Like God punished him."

They parked in front of the courtyard apartments. Maybe it wasn't the same Melanie, the hooker, he thought. No. Had to be, he thought again, as they weaved toward the apartments. Then be a guy in charge. He straightened up. This is your shot.

Tommy, though, was unsure of the apartment number, so they wandered around in the dark for a while, knocking on several doors. On door number four, a young woman, pink slippers on her feet, violet-eyed, answered. Goldsmith knew her instantly from the picture Carnes had given him.

"You're going to be in the movies," he said, aiming his finger at her like a pistol, just as he had at the old cop.

"How does she look?" Carnes asked gently the next day.

"Great. She's not fantastic, no offense. But okay."

"I meant, is she all right? Doing any drugs? Anybody living with her?"

"Nobody there. I didn't see any shit, either." Goldsmith hung his head a little, then lower to his knees as he sat on the chair in the jail visitors' room. Champagne was the worst pain in the morning, and wrap-party champagne was the cheapest and the worst of all. "Man," he said carefully, "what a head."

"You didn't mention me? Knowing me?"

Goldsmith put up one hand weakly. "Hell, no. I'm making an independent movie for TV production. She was very interested."

"Melanie's an ambitious person."

"How's Larson?" Goldsmith asked softly, pointing at Kaplow,

who sat apart from them in a chair at the other side of the room, back facing them. A clump of Kaplow's hair seemed to be missing from the back of his head. Goldsmith had the disturbing idea Larson was pulling his own hair out.

"Larson's not feeling too well. He wanted to see you, though."

Two sweet champagne-scented drops of sweat rolled down Goldsmith's cheeks. "What's wrong with him?" he whispered to Carnes.

"I don't think Larson's taking his medication anymore."

"Shit." Goldsmith half-rose in alarm.

"I'm kidding," Carnes said. "Larson? Can you say hello to Frank?"

Kaplow reluctantly turned in his chair. He waved. "How's my show?" His heart didn't seem to be in the question.

"On track. Moving along. We need some more okays from upstairs," Goldsmith said. "Nobody makes decisions at the networks now."

Kaplow nodded without much interest. Goldsmith wondered why his yearning for a deal had fallen so low. Kaplow furiously scratched at the bald patch on his head.

"He's not okay," Goldsmith said to Carnes. "I mean, I can see that. Is it safe here with him?"

Carnes looked resigned. "He's a little depressed. He's getting moved to San Quentin soon." Lower voice, "Death Row."

Goldsmith swallowed. There was something terribly real about a man no more than fifteen feet from you about to end up on Death Row. It had a tangibility that few things he could recall ever did. It seemed very mortal and very final.

Carnes brightened a little, sitting up. "Did Melanie talk about me?"

"Sure. I say, Sure, honey. I'll be in touch with Mr. Carnes. After the trial. After there's a verdict. After it's all settled." His hangover throbbed in the barred, airless, doom-laden room.

"She asked for your sign. She always does."

"She did some horoscope shit. I don't know. I didn't pay attention."

"You're not telling me everything, Frank."

Goldsmith nodded slowly. "Well. She says she's staying out of sight. Because of you."

"Me?"

"She thinks you'll hurt her."

Carnes shook his head in denial. In his jumpsuit, wristbanded and slightly redolent of the jail's cologne of ammonia, cigarette smoke, and old food smells, he seemed out of place to Goldsmith. Like a squinty, pudgy clerk got lost somehow.

"I loved her," Carnes said. Goldsmith believed him.

"Well, she's scared. She knows everybody in the city's looking for her. She's like something in an old TV show, woman on the run. She was very suspicious of me, let me tell you." Goldsmith recovered some of his usual confidence that had been driven out by the hangover and the condemned man near him. "So I had to give her a pretty fucking good pitch, Bobby. But, let's face it, scared or not, running or not, she's like everybody in LA."

"How so?"

"She wants to be in the movies."

"I didn't think she did." Carnes frowned. "How did you find her? I'm interested why she hasn't left the city."

Goldsmith shook his head. "Let's say I found her and leave it. Trade secret, okay? Now, why she's hanging around here, the cops, the DA, everybody trying to find her." Goldsmith shrugged. "Best I got was she says it's not right for her to move yet."

Carnes nodded. "I understand. It's in her stars."

"I'm going to see her again pretty fucking soon, nail all this down, as much as I got." Goldsmith didn't like Keegan's truculent dismissal the other night. "Then we'll see where we can go with it."

"The DA's screwed with her," Carnes said. "This trial's going to fold up."

"For your sake, Bobby, I hope so. Really I do," Goldsmith pledged with sincerity. "But, I can't tell you where she is. You understand."

"I wouldn't expect you to."

"I appreciate your trust." Goldsmith was going to talk about the deal specifics, something he and Carnes had not quite mapped out, when Larson Kaplow began crying loudly.

"They're taking me away," Kaplow said, twisting his hair.

Goldsmith was out of his chair. "Jesus."

Carnes went over, put his arm around Kaplow's trembling shoulders. The weeping grew more wretched. It hurt Goldsmith's head.

"I think I better go," he said.

"I think so, Frank," Carnes said.

Goldsmith buzzed for the deputy sheriff and was escorted out, hastily putting distance between himself and the unalterable fate behind him.

Carnes, three deputies, and the crying Kaplow went to the main cells. All the way, Carnes, who was acknowledged to be a calming influence on Kaplow by the jail authorities, talked quietly and emphatically to him.

"Remember what we talked about, Larson? Remember how that's going to help us both?"

Miserable, Larson Kaplow nodded, shuffling down the gray-walled corridors, inmates staring at him.

"Don't forget. I'll tell you when and how, very soon." Carnes became cheery. "I'll tell you how beautiful my lawyer looks in court."

Two of the deputies guarding the prisoners thought Carnes was actually singing softly. Perhaps it was merely humming. In any event, it soothed Kaplow, whose tears stopped presently.

In his office, Keegan had several sets of phones. The white one, beside the sofa, was a private line, and he chose it.

"Is this a bad time?" he asked when Lorrie Noves answered.

"No. I'm working late. I guess you are, too. What is it, six, your time?"

Keegan glanced out at the red-dotted skyline of the city and the formless blackness of the ocean after it. "Yes. Seven. I thought I'd see how your story's coming."

He paused, hearing her say something to someone else in the office in New York. Who? He waited impatiently for her, wanting to hear her.

"George, is this on the record?"

"Off," he sighed. It was professional.

"Just a friendly call," Lorrie said. "I can tell you that I'm working on a rewrite. The first drafts went through our senior editors, and they liked it. Is there anything new in the trial I could use?"

Yes. Very professional, he thought sadly. "We still haven't found my witness. But there are some promising leads on her." He rubbed his eyes. He felt like he was talking to a doctor or a tape recorder, not the woman he would have made love to if she had shown the smallest interest. "I've put on a lot of documentary evidence showing that Carnes and Ferrera were together in LA on May fourteenth, airline tickets, receipts for the bags they sent back to Nevada. The problem is that a lot of it is in Ferrera's name."

"Carnes was smart. Is there any chance you're going to lose?"

No beating around the bush, he thought. "Anything can happen in a trial. I remember that much from when I used to go to court all the time, and my senior deputies remind me all the time."

Say something, Lorrie. A kind word about anything, and I can make it personal. He knew how gruff and impersonal he sounded on the phone now. She must think I'm calling to find out about the slant on her story.

"How about the campaign? How's that coming? I've kept up on the polls anyway."

Keegan nodded, alone in his brightly lit office, tie loose, vast desk cluttered. "Aguilar and I are running even. Well, I don't regret taking this case. No matter what happens."

"Good for you."

"I appreciate that."

"Your kids are all right? I wish I'd had a chance to spend more time talking to them. They're very nice."

"I don't get a chance to see them much. Chris especially. He's at school during the week, sometimes all week. Elaine and I are like tenants. I see Innocencia more."

"I'm sorry, George. I know you care for them."

"There just isn't time for everything."

"No, I understand." It was perfunctory, almost as if she didn't want to allow any opening for personal talk.

"You're fine?" He couldn't break past the easy, practiced falsity of a politician's inquiry.

"Busy. Very busy right now. My daughter's got a birthday party tomorrow so I'm working late to take some time off. I'm the designated chauffeur for eight little girls."

He wondered if that was critical of him for being so absent from his children. "You do have your hands full. I won't keep you. I was interested in hearing from you. Are you going to get back here anytime soon?"

"Maybe. Before the election. I might, to satisfy my personal curiosity."

"I'd like to show you around."

"We'll definitely do that."

"Well, good night. Good luck tomorrow."

She laughed and hung up. Keegan sat on the sofa for some time, then got up and went to his desk. He used an old technique, honed after years of public service, of blocking everything from his mind except the work at hand. Witnesses for tomorrow. Reports, all inconclusive, on the mysterious Mazda.

He was able to sustain that concentration for about ten minutes, and then, his eyes softened, and he sat back. The sparkling city glittered outside, and he wondered about all the choices, made and avoided, that had finally brought him to this moment.

TWENTY

"LET ME TAKE YOU TO LUNCH," Frank Goldsmith offered, he thought, with some gallantry.

Melanie finished reading the agreement he'd brought, explaining how her rights to the story would be used, how she would be consulted during the writing of the teleplay. They were in her apartment, and the TV was on, sound off, a clip from the morning session of the trial running. She saw Carnes led in, saw Keegan standing, saw a young cop on the witness stand.

Melanie was unhappy. "I don't get to play myself?"

"Nobody does."

"I seen some."

"Well, look, honey, this makes an easier sale. The networks, they get to pick somebody they like." Goldsmith smiled warmly. He had been working on her for nearly thirty minutes. "How about lunch, kind of ease things along?"

"I don't know if I can sign this today."

He sighed. Just as Carnes warned him. "The stars aren't right or something?"

She shook the paper as if it were wet. "Legal affairs are not great today. Later this week." She held out the paper.

He took it. He wished he knew more about her, some angle to make her sign now. Another thought occurred to him. "Anybody else talking to you?" he asked suspiciously. "You getting offers? Because I've got enough story rights here, I'm going to make the best deal."

Melanie shook her head and got an orange soda. She had the windows open, and jackhammers down the street filled the room. Over the silent TV, radio music from the kitchen bubbled loudly. She bobbed her head to the beat. "Nope. Only one I talked to is Danuta at the school."

"Which is how I found you. She talked to my carpenter buddy."

Melanie frowned. "She got excited when she found out he was in the movies."

"Everybody does. The thing here is, honey, from now on, you don't talk to people like that, okay? Come to me. Talk to me, you have a problem or a question or you just, just"—he smiled—"want to talk. I love talking."

He idly poked around the room as he worked on her. He picked the habit up to get the lay of the land, how his audience thought and reacted. Goldsmith noted and cataloged at actors' homes, producers' parties, anywhere he went. Melanie was strictly tabloid, things from Kmart like the silvery lamp with its plastic cover still on. Nail polish in five small, bright bottles on the cracked coffee table.

She took her robe off and started dressing. Her clothes were heaped in a chair, and she plucked among them with sure intent, utterly oblivious to his stare.

"I keep in pretty good shape," she said.

"Jesus. Yes," he said.

"We're in business. That's all. No fucking."

"None?"

"I've learned," she said, straightening a sandal, "that fucking and keeping a clear head don't mix. Bobby showed me that." She grimaced at the TV, where Carnes was shown sitting attentively. She snapped it off. "I had this whole big dream, he was okay, everything was okay. But it wasn't." She sighed. "Not a bit."

They went to lunch at a Mexican restaurant, where Melanie ordered everything in clumsy Spanish. Beverly Hills Spanish, Goldsmith called it, the kind of half-phrases people learned so they could talk a little to their maids. Melanie said, "I picked it up from guys around where I worked a while ago."

Goldsmith hoped the waiter didn't get it all wrong. At lunch, he could see what Carnes liked about her. She was obvious, no byways or hidden roads. She seemed to talk right at you, and if it was an act, Goldsmith judged her one of the best he'd seen.

They had a very pleasant lunch, drank several beers apiece, and Goldsmith began to think there was another aspect to this whole trial story. The story of a young woman who started as a hooker and ends up . . . Where? He didn't have that part yet.

"Melanie." He took her small hand on the way back to her apartment. "I want you to tell me everything, open it all up, nothing you can't tell me."

And she narrated the whole time with Carnes. When she described the trips with Carnes, the two of them alone, her face was fresh, happy. She really did love him, he realized, and thought this little hard-edged angel was one of the loneliest people he had ever met.

He would have gently urged her to the bed in her apartment except that when she opened the door, the bed had been dragged into the center of the room and upended.

"Oh, my," she said almost primly.

Goldsmith stared nervously at the wreckage. TV shattered and stacked with the broken bed, clothes strewn around, even the carpet torn in a few places. "You got robbed. At fucking lunch, you got robbed. What can I do?" He saw himself transformed into her protector suddenly, sheltering her at his hotel.

Melanie put a finger to her lip, closed her eyes, and looked around again. "I want to get out of here," she said with utter firmness.

"No question. Get some clothes, whatever you need," he

said. His feet crunched on broken glass and plastic. Someone had methodically crushed or mangled nearly everything in the apartment. It was an appallingly thorough crime.

"Now," she said, turning to the door.

Goldsmith hurried to catch up to her, and they were met at the doorway by the sadly smiling old cop, blocking them. Behind him were cops in uniform. They were not smiling.

Win Conley looked at the apartment. "Housecleaning?" he asked.

<hr/>

At the moment Conley and Melanie met each other again, Keegan had put another witness on the stand.

The witness's chains rattled a little as he sat on the stand. He studied the jury, reporters, and whenever he moved his shackled feet, it sounded like he was crushing walnuts. Two deputy sheriffs stood behind him, protecting the jury.

Keegan had been wary of this witness, but without Melanie Vogt even the marginal witnesses had to be used. He held several file cards.

"Mr. Honeycutt," he asked, standing up, "where are you doing time now?"

"San Quentin," answered the witness. He was short, with very wide shoulders and a droopy mustache. His eyes were black specks. He wore a blue denim prison shirt and blue jeans.

"When were you confined to prison?"

"September. I got eight years off an armed robbery." He said it dispassionately, like paying a utility bill.

Keegan defused Goodoy's strongest cross-examination by showing his witness's weakest point himself. It did not help, he knew, that the jury understood that Wesley Honeycutt was a state prison inmate or that he had to appear in court guarded and in shackles.

But I've got to use him and make the jury believe him, Keegan thought. He put a picture on the witness stand.

"Showing you a photograph that's been marked People's Eighteen, Mr. Honeycutt, do you recognize the person in it?"

Honeycutt looked at the picture and smiled. "That's old Lee."

"Lee Ferrera?"

"That's him. That's me in the picture with him. Last year at Tahoe. We did some gambling and had some fun."

Ambrosini glared skeptically at the witness, and Goodoy seemed amused that Keegan had to rely on such a disreputable witness.

But who chooses the victims or the witnesses, Keegan thought.

"How long," Keegan said, glancing at his notes, "did you know Lee Ferrera?"

"Three years. Four years. He was in a band, so was I. We ran into each other, ran with the same people."

Keegan nodded. Honeycutt was a musician, not just a con, ladies and gentlemen.

"Mr. Honeycutt, this is very important." Keegan wore a serious, solemn expression. "When was the last time you saw Lee Ferrera?"

"Like about June second or third, maybe. We got together to party a little bit. Lee had some money."

Goodoy's hand went up. "Objection, Your Honor. Narrative."

"Ask your witness questions, Mr. Keegan. We don't want a whole recitation." The judge smirked at his remark.

Keegan barely heard it. On June fourth, Leah had taken her ride across the twisting roads toward the San Fernando Valley. At about the same time Honeycutt and his old friend Ferrera were sitting down for the last time. Connections in time, Keegan thought, a pattern I should be able to see if I were smart enough.

"Mr. Keegan?" It was Ambrosini, prodding.

"Yes?"

"We lost you again. This is the second time in a day."

"I was forming a question," Keegan said snappishly.

"Don't take so long with it. No question is worth waiting that long for."

The jury tittered and so did some of the spectators. Keegan glared uselessly at the judge. There was nothing he could do right now, but move along. He had been daydreaming. It was hard not to, anything lately set him off.

"You said Ferrera had some money." Keegan swallowed and spoke commandingly, as he did when he appeared before committees in the capital. "Did he tell you where he got this money?"

Honeycutt, chains rattling, coughed. "He scored."

"What did that mean to you?"

"Sold some dope. Crank mostly. Lee did some crank when he was low."

"Did he tell you anything about this particular deal?"

Honeycutt twisted to stretch his muscles, and the chains heavily clattered again. "We got real fucked up." He paused, said to the judge, "Excuse me," and got a grim nod in return. "And Lee goes, 'Hey man, I seen some major, major shit.'" Another nod to the judge. "'Little while ago.'"

"Did he explain at all?"

"He said somebody got killed." The dispassionate tone didn't vary. "He didn't say who."

Goodoy looked at Carnes, who was rubbing his chin carefully. "Hearsay, Your Honor."

"Exception, Your Honor," Keegan promptly broke in. "This is a statement against penal interest by Ferrera. He could have been charged with a crime."

Goodoy smiled. "Well, he was, Your Honor. Mr. Keegan did that."

"And dropped it when I found the right man."

"Your Honor!" Goodoy appeared shocked.

Ambrosini pinched his nose. It was a gesture of annoyance. He scowled at them. "No more of this posturing. I mean it very sincerely unless you both want to be present at a special hearing we will hold at the end of court today."

I'll bend, Keegan thought. He bowed slightly. "I was too quick, Your Honor."

Goodoy glumly nodded. "I didn't mean to provoke the court."

The childish apologies pleased the judge, who smiled abruptly at the two lawyers, then at the jury. "We can maintain dignity and decorum. It only takes the smallest effort from you."

And my reward? Keegan wondered.

His reward was the judge saying, "Overruled. You may ask your question, Mr. Keegan."

"Mr. Honeycutt." Keegan rested one knuckled hand on the counsel table. "Did Lee Ferrera tell you where someone was killed?"

"LA. He goes, 'Hey, LA's where all the major shit happens.' And he goes, 'It happened to me.'"

"He was unhappy?"

Honeycutt shook his head. "Hell, no. This guy was down. He was beat. I go, 'What's so bad, man?'"

"What did he say?" Keegan looked at the jury. Each one of them was watching Honeycutt closely.

Honeycutt leaned forward, talking to the watching jurors. "He goes, 'I got put in deep shit.'"

"Was that the last time you saw Lee Ferrera?"

Honeycutt sat back and nodded. "Last time."

"Did he mention anything about traveling or leaving Nevada?"

"Not to me. That's the kind of thing he always told me, man."

Goodoy, pen up, said, "Move to strike the last, Your Honor. Nonresponsive."

But Honeycutt, as Keegan also knew, was an old hand at the games of the courtroom. He spoke over Goodoy. "Lee was my bud, and he never said nothing about going anyplace."

The judge closed his eyes. "Wait for me to rule before you go on with your answer, Mr. Witness. The motion is granted. The jury will disregard the last part of the witness's answer."

Keegan sat down, letting a moment of suspense build in the courtroom. He said coldly, "When was the next time you saw Lee Ferrera?"

A puzzled frown from Goodoy, and a question to her from Carnes.

Their confusion was answered as Honeycutt took a stiff breath and answered, "Next time was when they got me out into the desert to look at his bones."

A short recess followed. When Keegan sat down as court went back into session, his assistant passed him small folded messages that had been left by the clerk. Keegan didn't even look at them, because Goodoy had started her cross-examination.

For the first time, Goodoy sounded contemptuous of a witness, and Keegan listened and drummed his fingers on the table.

She stood before the bench, to one side of Honeycutt. "Don't you have a nickname in prison? The same one you had among drug dealers?"

Keegan jumped up. "That is a smear, Your Honor. She is trying to attack the witness."

The judge sneezed. He seemed to be coming down with a cold. "What is the relevance of this nickname, Mrs. Goodoy?"

"It goes to this man's veracity. His truthfulness. He is known by a familiar name among drug dealers."

Keegan braced himself on the counsel table. It was time to fight for his disreputable witness and show the jury that even a drug dealer, a prison inmate, could be telling the truth about some things, like the last words of a friend. "She can't get at Mr. Honeycutt's testimony legitimately so she intends to throw a lot of garbage around here, confuse things, call names. It's a cheap, cheating way to go."

"Enough," the judge snapped.

"You are right." Keegan folded his arms.

"Enough, I said."

Keegan glanced at Honeycutt, who had half-turned to look at the house charts, unmoved, unaffected by the courtroom dramatics.

"The jury can detect stunts, Mr. Keegan. I am sure of that," Ambrosini said grimly. He put up a hand. "Mrs. Goodoy, limit your examination to matters going to truthfulness."

Keegan said curtly, "I hope the court gives me the same freedom when Mr. Carnes gets up here." He sat down, the folded messages crinkling under his hand.

"You are on thin ice," the judge said.

"Then I'll be careful."

Ambrosini subsided, not wanting to make an issue at that moment. But, Keegan realized, if the opportunity arose, the judge would swing in Goodoy's favor, not his. He hoped alerting the jury to Goodoy's tactics had been worth it.

Goodoy said, low and frostily, "Shorty, besides the felony conviction for armed robbery, you're also a drug dealer, isn't that true?"

Honeycutt snapped back, "Okay. That's my nickname. I don't like it."

"My question was whether you are a drug dealer."

Honeycutt shifted, Keegan keeping an eye on his irritability, the unseen walnut sound cold and hissing. "I've sold some dope. Sometimes."

"Thank you, Shorty. Now, Shorty, do you know the man seated to my right?" Goodoy gestured at Carnes.

"May've seen him."

"Yes or no, Shorty?"

His mouth tightened. It was good to know he was so chained up. Goodoy was deliberately provoking him to anger. "I think I seen him."

"With Lee Ferrera?"

"I don't know. Maybe."

"Shorty, do you know a woman named Melanie Vogt?"

"I know a lot of women."

"Tell me, Shorty," Goodoy began, and Keegan interrupted her, the jury attentive to him.

"Your Honor, Ms. Goodoy decided to belittle this witness by using a nickname he hates. She hasn't done that with any other witness. It's a cheap trick to anger the witness and make fun of him in front of the jurors." Keegan pointed at the jury box.

The search for truth and the struggle for justice often came down to a grade-school game of tag, each lawyer trying not to be the last one hit.

"This is cross-examination, Mr. Keegan, and I don't believe Mrs. Goodoy has gone overboard. Overruled. Please sit down." He sneezed again.

Goodoy went on for some time, poking here and there, but it was very hard to get a seasoned courtroom veteran like Honeycutt to say much more or less than he wanted to. Goodoy grew frustrated.

Finally, she said, "Have you talked to Mr. Keegan before you got to court?"

Honeycutt scrunched in his chair, half-lidded eyes on Goodoy. "Yeah, I did."

"More than once?"

"Couple of times."

"Did he visit you in jail when you were brought from San Quentin Prison to Los Angeles?"

Honeycutt nodded. He had heard this series of questions before, usually asked of witnesses against him. Keegan listened closely. "Yeah, he came to the jail."

"And you discussed your testimony?"

Again a nod. "Yeah, we did."

"He showed you police reports with your statements, didn't he?"

"Yeah, he did"—and Honeycutt slid in his knife—"and he told me to tell the truth. Just the truth."

"Nonresponsive answer, Your Honor. Move to strike," Goodoy appealed instantly to Ambrosini.

The return compliment for using the hated nickname, Keegan thought. He smiled slightly at the con's sense of revenge.

Honeycutt's droopy mustache rose in a smile, too.

Keegan, hurrying from the courtroom, was stopped by Conley and his chief deputy, each of whom took one of his arms. The trailing band of reporters and deputy DAs who came to see their boss in court murmured as he was rudely hustled from them, through a side door into one of the many labyrinthine corridors twisting around the building. Two of Conley's burlier investigators blocked the outer door.

"What's going on?" Keegan demanded as he was propelled

up the stairs, his chief deputy pulling him. He felt like he did on Christmas morning years ago, Chris and Elaine tugging him and Leah to hurry to the tree for the present-opening revelry.

"Things have happened like you wouldn't believe, boss," his chief deputy said excitedly. "Didn't you get my messages?"

"You want the good news or the best news?" Conley asked breathlessly coming behind on the stairs.

"Give me the good news."

His chief deputy smiled widely. "We got Melanie Vogt. Got her upstairs, tied down. Locked in."

Keegan smiled immediately and punched Conley and his deputy on the arm, a complete break from the usually formal rituals he had with them. "My God," he said. "I didn't even look at those notes. What's the other news?"

Conley almost shouted, his fisted hands in raised triumph, "Carnes confessed!"

TWENTY-ONE

AS THE NEWS OF MELANIE VOGT'S discovery spread around the city, it added excitement to the running soap opera of the Carnes trial. Within two hours of the news breaking, an AM radio station announced a Melanie Vogt look-alike contest, the prize winner to be flown for a weekend to Puerto Vallarta. Another radio station that had run a "Where's Melanie?" contest in conjunction with several dry cleaning businesses in Mar Vista closed down its promotion by offering a set of dishware and a month's free dry cleaning to whoever could come up with the most inventive first line Melanie herself would use to explain her disappearance.

Two stores in Reseda, on opposite sides of the street, took down their competing "Melanie Vogt, guess-which-day-she'll-be-found" posters, having boosted business five percent.

The more responsible reporters on local TV, both network affiliates and independents, began serious special bulletins implying that at long last Melanie Vogt could supply the proof Keegan needed of the sinister conspiracy out to wreck his trial and career.

For nearly the remainder of that afternoon, the reappearance of a young woman many people had driven by heedlessly when she worked around Washington Boulevard in Culver City was a major topic of media coverage in Los Angeles.

Even Celia Aguilar was forced at a campaign stop in San Gabriel to remark acidly that George Keegan finally had no more excuses for the conduct of the trial. He had his witness again.

The object of this short but intense interest was totally unaware of it.

It was not, Melanie thought, an unpleasant place. She coughed quietly, in part to hear herself, in part because she was bored sitting in the cork-lined room with only five chairs, a large brown table, and a man in a green sport coat who stared at her and smiled whenever she said anything but otherwise wouldn't talk to her.

"Do you have the time, please?" she asked.

The man shook his head. She pretended to sulk. "Do I have to wait much longer?"

The man smiled.

"Well. Maybe I'll get a drink." She stood up.

The man stood up and, with a smile, stayed in front of the only door in the windowless room. No sound penetrated from the other side of the door either.

"May I get by, please?" she asked.

Melanie and the man remained motionless before each other for some time. She thought if she didn't get out of the coffinlike room and away from her guardian-dog in fifteen seconds, she would start one long, very loud scream.

Keegan came in and seated himself at the table while Conley and his chief deputy found places standing up. He studied Melanie and wondered if she knew or cared how much trouble she had caused. He also wondered if she knew, as he had just learned, that a jail inmate was ready to swear Robert Carnes confessed the murders to him.

I think I'll rattle her first, he decided.

"Do you know who smashed your apartment?" he asked roughly.

She smiled and shook her head. "Can I have something to drink, please?" An emphasis on the last word, like a child. She licked her lips as if to prove her thirst.

"Two guys who just got out of county jail," Keegan said. "Carnes told them where you were. He wanted to find you."

"I know that. I told you," she said.

She was concealing her anxiety fairly well. But Conley's raised eyebrows meant he didn't believe her calm either.

"We need to clear up a couple of things, Melanie," Keegan said. "First, who was picking you up the night you ran away?"

A light knock on the door, an investigator handed in a paper cup of water, and Keegan passed it to her. He watched as she drank it down without pause.

"Am I under arrest?" she asked.

"You could be. I haven't decided." Keegan checked his shirt cuffs slowly, as if he were thinking. "Right now you were picked up on an accessory warrant."

She watched him.

"But you could get clear of that. Or I could charge you with possession for sale. It's up to you."

A small tic, he noticed, like an animal running up her arm, made the flesh quiver. Like a horse before a snake, he thought, the instinctive urge to flee mortal peril.

He pressed harder.

"So you could be an accessory to murder, Melanie. You could be charged with solicitation for prostitution. Sale of methamphetamine. A whole range of things. Or nothing at all. You could be free and clear."

"I don't want to be arrested," she said.

"You have to help me."

"What do you want?"

Keegan glanced at his chief deputy and Conley. They had talked about it before confronting her. Conley had the smug, satisfied look of a hunter who's brought down a prime catch. Keegan leaned toward her, and he became warmer, more personable. "I want your true and accurate testimony in court about the time you spent with Carnes and Ferrera. What was said. Where you were. What Carnes did."

She crushed the paper cup. "What we agreed to before? We got back to where things were?"

"I know about the Mazda. I want the name of who helped you to run, Melanie. Was it Celia Aguilar?"

Pause. She shook her head.

"How about the mayor?"

Keegan stared at her, and she lowered her eyes.

"Then I won't be arrested?"

"I'll give you a promise in writing that you won't be prosecuted."

"When do I have to go to court?"

Keegan said, "Soon. I'll call you as a witness soon."

His chief deputy quietly sat down beside her, and Conley shifted his weight to his other foot and sighed. It was coming together.

"Who helped you?" Keegan asked softly.

"I didn't kill anyone. I didn't know about anyone getting killed," she said defensively.

He sat back and watched her.

Melanie let go of the crushed cup. "This guy Koenig. He said he could give me a hand."

Conley raised his eyes to the pitted fiberboard ceiling and shook his head.

It had been a tough admission, Keegan realized. She had been scared by the violent destruction of her apartment. The knowledge that Carnes could work through felons just out of jail, who would do a favor for some reward, must have brought her danger into sharp focus for her.

Christ, he thought, I do not understand these people, how she thinks or why she does what she does. Here she is, not much older than Elaine, and Melanie was bargaining about being a prostitute, living with a murderer, being involved in drug-selling.

He saw Conley critically checking the shine on his shoes.

Maybe that producer Goldsmith was right. This is an LA story, where the limitless randomness produces any kind of collision. Where accidents govern everything.

Except that Keegan did not believe in limitless possibilities or accidents. No one escaped the pattern of his life.

"You'll give me a complete statement about what Koenig said to you." Keegan stood up.

"I want to leave when I'm done."

"That's your choice."

"How about before? Where am I going to stay?"

Conley broke in, leaning forward on the table. "With us, young lady. Safe and sound."

"You'll be in protective custody," Keegan said. "Until you finish your testimony."

She closed her eyes and took deep breaths. He was afraid she was losing control, the tic in her arm, the barely contained turmoil.

"That's the deal, Melanie," he said, looming over her. "All right? Can you hear me? All right?"

Her eyes opened on him, violet and intense. "Why fight it?" she asked.

Keegan, Conley, his chief deputy, got past people waiting to see him in his office. He had coffee brought in.

"I want her isolated," Keegan said to the two men. "I want to know who she calls and if she gets any calls in. And no visitors."

"That's a pretty rough time, boss," his deputy said.

"I'll put her on the stand soon, get her out, and she can go do whatever she wants to."

He avoided the spotlit gaze of Dr. Staggers's billboard outside and looked at the red line of taillights on the freeways and streets stretching arterially below him.

Conley smiled, hands in his pockets. "It was fine, George. The sweetest. I felt thirty years younger bringing her downtown."

"Congratulations, Win. Tailing Goldsmith was on the money."
Keegan was also relieved the accounts were balanced. He no lon-

ger blamed his old friend for the dilemma Melanie's flight created. "What about this asshole Goldsmith?"

Keegan's deputy said, "He still doesn't believe Carnes had him followed."

"Show him the jail records. Show him their names. Show him when Carnes was in the same tier," Keegan said, quickly going through the messages and papers that sifted inexorably onto his desk. "Where are these gentlemen now?"

"I'm keeping close to LAPD. We've got the car descriptions, their descriptions, times last seen. We might nail them."

"Win?" Keegan asked, throwing memos into file folders, signing travel authorizations and expert fee claims.

"Who knows? They could just keep going, too."

"I want you to continue to keep an eye on Mr. Goldsmith," Keegan said, sipping his coffee, served in a plain cup and saucer. "He's got a line in to Carnes, and maybe I can get something more out of it."

They worked on Melanie's housing, how she would be guarded and her identity concealed until she appeared in court. Keegan paused long enough to call home, talk to Elaine, and tell her once again he would miss dinner. She didn't chide him. Like Leah stopped doing, too, he remembered, when it became the order of the day. *It was assumed I wouldn't be around.*

"I've got the Koenig problem to think about," Keegan said, using another old trick, substituting an immediate problem for a personal, intractable one. "What Melanie's told us so far is obstruction, isn't it?"

His deputy nodded. "At least, boss."

He frowned. "It may go to Poulsby."

Conley grinned. "I'd like to arrest a mayor. Nice way to retire."

"I want this kept quiet, too. Like Melanie. Just between us. I'll decide what to do."

"You are going to charge him?" his deputy asked.

"I don't know yet."

Keegan could see the questioning expression on the other man's face. *I'm the one standing alone,* he thought.

He felt in charge again.

He said, "Win, can you come with me to the Men's Jail? I want to have a witness when I find out what Carnes confessed to."

They had a quick meal first, and then Conley drove to the Men's Central Jail. At night it was dark, hugely oblong, and noisy, and the spotlights gave it a stagy appearance, razor wire strung near it, on its top, around the parking lot, more like a vast military barracks than a jail.

There was a flurry of confusion when Keegan and Conley arrived. It was so strange for the DA himself to appear that the watch commander and two lieutenants personally popped up, checking the times and the interview room, making ostentatiously certain that adequate security for the prisoner had been taken, talking endlessly to Keegan about who was on duty, what he could expect, how good it was for him to come down.

He endured being shuttled from one office to another. It was their chance to shine, and he commented favorably on the sharp appearance of the deputies on duty, the wisdom of promoting some names he recognized.

He told a mild joke, at his own expense, and got the group laughing loudly.

He and Conley ended up with an escort of four deputies, two with shotguns. Their footsteps stuttered rhythmically along the concrete corridors.

The city in the city. The city few people ever see. Few voters anyway, Keegan thought. Here the outcome of the election was hardly of interest; only whether Carnes would shove it in Keegan's eye mattered.

In the small interview room was a large, powerful young man chained to his chair, free only to move his hands at his waist, or bend his head down to take the smoky cigarette from his mouth.

Keegan glanced at Conley. No reaction.

"I'm George Keegan," he said, sitting down. Conley stayed at the door, the shotgun-armed guards outside. A pipe carrying water or steam passed overhead in the room and squeaked loudly.

"Hi, dude. I know you," said the man, bending down again, dexterously slipping the cigarette back into his mouth. His torso was tied with chains in such a way that he could only twist a few inches to either side. Keegan looked at the rap sheet in front of him, one long variation on assault, all the way to murder.

"Mr. Williams," Keegan said.

"Call me Blue."

"All right."

"I'll call you Chief. Like the Indians. Big warriors."

Keegan knew about prison gangsters and their mythic posturing. As Conley reminded him on the way over, "This guy thinks he's some old fighting spirit. All those Aryan Brothers figure they're reincarnated tough guys."

It made Keegan wonder why the man would come to the prosecution.

"Look," Blue Williams said, cigarette wagging with each word, "I'm only talking to you because the guy burned a kid. You don't do that."

"That was my first question." Keegan looked coldly at Williams. "Why should I listen to you?"

"It's the truth. He broke the rules, dudes. Killed a kid."

Blue Williams bent again, straightened up without the cigarette in his mouth. He spat a bit of tobacco to the floor. "I get any help here? Like some time off? Like some privileges?"

"I'll give you a sentence reduction."

"How much?"

"Half off. You'll do no more than four years."

"I don't go to Pelican Bay, dude. No way."

Keegan nodded. None of the prison gangsters liked Pelican Bay, its single cells and cold, gray walls, where they were kept like dogs in a kennel, separate and forever.

"You won't go there," Keegan said.

"Okay, Chief. We got a deal."

"No," Keegan said even more coldly. "Here's the deal. You

must testify fully and truthfully. If you lie, if you refuse to testify, if I even think you're lying, the whole thing's off. You will go to Pelican Bay."

"You got my word, Chief. My word's all I got."

Spoken like a true proud rebel unjustly confined by a hypocritical society. He still didn't want a lawyer, either. It was his show.

It was time to establish his credentials as an informant. Keegan leaned to him a little. Conley stayed near enough to make a move, but the older man would be little impediment to Williams.

It was, Keegan thought wryly, the same kind of tension and ginger circling of each other he went through with the Board of Supervisors or a senator in Sacramento over a bill.

"Where were you when Carnes made his admissions?"

Blue frowned. "You mean when he copped out?"

"Yes." Keegan made no notes. He kept his eyes on Williams, trying to discern whether the man was truthful or not. Thus far there were no false notes. Keegan thought he was a good judge of truth and lies.

Williams cleared his throat. "First time, we was together at lunch. Shooting the shit, you know. I heard of him, he heard of me, that kind of shit."

"You'd never met him before?"

"Nope."

"So the first time you meet Carnes, he tells you"—Keegan made it sound incredible—"what he wouldn't tell anyone else?"

"Hey, Chief, he told that little cunt, too."

"Melanie Vogt?"

"Yeah." Williams looked at Keegan, then Conley. "She ain't said nothing to you, right?"

Keegan didn't answer. Conley was impassive, but his eyes betrayed concern. Like me, Keegan thought. Is she holding out?

"How many times did you two talk, Blue? How many times did Carnes tell you things?"

Williams rolled his eyes upward as if mentally counting. "Four times. You know, we end up together waiting for transport, sitting around, stuff like that. We talk. Hey, Chief, I'm an easy guy to talk to." He grinned. "He tells me everything."

"Why did he trust you, Blue?"

Williams shrugged his big shoulders. "He didn't talk to no-body. I guess he's lonely. Hey, being a celebrity, you know, it's lonely at the top." He grinned widely. "You made him one fucking big-time star." He shook, laughing. Then he puffed his chest out. "Anyway, he knew about me. I got a rap. He goes, 'Blue, you too smart to snitch. You too mean.'" He stared at Keegan. "Hey, Chief, you check it out. You see where Bobby Carnes was and where I was. You got the jail records."

"That's right," Keegan said sternly. "I can get the records. I can prove you're lying very quickly."

Blue Williams smiled. It was something that must have looked endearing when he was a child and innocent. "Hey, Chief, you put me in court, I'm going to give you everything you want."

Keegan and Conley left soon afterward. In the car, Keegan asked, "What do you think, Win?"

Conley shook his head. "I don't believe any of these guys. I don't think your jury's going to believe him."

"I know Goodoy will work him over. But he adds to the case, he gives some weight to what Melanie will say. Even if the jury doesn't buy him completely. I can't keep him off the stand."

"These guys, guys like this asshole, they can blow right up in your face."

Keegan nodded. It was a Los Angeles night when the murky air clings, and the stars are gone, and even the city's lights look distant, dim, and fearful.

"I have to put him on, Win. I've got to use all the evidence I've got."

Frank Goldsmith finished his eighth vodka grape surrounded by cronies at the Captain's Table on La Cienega, and a party of Mid-western tourists sang "Happy Birthday" to a beaming jowly man.

"You can still sign her up," one of his cronies said.

Goldsmith scowled at him. "How? How the fuck can I sign her up when I don't even know where she is and when every son of a bitch in town's going after her the minute she testifies?"

"She likes you, Frank."

The tourists started applauding and Goldsmith began working on the next vodka grape. "Someone's going to get to her, and I'm out. Out. Out. Out. I don't have a project. I don't have anything."

"So what, Frank? What's next?"

Goldsmith scowled at the tourists. "Everybody's lying to me, from that bastard in jail to the little hooker. But I'm not losing this project. This is mine."

"Right. Fight for it."

Goldsmith raised his empty glass. "Damn right. This is my town and my deal. I'll go down fighting for my deal."

TWENTY-TWO

A PRESS CONFERENCE in the district attorney's conference room, just off Keegan's eighteenth-floor office. Behind a lectern with the office seal, a powder blue curtain behind him, Keegan stood answering questions the next day. Every seat was filled, and the bank of cameras were nestled so close to one another that shots overlapped.

"It was good investigative work," Keegan said. "Melanie Vogt was located by members of this office after long hours, and a lot of good groundwork."

"Who helped her? Who's the plotters?" several reporters shouted.

Keegan stood alone against the agitated block of men and women. "I won't discuss her testimony before she appears. But she will have information about the whole incident."

A woman, near the back, louder and harsher, "Are you saying it's a conspiracy?"

"No comment."

"Was it your political enemies?"

"No comment."

More shouts and a jostling near the front; two cameramen dropped their cameras and a battery pack fell off someone's waist.

"Is Celia Aguilar involved?"

Keegan shook his head, hands on the lectern. "I can't answer. Ask her."

"She says you're the one behind the whole thing."

Keegan snorted. "Anyone who knows me knows how utterly ridiculous it is to suggest I would jeopardize a major trial and my own reelection campaign just to get some publicity."

"You got it, didn't you?" Another shouted question.

Keegan smiled at them. Phil Klein, his press officer, chewed vigorously on a cigar at the side of the room.

"Next question," Keegan said, still smiling grimly.

At the midmorning break, they sat in the judge's chambers.

"You can't let him put this witness on."

"Why not, Mrs. Goodoy?" Ambrosini asked.

"He's unreliable. It's plainly self-serving testimony. Williams says my client confessed. Williams wants a sentence reduction. He's lying."

"Isn't that for the jury?" Ambrosini ate from a small yogurt, tiny slurps, eyes on an upset Goodoy while Keegan sat pensively.

"What about that, Mr. Keegan? Mr. Keegan? Would you come out of your reverie? How reliable is your witness?"

Keegan looked at the judge. "I believe him." He had been trying to keep track of so many things, people, and impressions that he found himself losing track of individual moments.

More often, he realized. Too often.

Chris had been talking about going to the San Gorgonio Mountains on the weekend with his scout troop. I'll go, Keegan thought, get away for a couple of days. Elaine will be all right with Innocencia there during most of the time.

Maybe things will all seem clearer in the mountains. Maybe Chris will be easier to be around.

"If this man goes on," Goodoy said, "the damage will be done. The jury will be prejudiced."

"He's telling the truth. I suppose that hurts," Keegan said.

"Enough." Ambrosini licked his spoon, put it back in his top desk drawer, and threw away the empty yogurt. "You can put your man on, Mr. Keegan. It's a two-way street, of course. If your witness turns out to be a lying informant, you know what happens?"

"I'll demand a mistrial," Goodoy said.

"I'd grant it."

"I know the risk," Keegan said, standing up. I know all the risks.

During the whole late morning and early afternoon of Blue Williams's boastful, grinning recital, the courtroom was still. He seemed swollen in his jumpsuit on the witness stand, physically imposing and projecting a repellent, restrained brutality. His chains rattled fitfully.

As Keegan questioned, Carnes sighed, shook his head, whispered to Goodoy, made every appearance of being excited, nervous, angry. It was simple, devastating testimony. Williams said Carnes told him he'd gone to the Rotich house to steal drugs and money. He killed Lee Ferrera to avoid future trouble.

Keegan put the details of his deal with Blue Williams before everyone, deflecting any insinuation Goodoy could make. I'm hiding nothing, was Keegan's unspoken claim to the jury.

Finally, he asked a slouching, smiling Williams, "Have you been threatened by anyone to make you come in and testify today?"

"I have never been threatened, dude. And if I am threatened"— Blue Williams nodded to the jury—"that's the last threat the dude ever makes."

Keegan sat down, busying his hands.

Goodoy was on her feet, no closer than the front of the counsel table to Williams. He grinned at her, savage and hungry in his chains.

"Isn't it true," she said sharply, "you could have gotten everything you claim Mr. Carnes told you from newspaper articles or TV news broadcasts?"

"He told me. I didn't get nothing off the TV." He spoke the initials slowly.

Goodoy shook her head in disbelief, which pleased Keegan. She was genuinely at a loss with this witness, and he wondered if she might even doubt Carnes himself. She went over the deal Williams had gotten, adding sarcasm to his coming forward, implying he only wanted better treatment in jail.

She picked up a file folder. "Now, Mr. Williams, you've been convicted of four felonies, haven't you?"

Williams stared up, counting inwardly again. "Yeah. Four."

"You've never pled guilty, have you? You always go to trial?"

"I don't plead. I don't help out."

"You don't help the prosecution?" Goodoy asked quickly.

Williams smiled at her, easily, lazily. "I help myself."

The facts fit together, Keegan thought, and the jury would believe enough of Williams, if not all.

Conley slid into the chair to Keegan's right as Goodoy went on probing, ridiculing, trying to breach the testimony.

"If it's not about this case, I don't want to hear about it now," Keegan said, leaning to Conley. He assumed the nervous, anxious look on Win's face was about an office emergency.

"It is about this case. It's this damn witness." Conley pushed a page into Keegan's hand. "This fax just came in."

Keegan read it and felt a curious light-headedness. It was like a blow that doesn't knock you out, only drives everything from your thoughts.

When he rose, paper still in hand, it was without willing it. It was automatic, cutting off Goodoy's questions.

"Your Honor," Keegan said, "I request a short recess."

Still holding the flimsy fax, the damning fax, Keegan said to Conley and one of his assistants, "I can't tell Goodoy or the judge."

"It's discovery," his young assistant said timidly. "You have to inform them."

They argued in an unused jury room at the far end of the corridor. There was a smiling stick figure drawn on the blackboard.

"Goodoy will get a mistrial if I do that. Speedy promised her," Keegan said.

"Oh, Christ," Conley said wearily. "Fucking cons."

"I've got to fix it myself. I might be able to tie the judge's hands if I do that."

"Sir," his assistant said timidly again, "it sounds improper."

Keegan nodded. "You can't always play by the rules."

A deputy sheriff helped Blue Williams drink from a paper cup of water on the witness stand. It was a jarring, placid image.

Keegan chafed impatiently as Goodoy ineffectually ended her cross-examination. She's convinced he's untouchable, Keegan thought, glancing at the jury. So are they.

Ambrosini was engrossed in his note-taking on the bench and didn't notice Keegan's uneasiness. Nor did the spectators or the camera, which only picked up his back.

Finally, Goodoy sat down. Blue Williams grinned as Keegan jumped up. "Are you a member of the Aryan Brotherhood prison gang?" Keegan demanded.

Goodoy looked up suddenly, as did Ambrosini and then Carnes and the whole courtroom. Keegan's angry manner made her hesitate to object.

"The who?" Williams asked.

"The white supremacist prison gang, the Aryan Brotherhood. Are you a member?"

"No," Williams said.

Goodoy looked up, puzzled. "I think I have to object, Your Honor. It sounds like Mr. Keegan's trying to impeach his own witness."

Keegan shook his head and held an empty file folder. "Excuse me. All I'm doing is clarifying defense counsel's impression that this witness is biased because he has prior felony convictions. I need to clarify if he has a motive to lie," Keegan said. It was partly true, although neither the judge nor Goodoy knew how much.

"I don't pretend to see your purpose." Ambrosini sneezed. He wiped his nose. "But I suppose you can rehabilitate your witness."

Keegan swung to Williams instantly. "Don't Aryan Brotherhood members wear tattoos? Swastikas? Lightning bolts? Clover leaves?"

Williams shrugged his big shoulders. "I guess so."

"Do you have any tattoos like that?"

There was a pause. Williams's face didn't change. It was the same empty look he must have had when he stabbed his victims, like the lawyer who lived.

Keegan said harshly, "Do you have any swastikas tattooed on you?"

Williams said calmly, "A couple."

"And do you have any lightning bolts on your body?" When Williams again paused, the courtroom waiting, the jury looking at the witness, Keegan snapped, "I can have you strip down in front of everyone if that's what it takes."

Goodoy and Carnes whispered urgently, hands gesturing. One more moment, Keegan thought. I built this guy up, I have to tear him down to save my trial.

"You have all the tattoos of this gang, and you are not a member of the gang?"

"Nope. I said so." Williams was bland, sleepy-eyed.

Keegan opened the file folder. The fax lay in it. He said, "You know a man named Ed Langout, don't you? He's doing time at the California Correctional Institute at Tehachapi."

"I know him a little. We worked together in the Navy."

"Did you know Langout was a member of the Aryan Brotherhood?"

Williams frowned, unsure where the questions were taking him. "I didn't know that. You telling me he is?"

Keegan stared at the fax; his hands were steady, holding the open file like a preacher with a charged Bible. "Didn't you write Langout a letter last week?"

Blinking, chains rattling, Williams said, "I might have."

"Didn't you write to him and tell him, quote, 'I got my tale all ready, bro. I'm going to tell a story to get half-time. Maybe you can find some story to tell, too. It's not snitching if you lie.' End quote. That's what you wrote, isn't it?"

Williams stared defiantly, then glanced at Carnes. No reaction.

"Did you lie today, Mr. Williams? Is this whole story about a confession a lie?"

The defiant warrior rose to the challenge, as Keegan hoped. He said, smiling, "Sure. Big fucking deal."

Before Goodoy could get up and object and give Ambrosini the chance to entertain any motion she might make, Keegan marched toward Williams, the deputy sheriffs bracing suddenly.

"Didn't you lie to the jury and lie to me?" Keegan demanded. Let Goodoy try a mistrial motion after that, he thought. There's no prejudice when I've totally discredited my own witness.

Williams snorted and sat back, chained hands resting on his belly. "I said I help myself. So I help myself here. What're you going to do to me? Any of you sorry fuckers?" He stared at the judge, then the jury.

Goodoy did rise to ask for a recess, but as Keegan turned to his seat, he was certain he had avoided the chasm Williams had opened. Once off the stand, Goodoy somehow would have learned of the Langout letter. Probably from Carnes. Keegan looked at Carnes, who seemed a little put out things had ended so badly so soon.

Tricks. Always tricks, Keegan thought. Carnes looks mad for the same reason Leah used to get annoyed.

You can't get good help.

TWENTY-THREE

ON SATURDAY, AFTER an early start, Keegan and several other fathers drove their scouts into the San Gorgonio Mountains. At the last minute, he had gotten calls from Cabrerra, then Morganthau, urging he use the weekend to make a few campaign appearances. "No speeches, as usual, George. I understand about the trial and publicity," Morganthau said. "But at least let people see you."

"You go. Tell them I'm working," Keegan said, joking. He had to get away, even for a little while.

He and Chris sat together in the van, the highway ascending and the scrub and brown earth turning to pines and evergreens. The boys began singing songs, and suddenly, Keegan wanted to keep driving. Los Angeles slipped away behind him. It was the same vague dream he used to get when he was younger, running away until he got to a place where no one wanted anything, where his own voices didn't demand more from him. He couldn't remember when he gave up that dream.

The campsite was up the mountain, and the troop and fathers hiked under a glassy clear sky, past creeks and shadowy forest.

Along on the trip were the usual Beverly Hills parents, a noted eye surgeon, a psychiatrist, a concert pianist, and a retail store empire heir.

It was a rugged hike. On the way, Keegan tried to trade basketball and football stats with Chris. He had memorized many just to talk to his son. They managed some conversation under the warming sun on the trail.

Keegan was delighted with the way his son took charge of the twenty or so boys. Tents went up, brush was collected, the preparations made for cooking all the meals. The pines were stiff and spicy around them, and none of the other fathers, observing a Beverly Hills rule that professional problems were off-limits, even mentioned the campaign or Carnes trial. It was a world away.

Watching Chris direct so much purposeful activity, Keegan realized he hadn't reckoned on how mature his son had gotten, as if he'd gone from childishness to solemn adulthood in a moment.

They took a walk in the woods, and the concert pianist got a migraine and had to lie down. One of the boys tore his pants, and the eye surgeon and psychiatrist argued about which kind of surgical knots to repair them with. Then it was sunset, bright, purple and yellow and blue, and the air grew cold instantly.

By the time of the campfire, Keegan had set aside all of the things he had to face Monday. Cabrerra, for example, kept prodding him to find out what he could about the *Newsweek* story. He hadn't called Lorrie again. He needed to put off any definitive resolution with her, personally and politically.

The songs at the fire ended around ten, last coffee from aluminum cups, the old pines crowding in the darkness. The retail store heir, who collected secondhand clothes in a Rolls-Royce, sang several songs he remembered from his scout days, in a surprisingly melodious and sweet voice.

Everyone vanished into their tents, the fire sinking lower and Keegan sitting on a log beside it. The psychiatrist took a barbiturate to sleep, although he worried about the effect the altitude might have on the dosage.

Chris came out from his tent and sat down by Keegan. It was quiet, the tents green-black, half-lit by firelight.

"Can't sleep?" Keegan asked.

"I guess." Both of their voices were very low, scarcely above whispers, almost indistinguishable from the faint hissing of the resinous fire.

He's so tall, Keegan thought, glancing at Chris, so soon. "Well," he said to Chris, the word hanging in the cold air. "You certainly got everyone marching in good order."

Chris shrugged. "Mom said I got it from you."

"From me?"

"Telling people what to do."

Keegan chuckled uneasily. He did not want the conversation sputtering and dying out as it usually did. He tried to think how his father, dreamy, affable, so soft and pliable, managed to talk to anyone about anything and make it sound as though he were truly interested.

"Going out at all? You have time to take a break now and then?" Keegan asked.

"Sure. You met Julie. I told you about her."

"I remember her." But Keegan knew Chris detected the falseness in his voice. "I think I do."

"You met her," Chris repeated.

Keegan disliked these implied moments of accusation and feared the void of being alone with his son, without other people, the family, or some activity to occupy their talk together.

Keegan smiled to hide his restlessness and fell back on the family for security. "The other day, I never thought I'd hear it. Elaine actually said she missed having you at home. The way you used to fight."

"When Mom was alive," Chris said.

"Well. Still. For Elaine to say that . . ." Keegan tried to push on.

Chris said, "Mom would be alive if it wasn't for me."

The flat statement shocked Keegan profoundly. "Don't ever think that, Chris. It's not true."

"She was coming to see me."

"She had an accident. She could've had an accident anytime. Anywhere. We all can."

Chris got up, hands in his pockets, the forest breeze in his hair. For an odd moment, the tall young man was a stranger Keegan didn't recognize at all. Then the moment passed. This is still my son, he thought. He said, "You are not responsible. Never think it was your fault."

"You're telling me what to think."

"If you resented it before, you've got to accept it now."

"Why now?"

"It's the truth," Keegan said, certain only that Leah's death wasn't chargeable to Chris. Maybe me. Maybe it's what she wanted, but not him, not his burden to bear. "I wouldn't lie to you."

"Every time she came to see me, she was upset, real worried. Most of the time she'd start crying." Chris was embarrassed, the accusation more directed at Keegan.

"Your mother was having a hard time."

"I know. She told me. I'm asking why."

"I do not know. I wish to God I did, because then we could all stop beating ourselves for what happened."

Chris stared at his father, Keegan looked at the red and black dying fire. "You think you did it, too?" Chris asked.

"I blame myself. Yes, I do. I haven't talked to your sister, but I imagine she feels responsible herself. It doesn't make sense, but I'm sure she does."

Chris sat down again. "Jesus," he said.

It was as if an unspoken line had been crossed, a confession uttered that was real, not manufactured like Williams's in court. I had never told him I blamed myself, Keegan thought, knowing he couldn't say more.

"I didn't know what to do," Chris said. "Whenever she came to school, we'd go get something to eat. I didn't know what to do."

"Neither did I," Keegan said, wondering again if that was true. "People we love are sometimes very mysterious, I think. Harder to understand than strangers."

He wanted to say something more personal, to get beyond the abstract, tinny moralizing.

After a few minutes, a faint cough came from a tent, an ember exploded loudly in the fire.

In the new intimacy, transient probably, existing only in the range of the firelight, away from their lives, Chris said abruptly, "I'm not going to law school, Dad."

"That's kind of out of the blue."

"It isn't. I've been thinking about becoming a cop for a long time. When Mr. Conley visits the house, I talk to him. I decided that's what I want to do."

College and law school had always been inevitabilities, Keegan thought. "I don't like the idea," he said bluntly. "You'd be a much better lawyer."

"I don't think so. I like doing things that you can see right away, like this." He pointed around them. "Getting things together. Lawyers take a long time." He shrugged. "Besides, I don't want to run for anything."

"I haven't done so badly." Keegan bridled immediately.

"I didn't mean you. I meant I didn't want to. It's not me."

"You can't make a decision this quickly, Chris," Keegan said quietly. "Think about it again."

"I have thought about it. I told you." And the steely declaration was Keegan's legacy to his son.

They didn't get any further because a flailing figure broke into the campfire, scattering the embers. It was the psychiatrist, bellowing and laughing, drunk on the altitude and barbiturates.

The camp was awake and in confusion, trying to catch the giggling man, putting out the embers, Chris keeping the younger boys from disappearing into the woods or causing more trouble.

Later, in his tent, in a thick sleeping bag, listening to the still tumultuous camp laughing and talking about the incident, Keegan felt the cold all around him. He did not know his son or his daughter very well, and apparently, he had not known his wife very well, either. He tried to be concrete. I'll talk to Chris again about this idea of being a cop. I'll find out what Elaine wants to do, discuss it. Advise her. But crowding in, thickly and persistently, were his own doubts about the fame he had sought, and the duty he had to discharge daily. They combined with the feelings he'd had just now by the campfire with Chris, and Keegan was lonely.

TWENTY-FOUR

IN HIS COURT CLOTHES—gray slacks, loafers, and white shirt with the sleeves rolled up—Carnes helped two jail guards stack toilet tissue boxes in a tiled corridor.

"Most people," Carnes said as they worked and talked, "don't focus on a goal. My main discovery when I was young, very young, was that you need to figure where you want to go and then figure out how you should get there."

The older guard, nearly fifty and about to retire, was flushed from the exertion. "Say, Bob, you tell me what happens when some asshole puts a roadblock in front of where you want to go."

Carnes wiped his forehead with a paper towel. "Well, you need to figure out a way around that obstacle."

"Suppose there ain't no way?"

"You must remove the obstacle."

The two guards chuckled. The younger, hard-eyed one disliked Carnes and showed it. "I bet you don't care how, Bob. I bet."

"No," Carnes agreed, "if it's really between you and your goal."

They walked back into the jail's heart. It was breakfast time,

269

but Carnes was always good for a helping hand, all the guards knew that. Men shouted and metal rattled, and the air was heavy with smells of coffee and vats of scrambled eggs.

"Well, look, Bob," said the older guard, "I got this supervisor, and he's making it damn hard to get a full pension payout. My wife and I need that full payout."

He handed Carnes a cup of coffee when they paused at the guards' station, other men in uniform sauntering through.

Carnes nodded, sipping. "Well, you've got to make a plan and divide your goal, which is your retirement, into stages. Decide how you'll get to each stage. Don't let anything stop you."

He dispensed advice and assistance freely, and the guards had formed a benign wariness around him. Opinion did differ about Carnes.

As he walked away, heading for breakfast and then court, the older guard poked his partner in the chest. "See? He's not a bad guy. He gives you the time of day."

"I just need a couple of minutes," Frank Goldsmith said again to the unsmiling, unmoving, unmoved young guard at the security station near the jail's entrance. "Look. I been here before. You got the records. He always sees me."

"You're not his lawyer."

"I'm his producer."

"Carnes went to court an hour ago. I got a note here from his lawyer, and she says you don't see him."

"She says. What about him? You ask him?"

The guard shook his head and motioned Goldsmith aside. A line of people had collected behind Goldsmith, and he felt someone pressing against his back. He turned and found his face an inch away from the top of a very short, bristly-haired Asian woman. She cursed him.

Hastily, shamefully, he backed away from the line of people. For the third time, Carnes had refused to see him. Why? What was going on? Was he mad about the DA getting hold of Melanie Vogt?

Christ, Christ—Goldsmith squeezed his eyes shut as he stumbled out of the jail into the sunlight—that wasn't my fault.

He had one consuming thought. I've got to see Carnes. I've got to keep this deal.

"Not now, Barbara," Keegan said from his desk, "I've got my biggest witness coming up this morning."

Cabrerra paced in front of him. Her pale, full face was flecked with red from nerves. "Morganthau can't fire up the precinct people, George. You've got to do that. You've got to make some time."

"I've got the trial first."

She folded her arms. "The trial or getting reelected?"

"You know my answer."

"That's your answer this morning."

"That's my answer, Barbara," he said, ignoring the lights on his two telephones.

"Our own polling shows the trial isn't saving you, George. Win or lose, you and Celia are running about even."

He smiled at her. "So it doesn't matter."

She braced against his desk, impenetrable and immovable. It was how she customarily got heard by politicians who always had some claim on their time and attention. "George, I said the trial isn't saving you. It can kill you. With you all tied up, Celia's got these last couple of days in the campaign to herself." Cabrerra gestured out the window at the city's expanse. "You're not leaving any time to challenge her."

Keegan was thinking of Melanie and how the jury would see her. He had to put aside the other problem of Koenig helping her to get away, too. That was for another day and another confrontation.

Perhaps with Aguilar, who may have known. Lorrie said so.

"Don't worry about Aguilar," Keegan said, head down, working on the notes for his direct examination, as he had for days. "I may have her locked up." In every sense.

He didn't see Cabrerra straighten up, dismayed, puzzled, and stalk out.

▬▬▬

For several minutes, Keegan stood with his legal pad. The courtroom rustled, the jurors fidgeting, knowing what was coming and impatient for it to begin. They all wanted to see her for themselves.

When it was quieter, Keegan said, "The People call Melanie Vogt," and a bailiff at the courtroom's entrance motioned for Conley to bring her in from the corridor. She had come from the jail, dressed simply in a blue pantsuit that made her look very young.

He heard papers crinkling, whispering, the judge watching as she took the oath, sat down, and violet-eyed, stared at Keegan, daring him to ask a question.

Carnes sat back, sullen and irritable. A fountain pen, which he was specially allowed only in court, leaked blue, like a wound, from his shirt pocket. He was too intent on Melanie to notice.

All right, Keegan thought. Begin.

Her name. Her age, and if she lived in Los Angeles. Melanie answered quietly but boldly. She knows they're all watching, even the jaded clerks and reporters; the eyes are on her, he thought.

He lowered the legal pad. "Did something unusual happen on the evening of May thirteenth?"

"Yes. Two men invited me out," Melanie answered. She crossed one blue pantsuited leg slowly.

"Do you see either of those men here today?"

She pointed straight and directly at Carnes. "Bobby. Sitting there in the white shirt. With the stain."

Carnes jerked his head and saw the leaking ink, cursing softly as he yanked the pen out. He was clearly unhappy with her.

Goodoy patted his arm, and the record duly noted Melanie had identified Carnes. The judge stroked the side of his nose thoughtfully.

"Did you find out the name of the other man?"

"Lee Ferrera." Firm, simple, unhesitating.

"Did you go somewhere with these men?"

Melanie nodded and glanced at the jurors, reckoning their reaction. The men had folded their arms. "We went to a motel."

"What was the name of the motel?"

"The Half-Moon on Sepulveda."

"Did these men bring any luggage?"

"They brought two suitcases, about so big." She made boxes in the air and then let her hands drop as if heavy.

Keegan had to face the first of several potential hazards of her testimony right away. He went at it head on. "Miss Vogt." He emphasized the old-fashioned, more innocent sound of the address to take some of the sting out of what was to come. "Where did you meet the defendant and Lee Ferrera?"

"At the El Lobo restaurant. They came in, and Bobby came over, and he started talking, and they sat down, and they ate with me, and we all decided to go to a motel."

"Miss Vogt, was it their idea to go to a motel?"

Melanie hesitated briefly. "No."

"Why did you go with them?"

"Well, it was like a mutual plan. They wanted to party."

"Did you have a party?" He skirted the question of whether Melanie was a prostitute. He gambled that the jurors would listen to her story if they thought she knew her conduct was morally wrong, but not if they saw her as a willful lawbreaker.

"Yes. We celebrated for a while."

"How long?"

"Most of the night. I guess. I wasn't looking at the clock."

Two jurors, men, chuckled, and then froze self-consciously.

"Did the defendant and Lee Ferrera stay in the motel room with you all night?"

"They didn't leave until the next day. Before noon sometime."

Keegan nodded carefully, as if hearing this for the first time, making the jury and reporters aware of its importance. She could put everyone together at the same place and the same time.

"Did either the defendant or Lee Ferrera tell you why they had come to Los Angeles?" He knew there would be an objection.

Goodoy had one hand on Carnes's arm when she stood up. "That is absolute hearsay, Your Honor. One man is dead and he can't be cross-examined, and what Mr. Carnes said is pure hearsay."

"I'm not offering these statements for their truth," Keegan said with a wave. "I do want the jury to hear them to show how the two men acted."

Ambrosini thought, blew his nose, and said, "I will permit it for the limited purpose of showing the defendant's state of mind. Not for the truth of the statements." He turned to the jury. "Ladies and gentlemen, you will hear statements allegedly made by the defendant. You are to consider those statements only for the purpose of indicating how the defendant later acted, not as though the facts asserted in the statements are true themselves."

Keegan bowed slightly. A neat legal distinction that allowed everyone to know what Carnes was up to.

"Bobby said"—Melanie's face was small, alert, and tanned, as if she had come from the beach—"they were going to sell some drugs."

"What drugs was he going to sell?"

"He said they were going to see a guy named Rotich and sell him some crank." She paused as she had when they went over these questions the day before. "That's speed. Methamphetamine."

"Did you see any drugs in the motel room on the night of May thirteenth?"

"I saw some baggies with crank in them," Melanie answered. She told him before court that it would be all right. Her horoscope urged forthrightness. He wondered, as he had all night, what would have happened if the stars counseled secretiveness. In a way, Melanie was completely right. His trial and so much else depended on the divination of planets far away, because she thought so.

Goodoy was disgusted. She had stayed standing, as if anticipating a new objection. "Oh, Your Honor. She isn't a criminalist. She can't say what were drugs or not"—Goodoy swung to Keegan—

"unless the district attorney wants to qualify her as an expert in illegal substances."

It was harsh and swift and brought a smile to Carnes.

"This is character assassination," Keegan said. "You've got to warn Ms. Goodoy, Your Honor." He threw his pad to the counsel table. It was mostly a thoughtless gesture, but he knew it conveyed his anger to everyone.

Ambrosini sat up. "Stop it. Neither one of you is doing his case any favors with this bickering. I will hold you both in contempt." He pointed his fingers at them.

At the counsel table, Conley, who sat as an investigative advisor, whispered hoarsely, "You're getting close to the edge."

Keegan nodded slightly and whispered, "I know." He picked up his pad. "Your Honor, may I continue?"

"I'd like a decision," Goodoy snapped.

That settled Ambrosini, who sided instantly with Keegan. "Well, the objection is overruled. She can testify about personal knowledge. You can test her on cross, Mrs. Goodoy."

Goodoy sat down sourly.

"Did anyone use drugs on May thirteenth in your presence?" Keegan asked.

"Bobby did. Lee did. They took crank from the baggies. Bobby used it in some coffee." She spoke too casually, as if the acts were commonplace for her.

Keegan went to the clerk's desk and came back with a baggie recovered from Rotich's home. He showed it to Melanie, and she nodded. It was like the ones she saw at the motel, same size, same amount. He had her describe the rented car they had picked her up in and later drove away in themselves. It fitted with what Russell Dagowitz had seen.

The evidence came in relatively smoothly, Goodoy breaking in now and then, skirmishing with Keegan until Ambrosini stopped it. He, too, seemed more interested in putting the evidence before the jury than indulging his usual tactics of threatening the lawyers.

"When the defendant and Ferrera left the motel that morning—about ten?" Keegan asked.

"Ten. Eleven."

"When they left, did they take anything with them?"

Melanie sighed loudly. "They took the two suitcases, and they both took guns. The guns were in the suitcases."

"Could you see if these were revolvers or automatics?"

"They were big," she said, glancing at Carnes, whose head was down as he made a note for Goodoy. "Automatics. Bobby told me they were."

It was another crucial link. All of the ballistic evidence at the Rotich house and what could be gleaned from Ferrera's picked-over remains in the desert indicated the gunshots came from large-caliber automatics.

"Was there any discussion about killing Rotich or anyone else when the defendant and Ferrera left the motel?"

"No. No." She shook her head, finger pointing at Keegan. "I didn't like the guns, and I wasn't staying if they were doing anything like that."

"Did you stay at the motel until they returned?" She nodded slowly. "They came back around two, then Bobby goes, 'Lee and me got to leave right now,' which was not what we agreed to."

Keegan leaned back on the counsel table. "What had you agreed to?"

"Bobby wanted me to come with them to Nevada. To where he lived in Elko. We were going to all fly there."

"Did you go to Nevada?"

"Yeah. I did. Couple days later."

"Why?"

Melanie paused, her head cocked slightly to one side. "I liked Bobby. He liked me, and I thought we'd be together for a while."

Keegan peered briefly at flimsy credit card slips. "When you went to Nevada, you went by plane?"

"Yep."

"When you made those reservations, did you use your own name?"

"Bobby goes before he left, 'Make the reservations in your name and I'll pay for them later.' Yeah. He wanted to use my name.

We got a car in Las Vegas a couple weeks later, and he used my name on that, too."

"Not his own?"

"I never seen Bobby use his own name, sign for something in his own name. He always used me or Lee."

Keegan said for effect, "He used your name and Lee Ferrera's always?"

"Couple weeks I was with him, yeah."

Keegan nodded. The jury had the record from Rotich's home saying Ferrera was coming from Nevada. In a little while they would also have a slew of credit card slips for gas, meals, airplane reservations, all made out in Melanie Vogt's name or Lee Ferrera's. This guy is a manipulator, Keegan thought, and they'll see that, and they'll see how someone else's name usually meant Carnes was around, too.

"When was the last time you saw Lee Ferrera, Miss Vogt?"

"About May twenty-seven, twenty-eight, something like that. He came over. He lived about five miles away, and he and Bobby'd get together a lot, and after they came back from LA they argued, like at the motel."

"Argued about what?"

Melanie glanced at Goodoy, then up at the judge. "Selling a whole lot of drugs they got in some packages the day I came."

"What did these drugs look like?"

Melanie licked her lips and sighed again, as if to say she was growing tired and she had been very good so far. "They was in bags, clear plastic bags, big ones, though. Bobby and Lee, they went to pick them up at the airport. They shipped them from LA. Bobby showed me."

"Did the drugs in the large bags appear to be the same as the drugs you'd seen at the Half-Moon Motel?"

She primly put her hands on the witness stand. "Bobby said it was pretty good crank. He said this guy Barry gave it to them."

"Barry Rotich?"

She nodded. "Yep."

Keegan plucked one of the credit card slips from his sheaf.

Carnes had already claimed one dead man helped him, and now another one would, too.

"Miss Vogt, did Robert Carnes use the name Lee Ferrera to get a reservation at the Pueblo Cantina restaurant outside Elko on June four?"

He put the credit card slip in front of her, and she stared at it, even though she'd been shown it before. Keegan wondered if Melanie relived events, like psychics, by seeing or touching objects.

"Oh, of course he did. It was a birthday present. Even though my birthday isn't until July."

"Did Carnes sign this slip in your presence?"

"Yes."

"With whose name?"

"Lee. And he left a big tip." She pursed her lips in thought.

One or two jurors again smiled. Who hadn't wanted to spend freely with someone else paying?

Keegan had the slip marked and gave it to the clerk. "When did you discover Lee Ferrera was dead?"

Melanie's thoughtful expression faded, replaced by a blandly cold, armor-plated hardness, what she probably used when working. "Bobby and me had a big, big fight, and he threw me out, and I went back to LA. I went back by bus because I didn't have much money. I bought a paper to read when we stopped around Reno, I guess. I wanted to check their star chart, you know, a different one from the one I was using."

"Yes," Keegan said impatiently. "What else did you read?"

"I seen that they found somebody in Elko, a body. And I seen it was only about a mile from where Bobby lived, and then I seen it was Lee."

"What date was this?"

"June twelfth. I know the date on the paper. I can tell you the headline." And she did, and Goodoy cleared her throat quietly, and in the whole courtroom, it was the loudest single sound.

Keegan waited and came toward her. "So on June four, Robert Carnes used Lee Ferrera's credit card to pay for a restaurant dinner?"

"Yes, he did. And I go, 'So how come Lee's giving you his

card,' and Bobby, he goes, 'Lee said I could have it. He left. He ain't coming back.'"

Earlier forensic pathological testimony had established that Ferrera died sometime near the early part of June. The desert's relentless cleansing had made any definite date too hard to pinpoint.

But he sure as hell was dead on June fourth when that credit card got used, Keegan thought. And the jury knows it, too. He turned to Carnes, whose head rested on one hand. And he knows everyone knows.

Keegan stepped back. Outside the courtroom there was a media clamor about Melanie and a conspiracy to sabotage this trial. In here, under Ambrosini's unbending rule, the only question was whether she could tie Robert Carnes utterly and completely to the murders of the Rotich family and Ferrera.

She just did, Keegan thought. He was concerned about how she would endure Goodoy's cross-examination, its engine driven by information from Carnes.

"Miss Vogt, did Robert Carnes ever talk about Barry Rotich or his family while you were with him in Nevada?"

"Once." Melanie nodded.

"When was that?"

"Couple days after my birthday dinner, maybe a week after I saw Lee."

"What did Robert Carnes say?"

Melanie waved one hand slowly, as if stirring the air. With a natural performer's instinct, she turned to the jurors. "He goes, 'You know what happened in LA?' And I go, 'Yeah. I read it in the papers.' He goes, 'Melanie, Lee killed those people, all of them, and I couldn't stop him. I didn't want to tell you because Lee might've hurt you, and you been really good not talking about it while he's around, because he would've done something.'"

She paused.

Keegan broke in. "When Robert Carnes told you Lee Ferrera had left, did he say left town? Left the state? Left the country?"

Melanie sighed once more.

"I thought he meant, he's dead."

Goodoy said forcefully, "Objection, Your Honor. The witness is speculating. Also drawing a conclusion."

"Sustained on the latter basis, Mrs. Goodoy."

Keegan lowered his head, knowing that his own moment to dramatically end Melanie's testimony had come. He slowly turned over a page on his legal pad and put the pad down on the table, as though nothing more could be noted down.

"Miss Vogt," he said, folding his arms, facing her, "did you ever see Lee Ferrera after the day Robert Carnes said he wasn't coming back?"

Melanie blinked. "No. I never did."

Carnes coughed, and Keegan, in the theaterlike stillness of the courtroom, which had its own epiphanies and curtain calls, recalled Melanie's succinct explanation of Carnes's behavior: He turns you off.

Sitting down, his assistant congratulating him, Keegan noticed Carnes appraising Melanie.

TWENTY-FIVE

"ARE YOU A PROSTITUTE?" Goodoy asked calmly at the out-set of her cross-examination.

Melanie blinked tiredly, and sipped from a cup of water as Keegan said loudly, "Objection! Defense knows there's no arrest or conviction for prostitution!"

Ambrosini studied Melanie, then Goodoy. "True, Mrs. Goodoy?"

"I didn't ask if she'd ever been arrested or convicted, Your Honor."

"Unless there has been a conviction, it's irrelevant, and Ms. Goodoy knows it," Keegan said. Melanie's face had whitened, and she seemed fixed on Carnes, who smiled back at her. Keegan and she had gone over the real possibility of a question like this, but it still stung, and Goodoy's blandness was infuriating.

The judge shook his head. "I'm overruling your objection, Mr. Keegan. How she answers the question may impeach her."

Keegan sat down, his anger obvious and real. Yet part of the trial's narrative demanded that he show indignation, real or not,

281

Goodoy must show sorrowful reluctance at her job, and Melanie must show unflinching honesty.

"No," Melanie said levelly, "I'm not a prostitute."

Goodoy acknowledged this slightly with a nod. "You know that prostitution is against the law, don't you?"

"Yes." Melanie looked at Keegan. He smiled slightly to encourage her.

"You don't do illegal things, do you?"

"I try not to," Melanie said quietly.

"You know that a prostitute is someone who takes money for sex, right?"

Melanie nodded. "Yes."

Goodoy nodded again, as if teaching a slow student. "Isn't it true you took over two hundred dollars to have sex with Mr. Carnes and Lee Ferrera on May thirteenth?"

"I didn't ask for money. You ask for money, you're hooking. I did not ask."

"Did you have sex with these men?"

"Yes."

"Didn't you take two hundred dollars from Mr. Carnes after you had sex with him?" Goodoy asked, hands open toward Melanie.

The courtroom had come alive again, the stillness gone, as the cross-examination became more like a sport. There was a subtle undercurrent of muttering, giggling now. It dismayed Keegan, who prayed his witness would not go sideways or say something so outlandish that all her potent earlier testimony would dissolve in the jury's disbelief.

This was the worst moment of any trial, he recalled, when a major witness was on the stand and there was no way really to shield her from fatigue or nerves or a cunning examiner. Objections only served to buy a little time. Ultimately, Keegan fretted, turning a pen over and over at the table, Melanie had to rise or fall on her own.

I'm a spectator like everyone else right now, he thought.

Melanie answered, "I did take the money, but, like I said, I did not ask for it."

"But you are not a prostitute?" Goodoy asked with slight irony. Melanie shook her head. Keegan saw the point of Goodoy's pursuit of this area. The jury might say that Melanie was lying about her own activities and capable of lying about Carnes as well.

"Well, let's take a look," Goodoy said. "You'd never met these men before May thirteenth, had you?"

"No."

"You just knew they wanted to have a party. Meaning what? Alcohol? Drugs? Sex?"

"A good time," Melanie answered, and Keegan kept his fingers crossed that she still appeared trustworthy, the inner hardness he'd noted preserving her rather than making her stubborn. The jury'd hate that, he thought.

"How did you get to the Half-Moon Motel?" Goodoy asked, still skeptical.

"Their car."

"You got into the car with two strangers, what time of night?"

Melanie folded her arms across her chest. "Ten. Eleven."

"That late at night, you got into a strange car with two strange men from out of state to have a party?" Goodoy's voice was high, her feigned astonishment directed at the judge and jury.

"I don't know what you think is late, but ten or eleven isn't late."

"You've gone with other strange men at later hours?"

Keegan raised his pen. "Objection. Argumentative, Your Honor."

The judge nodded. He'd been watching Melanie closely, with a warm half-smile sometimes. He likes her, too, Keegan thought. "Yes. Sustained."

Goodoy went to the counsel table, and Carnes, helpful and harmless, gave her a computer printout the legal assistant had ready. Goodoy made the same show as Keegan had. She studied her document, as he had studied the file folder on Williams.

"Isn't it true you've used many other names in the last few years?" Goodoy asked without looking up.

"Like for a joke? What?"

"No joke. Haven't you used false names over and over when you picked up men for sex as a prostitute?" Goodoy waved the printout, and Melanie wrinkled her nose as if it stank.

Time to break up this attack and huddle, Keegan thought. But even as he stood up, objected, pointed angrily at the way Goodoy was flaunting a computer printout in front of the jury, Ambrosini began sneezing, and abruptly, in the midst of the noise and voices over each other, left the bench saying there would be a short recess.

"What names?" Keegan asked her when they were alone in an empty jury room. Sunlight slashed in through the old Venetian blinds on the west wall. "Is there anything else?"

She blew her breath out loudly. "It's nothing, just some names I made up. You know, so I didn't use my own."

"The jury'll think you were trying to hide your identity."

"Maybe I was."

Keegan had a cooling cup of coffee in his hand. The room was stacked with old file boxes and obviously hadn't been used for a long time. "The jury will think you are a hooker and were a hooker and that you are a liar," he said.

"I am not lying. You know I'm not." She huffed as if they were talking about an unfashionable dress.

"I know what you've done." Keegan sipped, trying to calm her. "I'm confident you'll tell the truth now. You've got to convince the jury you're telling the truth."

"I want Bobby to stay where he is."

"So is there anything else I need to know?" he asked softly.

"Nothing you don't already," she said bitterly. "All right. Maybe I got a couple busts."

Keegan put down his cup and stood up. Show no anger or fear. She could go sideways, and he'd lose it all. "Under other names? Names I couldn't check?"

She nodded.

"When we go back, Melanie, you'll start by admitting you lied.

You'll explain you're scared, and you lied about being a hooker."

She stared at him.

"You lied to me, and you just admitted it," Keegan said. It was weirdly like dressing down Elaine for staying out late or failing to clean her room. "You've got to admit it to the jury."

"What's going to happen to me?" Melanie asked, moving toward the sunlight, standing in it. It was the first show of fear he'd heard from her.

"I'm done with you after Goodoy's finished. I'll keep our bargain. The U.S. attorney's going to be in touch with you, probably the minute you get off the stand."

She faced him, arms folded. "About running away?"

He nodded. "And you tell the U.S. attorney the truth, Melanie. I can't help you. I'm involved because you were my witness."

"I don't need a horoscope to remind me," she said.

Goodoy finished going over the names on her list one by one. Melanie had used several, denied several, and answered feistily.

"You are prepared to lie if it suits you, isn't that correct?" Goodoy ended the reading with a snap.

"Because I'm scared he's going to kill me, too," Melanie snapped back.

"Move to strike," Goodoy said.

"She was answering counsel's accusation, Your Honor," Keegan said, pointing, relieved Melanie had survived the change from too innocent witness to frightened prostitute.

"The answer stands," Ambrosini said. "Move on, Mrs. Goodoy."

Goodoy took the setback with too much grace. She's got more waiting, Keegan thought, sitting down.

"When Bob Carnes and Ferrera left the motel room," she said briskly, unrattled, "you didn't go with them, did you?"

"No. I said I waited there."

"You waited because you'd get more money when they got back?"

"I stayed in the motel because Mr. Robert Carnes said he liked me."

"All right. All right." Goodoy was dismissive, the people in court alert to any new surprises from this long-awaited witness. "When Bob and Ferrera left, you didn't know where they went, did you?"

"To this guy. Rotich."

"Do you know where he lived?"

"I think in the Marina. I think I heard Lee say that."

"But"—Goodoy was more dramatic—"you haven't the slightest personal knowledge that's where Bob and Ferrera went, do you?"

"Except that they said—" she began. Goodoy walked to her.

"You weren't with them, you didn't watch for their car the whole time until they came back, you can't have any personal knowledge where they actually went, can you?"

Momentarily confused, Melanie looked at Keegan. He made no sign. Just what the reporters and jurors, not to mention Goodoy and Carnes, would need, he thought. DA coaches his witness.

She finally said, "I guess I can't."

"Thank you for telling the truth." Goodoy marched away.

Keegan called out, "Objection. She's commenting, and she's argumentative." Melanie took a deep, nervous breath.

"One final time, Mrs. Goodoy." The judge's nasal irritability filled the courtroom. "Ask questions. Leave the rest to me."

There was a mild ripple of amusement through the crowd, and Keegan was relieved again that Ambrosini, perhaps because he liked Melanie, was giving the brunt of his crankiness to Goodoy.

A trial was not so much the objective product of impartial, sexless mentalities clashing, as it was ordinary human beings fighting their opponents and themselves over what happened in court.

Because he was a politician, Keegan had long ago lost any deep illusion that a courtroom was a heavenly tribunal.

Goodoy turned from the counsel table and the genial-looking Carnes. He likes Melanie's discomfort and unease, Keegan thought angrily.

"Give me a simple yes or no. You do not know if Bob and Ferrera stayed together when they drove away from the motel, do you?"

"They came back together."

Goodoy sighed obviously. "I understand you want to avoid my questions."

Keegan had no opportunity to object because Goodoy both bowed slightly to the judge and apologized even as Ambrosini began wagging his finger at her.

One red flag did go up for Keegan, and he made a note. Goodoy inserted it too quickly, too gently.

"You have no personal knowledge, do you, if Bob and Ferrera even stayed together once they drove away from the motel?"

Melanie frowned. "I don't know."

"You don't know if they split up, one going one place, the other somewhere else?"

"No."

Keegan starred the note, handed it to his assistant. This was the heart of whatever defense Goodoy was preparing. The problem was that he had no real way of meeting it until he knew exactly what it was. "Get the dicks checking right now. If they missed something," Keegan whispered. "I want people in my office at the end of court."

His assistant slipped away.

Goodoy went over Melanie's testimony again and again. Time knotted up for Keegan, and the climax of Melanie's appearance came when Goodoy asked, "You stayed with Bob at his home in Nevada?"

"I said so."

"How long again?"

"I said about two weeks."

Goodoy nodded. "And for almost that entire period, two whole weeks, you knew the Rotich family had been massacred?"

"I thought Lee did it."

"So you had no doubt whatsoever that Bob Carnes"—Goodoy was gentle in tone, hard in meaning—"had not committed those crimes?"

"I . . . Let me . . ." Melanie fumbled oddly, her face contracting.

"Well, would you have remained in his house for two weeks if you believed he was a killer?" Goodoy sat back waiting for an answer she was certain would help Carnes.

Melanie looked at her. "I thought," she said, "he loved me."

There were more questions and Keegan let Melanie go without asking her more himself. It had been, he thought, an affecting appearance. He stood as the jurors filed slowly, a little awkwardly, from the jury box, court recessed for the day. They heard her, and they know it was the truth. He did love her, and she thought so, too.

When the jurors were gone, the reporters lurking in a noisy mass just outside the courtroom, Keegan said to Melanie, "Thank you."

"Yeah," she said, tiredly. "They from the government?" She pointed at the men waiting at the courtroom door. "Let's get it over with."

"You're not in custody. They just want to talk to you."

"Sure. I know. Like you. Look, I tell you something I told Bobby when I first met him. I told him about my daddy and how he didn't listen to what's going to happen, thought he could just get away, get through it himself. But, you can't. I can't. Bobby can't."

"I'll check my stars."

"You think it's a joke," she said and walked from him to the lawyers from the U.S. attorney's office. From the Criminal Courts Building, she would go across the street, concealed somehow, into the white stone monument of the Federal Building. She was caught, and she was right about that.

Several deputy DAs waited for Keegan in the nearly empty courtroom, and they all had questions or problems or answers he had directed them to get.

But, as he gathered his own papers, handing the heavy briefcase to another assistant, he wanted to know what Lorrie Noves had been doing sitting in the courtroom, watching him, and then getting up, taking something from her olive-colored bag.

TWENTY-SIX

THEY WENT TO A SMALL SPANISH restaurant just off Olvera Street, where the billboards were Spanish and the freeways rising nearby seemed to be running away. It was dark already, winter's approach, and the restaurant's bright lights burned against a gathering season's inevitability.

There were only a few people in the dining room. A small black-and-white TV was tuned to a Spanish variety show.

Keegan finished reading the proof sheets she had given him. She looked at her water glass and waited.

"It's quite an article," he said.

"I thought I'd be fair, let you see it before it runs in the next issue."

"Can I keep this?" He held the sheets and the damning piece she'd written about him, and his hands didn't tremble with anger at all. The waiter brought their margaritas, and she drank hers.

"No," Lorrie said, "I mean, I'm not supposed to let an article out. Oh, what the hell. Yeah. Keep it."

Keegan folded it and put it in his coat. "Coincidentally, I've got a campaign meeting tonight. This will give them a little time to have a defense ready." He half-raised his glass to her. "You're giving Celia Aguilar a real boost."

"I didn't have anything good to say about her. I think she's too parochial to be DA in this city."

"Well. You didn't have anything good to say about me. And I'm the incumbent."

Lorrie shook her head. Her hair was pinned back, perhaps because of the East's already vicious winds and winter. She looked unlined, unworried, a diligent technician. "I think, if you think about it fairly, you'll see it's a balanced piece. I mentioned the positive things you've done. Environmental lawsuits. Minority hires. Lots of convictions."

"Excuse me if I'm not very objective." He drank, still smiling a little. It was a stiff smile. The waiter came over, and they ordered quickly, thoughtlessly. A few of the people in the room recognized him. Two clapped. "I have some fans left," he said.

"You knew going in I wasn't going to do a puff piece," she said. "It's not a critical article. It just tries to give a full picture of you."

Keegan sighed wearily. "Unbending. Driven. Impulsive. Possible domestic problems that led to the death of a glamorous wife. The child of middle-class parents trying to show everyone he can pick up all the marbles. I don't need a full picture like that."

Lorrie ran her finger around the glass's rim, licking stray salt. "I left out things. You know I did."

Keegan nodded, sad and sorry at the same time. "I didn't think you'd write anything because I made a clumsy pass."

"I didn't even think of that," Lorrie said quietly. "No, I meant, I felt . . . I felt sorry for you."

Keegan felt his mask of stern impassivity slipping into place, just as it had when he and Leah fought or when the kids wanted attention. "I don't feel sorry for myself. I don't need a stranger doing it for me."

"I'm sorry. I didn't mean to upset you."

"I'm annoyed at myself, frankly. I thought . . . I imagined there was a moment of mutual interest the night I took you around." He sat back as the waiter dropped a towel-handled hot plate in front of him, then Lorrie. They both sat, the food steaming, untouched.

"There was," she admitted.

"I'm not saying you're trying to get back at me in what you wrote. I don't like making misjudgments."

Lorrie glared at him, her hand clenched on the table. "Look, first time, no bullshit, I told you I was married, I told you I liked what I did. I liked my husband and my family, and that meant that's all."

"Then I apologize for overstepping."

"Look, George. One thing I didn't put in the article. One really major thing is how damned self-centered you are. It's going to come as a shock someday, but the whole world doesn't revolve around you."

"I never thought it did," he said stiffly.

"Untrue," she said slowly. "From what I've seen, you've got it worked out that the whole place, your office, the trial, your wife, it's all connected to what you think or what you do. People have their own agendas."

"Obviously."

"Look, I don't wish you any bad things. I think there are a lot of impressive things you could do for this city."

"You aren't making it easier," he said. His hands were flat on either side of his plate, and he didn't move at all. He had the odd sensation that his skin was freezing solid and he couldn't move. He couldn't even show how sad he was that this desirable woman was beyond him and maybe even right in what she said.

They both turned when the sound of his name came over the TV. A Spanish-language campaign ad ran swiftly, his face filling the screen. The two clapping diners clapped again.

"I have to tell the truth," she said, zipping up her bag.

"Why?" he asked.

"It's what I do. My job." She stood up. "You may not believe me, but I will be rooting for you on Election Day."

"I believe you," he said. "Don't you want to eat?"

"I'm not cold-blooded enough to sit here knowing how you feel."

She hesitated and put out her hand. He shook it quickly. Quick tactile impressions flooded over him. Cool, dry, smooth skin. Then she was gone. Keegan sat motionless for several moments, realizing he wasn't hungry, and paid and left, too.

In the parking lot, the asphalt seemed blacker than usual, the lights overhead fainter, and the drifting snatches of salsa music like incoherent cries. He got into his car. The police radio scanner was lit up, running up and down channels, calls coming in silently, crimes, calls for help, shrieks turned into little glowing lights on the scanner's face. He hit the steering wheel once, again, harder another time. It was, he tried to tell himself, just another of LA's endless, meaningless collisions. Like pool balls knocking each other. If Carnes hadn't been greedy, if Mrs. Harrold hadn't written her letter, if he hadn't wanted fame, if Leah hadn't driven that night.

It makes sense, he thought, somehow it does, and if I can only convict Carnes I can find the solution. It's impossible to be overwhelmed by guilt and loneliness if you balance the scales. Carnes for Leah. Carnes for the dead.

Carnes for me.

Two hours later, his senior campaign staff sat around Wylie Morganthau's large living room, a fire spitting and guttering in the brass-fixtured fireplace. Two spoiled and careless great brown dogs loped among the men and women.

Cabrerra pushed her glasses up. "I warned you, George." She handed the article proof sheets to Morganthau.

"Can you do anything?" Keegan asked. He sat in a padded chair, legs crossed, head low, his voice still firm.

"I can underline all the good adjectives. 'Intelligent. Decisive. Aggressive.' Send them to the news outlets."

Morganthau whistled softly in disappointment as he read.

"It's not a movie review, Barbara," Keegan said angrily. "I want you to defuse it. That's why I got it for you."

She smiled thinly. "Yes, sir."

Morganthau passed the article on to the next person. One of the dogs began barking at the other, and Morganthau swatted its head.

"One more problem," Keegan said. "I've got LAPD checking. I think there's some surprise in the trial coming up."

"Oh, peachy. Peachy," Cabrerra said. "More good news?"

"Cut it," he snapped.

"Don't bark at me, George."

Morganthau, always diplomatic, broke in, "Okay, so you have a hitch in the trial. How long's it lasting now? A week?"

"I still think we'll be finished before the election."

The rest of the staff, finance director, media buyer, precinct director, all glanced at one another.

Cabrerra said, "At the risk of you snapping at me again, I want to point out that all of our polling, all the media polls, everybody, says the campaign is a draw right now. You need a victory in the trial."

"I need a lot more than that."

"It's no guarantee," she said. "But if you lose, it makes everything Aguilar's said look true."

Keegan stood up to help Muriel Morganthau when she came in with a tray of coffee. The dogs romped around them. It had been hard to fully concentrate during the meeting, but suddenly, he had an idea. Maybe it was thinking of Melanie going off with the marshals that afternoon, or the indecisive meeting with Lorrie.

Keegan felt he could grasp the campaign and trial. He could force Aguilar out.

"Wylie," he said, passing the china coffee cups, "can you get hold of Aguilar's campaign manager? The two of you still talking?"

Morganthau was puzzled. "Sure we're still talking. Professional courtesy."

"Then set up a meeting with Aguilar right away. I'll bring along a couple of people." He thought of Poulsby and Koenig.

"Okay. What's my pitch, George?"

Keegan gave a cup to Cabrerra, an inquiring look on her face, too. "I want to settle the campaign. Tell him the campaign's over."

But Keegan didn't go home after the meeting at Morganthau's. Even as he avoided answering the exclamations from Cabrerra and everyone in the room, a call came, and he rushed out.

He was driving downtown with Conley and the Branch and Area chief. They bounced along quickly, the buildings and sidewalks alternately dark and garish. The heat was on high in the car. Conley sat, grumbling, in back.

"Who's seen him?" Keegan asked sharply.

"The doctors. The guys who called it in," Conley answered.

"Are the doctors moving him?"

His bureau chief shook his head as he drove. "Don't know. Win and I were working late."

"So we heard it first. Lucky," Conley said sarcastically.

Keegan was frustrated when he didn't have information or any idea what was going on. He couldn't hide his impatience. "Somebody tell me why he's in Los Angeles."

Conley leaned forward, the car bouncing over dips in the street, his face shadowed, then lit, shadowed again as the lights rushed by him. "Mr. Kaplow was brought down from San Quentin yesterday morning, George. A special trip. He was supposed to appear in Department 167 for pleas on some old four-fifty-nines he had left over."

"Christ Almighty, why the hell are we going after old burglaries when the man is on Death Row?" Keegan asked, eyes fixed ahead.

"In case something happens to the capital case," his bureau chief answered. "We could still hold him on the burgs."

Keegan swore. "Get me every report from everyone on duty, who transported him, his visitors. I want a complete record of his activities until he tried to kill himself."

Conley sucked his teeth and nodded. "Pretty coincidental."

Keegan swore again. "No coincidence at all. Carnes rigged this like he did that phony confession."

They drove in tense silence until they got to the Men's Central Jail. Keegan jumped out and led a taut, angry parade into the building. The staff was waiting for him, and the parade went on, growing as he passed through the jail's administrative section, the commander and assistants joining, then into the security and transportation sections, busy at that late hour. Conley and the bureau chief stayed near the rear. By the time the parade got to the double-doored hospital section, it was three abreast going through the corridor.

"She's not his lawyer," Keegan said tersely to the commander. "You did not have to let her in."

"The doctor said it might keep him quiet." The commander was defensive.

Keegan turned his frustration to one of the physicians, just inside the door, the brightly shining control booth to one side. "You don't make security and legal decisions, Doctor."

"Mr. Keegan—" the man began.

"What kind of injuries does he have?"

The doctor, short and thin-haired, put his hands on his hips. "We've only got an antique X-ray to work with. It shows a hairline skull fracture. I think he's also got a concussion."

"Is he going to die?"

"I don't know if he's bleeding inside the skull. We need to move him someplace with decent equipment."

The jail commander and doctor began arguing about conditions in the jail as they all briskly walked into the hospital section, its walls and floors cinderblock green, even the grilled windows and doors painted green. Keegan smelled a distasteful acidic odor.

Larson Kaplow lay in a single bed, in a small, windowless two-bed room. He was covered with white sheets, and dusty medical equipment was around him. Beside the bed stood Goodoy and two deputy sheriffs.

Keegan, tight-lipped, said to her, "I'm here. As requested."

"I thought you'd like to hear it from him. I think you'll agree it changes the trial. Completely," she said calmly. She had a raincoat over her dress and no makeup and looked starkly alert.

Keegan looked at Kaplow. His head was bandaged, his mouth partly open, and fluids drained in and out of him. He was still in his jail jumpsuit. "Is he conscious?"

"I've got what he said just now." Goodoy opened a small beige notebook.

He waved her back. "I want to hear it from him. I want to know how a man in an isolation cell can try to kill himself."

The doctor, watching disdainfully, said, "He ran into a wall headfirst. Hard enough to crack his skull, Mr. Keegan. Several times into the wall. If you want to kill yourself, you can do it anywhere."

"I don't think he wanted to kill himself. It's an act," Keegan said. "Carnes set it up."

Goodoy's raincoat rustled as she put the notebook away. "He just told me where the gun that killed Lee Ferrera is."

"Carnes told him where it was. This man"—Keegan pointed at the sheeted figure on the bed—"wasn't anywhere near Nevada when Ferrera was killed."

On the bed, Kaplow suddenly opened his eyes and made a motion toward his mouth. The doctor bent to him. "Water? You thirsty? Food? What?"

"Gum," Kaplow said.

"Gum," the doctor repeated.

"Give him some goddamn gum," Keegan ordered. Goodoy gave Keegan a page from the notebook. He held it tightly.

"You'll check out that information about the gun's location?" she asked. "As an officer of the court?"

Keegan nodded sourly and wanted to end this grotesque show. He believed Goodoy knew Kaplow was phony, but found his information too useful. Just like me with Williams. Carnes is playing us all. The idea infuriated him.

He stood closer to Kaplow, now placidly and slowly chewing on his gum, thick, black-haired hands folded across his sheeted stomach. "Do you know who I am?" Keegan asked.

Larson Kaplow nodded, staring. "Captain Kangaroo."

Someone beside Conley snickered, and Keegan glared at him. "I'm George Keegan," he said to Kaplow. "I'm the district attorney. Did you try to kill yourself this evening, Kaplow?"

"Shame, shame," Kaplow murmured, mouth stopping, gum lying like a pink pill on his tongue when he spoke.

"What shame?" Keegan demanded.

Larson Kaplow took a deep gurgling breath, his hands going to his sides, and Keegan stepped back. Kaplow said loudly, "I killed them. I shot that poor little boy."

When he got home, Keegan took the bottle he'd put under the cabinet in the bathroom and poured it out down the bathtub, running water after it. Kaplow and Lorrie both had struck him into hard, unregretful action. The bottle was a symbol of Leah, self-indulgent and self-pitying.

I don't have room for that, he thought, taking the empty bottle and putting it into the kitchen garbage. Carnes and my enemies are making new rules, and I've got to fight back.

He sat in the living room, too tired to sleep yet. Elaine came in and took the chair opposite him, legs folded underneath her.

"You like it so dark?" she asked. Only one lamp was on at the far end of the room, gleaming on the polish of the grand piano, which Innocencia shined every day and no one played anymore.

"I do," he said. "Put on another light if it bothers you."

"No. It's okay. I only get to see you late like this."

"It's late for you," he said.

"You're gone in the morning before me." She was matter-of-fact, chatty, unlike her silent brother. Keegan thought of them as children, when they had to be different deliberately. Chris would wake up happy, so Elaine woke up grumpy. He pictured them going on into adulthood, contrasting each other as they lived their own lives.

"Tell me about your day, honey," he said.

"I put some bumper stickers on cars at school."

"Thank you."

"We did relay races. Are you listening? You look tired."

"I can hear you. I just had a long day."

"You want to be alone?"

"No. I like your company."

She smiled, and it was still the smile of a little girl, and Keegan wished, with absolute fervor, that life wouldn't change and had stayed the same as it was only a few months before.

"Maybe it is late." Elaine yawned suddenly. She uncurled her legs and stood up, tall and graceful as her mother had been.

Keegan got up, too, and put his arm around her as she guided them up the small steps from the living room to the foyer. "Honey," he said hesitatingly.

"What?"

"Would it matter to you if I wasn't an important man?"

TWENTY-SEVEN

THE NEXT MORNING a fresh and unexpectedly warm day broke over the city. Heavy white clouds hung over the suddenly visible, impossibly distant mountains, and the commuters plodding along the tangled miles of freeways thought more of the humidity, the alarming fruit flies found in Torrance and Santa Monica, and the probable need for more helicopter spraying than they did the Carnes trial or the election. The latest estimate from the county registrar was for a lower than average voter turnout.

Keegan, damp already in his suit, didn't care about the weather or the flying pest returning. He and Goodoy and Ambrosini were arguing before court about Kaplow.

"The preliminary information I got just now," Keegan admitted tensely, "is that the gun they found in Nevada might be the gun that killed Ferrera."

Goodoy, who always looked cool and bone dry, said in mock amazement, "Might have? This is exactly the kind of gun your pathologist said Ferrera was shot with. Exactly."

Keegan said nothing, holding the back of the chair in front of the judge's desk. He had listened only a few minutes before as the sheriff of Washoe County, Nevada, described the late-night, early-morning search for the missing weapon. Two large searchlights borrowed from a used-car lot and men with flashlights crossed the desert a mile from where Ferrera's dried remains had been found. Grimly, Keegan heard that in a small drainage pipe, partly buried, a .44 caliber automatic had been found.

Just where Kaplow told Goodoy it would be.

Just where Carnes told Kaplow it would be, Keegan thought.

"What you'll find, when you test it," Goodoy went on casually, "is that gun fired a couple of the shots that killed the Rotich victims. Ballistics will confirm it."

"Larson Kaplow didn't kill any of those people."

Goodoy snorted. "Kaplow's a mass murderer. He had the gun."

Ambrosini arranged several pill bottles in front of him. Vainly he had tried to cure his unshakable cold, and he glumly studied the bottles. "What are you saying, Mr. Keegan?"

Keegan said, "Judge, Carnes put this man up to these statements. You can't let him go in front of a jury. You've got to weigh his evidence yourself first."

Then Ambrosini, who pocketed two pill bottles, did something Keegan had hoped for and never expected him to do. He smiled a wintry smile and said, "I don't propose to let anyone waltz into my courtroom. We're going to the hospital first."

"We're convening in the matter of People versus Robert Carnes outside the presence of the jury. The defendant is not present. Appearance waived for this special hearing. Both counsel are present." Ambrosini sat on a high white stool, his black robe falling around him.

Keegan and Goodoy stood. Kaplow lay on the bed, in nearly the same position as the night before. Three deputy sheriffs were grouped around him, and his right wrist and ankle had been manacled to the metal bed bars.

Keegan had talked with his senior trial lawyers. The conclusion was unanimous. Kaplow, at all costs, had to be kept away from the jury. They had reviewed the records of Kaplow's true crimes and discovered gaps in time. Goodoy could argue he had been in Nevada. Goodoy asked summary questions, and Kaplow answered sluggishly, as if bored. His hands plucked at the gray blanket covering him.

Keegan stepped near him when his cross-examination began.

"Captain Kangaroo," Kaplow said warmly.

Keegan didn't respond. Kaplow, lying so stiffly, with guards stiffly around him, looked like a dignitary lying in state.

"You claim you killed Barry Rotich because he was cheating you?" Keegan asked. The court reporter, ten feet away, nervously watched Kaplow.

"Oh, he was a cheater all right."

"And you shot him. You strangled all your other victims. Why did you shoot Rotich?"

"I can do whatever I want to. Anyway," he said indignantly, "Ferrera shot first."

"When did you start dealing drugs?"

"Off and on for years." He shrugged. "A sideline."

"Where did you meet Ferrera?"

"Los Angeles, a year ago."

Vague and maddening answers that could be verified only so far, and that was their danger. It would be hard to disprove what Kaplow claimed, and against Keegan's disbelief was the hard fact of the .44.

"How did you know Ferrera was in Nevada?"

"I followed him."

"Why did you kill him?"

Kaplow paused. "He was cheating me like those others."

"Do you know Robert Carnes?"

"We used to play cards together." Kaplow rubbed an unsightly bald patch on the side of his head, the skin inflamed.

"Is that when he told you how to make up this story?"

"That's a trick question."

Keegan stepped back a little. He had not dented Kaplow, and if he could not, Ambrosini would let the man testify. The judge fished under his robe and took out a bottle of amber pills and checked his watch. Jesus, Keegan thought. Kaplow will inject reasonable doubt, and Goodoy could walk Carnes out the door.

Keegan had spent years dealing with liars, and he was not going to let a murdering one get the better of him. He said coldly, "When did you meet Rotich?"

"A while ago."

"Where?"

"I don't remember. Maybe LA."

"How tall is he?" Keegan's voice was sharp, brutal in the closed little room.

"My height."

"He's five inches shorter than you."

"I can't estimate. I'm not good at it. Maybe I was on medication." Kaplow was petulant, pulling the blanket higher.

"What was he wearing the day you shot him?"

"I don't remember."

"Try."

"Oh. Oh. A coat and pants."

Keegan glanced at Goodoy and the judge. "Shorts. And a short-sleeved shirt. It was a hot day. When you killed Ferrera, what was he wearing?"

"A shirt. Jeans. Who remembers clothes?"

"A Windbreaker and shorts." Goodoy had started tapping her foot lightly on the linoleum, the steno machine softly clacking. "What room in the house did you shoot Rotich?"

"Bedroom."

"Which one?"

"There's more than one?" Kaplow frowned. "The big one."

"He was shot in the rear den. Not any bedroom."

"That was a trick question," Kaplow said.

Keegan stood back. "Just like your answers."

Mayor Poulsby had been eating pancakes and sausage from a paper plate at a wedding reception in the backyard of the nephew of his water commissioner, and the guests were delighted to have him, and he smiled and seemed genuinely pleased to make them happy. Cars going by on the sunny, muggy street honked, and he waved.

He kept checking the time. At a certain moment, he put down his plastic glass of champagne, kissed the new bride, waved, was applauded, and hurried to his city car, the engine running. He got in beside the driver and poked him. "Let's go," he said. "Use the siren. The bastards wouldn't let me leave."

At the same moment, Martin Koenig excused himself from a meeting of city officials downtown. He nervously took the elevator to the basement garage and drove out, fearful, sweating, heading west.

As Koenig drove, Celia Aguilar finished her second speech of the morning, and with uncharacteristic mystery, told her two campaign workers she was going someplace, would not say where or to see whom, and before they could press her, she strode to her car and left them wondering whether the schedule for the remainder of the day was still good.

Keegan came alone to the marina, taking the precaution of wearing a warm-up jacket over his shirt instead of his suit coat. It was a small concealment. The day was briny and warm, and as he stepped from the swaying dock to the yacht, he saw massed boats, their sailless masts bobbing back and forth as if to a soundless tune.

Below deck, he found Aguilar, angrily talking to Koenig. Nelson Poulsby reclined in a chair with his eyes closed.

"I had no idea I was meeting with these two," Aguilar said to Keegan. "I thought this was you and me. You and some bizarre threat."

Keegan took off his jacket because it was hot in the cabin.

Poulsby opened his eyes and smiled. "Hello, George. Like a wee small drink?"

"I want to keep this brief," Keegan said.

"I protest. I don't understand why I should be here," Koenig said.

"Because I said you should, Marty. Now, shut up and let's find out what George's got on his mind." Poulsby sat up and then went to the bar and mixed a large drink for himself.

"I don't know if this concerns all of you. I don't know if you're responsible"—he pointed at Aguilar—"or it's them alone."

"The strain of actually doing a trial has driven you around the bend," Aguilar said. "You are nuts."

Poulsby drank. "So, what is it?"

Keegan stood near one of the portholes. He could see the spray from powerboats refracting the sunlight against the stone breakwater, delicate greens and blues glimmering. He was acutely aware of being on Poulsby's turf. The mayor suggested the yacht as the most inconspicuous place for them to gather and then pricked Keegan's curiosity by saying Aguilar already knew the way.

"Melanie Vogt has told me that she was called, assisted, and then met in a car driven by Koenig. The purpose was to drive her out of the city. So she wouldn't have to testify."

"I did nothing wrong." Koenig's yellowish skin was going white, and he wiped his cheeks with a paper napkin from the bar. He looked at the mayor. "I informed people."

"After the fact. Way, way after the fact," Poulsby said.

Aguilar's rigid expression was contemptuous. "You're a moron, Nelson. I always thought so. And you're a double moron because you work for him," she said disgustedly to Koenig. She faced Keegan. Just like the meetings in his office, the same imperious, untouchable certainty. Juries either hated her or worshipped her because she allowed nothing in between. Keegan said, "Did you know?"

"I did not know. I told these two morons they were to stay away from witnesses, George. I don't care if you believe me. I think you know one thing about me. I wouldn't screw up a trial."

"But you'd like to beat me."

"I'm going to beat you," she said. "But I don't win that way."

"Prove it," he said.

"George, I'm not on trial. I don't have to prove a thing." She looked at her watch. "I've got a taping at KTLA I can still make."

Keegan said bluntly, "Celia, if you've got anything to do with this thing, you'll have to withdraw."

She shook her head. Unflappable, he admitted, unmoved by even that kind of declaration. He was sorry so vigorous a deputy DA had no room for compromise with him. "Go to hell," she said.

"I guess that wraps things up," Poulsby said. "Sure you won't have one for the road?" He made another drink and sourly eyed a fidgeting Koenig on the couch.

Keegan folded his arms. "I decided I couldn't file any charges because it would look like a conflict in a campaign year. Melanie's over at the U.S. attorney telling them exactly what happened."

"Oh, my God," Koenig whispered.

Poulsby thoughtfully drank. "Well. What's your point?"

"I'll use whatever goodwill I've got over with the feds if Martin or Celia will make a public statement. I need proof there was a plot to hide my witness. For political gain."

Keegan waited to see who jumped. He did not know whether Aguilar was a conspirator, but he was willing to force her to take a stand. It might get her out of the campaign.

"Well, George," Aguilar said, walking toward him and obviously intending to walk out, "do whatever you want to. I never met your hooker. And I know damn well Martin isn't going to lie about me. Not if he knows what's good for him."

Koenig shrank back slightly, then sat down with a thump. His shirt collar was loose on his neck, and Keegan thought he might be working so hard this election year he was getting scurvy again.

Poulsby said, "Marty's not making any statement for you. The best you can do is put your hooker on the air and cry about what happened." He grinned, put his glass down on the bar with a clink. "But, knowing our federal friends, they won't let her make any public statements until they're done investigating. You're out of luck, George."

"I didn't break any laws. I didn't do anything illegal," Koenig said from his chair.

"Right. That's another thing. Marty didn't break any laws," the mayor said.

Keegan started to leave with Aguilar. "I believe you. I don't think you're involved with them."

"Thank you. It makes my day."

Behind him, as he followed Aguilar out, Keegan heard Poulsby say cheerily, "Besides, what can you do anyway? You're going to lose, George."

On the dock, squinting into the hot sun, the thick white clouds pressing low, Keegan said, "If you were responsible, I was going to tear you apart."

Aguilar stopped. She was tall, rigid, and as the dock shifted with the swell, she barely moved with it. Like her personal virtues. And failings, Keegan thought.

"Look, George, Poulsby's right. You don't have much of an obstruction of justice case. What did you really think you'd accomplish today?"

"Force you out. If you were dirty with them."

"I'm in for the whole thing. You know me."

Keegan nodded, and they walked to the parking lot. Tanned boaters of all ages strolled carefree to their boats. "This is how it's done, Celia. Sometimes the threats work. Sometimes you find out you're even right."

For the first time, Aguilar, her brooch flashing in the sun, looked worried. "God. Maybe I am making a mistake."

He left her and drove downtown, sweating hard even with the car's air conditioner on high. The dark canyons of old buildings on Grand as he headed for the Criminal Courts Building were like coals in the late-season heat. Keegan felt a little carefree himself. He had come away with few things settled, and he was still going to be dogged publicly about proof of the conspiracy charge. He could only refer the reporters to the U.S. attorney.

But he had stopped short of the warfare he had engaged in for so long. He withdrew when it was right to do so and didn't press on until the battle between him and his enemy became bloody. Before this trial, he would have taken the threat against Poulsby or Koenig or Aguilar to the limit.

Maybe I'm getting closer to my childhood ideal, a workman rightly dividing the truth. Not just a blind winner.

And, as one of his smiling campaign posters slapped on an RTD bus rumbled by, KEEGAN'S THE WAY finally made sense to him.

Besides, he thought, riding the elevator up to court, poor Celia obviously doesn't know what she's getting into.

At least I do.

━━━━━

"No seats? No standing room? What? One seat. That's all I need." Frank Goldsmith tried again with the deputy sheriffs sitting around the metal detector outside Ambrosini's courtroom.

"Look," said one sheriff, standing up, towering over Goldsmith. "The courtroom's filled. The judge doesn't like people coming in and out." He pointed at the dozen or so people milling around in the corridor. "See them? They been waiting all morning. One goes in. One comes out. Nobody's come out. So nobody goes in."

Goldsmith blustered. He named actors and movies he'd done. He tried walking straight for the courtroom's faded brown-veneer doors. The deputies actually grabbed his coat and pulled him back.

He felt it all slipping away. At the DA's office, a crusty old woman guarding Keegan's office wouldn't let him in. He was barred from seeing Carnes; Melanie was gone again, rumor said with the feds or something. That left Keegan to put his deal together. And Keegan wouldn't see him. Perhaps he could see Keegan.

He had little plan beyond getting into the courtroom. But he realized he probably wouldn't get close to Keegan in there, either. More deputies. With guns.

It had come to this. He was alone. He had no wife or home. The hotel didn't count. He had no employment. His only steady income came from the rented actors. His grand deals, especially this last saving one of the trial, vestiges of years of schemes and jiggering, sizzled away in the day's sunshine.

Nothing was left without this project, and he didn't have this project without having someone signed up. All doors were closing in his face.

I'm desperate, he realized. I am a desperate guy.

I must get in. He faced the annoyed deputy sheriffs at the

308 WILLIAM P. WOOD

security checkpoint. A tap on his shoulder. It was the old cop who had dogged him for so long and actually helped wreck things.

"What's up, Mr. G?" asked this phony Gary Cooper genially.

"I got to get in."

"Nobody in there wants to see you."

"All I need is a minute. Let me see Keegan."

A shake of the head, sad smile. "No, sorry, Mr. G. You pretty much burned your bridges fooling around with Carnes."

"This is LA. Nothing's in concrete," he said, his old swagger automatically surging. "I got you your best witness."

People in the corridor started to stare nervously at Goldsmith. He didn't care. He had the old cop in front of him, and he knew the deceitful old man could get him through the door right to Keegan.

"Look," he said confidently to Win Conley, "do you want to be in the movies?"

TWENTY-EIGHT

"WHO IS SHE?" Keegan urgently whispered to Conley, who sat down quietly at the counsel table. The defense was about to begin. Goodoy had called a witness, the bailiff went to the doors and brought the witness in.

Conley checked with an assistant who kept the evidence index and witness names. "She's not on our list," he told Keegan.

"This is Goodoy's surprise, I think," Keegan said. A short, thin, nervous woman, in pants with a nylon Windbreaker on, came in and took the oath. "Find out who she is and get on it," Keegan ordered. Conley nodded and slipped out again.

Keegan hunched forward. Goodoy stood at the counsel table, Carnes holding a pencil to his lips.

Goodoy said, "Mrs. Slavik. Do you mind if I call you Lana?"

On the witness stand, the courtroom's curiosity focused on her, the short woman said gratefully, "I'd prefer it. I'm a little scared here."

"Well, try to relax. Keep your voice up." Goodoy cast a glance at Keegan. Here it comes, he thought.

"Where do you work, Lana?" Goodoy asked pleasantly.

"At the Oasis Coffee Shop on Venice Boulevard. I'm a waitress," Lana Slavik said, warily looking at the enormous black eye of the camera at the rear of the courtroom.

"Were you working at the Oasis on May fourteenth?"

"My usual shift is eight to two, but I changed with a friend, so I was on during the day, yes."

"What hours?"

"I came on at noon and went off at six. In the evening. The afternoon." She was flustered. "The evening, six in the evening."

Goodoy smiled reassuringly. "It's all right. While you were working, did someone you see in court today come in?"

Keegan tensed. He had no doubt who the witness would pick out. She was an alibi witness for Robert Carnes.

Mrs. Slavik nodded and shot her arm out toward Carnes. "He came in, sat around."

"May the record reflect she's identified Mr. Carnes?" Goodoy asked softly to the jury.

"Yes." Ambrosini coughed. "So reflected."

Keegan sat back in frustration. He did not recall the woman's name on any police report, which meant she had not been interviewed. Carnes had given her name to Goodoy.

"What time did Mr. Carnes come into the coffee shop?"

She thought, hand at her mouth. "About three. I'm not absolutely sure of the time. It was about midday for me, just before my break."

"Did he stay long?"

"Half hour. Until I went on break. Then he left."

Goodoy walked toward the witness stand. Everyone in the courtroom understood how devastating Lana Slavik was to Keegan's case. She was an apparently independent witness who could place Carnes elsewhere than at the Rotich house at about the time the killings took place.

And she says he was alone, Keegan thought. Ferrera is supposed to be away killing everyone.

"Did Mr. Carnes sit alone the whole time?"

"Yeah. In a booth. We don't like people in them if it's only one. I told him, booths are for parties. Not singles. He says, 'I'm waiting for my party.'"

Goodoy glanced defiantly at Keegan, daring him to make a hearsay objection. But he wanted to hear it all at once. He needed to know immediately exactly what kind of alibi Carnes had constructed for himself.

"One person?" Goodoy asked. "Party singular?"

Mrs. Slavik recited, "His friend was away, busy, and he was waiting for him."

"Did someone join him just before he left?" Goodoy was leading and knew it and boldly challenging Keegan. He sat silently.

"A man came in just as I went on break. He sat down. Or he just sat down, and they got up again. He was in a big hurry."

Goodoy went to the clerk, got a photograph, and put it in front of Lana Slavik. "Take a look at this man, Lana. This is a picture marked People's Thirteen. Do you recognize this man?"

"That's the party who came in. The jumpy one."

"The jumpy one," Goodoy repeated carefully, taking the photo. "This is a picture of Lee Ferrera. Can you describe Mr. Carnes's behavior while he was at the coffee shop?"

She shrugged. "Sitting. Quiet. Cup of coffee. No. Tea. He wanted a second cup of hot water."

"They both left? Together?"

Mrs. Slavik nodded, relaxing a little, smiling as most of the witnesses had, sooner or later, for the audience in and beyond the courtroom. "Soon as this other man showed up, they were gone. I kind of figured this one"—she pointed again at Carnes—"was one of the sitters. You know, they come in, have some coffee, read the paper, just sit. But he didn't sit there too long after this other guy showed up."

Goodoy nodded and sat down, and Keegan waited until Ambrosini peered irritatedly at him. "Are you going to ask any questions?"

Keegan stood up. "Your Honor, this is an unexpected witness. Before I can usefully ask her any questions, I'll need time to prepare."

"Approach the bench, both of you." The judge beckoned.

At the side of the bench, their faces only inches apart, the judge said sourly, "I imagine this one stings a little, Mr. Keegan."

"Like hell."

"You'd like time? How long?"

"A day."

Goodoy groaned loudly. "That's ridiculous."

Ambrosini winced in impatience. "We've had a disrupted schedule already today because of one defense witness. You can have a break now, Mr. Keegan."

"Thank you," Keegan said.

"Until nine-thirty tomorrow morning, when we reconvene."

Keegan caught Ambrosini's sly pleasure at the truncated break. He loves making me run, Keegan thought.

"There must be something. She's got some weak spot," Keegan said as he gathered his trial staff in his office. "We've got a couple of hours to find it."

He divided the staff into ad hoc task forces. Conley took the police agencies with his investigators. They searched for any records relating to the Oasis Coffee Shop or Lana Slavik. Other deputy DAs went through the old case files. They checked with the FBI and the Department of Justice in Sacramento.

Keegan kept track of everything as bits came in. He found time to call Chris, then Elaine, as if reaching out to his children might ease his burden.

At six-thirty in the evening, Keegan took Conley and three investigators and drove to the coffee shop.

"I've accounted for Carnes and Ferrera until around noon on the fourteenth," he said to Conley. "The time of death for the Rotich family is about three in the afternoon. Then we've got them back at the motel with Melanie and on a plane to Nevada by five, all the crank shipped around four-thirty in Ferrera's name."

"She's clean herself," Conley said. "Nice little lady."

"Too bad," Keegan said grimly.

They strode into the Oasis Coffee Shop, through the swirling crowd along Venice Boulevard. A long neon palm tree buzzed electrically in front of the building, and skateboarders and bikers went in and out.

It was busy inside, too, and smoky, and Keegan was a little amused to see how much he and his lawyers stood out. The investigators found the manager, short and nervous enough to be Lana Slavik's brother, but they weren't related. Yes, she was a solid worker. It was lousy she had to miss work to go to court. Yes, everybody followed the trial.

"I think," Keegan explained to the manager, "Carnes came here to set up an alibi. By sitting alone. Ordering tea, asking for water, things that might be recalled, if he needed a witness."

"I'm amazed he came here." A hand brushed over his thinning hair. Nerves.

Part of the pattern I still don't see, Keegan thought. Collisions that somehow reached from a drug dealer's home in Marina del Rey to involve the whole city, the mayor. My family. Maybe I shouldn't be so dismissive of Melanie's fate ideas. It might all make perfect sense.

For two hours, with the manager's help, they went through checks, meals eaten and forgotten already, until they discovered that the ones for May had been destroyed. Like the burnt files. Obscuring the patterns to make the game more fun, he thought. He wasn't deterred. There had to be something. He had not come so far to have Carnes successfully put up a wall against him.

In the manager's office, the music from the coffee shop leaking in, Keegan and the others waded through boxes of old employee records. Cabrerra would have a fit if she knew I was doing this instead of something really worthwhile like raising money for TV ads, he thought, putting another pile of records by Conley.

At nine-fifty, after more than three hours, Keegan found what he was looking for.

The next morning, he spoke carefully and slowly to Lana Slavik, his manner unthreatening. She held her hands in her lap on the witness stand.

"On a normal day, Mrs. Slavik," he asked, "you see, what, a hundred people?"

"Normal?" She grinned. "Maybe two hundred. Lunch is our big time, you can't even move."

"Two hundred a day." Keegan raised his eyebrows, impressed. His evidence lay on the counsel table, waiting. "In six months, at two hundred people a day, thirty days for each month." He frowned, pretended to compute the vast number. "You've seen a few hundred thousand people since May fourteenth, haven't you?"

"Well, we get repeats. But I've got the bad feet to prove it."

Keegan allowed the mild laughter that undulated through the courtroom, and he smiled, too. "I imagine you do have repeats. But that man"—he pointed slowly at Carnes—"he only came in once, one day, didn't he?"

"I believe so."

"Did he come in again? Do you think you saw him some other day?" Keegan grew sharper in his questions. Goodoy and Carnes were in close conference, heads together. Probably telling Goodoy how innocent he is, Keegan thought.

Mrs. Slavik pursed her lips. "I think he was in just the once."

"You aren't sure?"

"I'm not sure," she admitted.

She's an honest woman. The jurors see that, and they'll take her word or discount what she says because she won't color it.

Keegan picked up his evidence, a small white card. He had just put a large hole in Carnes's alibi. "You said you took a friend's shift on May fourteenth. It was not your usual shift."

"That's right."

"Things were hectic, you were rushing around, you weren't thinking clearly about every detail."

Mrs. Slavik squinted and was sour. "I kept my head on."

"So you were focused on details, on the things happening in the coffee shop?"

"You bet I was. Get trampled if you're not."

"I'd like this card marked People's next in order," Keegan said, putting the card in front of her. "When you come to work you fill in your hours worked, the date, and your initials, don't you?"

Goodoy said suspiciously, "I haven't seen that, Your Honor."

"I'll show it to counsel in a moment," Keegan went on quickly. He didn't want to break his questioning now. "Don't you fill out an important record like your hours worked, Mrs. Slavik?"

"Yes." She peered at the card closely.

"You would fill it out because your pay depended on it, and you were keeping track even of details on May fourteenth, isn't that so?"

"I must've forgot." She pushed the card toward Keegan and looked sheepishly at the judge and the jury.

"What was that?" Keegan also looked at the jurors.

"I forgot to fill in my hours for the fourteenth."

"You forgot," he repeated, handing the card to Goodoy, who ran her finger down it, checking the numbers. "You forgot something as important as the hours you worked, which would mean how much you got paid."

"People forget. I should've filled it out."

"But you do have a clear, absolute recollection of this man coming in at three or three-thirty in the afternoon, six months later, two hundred thousand people later?" Keegan asked.

Mrs. Slavik, who was used to rude customers and complaints about service and food, stared back at Keegan. "Maybe it's not so clear."

"You don't know what time, what day, or really even if this man came in at all, do you?"

Mrs. Slavik sighed. "Put it that way, no. I guess I don't."

Keegan sat down, and a reporter caught his eye, giving him a thumb to the floor. He did not know whether that was a comment on him or Carnes's punctured alibi.

Keegan whispered to his assistant. The irony was, of course, that Carnes had been in the Oasis Coffee Shop to set up his alibi. But the essence of the trial, like life in LA, was to turn fact into falsity and illusion into reality. It was a political campaign, too, in which a man was depicted, and he might have little relation to the depiction. A man, Keegan thought, who made a personal yearning for solace and absolution sound like a public call for justice.

Goodoy gestured toward the witness stand and the deputy sheriffs behind Carnes rose when he did.

There was one major figure left and he was about to take the stand.

The first shock for Carnes was how big the courtroom looked from the witness stand. Coming in, sitting at the counsel table, facing only the judge and the clerk and court reporter, he lost a sense of the crowd behind him, even when he glanced back at them.

Now they spread before him, faces in rows, suits, eyes on him, and at the very back, a fat man behind a camera. It was like the opening of a great flower, startling. Carnes nervously cleared his throat. He wore a tie, at Goodoy's insistence, and he had rehearsed this moment with her over and over. He knew his lines.

Yet he hadn't felt confident enough to tell her about the two nearly sleepless nights before today. He heard everything in the jail, all night, the rustling and creaking of other bodies, and sobs, tuneless singing, the laughing guards walking on the concrete.

He knew how much depended on his appearance in the trial's final days. He saw Keegan, large, hateful, glaring at him. The courtroom's light seemed brighter, and Carnes blinked. He strained to control himself. At his right, two jurors studied him.

When he was very young, Carnes had gone to the Barnum and Bailey Circus in New York City. His parents bought seats high up in Madison Square Garden, and when they finally got up to the seats, coming into the vast arena writhing with thousands of people, lights, noise, an explosion of sensation literally hundreds of feet up, Carnes covered his eyes. Then he screamed.

He felt the same terror on the witness stand, and it took all of his energy to remain outwardly calm and unaffected. He gamely returned Goodoy's smile.

She was an angel in gray, with a white lacy blouse and yellow legal pad.

She began with simple questions. Name. Age. Where he went to school, and he relaxed a little, even with Keegan's baleful presence so close by. Goodoy showed him a picture of Lee and asked when they met and how they became acquaintances.

As Carnes spoke, he wondered how Blue Williams and the waitress had affected the unfathomable people in the jury box. Or how Kaplow would have impressed them. He felt if he could come down and talk to them, as he did with the jail guards, they would believe him, but it was much harder and unpredictable working through third parties.

Goodoy asked him about going to Los Angeles in May.

"Mr. Ferrera said he was going to visit some relatives." Carnes twisted his neck unconsciously, the restricting tie irritating him. "He agreed to pay my travel expenses. He said these relatives were unpleasant, and he would probably like to stay a short time."

"Did he tell you anything about the purpose of his visit? The name of his relatives or where they lived?"

Carnes shook his head. He eased more, seeing how Keegan scribbled so fast and the way the judge peered at him from the bench. In fact, he started to like the way everyone in the courtroom watched him. It had a tonic effect on him.

"He had a girl with him. The girl who was here earlier."

"Melanie Vogt was with Lee Ferrera when he came to your home in Elko?"

"Yes, she was. They were going to take some kind of vacation after this Los Angeles visit. I had the impression."

Keegan raised his pen and said loudly, "Objection. He can't state impressions, only facts."

"Sustained," Ambrosini said, not unkindly, Carnes thought.

He nodded politely. It was like a game sitting there, his beautiful, wonderful lawyer protecting him, the rules so neat and defined, and the whole crowd watching him. More. Thousands upon thousands watching him through the TV camera. It was a new sensation, he realized, like a tickle of electricity from his feet to his hair.

"Bob," Goodoy asked matter-of-factly, "did you know what Lee Ferrera did for a living?"

"I later learned he sold drugs. I didn't know it when we lived nearby in Nevada."

He described meetings that never took place, conversations that never happened, as he created a whole new May fourteenth. It was a believable story, Ferrera renting the car, Ferrera out to sell drugs, Ferrera renting the motel room and picking up Melanie Vogt, who was waiting for him. The one true thing he slipped in was a shy admission that yes, he and Melanie had sex. Then there were the baggies of white powder Ferrera left around the motel room. Yes, Carnes said, low, he knew they were drugs. No. He wouldn't risk taking any himself.

He asked for some water. He took off his glasses and wiped them and tapped his finger on his chin before answering. He painted a vivid scene of Ferrera dropping him off at the Oasis Coffee Shop while he went on to visit these relatives. When he came back, Ferrera was very upset, and only at the motel, as a frantic Ferrera and Melanie packed, did he learn the horrifying truth.

Carnes remembered Frank Goldsmith's description of pitching a story for a movie or TV episode to the people who could okay it. He imagined himself pitching a story to the jury, and he wanted them to buy it far more desperately than Goldsmith ever wanted a mere idea purchased for production.

"I was afraid," Carnes said, "that Ferrera would kill me, too. I know I should've reported him or something to the police."

Goodoy nodded sympathetically. Through her, Carnes told the world how these two violent, wild people, Ferrera and Vogt, took over his life. Used his credit cards. Used his home. It was terrible.

By the time they broke for lunch, Carnes had told a wholly new, concrete version of what had happened and portrayed himself as foolish and frightened. Which was, he knew, how he looked to most people anyway, a dull, pasty, plump man who would not, could not, hurt a fly.

As he left the witness stand, Carnes barely suppressed a smile. He wanted to take Goodoy's hand and show his triumph over the vain politician, the oafish man sitting at the counsel table who had obviously taken on more than he could handle.

Originally, Keegan's involvement in the case had infuriated Carnes because it put so much pressure on his defense, made everything so open and vulnerable. But now, Carnes was glad Keegan had stupidly done the trial himself.

He was going to lose everything. His job and this case, too.

Around two-thirty in the afternoon, Keegan began his cross-examination. He had dissipated his anger at the stream of lies Carnes so blandly told that morning, shouting at his staff, anyone who came near. "He's a liar. A damn liar and a killer," Keegan swore in his office to his chief deputy.

"Then you have to bait him and reel him in carefully, boss," came the quiet answer.

I've got you, Keegan thought, drumming his fingers on his notes as he waited to ask his first question. I'm not letting you go until you're dead.

"You say Melanie Vogt is a liar?" Keegan asked abruptly.

"She told some lies."

Keegan squared his shoulders, walking a few steps toward Carnes. "Tell me if these statements she made are lies. You came to LA to buy crank from Barry Rotich."

"That's a lie."

"You picked her up for sex."

"A lie."

"Lee Ferrera was your partner in the drug deal."

"Lie."

"You brought a .44 caliber automatic to the motel and took it with you when you went to see Rotich."

"She's lying."

"You brought seven baggies of crank as samples for Rotich."

"That's another lie."

"You promised to take Melanie with you to live with you."

"Lie."

"You made her change the plane reservations to Nevada."

"I did not."

"She's lying?"

"She's lying."

"You made her make plane reservations in her own name."

"Lie."

"You used Lee Ferrera's name for hotel and dinner reservations."

"I did not. She did."

"The drugs arrived at your home in Nevada later, and you were going to sell them."

"Lie."

"You told her Lee Ferrera killed three people."

"Lie." But Carnes hesitated. The questions and answers had gone on with a staccato, thoughtless swiftness. He sat back, warily looking at Keegan, then Goodoy.

"Lie or truth?"

"That last statement is the truth."

"You did tell her Lee Ferrera had killed those three people, and she did truthfully come in here and repeat it to us?" Keegan demanded.

"Yes. I think she knew he'd killed them before I told her."

"Don't look at your lawyer for cues. Look at me."

Goodoy was shocked to her feet. "That is objectionable, Your Honor. I am not giving Mr. Carnes any cues or helping him in any way."

Keegan waved his legal pad at Carnes. "I don't know what they've worked out," he said.

The judge coughed, and his head stuck out like a turtle's from the black robe's protection. "I think everyone's trying to be professional. Objection's sustained as to the last remark. Remember the jury is watching you both."

Keegan nodded. He'd heard that Ambrosini's cronies warned him he looked too sour and nasty on TV. The great eye on them all mellowed even the judge.

He walked closer to Carnes, pleased to see sweat-dabbed white cheeks. He's not enjoying himself anymore, Keegan thought. "So the one time Melanie Vogt tells something that helps you, she's not lying. Is that your testimony?"

Carnes shot back, "I don't know why she lies or tells the truth."

"But we know why you'd lie about her."

"Objection," Goodoy called out.

The grueling afternoon went on for hours like that, Keegan determined to highlight everything Carnes had done as much as Goodoy tried to erase it. He went over every document, every piece of physical evidence, every statement, showed the photos that together demonstrated how Carnes was at the Rotich home, planned the drug theft, and covered it up by murdering Ferrera later.

Near five, the court reporter hung limply over her machine, and the spectators drooped. Keegan stayed on his feet the whole time, as Carnes struggled with each accusation. Carnes drank water, loosened his tie, and his impassive face sagged, but he had not admitted anything.

It was the accumulation of details Keegan wanted. It was a pattern he saw and understood. Each lie Carnes claimed someone told about him went into the pile. Every document, rental slip, credit card slip, shipping tag that required explanation or denial, was another slice at him.

All the people lied. The evidence had been misconstrued.

I will never allow the jury to accept that, Keegan thought. He swung from the counsel table, still energetic, to Carnes.

"You didn't turn in those bags of methamphetamine that showed up at your house, did you?"

"Turn in?"

"Give them to the police." Keegan pantomimed talking on a telephone. "Making one phone call to say drugs had come to your house."

"No. I thought—" And Carnes prepared to continue one of his lengthy answers.

"That's enough. You answered. I'll ask another question," Keegan snapped. Never let a defendant forget who controls the courtroom, who keeps him on the stand, who harries him. "Did you tell your neighbors about the drugs?"

"No."

"How about an anonymous tip to the police?"

"No."

"Anonymous call to the local TV station, where they could find a whole lot of illegal drugs?" Keegan suggested caustically.

"I didn't tell anyone." Carnes smiled faintly. "I threw the drugs away almost immediately."

Keegan leaned back as if hit. An act. "Threw them away?" he demanded.

"That's right. I tore the bags open and let them blow away in the desert."

Keegan shook his head, hiding his delight at this unprepared answer. Carnes could script almost everything, as he tried with Williams and Kaplow and Slavik, but he had to improvise now and then where he was weak.

"You mean," Keegan said slowly, "you stood there and let all that crank blow away?" He flung his hands up.

"Yes," Carnes said bravely. "I hated it."

"You knew it was evidence in a major murder case, didn't you?"

"Yes." He paused again, obviously trying to think, and Keegan was certain the jurors heard those mental gears clattering. "I knew that. I didn't know what I could do. I told you, I was frightened by the whole thing."

"You did say that." Keegan nodded. "Didn't you also know that so much methamphetamine was very valuable?"

"I didn't know exactly."

"Didn't Ferrera tell you how much this haul was worth? He told you everything else, you said."

"I don't recall."

"But you did know he'd been willing to kill three people to get his hands on it. That meant it was extremely valuable." Keegan had moved to within a few feet of Carnes and spoke harshly.

"I didn't think about that."

"Weren't you afraid Ferrera would kill you, too?" Keegan asked suddenly.

Carnes stared. Thinking. Time passing.

"Did you know Ferrera was dead already?" Keegan asked.

"No."

"Maybe you weren't afraid of him because you were going to kill him," Keegan suggested.

Carnes shook his head. "I didn't kill Lee. I don't know who did."

"Then you certainly took a very big chance, someone as scared as you were, just throwing away Ferrera's drugs, didn't you?"

"I didn't want them around," he said lamely. He was growing tired.

Those were stupid lies, Keegan thought, looking at his pad, and everyone knows it. You know it, too. He stared at Carnes.

"How many bank accounts do you have?" Keegan asked, changing subjects suddenly.

"One. In Elko. In my name."

Keegan tossed several papers in front of Carnes. "Are these records of your account?"

"They look like it."

"How do you earn your income?"

Carnes smiled, assuming he was back on firmer ground. "I've worked as a salesman for several companies. I have a degree in metal engineering. I've worked for two construction companies."

"Stop." Keegan put a hand up. "When did you work for Belton Construction, your last job?"

"About a year and a half ago."

"All the salary you earned shows up in deposits in those bank records?"

Carnes looked down briefly. "Well, except for what I used to live on."

"You invested a lot elsewhere?"

"I didn't make that kind of money."

Goodoy said, "Your Honor, these questions are irrelevant. Also argumentative."

Ambrosini shook his head and took a drink of water. "No. They go to credibility. Don't they, Mr. Keegan?"

"They do, Your Honor." A pleasant change of attitude from the judge as the trial wound down. Maybe he also thinks I'm going to be reelected, Keegan thought. Maybe he wants a TV show.

Keegan then took utility records, property tax assessments, and a bill for a new septic tank from his assistant. He put the papers slowly, one by one, in front of Carnes.

"You paid all these in the last year, didn't you?"

"They're all marked paid." Carnes frowned and loosened his tie a little more. He frowned at Goodoy.

"And you paid for all your groceries, your gas, your taxes, any little trips, repairs last year, didn't you?"

"I owe a little," Carnes said.

Keegan nodded. "Look at your bank records again. Look at the balance. You made two withdrawals all last year. The withdrawals barely cover your property tax bill."

"Yes." Carnes frowned again.

"So where did the money come from?" Keegan asked rudely.

"I had it. I did odd jobs."

Another stupid lie.

"Odd jobs that covered all of your bills for an entire year?"

"Yes."

"With all these bills, you say you threw away thousands and thousands of dollars worth of drugs?" Keegan was close enough to put his hands on the witness stand.

"I did. I said that and I did," Carnes repeated, a steely stubbornness showing through.

"The jury will have all of these records to look at," Keegan said, walking back to his seat. "Do you want to change or modify your testimony at all? This is your chance."

"I don't need to change anything." Carnes smiled.

Keegan sat down. "I'm finished," he said.

"I've only told the truth," Carnes said.

"I said I'm finished," Keegan repeated. "He has nothing to say to me."

He took a deep breath and sat back. The jurors were lost in thought, heads lowered, then raised to look at Carnes and Goodoy as she said she would resume her redirect examination in the morning. One of the jurors, an older man, rubbed at his eye repeatedly. A woman seemed intrigued with her hands.

Tell twelve people who have to scramble to pay their bills that you found money somewhere, somehow for a whole year, Keegan thought. Let them touch those gas bills and tax bills. Leah would never have thought of this line, the one that sends Carnes to the gas chamber. She never thought of money tangibly at all.

Keegan breathed deeply again. But my father and mother thought of money, how to get it, how to hold on to it, how to pay for all the bills that seemed to come in the mail endlessly. Just like the men and women on the jury.

Just like me, before I married Leah.

TWENTY-NINE

"THE JURY'S BACK," was the single phrase Keegan waited for impatiently for three days after he finished his final arguments. There are no straight lines in Los Angeles: everything from the streets and freeways to the architecture and even the light seems to bend and deform to other forces. The jury did not come back immediately after they marched, stolid faced and single file, from the courtroom, and the TV camera's light went out.

Keegan had meetings in his office with the staff. Problems that had accumulated while he was tied up in court now flooded over him. Hiring decisions in Compton. Disciplining two deputies arrested with cocaine. Straightening a morale problem in his Long Beach office, which was, because of the distance, a world to itself.

On the third day, the city was cold, overcast, and gray, the black skyscrapers and towers sullen, waiting for rain.

He paced his office, unable to think about the campaign, however much Cabrerra barged in, harangued him, and left. What could the jury be doing? He asked his senior lawyers, and they said a trial of this kind usually meant deliberations for a week.

Phil Klein, cigar rolling in his mouth, unlit, said, "Boss, the boys and girls are coming at me about this *Newsweek* piece. They've heard about it."

"It'll be out in a couple of days," Keegan said distractedly.

"They're sharpening the knives now. Don't you want me to get something, you know, to give them, make it sound better?"

"Talk to Barbara again, Phil. She's the angle-maker."

The phone rang, the black one on Keegan's desk. It was eleven in the morning and going to rain.

"The jury's back," he told Klein, when he hung up and got his coat.

Keegan kept his back straight in the chair. It had been an ordeal working through the people lined up outside the courtroom. On the sidewalks, others stood in the spattering rain under massed umbrellas.

He'd listened to his trial deputies describe the odd sense of disorientation waiting for the jury in a big case. Time and color and shape all lost coherence, as if in a dream or fugue. But Keegan, as Ambrosini sat down and called them to order, then called for the jury foreman to stand, was concretely aware of everything. He was completely in control.

"Mrs. Lutz, has the jury reached a verdict?"

Young, composed, black, she shook her head. "No, we haven't."

Keegan forced his back hard into the chair, and someone said, "Christ," in a despairing whisper. Carnes, he saw, had closed his eyes, head shaking. What are your nights like, Keegan wondered.

The judge cleared his throat and shuffled papers. "Are you saying the jury is deadlocked?" Dry, nasal, and unemotional.

"Yes." She glanced across at her fellow jurors. "We are deadlocked, Judge."

Keegan bent to his assistant. "Can I do anything?" he whispered.

"It's out of your hands now."

He sat back, trying not to show the painful betrayal he felt. I showed you everything, he wanted to say to the jurors. I trusted you to do the only right thing.

Over the continuous rustling and murmuring sweeping the courtroom, Ambrosini went on, "Without giving me the number of jurors or the direction they are leaning, tell me if the jury favors one position more strongly than another."

The forewoman shrugged. "Yes, we do. Everybody's got pretty definite opinions."

"Would further deliberations be of any use?"

Several jurors vigorously nodded. "I suppose it might," Mrs. Lutz said without enthusiasm and sat down.

"Then I will direct you to return to the jury room and resume your deliberations. Please notify the court, through the deputy sheriff, when you have reached a verdict or you wish to return to court."

Keegan stood as the jurors again filed out, and he swore vehemently. The spectators got to their feet, the voices, questions, very loud.

"What more do they want?" Keegan asked furiously. "What else do they want me to give them?"

Midafternoon he found out.

He held his press conference in the DA's office, standing at the podium in front of the blue curtain, facing cameras and forty reporters—hands and voices raised—who fought for his notice. Conley and the bureau chiefs flanked him, and deputy DAs filled the doorways, faces pressing in like kids solemnly watching adults.

"My first reaction?" Keegan had a rueful smile. "I was appalled. I thought the jury was stuck, and I'd have to do it all over again."

"Are you ready for the penalty trial?" a woman in back called out.

Keegan wiped his chin and lower lip, sweating in the lights. "As you all heard Judge Ambrosini say, we'll start the penalty phase of this trial in about five weeks. I'll ask for the death penalty as I've said all along."

They asked him about the wisdom of the jurors, and he said most people used common sense and that doomed Carnes.

"How about Goodoy? She okay?"

Keegan nodded seriously. "I have a high regard for her. She did a fine job. She just didn't have the truth on her side."

He wanted this to go on forever. I made the right decision to take the trial. I didn't fail like so many of them—he looked around even at his own deputies—thought I would. Cabrerra sidled to one side of the curtain and waved at him. Before the press conference she said, "All right. You got your guilty verdict. Now you've got five days left to run flat-out." She patted his shoulder. "Then you get reelected."

"Are you going to take another case to trial? Make this a habit?"

Keegan grinned widely. "Like the old vaudevillian, I want to stop while they're still applauding. One trial a term is enough."

He gave a small salute to the deputy DAs crowding into the room, and they obligingly broke into applause. It would be, he knew, a good picture on the TV news.

Later, the senior staff filled his office, bringing bowls of punch and glasses, and he took the many congratulations gracefully standing at his desk.

"Don't let it go to your head," Conley said.

"Give me some credit, Win."

"Okay. It was a good victory. This place would've been pure hell if you'd lost." He shook Keegan's hand.

Keegan called Elaine and Chris and said they'd all go out to dinner to celebrate.

Cabrerra came in and put the fresh issue of *Newsweek* in his hand. The article Lorrie had written wasn't the cover story, but it filled pages in the magazine. "Sorry to spoil the day, George," Cabrerra said. "It just hit the stands."

"Well, I think you've muted it a little," he said. "We knew it was coming."

"Right. Yes. Upbeat. One verdict down. One verdict to go

on November fifth." She got a glass of punch from Conley, and Keegan put the magazine in his desk.

From the window he looked at the gray skyline, the New Otani Hotel like gray ice and the sea invisible in the overcast distance, and he still didn't know what the charged, upraised hand of Dr. Staggers on the billboard below him meant.

NOVEMBER

THIRTY

THREE DAYS TO THE ELECTION.

Headlines no campaign could buy. Keegan and Cabrerra passed them around, driving from campaign stop to stop, the heavy sound of one newspaper slapped over another satisfying beyond measure.

His schedule was kept heavy. Coffees in homes, four in the morning, twenty minutes each, a minimum of thirty people at each. Neighborhoods from Bellflower to Lennox, back up to Westwood, down to Burbank. Over to San Gabriel and its neat houses, back to aging Rosemead, he crossed and recrossed the county, spending most time in the cities with more people. He was on the phone every morning, at Morganthau's direction, calling donors to keep the money for the TV and radio ads coming in. He held press conferences when he paused in his photogenic door-to-door walks in Compton. Against the backdrop of poor homes and empty lots, he gave stern lectures about crime prevention and sterner warnings about prosecuting drug dealers. The obvious use of his trial victory was sometimes criticized.

Cabrerra decreed three speeches a day. Keegan spoke at lunch and dinner, Kiwanis, Rotary, the Signal Hills Crimefighters one day. He was a celebrity everywhere, and people smiled and surrounded him. Years of public office hadn't meant anything like this attention he got from a month of a televised trial. He began to feel as if Celia Aguilar no longer existed. It was a dialogue solely between him and the people of Los Angeles.

In the car, he tossed aside critical news stories.

"Is this stuff hurting?" he asked Cabrerra as they were driven to the next stop.

"I don't really know," she said carefully. "Our tracking polls show people are still nervous about you."

"Me? Why?"

"Oh, it's probably just LA, George. They like to change the show for the hell of it no matter how good you've been."

He shook his head. "I've never gotten public support like this."

"We're still in a dead heat with Celia."

Keegan patted her leg. "You get them to the polls. I'll get their votes." He felt full of confidence.

At the next stop, with several crime victims and cameras, Keegan took a ride over Los Angeles in a blimp. It occurred to him that he hadn't seen anybody except campaign staffers lately. He hadn't even seen Conley since the trial ended.

As they drifted over the city, the blimp's engine chugging like a feathery tugboat, Keegan gave his speech about neighborhood watch programs and how he'd gone after polluters. He thought, as he talked, he'd get Win and the kids together and have dinner just before the election. It's one thing to have a thousand people slap your back, he thought, holding onto a strap in the blimp, but I've got to have my family and a good friend near now.

The day before the election.

Innocencia made pot roast because she knew he liked it and it was a cold day. For hours the house smelled magnificent, and Keegan started a fire. Chris and Elaine treated the evening like a holiday.

At dinner, Keegan said, "Win, Chris wants to join the police."

Chris looked up. "I haven't made up my mind."

"I don't believe it." Elaine rolled her eyes.

Conley went on cutting his food, eating, eyes on his plate, listening and nodding. Keegan knew he was thinking.

"What can you do, Win?" Keegan asked.

Conley sniffed and put down his fork. "Not a damn thing."

Keegan grinned at the joke. "I appreciate it."

Conley looked at Chris Keegan across the table. "No. I mean I won't do anything for you."

Defensively, Chris said, "I don't want anything. I didn't ask for any help."

"Well. Whatever you can do will be appreciated, Win," Keegan said.

Conley said, "You're not listening, George. I mean it. If Chris's really planning on joining, I won't help him. I won't let anybody I know help him. If I find out you found someone, I'll make life hell for them."

Keegan's smile left him. Innocencia came in, took the plates and compliments. He wiped his mouth. "I don't understand."

Conley pushed back a little. He had, as he usually did when eating at home or at Keegan's, loosened his belt, and it made him look much older. "The worst thing that could happen to Chris is for his fellow recruits, his fellow officers, to think he got special favors. Someone was looking out for him. He's going to have a tough time anyway because he's your kid."

"I'm going to do things my own way," Chris said.

Elaine frowned. "It's a bizarre idea. Mother would have hated it."

Keegan said, "I've got enough respect among cops. No one's going to take any resentment out on Chris."

"Can we drop it?" Chris asked. He got up. "I still haven't decided. I want to decide on my own."

Conley nodded. "Think about it, Chris. Like it or not, being George Keegan's kid is going to make your life as a cop harder. It won't matter how good you are. Or how bad. If your dad gets to Sacramento, I know what kind of career you'll have with LAPD."

"That's not fair," Keegan said in annoyance. "Chris can handle things himself."

"Fairness isn't part of it."

The conversation and the whole evening had suddenly gone sour, and Keegan didn't know why. They left the table soon, Chris and Elaine watching TV in the living room while Keegan took Conley into the kitchen. Innocencia was washing dishes.

"I'm going to vote early tomorrow," she said.

"Vote a couple of times. I may need it." Keegan got glasses for Conley and himself as she giggled.

They poured drinks and walked back to the living room, stopping where they could see the kids from the back. Keegan relaxed, the fire and the kids making him realize it would be over soon, the trial ended, the days of speeches and walking and smiling. He had done all he could do. He didn't want to chastise Conley for being rude, either.

"Quiet night," Conley said.

"I had them stop all calls." Keegan drank.

"Good kids," Conley said, watching contemplatively for a moment. "I'd like to see mine more."

But Keegan couldn't let his annoyance pass entirely. He said, "You shouldn't have gone after Chris."

"I went after you."

"Me?"

"Important people get it into their heads they can do anything. Set up everything. Run everybody. Look"—Conley's loose belt barely stayed closed around his thin waist—"people have to make their own mistakes. Let him fall on his face, for Christ sake, George."

There was a loud thump and a rustling on the side of the house in the hedges that formed a living wall between Keegan and the next home. He raised his eyes. The rustling was louder.

"Cats probably," Keegan said. "They're all over the neighborhood."

Conley said nothing, but Keegan noticed he was tensing, from reflex, at the unknown and unforeseen.

Innocencia called out in fright from the kitchen, her voice carrying over the TV, which Chris instantly shut off. Keegan and Conley hurried back, and met her, hands in a wet apron, coming toward them.

"What's wrong?" Keegan demanded.

"There's someone coming around the back of the house," she said. "Creeping around. I saw him when he got past the kitchen window."

"I'll go check," Conley said. He cinched his belt up. He had on his shoulder holster, and he had kept his sport coat on during dinner to keep it out of sight.

"I'll come, too," Keegan said, setting his glass down.

"No. You stay inside," Conley said, and it was a command, not a friend's suggestion. "You're an important man, George."

Keegan nodded. "I'll wait." And his children and Innocencia were beside him. Conley had gone out the front door.

"What's going on?" Chris asked.

"I don't know. We'll find out." He noticed again how big both Chris and Elaine were, and had again the giddy feeling he'd gone to sleep one day and awakened to find years had passed. Innocencia seemed to hold her breath. The trial and campaign had made them all tense and jumpy.

"It's probably just someone crossing through the yard," Keegan said. He thought of all the people he met, who had seen him, who had been angered or offended during his years in office. He thought of Carnes, plotting, enraged, the men he sent to find Melanie still fugitives. He thought of Poulsby and a frightened Koenig.

A heavy crash hit the side of the house, and shouts flew up immediately. One loud crack, snapped off at the end, meant a shot fired.

Keegan didn't hesitate.

"Okay. Okay. Everybody upstairs and get down on the floor in my bedroom, come on, let's go." And he forcibly herded them up, almost running. Don't think. Don't worry. It was like the night he found out about Leah's accident, the same dark panic. But this was different. He didn't know who had fired or at what. He didn't know what the threat was.

Once he was sure the children and Innocencia were protected by the bed and bureau, and low to the floor, he pushed the button that summoned the Beverly Hills police. Two minutes. Alarms ringing in the Spanish Gothic sandstone building at the foot of City Hall, shock when they saw who was calling for help, maybe even a crack or two about the other time, when little Elaine had caused so much unnecessary turmoil.

Keegan crouched down, staying away from the window. He heard more rustling and crashing outside, and a dog next door started barking frenziedly. It was soon joined by a chorus of dogs, all barking and growling at one another, into the damp and dark night.

Chris slid near him.

"Stay down. Jesus," Keegan said pointlessly.

"They're fighting outside."

Keegan reached for the phone as it rang. A sergeant from BHPD calmly asking for details. Three units were on their way. Keegan tersely said there was someone outside and one shot had been fired. He gave the last location, and even as he was speaking he heard the sirens, the red and white lights flew onto the bedroom's darkened ceiling from below, and voices called out. Car doors opened, and he crouched lower, coming toward Chris and Elaine, Innocencia stone-faced beside them.

A deep, unnatural silence blew in, like a great dark wind, and in it was only the faint sound of light rain outside.

Keegan felt the heavy quilt on the bed against him. Leah liked to cuddle underneath it in the early morning.

He did not feel fear. It was more a mental confusion. He could not decide whether to get up and see what was happening or stay where he was. Elaine pressed near his ankle.

"It's all right," he said very softly.

At that moment, there was another shout, two shouts, and four gunshots so closely fired they reverberated against the houses like one great blast.

Keegan heard Innocencia praying in Spanish. It sounded like the TV in the restaurant where he had last seen Lorrie. He desperately hoped Conley was safe.

He heard his name called over a bullhorn, and he went to the bedroom window. It was hard to see outside, but all the lights had come on along his block of Rexford. He saw four squad cars angled around the sidewalk in front of his house, men with flashlights, and his name was called again.

"I'm fine," Keegan called back. "We're all right."

He turned to the others in the bedroom, just starting to get off the floor. "Chris, please keep low and stay here until I see what's going on."

"I want to come."

"No. I would like you all to stay here," he said. He walked downstairs. He heard sirens, undulant ambulance and police sirens, and he was met as he came out the door by two Beverly Hills cops. He looked around for Win. It was important, at a moment of chaos and tension, to maintain an appearance of calm. He wore his mask of resolution.

He asked calmly what was going on. The younger cop began talking, all the time leading him toward the flowerbeds in front of the house. A man, on the grass, being handcuffed, babbled fearfully. He was dressed in black sweats.

"It's some kind of mix-up, ask anybody. Look, they won't let me get near anyone. I get shut out of the trial, I can't see my people, so I'm left hanging out. I've got obligations. Look, I did some favors, too," the man babbled on, was pulled upright, his face going from cop to cop as he was pushed quickstep to a squad car.

"So all I'm doing is coming to see Keegan. He knows me. Ask him. He knows me. We used to live near here. Shit. I used to live in Beverly Hills, you guys probably know me, too. I'm in the business. All I'm doing tonight, really, is thinking, If I sort of pop up in his living room, a gag, you know? He'd talk to me. Do some business."

Keegan watched, said to the young cop bringing him forward, "His name's Frank Goldsmith." He was icy calm. His mind was a noisy fireburst, and like that night when the cops, just like this, brought him to the wreckage, pushed him to it, forced him to see, he would not show any emotion.

Goldsmith was put, head down, into the squad car as two ambulances and more cars arrived, and the homes along the block emptied their occupants onto the sidewalk, in robes and pajamas and sweats. It's the lights, Keegan thought, all these red and blue lights, the flashlights swinging around. It makes you dizzy. It's out of focus.

Goldsmith was still talking. "So all I'm doing, swear to God, is checking around the house. I'm going home. I said, Fuck it, who am I, I'm climbing into someone's house? I'm not a fucking stunt man, I'm a producer. So this guy, he's got a gun, he's on me, and I swear to God, he fired at me. Is he dead?" Goldsmith's voice was cut off as the squad car door slammed shut.

Keegan sensed his son and daughter beside him, their steps slowing, drawing even, and the trio stopped at the flowerbed. The young cop pointed.

Chris put his arm around Keegan, and Elaine drew her hands to her mouth and coughed. Keegan put his arm on her.

It's the lights, all these lights, Keegan thought. Like the night on Mulholland Drive, lights whirling and slashing through the darkness, illuminating things that should stay in the dark. The shadows danced along the crushed birds-of-paradise and ferns where the struggle must have taken place, where at least one dark form with a gun would have been seen by the cops when they hurried up. The light rain was cold, pricking icy needles on his face.

Face up, arm thrown over his head, Win Conley lay dead in an otherwise elegantly maintained Beverly Hills flowerbed.

THIRTY-ONE

ELECTION DAY.

The rain had turned to showers that swept across the wide LA basin from the mountains to the sea, and a gray opacity descended, and there were the usual fears that the stilt homes around Malibu, built above the endless traffic along the Pacific Coast Highway, would not wait for the great earthquake to slide down the hillsides.

Gray, grainy photographs in every newspaper of Keegan at the hospital, with his children, outside his home, hair stuck flat and disarrayed on his head, raincoat soaked, slowly dissolved on the sidewalks where they were discarded or were picked up by the water rushing into sewer and drainage ports in the streets, the sad faces and awful headlines decomposing and coming apart until only sodden bits of paper were left to find their way to the ocean. After all, they were only images in a city of images, and more would appear the next day to take their place.

At various restaurants on the Westside, many with stark Italian logos, shocked and yet boisterous groups of movie people shook their heads at the paradoxes in life. The shooting in Beverly Hills

340

involving the district attorney himself was the only topic of luncheon exclamations. At a fashionable restaurant in Brentwood, men vied to recount Frank Goldsmith stories, some based on personal knowledge, but good stories from any source. At the Captain's Table, Goldsmith's actual cronies made their way in a denser crowd than usual and speculated what he was doing at Keegan's home and why he was spared a shooting death.

As the county's several million voters went to the thousands of polling places in the rain, a twinge of recognition struck each one upon seeing Keegan's name on the ballot.

Keegan nearly didn't get to the district attorney's office because he slept an hour between the hospital and coming home, too sick at heart to think, too weary to move.

When he did arrive, the gloom outside dripped from one floor to the next. Everyone was shocked into silence or bewilderment, cops, investigators, and deputies. He rode up the elevator, got out, and walked the corridor to his office, stopped every few steps by someone who wanted to express loss or misery. Quite a few clericals were crying, and very little got done on the eighteenth floor except in the Major Narcotic Bureau where no one death slowed anything.

Keegan sat at his desk, his assistants and staff clustered in his office. He felt old and tired and puzzled, filled with a cold sense of inevitability, as if exchanging Carnes for Leah as a method of atonement had been rejected by fate and Win Conley's death added to his burden.

He was amazed that a man who had survived everything the streets of Los Angeles had thrown at him, been amongst the wreckage of a burning plane to save Howard Hughes, had died violently on the quiet and haughty streets of Beverly Hills. It made little sense.

Keegan's chief deputy, arms folded, standing in front of the staff, said, "We've decided to start an achievement award, boss. For the investigators. It'll be in Win's name."

Keegan stood up and was lost, unable either to speak or say anything. It was a strange sensation, everyone watching him, waiting for him to say something, and nothing happening at all. He looked at the gray, water-streaked windows. He was aware of the unease his silence was causing, the bureau chiefs looking at one another.

He wasn't frightened by his own paralysis, only curious. Then, as if he hadn't willed it, his mouth opened, and he said, "We've lost a good friend."

People nodded, and he sat down, and when it became obvious he wasn't going to say anything else, his chief deputy decorously shepherded everyone out.

Cabrerra remained behind.

"You look rocky, George," she said, her glasses as gray as the windows, her plump face pale.

"I'm fine."

"You could go home. There's nothing for you to do now. Here or at headquarters."

He shook his head.

She sat down. "The bad weather's hurting us. Our people are fair-weather voters, and it's tough today. Aguilar's got a hard core of true believers. They'd come out in an earthquake."

He looked away, then at the photos of Leah, the children, on his desk.

He heard Cabrerra, in a softer voice than he had noticed before, say, "George. I am very sorry."

———

"Get me out," Goldsmith said huskily to his lawyer.

"Can't do it, Frank. Bail's two hundred thousand. Judge won't go lower."

"I can't make five grand, much less twenty. Look. What's going on? They sticking me with what happened?"

"Well, right now, right at this exact moment, it's not clear what you're ultimately going to be charged with. The DA hasn't filed charges yet."

Goldsmith groaned. He didn't like the chafing of his jail jump-suit, and he was furious with his lawyer, who had a Century City law firm behind him, for being so slow to answer the all-night-long distress calls he'd put out. The man had a brace of gold-topped pens in his European-cut suit pocket.

"The DA? The DA?" Goldsmith repeated incredulously. "It's his goddamn house. I'm crucified."

"Frank. The DA will not handle the prosecution. It goes to the attorney general. Guaranteed. Conflict of interest."

"So get my bail down. Get me out. Out," Goldsmith pleaded.

"I'm working on it." His lawyer got up, checking his suit to make sure no bits of anything odd from the jail were sticking to him. "One good thing," his lawyer went on, "I'm getting some feel-ers from Underbridge Productions."

"That cocksucker Mark Rubins?"

"He says, he says it casually, your story's interesting."

Goldsmith raised his throbbing head, the sparkling migraine that had appeared with dawn making the lights take on auras. "My what?"

"The whole situation. Everything. He says, again he's very casual, he says, it has possibilities."

Goldsmith thought his lawyer's face had suddenly acquired an aura itself, like an old painting of a saint. "If we're starting any negotiations with Rubins, I want some script control. No." He wobbled to his feet. "I want to write the goddamn script."

It was, he thought with the painful clarity of a migraine, his story to tell.

———

Shortly after the polls closed at eight P.M., Melanie made her televi-sion debut on KCOP. She sat to one side of a gravelly voiced host who was sunburned the color of a baked apple. It was a local talk show, and she was the first guest.

She wore a bright blouse and jeans, and she smiled beatifically on the spare set, one leg under her when she sat down.

They chatted for a little while, talking about her childhood and her trainer father, who she said she hoped was watching, and she described her love of all animals, especially the majestic horse.

"All right. All right." The show's host tapped some papers, looked at her as if she was the next bout on the night's card. "You've been close, very, very close to one of the biggest stories in this town in years. What about the verdict?"

Melanie had not really come to a firm reaction to Bobby's guilty verdict. She had a sense he might still beat the final jury decision and spend the rest of his life in jail rather than die in the gas chamber. He was clever enough to do that. The U.S. attorney promised her all kinds of protection if it appeared she needed it. There was some excitement, which of course she couldn't even mention on TV, about indicting the mayor and his chief aide.

"My feeling about the verdict is that I'm sorry for all the bad things Bobby Carnes did. I did, the morning he went out, tell him to be careful."

"You? You told Robert Carnes, killer, to be careful?"

"Yes, I did."

"It sure looks like he should've listened to you."

"Yes, he should."

"The stars helped you?"

Melanie nodded primly. "I get a lot of help in my life from the stars. It's just like it's plain good advice."

"All right." A smile from the host, the lights like holes of white punched in the space in front of the set, they were so bright. "All right. George Keegan. District attorney. High-risk strategy doing this trial. Up for reelection. Polls are closed. What do the stars tell you about him? Win or lose?"

Melanie uncurled her leg and studied her feet. "I think Mr. Keegan and his friend should have listened to me."

"Oh. You warned Keegan and the victim last night, too?"

She nodded. The desk the show's host sat at was made of plywood, and she thought it might break. The whole place was awfully flimsy. "I did warn them."

"He wins the election?"

"I think so."

"Maybe he should have taken your advice. Maybe we all should. You're right about a lot of things. Maybe you've got a new career."

Melanie had not considered what she would do. Her life as a cosmetologist seemed over and trivial compared to what had happened.

The host said, "I've got some advice for people watching. You keep your eyes on this little lady. She's got a bright, bright future."

She smiled, as comfortable before the blind cameras as she had been at home with her father or with any of the strangers who passed through her life like Bobby.

They all wanted something from her, and it was only a matter of figuring out what to give them.

At nine-forty, with early returns coming in and the DA's race listed as inconclusive, Carnes walked toward his cell, along a brightly lit, almost shiny jail corridor, hands in his jumpsuit pockets. He had just gotten a piece of dryish pound cake to eat later.

His soft-soled sneakers squeaked on the polished concrete floor, buffed lustrous. He was preoccupied and disturbed by the trial's outcome and had not, even after diligent mental exercise, been able to shake off a feeling of doom and despair.

He passed two guards, chatted briefly with them, and was a little buoyed by their good wishes. He was treated with more severity and restriction since the guilty verdict, but the earlier tolerance remained.

He turned the corner, down an identical corner, lost in thought.

He looked up at the footsteps beside him.

"Seymour, I didn't see you."

"I saw you," Belik said with a grin. He had his hands in his pockets, and he was stouter than Carnes recalled during the bridge-playing days.

"You're back?"

They walked, Belik panting slightly, his head swiveling on his thick neck. "I'm coming in for my Vacaville report." He had spent several weeks being observed by psychiatrists at the California Medical Facility at Vacaville to see whether or not he could be sent to state prison.

"I'll talk to you tomorrow. I've got a lot on my mind." Carnes walked on, still preoccupied. He had watched Melanie on TV, and seeing her again upset him. She was not supposed to have gotten away.

"Still playing cards?" Belik at his side again.

"The group broke up."

"Sure. Larson's gone. I'm gone. You're going away."

"We'll see. My trial's not over." He tried to shake Belik off. The lights overhead were stark, very hard white, all shadows gone.

"So no cards," Belik said.

"No cards, Seymour."

"No one to pick on."

"Pick on?"

"Do things to, make him mad, make everybody laugh at him. Tell everyone he's stupid."

"No one said you're stupid." Carnes shook his head at this idiot who had returned so inopportunely to haunt him.

"I'm not stupid. Ask the doctors," Belik shouted.

Carnes looked sharply at him, and saw the long-bladed knife Belik must have been working on for some time.

Nelson Poulsby burped, patted his mouth, and held out his hand for another drink, which a waiter, harried and snide, filled as he passed around the crowded suite once more. The mayor tossed a salty canapé into his mouth.

"Why wait?" he chewed and mumbled to Celia Aguilar.

She and her family, husband and children, mingled with the people aimlessly flowing in and out of the suite at the Century

Plaza Hotel. Three TV sets, all on different stations, blared at one end of the room, and a gaggle of drunks huddled close to them, cheering or cursing whenever the DA's race was reported.

Aguilar did not like having her family share such intimacy with Poulsby, the mayor's people, and the others who insisted on coming in and shaking her hand or hugging her. Her hand ached, and her shoulders were sore from being squeezed, and she was tired of introducing her husband and children. She fanned her face. The air conditioners struggled with so many bodies. A window had been opened, but the suite was still humid and oppressive. Damp wind blew the curtains.

"I said, why wait?" Poulsby grinned at Koenig sitting at the other end of the sofa, a drink he'd been sipping for two hours in his hands.

"He's got to give up first. I'm not marching downstairs and having Keegan say he's waiting for all the votes to be counted." She was curt and absolute. One of her daughters came by. "No more anchovies," Aguilar ordered.

"Hell, Keegan's going to draw this out all night. He lost. He doesn't want to admit it. Just go out and tell everybody you won."

"Nelson, I don't know I've won. For sure."

The horrible part was that her husband actually enjoyed shaking Poulsby's hand, meeting the man. She looked around. All of this might never end.

The drunks began cheering. Aguilar, with a first and unfamiliar twinge of fear tickling her, looked at them, as they hopped up and down.

"Looks like we know for sure," Poulsby said, empty glass out for another refill.

Across the city, at the purple, glass enormity of the Bonaventure Hotel near the Music Center and the ceaseless commotion downtown, Wylie Morganthau and Keegan were with Barbara Cabrerra in the campaign suite.

"What's the point, George?" Morganthau said again. "It's done. You did your best. We all did. It didn't work." Morganthau drank his vodka neat, put one finger in his ear to block some of the noise in the teeming room.

"I want Barbara to tell me what happened." Keegan was stubborn. A little drunk, if you wanted the truth, Morganthau thought. George had that squint-eyed fierceness he used to get, before the accident, when he'd take on anybody, the police department, developers, gangs, anybody he thought was doing wrong. It seemed to go out of him during the trial, like he was running on automatic almost.

"Tell him." Morganthau threw up one hand. "Christ. Then we can get loaded."

Cabrerra nibbled a cracker. "Two things did it. One was the shooting. It gave people a reason to vote against you. Second. The article. You came across like a ship without a rudder, George."

Keegan seemed to take that, then Morganthau almost yelped.

"What did I do wrong, Barbara?" George asked again.

"Christ. Not again. Look, George, tell you what. We'll open those." Morganthau pointed at the bottles of victory champagne stacked on the wet bar. "We'll get really loaded, and everybody can take a flying fuck, okay?"

Keegan stared angrily around at the subdued yet noisy, listless welter of people in the suite. Several, drinking heavily, watched the TVs. In the last hour, Morganthau noticed that as George's chance for reelection grew dimmer, he seemed to evaporate. People talked like he wasn't there. They walked by him, not discourteous, the bastards, just like he'd become a ghost.

So, I understand if he's a little angry. In the last twenty-four hours he's lost a dear friend and his job. He should get drunk. He should get out of here anyway. Bastards eating and drinking on his tab.

Muriel Morganthau was downstairs in the Santa Barbara ballroom, with a few hundred diehard supporters, waiting for Keegan's appearance. It left Wylie free upstairs to look around at the available ones strolling around the suite, and he spotted a tall, freckled redhead, who kept looking at him over her glass.

The night, if it was a disaster, shouldn't be a total disaster.

Muriel was babysitting George's kids.

"What're you going to do, Barbara?" Keegan asked Cabrerra.

She smiled sweetly. "Back to Sacramento. I've got a couple Assembly races that look interesting."

"How long should I prolong this wake?" Keegan asked.

"George, you're coming in only two, maybe three thousand short. You did good," Morganthau said. He was a little tired, even if he sympathized, with George's maudlin behavior. Too much depressing stuff happening lately, Leah, the campaign, the old guy. The thing was over, school's out, and it was time, Morganthau decided, for a vacation.

"Excuse me, you two. I've got to see someone." Morganthau patted Keegan and headed for the redhead.

As he pushed people aside, he saw that *Newsweek* reporter, who stabbed George in the back, going over to him.

![divider]

He took her into the suite's bedroom. Coats and jackets had been heaped on the bed and chairs after the closet filled up.

"You came to gloat?" Keegan still held his glass.

"I'm doing a wrap-up story. Winners and losers."

"You've got courage." He drank and noticed she had on a water-spotted raincoat and little makeup. It must have been a hasty decision to come to the hotel.

"I'm very sorry about what happened last night."

"All right."

"I don't want there to be any bad feelings. You may not believe me, but I admire you. You're willing to take risks."

He grinned without humor. "You didn't help me at all."

"Even people like you don't win all the time. They don't win everything."

"I lost everything."

"Not the way I see it. That's not the story I'm writing."

Keegan put his glass down. "Come downstairs with me. I'll give you something for your story."

She was puzzled. "What?"

"My farewell."

He was silent in the elevator ride down to the ballroom, and the vertigo as the elevator descended left him confused. He did not know how far he would fall.

The ballroom was spangled, and a banner—KEEGAN'S THE WAY FOR DA—hung across the stage, and a ten-piece orchestra, Morganthau's extravagance, in tuxedos, played for a dwindling, frenetic crowd. He hadn't told anyone except Lorrie he was coming down, so his sudden appearance at the podium was not noticed until the orchestra began playing drumrolls into the vast, emptying ballroom. The TV lights went on, and the stage was white-hot in their remorseless glare.

He stood looking out, the people darker away from the lights, mostly shapes and shadows shifting, shimmering, moving without his being able to do anything about it. Lorrie stayed in their midst. Chris and Elaine, detaching themselves from Muriel Morganthau, joined him on the stage. They were dressed formally and looked sad.

He recognized some faces from the office, deputies with wives and husbands and a loud bunch from Conley's bureau.

The microphone squealed electronically, and the crowd started applauding and chanting his name. Like the ugly night at Park's home, when some stain of corruption or failure shone out enough for them to think he could be bribed. Keegan waited. He looked at his children and the senior staff on the stage around him and an immense pride broke over him. I have done all right, he thought.

He began speaking, thanking everyone, and he was interrupted again and again by applause. Like I won, he thought.

"Some people," he said, "don't have the advantage of being guided by a principle. I am lucky. When I was young, I found a principle, and it has guided me every day since then until this very moment." He recited from II Timothy, the old lesson in morning chapel.

"And more than that. Much more. I had the inspiration of a woman I never met to help me win a tough case." Keegan took out the letter from Mrs. Harrold and read it, and when he was finished, the silence endured until a great tide of clapping rose.

"Public service was a duty for me and my late wife. And for Win Conley, whom many, many of you knew. And respected." He stopped. "I think the paths of our lives are guided by things like respect and what's right. I think our lives are formed for us, and we follow them, as best we can, wherever they lead us." He stopped again. It was what he had always believed, and yet it was becoming murky in his mind.

"I don't blame anybody for where I am tonight. I didn't quite make it. We didn't make it," he said with forced lightness. He wanted to hold his daughter, and could only see her profile down the stage from him.

"But I am the luckiest of men to have the support and affection of you here tonight. Tomorrow is another day. I only wish absent friends and loved ones could join us." He held the podium and felt very heavy.

His name was rhythmically chanted, primitive and pure, and he raised his eyes, feeling tears. I've tried, he thought, all my life. The voices merged, his name rose to the dark ceiling of the ballroom.

He felt Chris, saw him take his arm. "We better go," his son said firmly to Keegan.

Keegan let himself be moved from the podium, along the stage, his name roared and shouted at him. He felt like he was rousing from a dream. He was thumped on the back, people hugged him, shook his hand as he walked slowly off the stage, Chris supporting him, Elaine at one side.

They were all around him, and he was ashamed to be weeping.

"Yeah, get me out of here," he said blindly to Chris or whoever was nearest. "They'll think I'm crying because I lost."

ABOUT THE AUTHOR

WILLIAM P. WOOD is the bestselling author of nine novels and one nonfiction book. As a deputy district attorney in California, he handled thousands of criminal cases and put on over 50 jury trials. Two of Wood's novels have been produced as motion pictures, including *Rampage*, filmed by Academy Award–winning director William Friedkin (*The French Connection, The Exorcist, Rules of Engagement*), and *Broken Trust*, filmed by Jane Fonda Films with the screenplay by Joan Didion and John Gregory Dunne. Wood's books have been translated into several foreign languages. He lives in Sacramento, California.

CPSIA information can be obtained
at www.ICGtesting.com
Printed in the USA
JSHW010741260720
6859JS00004B/13

9 781620 454732